The

ROAD

Beyond

RUIN

ALSO BY GEMMA LIVIERO

Broken Angels

Pastel Orphans

Marek

Lilah

The ROAD *Beyond* RUIN

GEMMA LIVIERO

LAKE UNION
PUBLISHING

Text copyright © 2019 by Gemma Liviero
All rights reserved.

No part of this book may be reproduced, or stored in a retrieval system, or transmitted in any form or by any means, electronic, mechanical, photocopying, recording, or otherwise, without express written permission of the publisher.

Published by Lake Union Publishing, Seattle

www.apub.com

Amazon, the Amazon logo, and Lake Union Publishing are trademarks of Amazon.com, Inc., or its affiliates.

ISBN-13: 9781503904767 (hardcover)
ISBN-10: 1503904768 (hardcover)
ISBN-13: 9781503901018 (paperback)
ISBN-10: 1503901017 (paperback)

Cover design by PEPE *nymi*

Printed in the United States of America

First edition

To Oscar & Stella

MAY 1945

CHAPTER 1

ERICH

The color of Erich's hair was scarcely visible amid a field of yellow wildflowers. He lay very still on his stomach, one eye closed, the other trained on the muzzle of his rifle pointed toward the people at the base of the hill. An older man and a female of indeterminable age walked slowly, their pace encumbered by the failing legs of the man, with his uneven gait.

Erich's finger pressed lightly against the trigger, testing the weight of its resistance. No one would miss them, he thought before movement off to the side distracted him. He changed his aim to his originally intended target, saw the grasses quiver. When he caught a glimpse of the rabbit's gray-brown legs disappearing beneath its tenuous cover, he pulled the trigger, and the sound of the small explosion traveled far across the valley. All movement in the grass ahead ceased, and he stood up to mark the spot, shirtless, his narrow torso suntanned, red in places, his browned face burned and peeling. He walked to claim his quarry, enjoying the temporary freedom that had been afforded him.

The people on the road had quickly disappeared from view. It mattered not to Erich that the sound of gunshots was a recurring nightmare for them. Like so many others, he assumed, the pair traveled the roads to reach a home that was repossessed or no longer standing. He picked up the rabbit by the legs and set off toward his two-story weatherworn house that in recent times had lost its self-respect, with mold under the eaves and shingles missing from its roof. The quaint storybook windows that had once been open to possibilities were kept shut against a hostile present. And the building that had once been beautiful, with its milky walls and chocolate gables, had become little more than a temporary refuge.

Erich squinted toward the sun and a powdery gust from the east, which carried a familiar yet vastly different smell from that of the acrid fumes and smoke he had grown used to elsewhere. Something was stirring up the dirt in the far paddocks, and the scent triggered memories of his sister, Claudine, running wild, uncaring about punishment and consequence, hands covered with dirt to smear the faces of the younger ones.

On the far side of the paddocks, he could see a haze of dust and hear the groan of several engines, and a sense of urgency replaced the feeling of freedom.

He turned and ran through the front door.

"Mother, trucks! Russian!"

His mother shoved the plates she was holding down hard so that they rattled together on the table.

"Get the matches. Hurry!" she said.

While Erich followed this instruction, she hurried into her bedroom and returned, carrying a wooden box. During Erich's childhood the box had been untouchable, something that held secrets shared only between parents. As an adult he had learned the value of its contents, and more recently it had become a threat to their survival.

His mother withdrew from the box letters, photos, and papers and threw them into the fireplace. Erich struck a match and held it to the pile, which quickly caught the flame. It was their names, their past lives they were burning, but Erich, born to survive, felt only a sense of relief watching them shrink and blacken as he fanned them into charcoal ash.

"They might not stop here," said Erich.

At the bottom of the box were several other documents that consisted of both drawings and text. His mother examined them carefully, lovingly almost, as he had seen her do many times before.

"Keep them with you," she said to Erich, shoving the papers into his hands. "You must not let people forget your father, forget what he did."

Erich looked at the papers, then at his two younger brothers at the dining table, serious faces, their hands in their laps, the middle brother on the threshold of manhood. They were growing used to these moments when they had to wait and hope. The empty chairs at the table said much about their family. The space told of change—how much they had lost.

Erich watched his mother's familiar stoic and unchangeable expression. He had absorbed much of her strength. She had given so much of it to all of them over the years. Though the resilience had remained unshakable, her body was not coping with their change in fortune. She had lost weight. The flesh around her jawline had melted away, her chin becoming more prominent, and a purple tinge to her hands stubbornly remained after a long winter without coal.

"Is the war over, Mutti?" asked the middle brother.

His mother held his gaze, but there were no secret messages, no more plans. Nothing to suggest they could do anything more. Those times had gone. Then her eyes drifted toward the window to the trucks now coming up the hill, along the dirt track that led to their door.

"No," said his mother.

AUGUST 1945

CHAPTER 2
STEFANO

Berlin is underwhelming. The city described by Germans as the most progressive in the world, occupied by intelligentsia, superior order, and robust architecture, is little more than a puzzle now, what remains of it, slowly being pieced together. Buildings, unusable, with their insides garishly hollowed, mock the crushed regime. Windows, from where Germans stretched their arms to salute their führer, to clap the soldiers in the street, are now empty, elitist dreams.

There is an absence of men of working age here, men who were killed or imprisoned, along with many too young to wear a uniform and too old to shoulder such loads. The Third Reich no longer had age restrictions in the final days.

Beige women, in belted dresses and headscarves, walk in groups along the pavement of streets cleared of debris, clutching handbags as if they have somewhere important to be. They appear to acknowledge Stefano as he passes, but they don't consider him for any length of time. It isn't from fear or guilt that most avert their eyes; Berliners no longer care about the people who walk their streets. They have thrown away caution and replaced it with apathy. Without the Nazi symbols of false superiority, there is nothing to measure themselves against. Among the debris and the shards of a broken city, they, too, are free.

Stefano was stopped earlier by British soldiers to show the mark on his arm. It is as good as an identity card. In fact, it is better; the mark means that one is no longer answerable. He is left alone, unquestioned. The Russian soldiers ignore him. The British soldiers nod formally. The Americans stare longer, curious. Stefano is thin, worn, gaunt, haggard, all the words that his mother would have used to describe his condition. She would be horrified by the state of him, but he has seen others in worse condition. He is a survivor—one of the lucky ones who ordinarily wouldn't consider themselves lucky.

Tall, muscled, he was once a swimmer, a student of languages. Stefano's family had used words like "tender" and "loving" to describe him after he left them the first time. Then more words the second, then no words on the last trip, because, by then, as war raged with a new sense of recklessness, thoughts of inevitability had replaced any promises of return. He is twenty-three, but his experiences make him twice as old.

He passes another group of women, the *Trümmerfrau*, the rubble women. The Allies have assigned them the task of cleaning up the city. They collect the fallen bricks and place them in a barrow that is already overflowing. An elderly man wheels it away, disappearing down a street between the ruins. The women wipe their foreheads and rub their weary backs before bending down to retrieve more bricks to place in another empty barrow that has just arrived, wheeled unsteadily by a small boy.

Two children scoot past Stefano from the opposite direction. They converse between themselves and accelerate when one points to something ahead, toward a pile of scrap, another playground. Two small girls carrying sacks walk confidently across hills of broken things, every so often bending to examine something shiny, something of value to them that they place in their sacks. One stops to push some hair from her face with her grimy hand. She catches sight of Stefano, smiles, and waves. This simple gesture confuses him at first, as he is unaccustomed to children who are readily accepting of change, who rise quickly above setback. By the time he raises his hand in response, her attention has been diverted, one tiny arm reaching deeply into the rubble for something she has spied.

One woman shakily wheels a pram filled with bricks before it finally tilts and falls on its side. Stefano wants to walk past, to leave it, but it isn't in his nature. Even now. He stops to help, and she matches his pace, brick for brick, returning them to the pram. When he is nearly done, the woman stops to rest, to view the man who is helping her.

"Danke!" she says, and then she looks down at his left hand to the bandage that has come unwound. There is no trace of repulsion at what she sees underneath.

"Do you want me to fix the bandage for you?" she asks, her eyes darting several times between his face and his hand, and then to the numbers on his arm.

He shakes his head.

"Ein Konzentrationslager?" she queries.

"Yes."

"I had a son your age," she says. "It would be good to have him here now." She returns to her work, uncaring whether Stefano responds, whether he might be curious about her son's fate. Such questions are pointless now, and he leaves before he feels compelled to do anything else for these people.

He wears the new shirt and trousers the Allied administration gave him, and shoes that fit well. Over his shoulder Stefano carries a satchel that contains a tin of meat and beans, several military chocolate bars, a flask of water, a spare shirt, an extra pair of socks, a torch, some money, a map, and a watch that belonged to a dead German. But most importantly he has a document that says he is free.

On the south side of the city, a truck is waiting where he was told it would be. He is relieved that he can see the end of the city's destruction and open landscape ahead, but beyond that is an interminable postwar chaos.

He steps up to the window of the truck, shows his paper, then climbs into the back. Inside, several faces look at him vacantly, a sign they are used to changes, to strangers. There are mostly children—washed faces, borrowed clothes—and mothers. Polish refugees, he thinks, from the look of them, the fairness of them, and from the fact they have no homes here. He does not converse with them during the trip, and partway into the journey as the sun begins its descent, the vehicle stops and the driver taps the side of the vehicle to signal for Stefano to climb out.

"*Do svidaniya!*" calls the soldier.

"*Do svidaniya,*" he replies.

He watches the truck veer west at the intersection and head toward a displacement camp; then he turns southeast in the direction of Dresden and, beyond that, to a Mediterranean winter above the cliffs of Amalfi.

1932

Stefano woke to the sound of boat motors and the slapping of waves against the rocks below. Summer brought many fishing and tourist vessels to his Mediterranean doorstep. The house was not yet hot, the sun not yet high, but the water was already reflecting its silvery surface onto their white sandstone walls and through the windows into their living room.

Agatha, who had been on his bed when he fell asleep, was missing. Stefano stretched out his arms across his bed, eyes not staying open willingly, and he felt blindly at the end of his bed. With hair tousled and his eyes still puffed with sleep, he pulled on trousers that would soon be too small for him and his fast-growing body. As he had done every morning, he rubbed his finger across the top of his lip. Already he felt some soft hair growing and prayed daily that he would soon have a handsome mustache like his father.

His sisters were quiet from their bedroom. The younger, Nina, would not rise for at least another hour. His older sister, Teresa, would be up soon to order everyone around. It would do him well to be out of her way when she first rose. She was always looking for reasons to be angry.

The crunching and scraping sounds of sand and gravel led him down the steps from their terraced balcony to a garden below. Beyond the garden was a cliff face with more steps down to the sea.

His father was mixing cement, and beside him was a pile of white bricks; also beside him on the grass, Agatha watched. Nicolo had commenced constructing a small square structure. Agatha wagged her tail, happy to see that Stefano had joined them. She was a small black-and-white dog that Stefano had found as a puppy. After two years with the family, she was still mischievous.

"What are you doing, Papa?"

"I'm building a little house for Agatha."

Stefano studied the bricks and the careful way his father was spacing them apart before the kindness of this action suddenly struck him. That his father would do this for his dog was another reason to love his papa.

Though, in Stefano's heart, he knew that Agatha was just as much his papa's dog as she was his.

"What will it look like?"

"About this high," said his father, his hand stretched flat and placed level against his hip. "Though at the back there will be a long, narrow window so Agatha can look through and see the sea to make sure there are no marauders heading our way. And she can bark and warn us."

Stefano looked out to sea, then back to his father, whose mouth had stretched into a grin. His wide smile, so genuine, with his mustache reshaped into a long, thin line, had always been infectious, and Stefano couldn't help but smile, too.

"There are no marauders, Papa," said Stefano, and his father stroked his head roughly with affection. Stefano liked his father's playfulness, but he liked even more that Agatha was about to have her own house also. "But why can't she sleep with me on my bed?"

"Because she pees on the floor, because you sleep so heavily you don't hear her whining to get out. Besides, she loves to contemplate the Mediterranean. She loves to see the colorful tourists on their large yachts."

His father was right. Agatha loved her perch at the balustrade to watch people and the water below and afar. It was the perfect vantage for her watchtower.

Stefano gave Agatha a hug and rubbed his cheek against her fur. She rewarded him by licking his arm.

"Can I help you, Papa?" asked Stefano.

"Of course."

They worked all morning. Stefano helped his father mix the cement, then passed the bricks to his father to position. Sometimes they would swap roles, but Nicolo would straighten Stefano's row of bricks without him seeing.

By the time they finished, it was just after lunchtime, and they dived into the sea to cool down—Agatha, too.

When they came back up the rocky climb, and the many stairs up to the ground floor of their house, his mother greeted them with chilled lemon water, and the three of them sat on the terrace to watch the boats. These were the moments that would stay with Stefano through life, the rafts he would hold on to when he was sinking.

The following year his father fell from the roof of a laboring job and died on the way to the hospital. Agatha barked for weeks from the terrace and for several days did not use her little brick house at all. And the anchor that had been his father was hauled up and buried with him.

Present-day 1945

Stefano is startled awake by the sound of voices close by—a group of people walking, wheeling carts, and carrying children on their backs. It is instinct to stay motionless at every sound, to assess, and then to react. His body has been trained for different sounds and smells. He has seen many travelers heading home since the end of the war, carrying clothing under their arms, some with items tied to their backs with rope. They have emerged from the remnants of Europe, across many foreign lands, but their resentment and their hunger bind them. He does not choose to travel with anyone. He does not wish to reflect upon the war or hear their stories. He has too many of his own.

He puts his head back down, hidden behind the tall gully grasses, and rolls over onto his side. The ground is hard and damp, and Stefano grew cold during the night. He raises his eyes, then sits up suddenly. Lying close by is a woman. On her back, she appears to stare at the sky, and he wonders if she was there when he first lay down in the field. Under a quarter moon he had not seen the dullness of her coat, the gray scarf wrapped around her head. But she is not the sole object of his curiosity. Beside her, sitting and watching him, is a small boy, clutching a basket that holds a bundle of linen.

Stefano stands up carefully and walks nearer, the boy eyeing him warily.

"Are you all right?" he asks, but the boy only stares, eyes heavy with resignation and rimmed in red.

Stefano edges near the woman, slowly, so as not to upset the boy, and crouches to examine her. She has her eyes partially open, the color unseen, disappearing to the backs of her eyelids. She is rigid.

He has seen many dead bodies before, but this one is different: there is no obvious cause of death, no shrapnel embedded, no cotton saturated with blood. She is intact.

"Is this your mother?"

The boy says nothing.

"Where is your father?"

The boy says nothing. Stefano tries French and asks the same questions, but still the boy says nothing.

"Are you hungry?" Stefano asks once again in German.

The boy nods. Stefano retrieves some pieces of chocolate from his satchel. The boy takes them eagerly, shoves the palm of his hand to his mouth, and chews, forgetting all else but the food that will barely fill his stomach. He is ravenous and has likely been this way for days.

Stefano looks around him to the empty spaces, the fields that go on forever. The lack of humans, the lack of anything that will give him answers to the plight of the boy. The group has now passed into the distance. There is nothing he can do here, he thinks. He will have to leave him, hope that a farmer finds him, a soldier, someone to take him in. He looks back at the dead mother, then the boy, and shakes his head gently. There is nothing Stefano can offer him.

"Are you from Berlin?" he asks the boy, who is sitting and watching Stefano's pack, knowing now that the satchel holds more of the food he yearns for.

"You must go up that way," Stefano says, standing up and pointing north, "where there are houses. Knock on doors."

He walks backward a few paces, and the boy starts weeping, bottom lip forward and the fingers of his free hand plucking nervously at the side of his shorts.

"Good luck!" Stefano says.

The boy starts to whine and lays his head on his mother's chest, the food now forgotten, his despair reignited. With the basket now slightly tilted, Stefano can see the contents: a baby's forehead and nose exposed, skin blue and bloated with death. And Stefano feels something gnaw at the soft belly of his human condition, at the piece of his makeup that can still feel pity, the same piece that made him stop to help the *Trümmerfrau*.

"I'm sorry about your mother," he says more gently, presuming that she is. "You must go on without her. Find help, yes?"

The boy keeps one arm across his mother and the other holding tightly to the handle of the basket. He bends down to kiss the baby's forehead, and Stefano has to look away, unprepared for the small lump that has formed at the back of his throat, at the sight of the gesture, believing he'd grown immune to such things.

"We should put her coat over both of them to keep them warm in the night," Stefano says, thinking of his own mother. And the boy sits up to watch as Stefano takes off the woman's coat and uses some force to bend the limbs that are stiff and empty of life. Then he lifts the almost weightless linen bundle from the basket to lie beside the mother and places the coat over both faces. That at least, so they are not staring into the sun.

The boy watches all this silently.

Stefano is about to say a prayer, then changes his mind. It is too late for prayer. He sighs, wishing he had chosen somewhere else to stop, before turning to walk away. He is of no help to the boy. Not now.

As he steps toward the main road, the boy jumps up to follow him with the now-empty basket. He is wearing shorts, long socks that have no stretch, and shoes that are battered with wear.

"Wrong way!" Stefano says, pointing back in the direction he has come. "That way!" When the boy doesn't move, Stefano steps forward, touches his shoulder, and feels the warmth of him; the living warmth a sharp contrast, he thinks, to the mother and baby he also touched.

"You must not follow me," he says. "I have far to go."

Stefano turns back to look at the long quest ahead, then back down at the boy.

The boy fiddles with the tips of his fingers, looks back at the pile that was his mother and baby sibling, and Stefano knows he is thinking the same. He has no one now.

"What is your name?"

A small frown appears on his face, and the boy looks down briefly, then back at Stefano.

"No name? How old are you?"

Still nothing.

"Five? Six? Four maybe?"

The child nods.

"Four?"

He nods again.

"Do you have a tongue?"

Nothing.

"I can't take you. I have things to do."

Nothing.

Stefano sighs. He rubs at the dull ache at the front of his head, thinks briefly that he could trick the child, tell him that he will return and leave him there, before deciding otherwise.

"Come with me," he orders, suddenly frustrated, and the boy follows him back to his mother. Stefano bends to search the woman's coat pockets. There is nothing to say who she was, where she is from, who the child is. "You must leave the basket," he says. "It will only slow you down." But the boy grips it harder.

Stefano links his hands behind his head, paces in a circle, and curses under his breath, regretting again that he found the child and is now burdened with the task of finding him a home.

The boy looks at him with eyes that tell him nothing. He is lost, like I was, thinks Stefano suddenly. Life has turned its back on him, too.

"All right," he says. "The basket, too."

Stefano continues heading south, the child half running to keep up with him. Twice he stops at houses to ask for accommodations for the boy. Twice he is rejected. He is told there are many orphans now, and beggars, and the people who open their doors are quick to close them again.

The child grows weary and drops back several yards, his small legs slowing. Stefano stops to wait for him to catch up this time, the traveler frustrated now that he has to slow his pace.

They stop at another house, the front door missing. Stefano checks his map and enters curiously. There are bullet holes in the walls upstairs and traces of blood at the top of the stairs. He is certain there were bodies here that someone has moved, and out the back there are mounds of earth and crosses above them to suggest where they might now lie.

The previous evening he saw Dresden in the distance, across the river, scorched earth and stalks of buildings reaching up to escape the detritus of war. Farther east, the signs of damage lessen in towns and villages clustered between the river Elbe and densely wooded cliffs.

They reach a village that appears unbroken. A working clock in a tower in the center square, surrounded by square buildings with more windows than walls, announces that time hasn't stopped here. Shop doors are open, and people converse in doorways, in groups, a sight rarely seen publicly since early in the war.

There are still signs, however, that the town has yet to stand on its own. Russian military vehicles, small trucks and vehicles in camouflage green, are parked on the street. A hotel is boarded up with a sign advising that the owners will be returning, but it doesn't give a date, and a bakery, though open, does not have bread or cakes on display in the windows. A fish shop, its shutters wedged shut with age and time, has words scrawled angrily across a faded wooden sign: "No Fish."

Farther down is a café more inviting. Its sign reads "Open" at least. He steps inside, and the woman behind the counter views Stefano suspiciously. She has already surmised that he is not German and that he does not belong here, and there is curiosity, brief, about the child, but only that. It is perhaps the look of him, battle scarred and weary, something he does not need to feign, that makes him less of a threat, along with the child. But there is no mistaking the distaste and distrust in the

lines between her eyes. In his head he reminds her that certain rights
have been forfeited, that arrogance is one of them.

He asks what is available since there is no menu visible, only a
doorway to a kitchen and the smell of boiled cabbage. She is at first
reluctant to respond, to move. He opens his bag and holds out some
German marks. She says there is talk of a new currency, and these marks
will be worthless soon. She takes them anyway. The way she stared at
the money too long told him that she would. And though a foreigner,
darkly Mediterranean, he is better than no customer at all.

"Is the child ill?" asks the woman, looking over the boy.

"No," says Stefano, then wonders himself. "What do you have?"
he asks her.

She steps aside to point to a chalkboard on the floor against the
wall behind her. Most of the handwritten items have been crossed out
and new ones written with a careless, resentful hand.

Perhaps a lack of company and conversation drives her to talk
regardless of her prejudice and suspicion. She tells him that she attracts
many beggars that she has to send away. The Russian military police
come there, too, which is the only reason she can stay in business now.
They used to harass her and other shop owners, but this happens less
now. They seem to have other things to do. However, the relationship
with them is still tenuous. Sometimes they pay, and sometimes they
don't. She says she grows her own vegetables. She says her husband
came back from the war changed. He is old, she says. He was not worth
imprisoning, but he is even more useless now, she says.

There used to be fish, but the river is poisoned from the Russians
and the bombs and their Russian piss. They are uncouth, loud, they
drink too much, but they come to her café. Her café is reputable at least.
There are no dogs on the menu. She repeats what others say because
she knows very little, he thinks. She is walled in, surrounded by gossip.

She wishes that things were the way they were in the war. Her café
did well, frequented by soldiers and civilians with money. The tourists

were mostly German, which was better, she says, though she does not look at him at this point. She has not forgotten to whom she speaks. There are no pictures of Hitler, but her loyalties still lie with the country before the surrender.

"The town is busy. Have new people moved here?"

She asks him to repeat the words. He is unsure if it's his accent or if she is hard of hearing. He asks the question again.

This time she shrugs and shapes her large lips into those of a fish. She does not care to provide an answer, though she likely has one. She is happy to say only what she wants to.

He doesn't think ill of her. She is too ignorant. Perhaps she is miserable enough as it is. He thinks about asking if she will take on the child, but the thought of him with her is almost as bad as leaving him with his dead mother. There is little compassion, little interest in the child so far.

The boy and Stefano share a thick pink-red soup with a strange chicken flavoring that attempts to mask the bitterness of the underripe beets. He has to grab the wrist of the child at times to stop him from rushing the spoon to his mouth and spilling some of the contents, but he gives up this battle halfway through.

He orders some milk, but the owner says that they haven't enough and offers some coffee instead. It has a tinny, bitter taste, and something added that isn't caffeine.

He says *danke* as they leave, to which she nods. He stops at a grocery store and the pharmacy to ask several questions, one about a place for the child, but there is none. He also stops at the post office.

"You are going the wrong way," says the postmaster while customers view the newcomers curiously. "You had best head back toward Dresden if you are looking for transport."

He is back on the road. It has grown hot. A truck speeds past them, and its engine roars suddenly. The child ducks and falls to the earth.

"No more bombs," he tells the boy. He reaches down to take his hand, and the boy looks at it, for a length of time, as if it is something

21

he hasn't seen before, then tentatively takes the larger hand. He helps the boy upright, then crouches down beside him and tells him to climb on his back.

He continues his journey, with short, thin legs looped under his long arms, the boy's head resting against Stefano's back, the basket now carried by Stefano, whose steps are slowing, his limp more noticeable.

They both have weight they must carry. Stefano thinks back to the bombs and the bullets and the fire, and he looks down at his bandaged hand. It is no longer a wound. It is now a reminder, among many scars, that will be with him forever.

CHAPTER 3

ROSALIND

In the quiet of early morning, a dog barks from somewhere across the river, and the *plock* of a broken cuckoo clock and the piping of a goose herald the start of Rosalind's day. They are just several sounds of time that alert her to the surroundings, beckon her from bed, and push her into the drudgery that is now her life. She lowers her feet to the cool stone tiles and heads toward Georg. At the top of the narrow stairs, she walks immediately into Georg's attic room, with its vaulted wooden ceiling, which expands the length of the house. His bed sits against the room's only window facing the wood. Light enters the crosshatched, partially boarded window at daybreak, stamping squares of pale-yellow light across the room's shades of early morning gray.

Georg, lying on his back, emits an evenly spaced burst of gargles from the back of his throat. Gangly, his long legs take up much of the bed, his toes hanging over the end. Rosalind lifts up the sheet and climbs in next to him. Lying on her side, she watches him sleep, studies his profile, the mixture of pale-red strands in his hair, and his skin, youthful and firm like hers. He sleeps rarely, sometimes haunting the house at night, but when he does, his slumber is deep, like a baby's.

"You need to tell me what's in your head," she asked him several nights earlier when she had awoken just after midnight, and, like many other nights, found him pacing the room and whispering to himself. Communication has been difficult with his new state of mind; his mind can only be reached intermittently now.

"I don't know," he had answered, shocked at the interruption. "There are things I need to do."

"There is nothing you need to do right now."

"But she's in danger."

"Who?"

The question was out before she had time to stop herself. She knew the answer despite the fact it wasn't spoken. He was thinking about Monique, worrying about her. She had become his obsession after the war.

Monique can take care of herself, she had wanted to say but couldn't, because she'd tried that once before, and his reaction was frightening. The mention of her name these days can cause him anxiety and set about events that Rosalind is sometimes unable to control. To keep him somewhat stable, since the war took part of his mind, she has found a solution to his depression and his outbursts. But lately his mood has worsened. Lately he has raged and broken things, frustrated by thoughts and images in his head.

Rosalind rests her head on the side of his pillow to ponder. His mouth is open, suspended with the effects of sleep. There are blue veins around the edge of his jaw and down the side of his neck. With her fingers she traces them. This is his good side, how he looked before his final campaign. On the side that is hidden, there is a puckered red scar that runs from the top left-hand side of his temple to halfway across the side of his head, making a track through his hair.

He stirs; his eyes flutter slightly. His body is warm, and she shifts several inches closer. She wears a lavender-colored silk chemise that finishes just below her knee. He bought it for her as a gift on their wedding day, three years earlier. Apart from her gold wedding ring, it is the only precious item she has. Other things, other jewelry, her collection of books, her parents' wedding china and silverware, have all been abandoned, and her parents' life, her life, is now just rubble in a street in Berlin.

Georg opens his eyes and stares at the ceiling, adjusting to the new day. She wants him to look at her, but he doesn't turn his head.

With her hand she forces his chin toward her, but still his eyes do not find hers. They stare over her shoulder to something his mind doesn't really see. She lifts herself up on one elbow so that he can look into her eyes. Visual stimulus works the best with Georg, and soon his eyes are focusing as green stares into blue.

She remembers the first morning after they were married. She remembers the first time he looked at her. He must have loved her then. *Did he?* It was just later when other things got into his head.

She reaches under the cover and slips her hand into his shorts. She rubs gently at first, and his body shifts slightly, his eyes closing involuntarily. He is partially aroused, but she knows that little else will happen. Even though his body reacts, his mind and heart aren't hers anymore, even in this state. Perhaps they never were.

"I love you," she says, eyes welling with tears.

And he looks at her vacantly. He doesn't recognize her, not this morning, and not the ones before.

1933

"Here she is," said Rosalind's mother, Yvonne, lips flattened together. It wasn't said like a genial introduction, but the tone of it, the way the words sank at the end, suggested Monique was something now they all must bear.

Monique, twelve years old, a small face lost in a large mass of dark curls, fists in and out of her eyes, emitting sounds like those of a lonely puppy. Yvonne stood beside Monique, holding her hand and staring at Rosalind under rows of lines and invisible brows, agitated, angry, or disappointed. Rosalind couldn't be sure exactly which. Her mother was difficult to understand and never good at conflict, or anything that took her away from herself. And that day, it was up to Rosalind to rescue her mother. "Children" were a territory Yvonne preferred not to understand, once confiding to her daughter that she had never planned on any at all.

Rosalind's father, Max, she believed was somewhat happier at his daughter's arrival. Rosalind was a good girl, he said often, when she showed him her schoolwork, and these words would come to be highly prized by Rosalind when he came home from a shift on the trams. There was nothing of great substance in the relationship with her father, just more an understanding that she was part of the same enduring grind, attached, the three of them, by the ties of birth.

Why her mother had seemed so bitter at times, Rosalind never really considered, until Monique brought it up when they were some years older. She concluded that there were those who were born with a frown and those born with a smile. And a little after that, Rosalind would realize that she was born with a frown also, that one's nature was difficult to alter.

"Do you want to see my room?" Rosalind asked her younger cousin, whom she'd not met before that day. She was surprised that Monique could still hear her through the whimpering that had risen to more of a howl. In Rosalind's bedroom at the back of the house, Monique sat on the spare bed.

"I'm sorry about your parents," said Rosalind. "They will come back, and you can go home again soon, I am certain." Monique's crying lessened, the volume lowering. "Sometimes people only go to prison for a short time."

But it would prove to be untrue. The incarceration of her parents in Austria, where Monique was from, was permanent. The new government had been imprisoning those who openly opposed the regime, and Gustav and Ada, Monique's father and mother, were two of them. To add to their crime of dissidence, they were caught helping funnel other objectors out of the country.

Monique at first was seen as an infiltrator, another mouth to feed, and someone who brought with her an undesirable amount of noise. But the silent grudge that Rosalind's parents held toward their niece slowly disintegrated over time, and they would come to appreciate Monique's bright personality and lust for life, and her ability to remain herself, untouchable, despite the chaos that Berlin was entering. She would prove a welcome distraction from the gray.

Two years separated the cousins, and Rosalind, who at first liked the idea of looking after Monique, of taking control of her, of shaping someone of her own, quickly realized that her younger cousin needed little nurture.

Her parents' acceptance of the new situation and Monique's strength and independence seemed, to Rosalind, to highlight the differences between the two girls, an observation that led her to feel, sometimes, less than. But it was not until the first riverside summer together, with Georg, that Rosalind's resentment of Monique really began to take hold.

Present-day 1945

Two geese rush toward the grain that Rosalind scatters to the ground. It is a treat that she gives them every so often, in place of the grass she collects from the empty paddocks across the road. Her intention was to breed geese, like her grandmother did, to expand the goose farm. Her grandmother had many geese once and wasted no part of the birds, the flesh and the fat for consuming, and feathers for stuffing linen.

Only these two were here when she arrived after Berlin was taken. The others were likely stolen, the gate to their pen broken, palings taken also. The pair, with their wings clipped, had somehow managed to stay hidden in the woods, and she had repaired the fence and restored their home. More recently she welcomed the connection she had with these two interesting white females. As if their survival had not been a coincidence. As if they had been spared to await her return.

At the back of the enclosure is a small shelter for the geese, and inside here she discovers a miracle. The geese did not lay any eggs over the spring, but inside are two, side by side, as if they conspired, as if they thought of her. She picks up the eggs, kisses each of them, amazed at the size.

"Thank you," she says to the geese as she passes, placing their offerings in the bucket that she used to carry the grain. She has not eaten any eggs for weeks. When there are chicken eggs at the market, they are overpriced to compensate for the Russian military that expects them for free. With these precious deliveries, Rosalind is imagining making an omelet for Georg with the remainder of the bacon and the peas she has stored and used sparingly.

The sudden crunching of gravel alerts her to visitors, and a motor vehicle makes its way toward her, stopping in front of the house and several yards from the pen. The roofless vehicle idles as two Russian soldiers discuss something between themselves, one of them watching her carefully. She waits, her heart beating fiercely against the walls of her chest. There is no point walking to the door of the house, nor does she trust her legs to walk close to the car. This is the third time soldiers have come here since she returned from Berlin. The first was to search for German soldiers, the second time to inspect the property and the vegetables she grows behind the house.

She bites down hard so that they do not see her lips tremble, and she steps forward. One of them, the passenger, alights from the vehicle. The driver stays in, engine idling, revving occasionally. It is a good sign at least. They do not intend to stay long.

The soldier stops just short of the pen and waves her forward. Rosalind opens the gate and moves close enough to see that his fingernails are clean. He is young and handsome, possibly even younger than her, with dark hair and lashes, and light-brown eyes. His uniform is a light-tan color, with baggy trousers tucked into boots. He wears a small cap that has a small red badge.

"Geese," he says slowly, in German, pointing behind her to the pen.

"I only have two."

"We take."

"But they are laying eggs."

He looks at her briefly, then turns to the other soldier in the car. He says something in Russian. The other one barks back.

"When finish, you give," says the young interpreter.

She nods, thinking it is now the end of the conversation, but the driver barks more Russian to the younger soldier.

"Who else here?" the younger one repeats in German.

The question confuses her briefly because she knows that both telling the truth and lying have consequences.

"We must have number," he says more firmly.

"My husband and I. There are two."

He calls back to the driver.

Rosalind's breathing is shallow and fast, and her throat feels tight and dry. She nurses the bucket that holds the two eggs. She is already calculating the time it will take her to get to the front door if she needs to. Though she wonders what good it will do.

He nods again and notices the eggs in the bucket.

"Please have!"

Rosalind looks in the bucket and back at him, her blue eyes smaller with the weight of her frown. He sees this or seems to. His tone is suddenly softer and no longer a command.

"Just . . ." He holds up one finger. His brown eyes are crinkling slightly, his hand well away from his gun. She reaches inside the bucket and hands the soldier an egg. He nods and turns back toward the car.

She breathes out deeply, remembering another question posed to her in Berlin. She remembers the tone that was not soft at all. She remembers the sounds of another girl begging, and wanting to cover her ears. The Russian soldiers were not thinking when they came through the first time. Primal revenge drove their will as they stepped roughly over bodies of male children, bearing arms, kicking them to check if they were dead. She shivers slightly as the soldier climbs back into the vehicle with his oversized boots.

The click of the front door alerts her to Georg. He doesn't move but stares at the men in the vehicle. Her husband is fully dressed in a shirt and trousers. He looks alert, undamaged, she thinks in the instant before she understands the danger here. His green eyes look greener, angrier in sunlight. He holds a rifle, not aimed at them directly, but raised partway upward from his leg.

The Russians stand up quickly from within the car, rifles braced and aiming.

"Wait! Stop! He is ill," she says, tapping her own head. "He does not know who you are."

"Tell him to put gun down!" says the soldier.

"It doesn't matter. There are no bullets . . ."

The driver is shouting over her. He is not listening or doesn't appear to understand her, and the younger one has again stepped out of the vehicle.

"I will get it from him. Please wait!" she says, putting up her hand toward the soldiers.

She drops the bucket that has the other egg and walks to the front door. Georg does not look at her, his eyes fixed on the men.

"Where is she?" Georg calls to them.

"Ignore him, please," she says, frantically taking the gun from his hand and pulling back the bolt to show them there are no bullets.

The Russian outside the vehicle lowers his gun and brusquely waves her forward.

"Is he . . . from battle?" he asks while he reaches for the weapon from Rosalind.

"No," she lies, understanding the missing word as "injured." "He was not a soldier. I have already explained to others who have been here. He was attacked by thieves. I can get his card if you wish."

The spokesman explains this to the driver who smiles scornfully.

"*Kar-bang,*" says the other Russian, holding two fingers in the shape of a gun toward his head. He laughs at his own joke, colder and desensitized by damage, but the younger remains serious, not yet over the fear of being shot.

"Good day," says the young soldier before jumping over the car door and onto the passenger seat, taking Georg's rifle with him. The older driver says something in Russian as he revs the engine to turn the car around.

"Inside!" says Rosalind to Georg. "There is nothing to see."

He turns and heads back inside, and she watches and waits for the car to disappear.

As she bends to retrieve the dropped bucket, she sees the remaining egg is now broken, and pieces of shell float in a pool of yellow on the ground.

CHAPTER 4
STEFANO

In the late afternoon Stefano enters a track between the thick band of conifers that line the roadside. The trail opens up to a clearing at the edge of the river, and to the right it bends sharply before continuing briefly to finish near two houses nestled in woodland. Stefano considers the houses for a moment before he leaves the track to cross the clearing toward the water.

He peels the sleeping child off his back and lays him down, then steps down the embankment to perch at the edge of the water. He splashes water on his face and hair, and the boy, sleepy but awake, steps down to mimic him. Behind them, from this position, and through this sparse section of wood beside the river, he can glimpse the houses at the end of the path.

The house closer to them looks more neglected, possibly abandoned. Only weeds and the dying remains of a plant fill the small garden bed by the door. A pane of glass is broken on a set of windows on the top floor.

He waits and watches. The boy sits beside him patiently, watching Stefano's movements and waiting for his next cue. He has a small narrow face, dark hair and hazel eyes, and thin limbs, and the skin on his nose is burned and blistering. His legs are infested with insect bites that have scabbed from scratching, and his knees are cut and bruised.

At dusk, a short while later, a light appears inside the farthest house at the end of the track, followed by puffs of smoke above a chimney. Stefano watches for lights to appear at the other house also.

Drab clouds smother the sunset behind the willow trees that hang dispiritedly above the river on the other side. Grayness looms, and Stefano estimates the time he has left before nightfall and the rain that will shortly follow.

He waits a few minutes more to make certain the second house is empty before turning to the boy who sits silently on the embankment, studying the darkening water below him.

He is not yet old enough to contemplate his future, now in the hands of Stefano. It is a responsibility that suddenly dawns on Stefano, making him ponder the decisions that led him to this fate, decisions that were forced upon him, and those he made himself, the consequences of which he now must bear. That there should be another twist seems suddenly unreasonable.

There was a moment earlier, as he put the child down to study markings on a map, the child distracted by people in the town, when he wondered whether to leave him, to disappear quickly from his view. It is unsettling in a way to have the responsibility; yet, just as unsettling, perhaps more so, is the thought that he still might be capable of abandoning him.

"You must remain silent and stay here," he says quietly. "Can you do that?"

When the child doesn't answer, he wonders whether German is the boy's first language, though the child does stay by the embankment as Stefano crosses the track.

At the rear of the silent house, where he is least visible from the other house's occupants, there is a small space of yard that holds a water pump and a partially fenced pen where animals were once kept. Behind the pen is a badly damaged shed, and beyond that, for both the houses, is a pine-covered ridge that separates them from the road to the remains of Dresden. On the wall beside the back door leans an ax. Stefano examines it, smells it. There is no scent of freshly cut wood along its blade.

Near the shed, a pyre contains the remnants of burned and barely recognizable household items. In the dimming light, sticking out of the soil and debris, like a bent human arm, is a metal hatstand. Clothing, pillows, and linen are strewn and singed, along with bent and twisted pieces of metal resembling coat rails, pails, and picture frames. A blanket lies nearby, blackened and stiff, damaged more from the other elements than the fire. He moves closer to see scorched metal cups that were once trophies of some kind. He picks up one, its wooden base mostly burned away, searches unsuccessfully for a name before placing it back on top of the pile.

Inside the shed, part of a wall has been blown away. Pieces of wood lie strewn across the floor. The damaged wall looks interfered with as if, after harm by shells or air fire, someone, seemingly enraged, has continued to pull it to pieces, panel by panel. Looking closer, Stefano sees that some of the broken wood is not from the walls but from pieces of furniture that might once have been a crib and a nightstand.

1935

Stefano climbed up the rock wall and followed the steep road back to his aunt Serafina's house, built into the side of the cliff. After his father died, his mother, then struggling financially, brought him and his sisters to his aunt's house. In the days before they left, he had begged and argued that Agatha come, too. There were new rules now, his mother told him. Rules made by his aunt and uncle and ones that did not include pets.

His new home had a terrace, like their old house several miles away, but jammed between lots of others and without a patch of grass for Agatha, had she come. Above them were other houses with terraces. Washing dotted the coastline and caught the warm breezes. Tourists chugged past in boats to gaze upon the coastline and the yellow, red, and ivory buildings that jutted out from the rock.

A short set of stairs led from the terrace down to the cliffs above the water. On fine days the shimmering water was blinding, and he lived for these days when the sun was high and the water dazzled. There were no low rocks to climb down to the sea, not like at his old house. It was a high dive from the cliffs into the water. His cousin had taught him to dive, and they swam together most afternoons.

His cousin, Beppe, just turned eighteen, five years older than Stefano, was tall, lean, and muscled, with skin roasted a dark golden brown from the sun. The girls on the terraces above would sit outside to watch him and his friends dive in their tight-fitting swimming trunks. Beppe knew they were watching, and he basked in their admiration.

Stefano was also growing tall for his age and bronzed, though still lean and yet to grow muscled like his cousin. He had an *old face*, his aunt would always tease: *Like you know things that you wished you didn't. Like all us adults. Perhaps it is from all the books you study.*

After his swim one day, Stefano entered the front room, its slate tiles warmed from the afternoon sun. His mother drew the curtains and told him to sit down.

Serafina stood in the kitchen to supervise whatever was about to be told. Stefano's mother, Julietta, had looked up to her older sister, and trusted her with most family decisions. Julietta then told him that Italy had invaded Abyssinia.

"Why?" said Stefano.

"Because Il Duce wants to make our country stronger," said Serafina, taking over. "We need to strengthen Italy's power. We have lost so much over time."

"Will we win?"

"Of course," said Serafina. "With a great leader in charge, everything is possible."

Stefano was skeptical. He had heard people say otherwise. He liked to sit near the shops in the center of the town and listen to the old men speak in the cafés. They had talked about Il Duce, Mussolini, but not in a good way. He had heard that not all men liked their leader. But he didn't dare say that. He had learned very quickly not to give his thoughts away, especially to Serafina, who was fiery, and Uncle Enzo, who was always so serious, so passionate when there was talk of politics and war. Stefano did not remember his father being anything like that. He remembered that his father hated war.

"Mamma, I want to fight," said Beppe.

Beppe's father agreed. Enzo sat there with his one good leg, the other lost in the great world war. Even then Stefano was curious why they were keen for their only child to go to war when Enzo had nearly lost his life.

"Yes, you must!" said Beppe's father.

Julietta looked at her son, Stefano, and he could read the fear. She would rather go herself than send her only son. But Stefano was tired of being the baby. He was tired of his mother always wanting to protect him, wanting to know where he went. Always fussing about the way he was dressed, putting him in trousers and starched white shirts for church. He wanted to be a man like Beppe was allowed to be, who seemed to have the freedom to do as he wished.

"Then I will fight, too," said Stefano.

Beppe laughed, but his laugh was not spiteful. He patted him on the head. "You are too young. One day when you are big, but now you must stay here and look after your mamma."

And Stefano resented this, that he was the only male in the family, old enough to be the one who must stay for his family, but still too young to go to war.

Julietta closed her eyes and said a prayer. She didn't believe in war either. Stefano saw it all the way back then: that the two sisters were so very different. And later when loyalties were tested, he would remember the heat on his back from the glass behind him; he would remember the moment. If they had stayed there, if they had never moved north, his losses may not have been so great.

Present-day 1945

The back door is partway open, and Stefano pushes it back farther on its bygone hinges that faintly squeal. Old leaves that had remained peacefully undisturbed on the threshold scatter at the intrusion.

The air inside is pungently stale as he enters a narrow hall between a small storage area and a bathroom, before the front room opens up to reveal a living area, the kitchen, and what appears to be a bedroom at the far end of the house. The rooms are unable to catch the remaining light from the horizon, and Stefano switches on his small torch to survey in detail.

The front room is sparsely furnished, and there is more wreckage on the wooden floor, as if it has been dragged from the pile of burned rubbish outside. Shattered crockery along the perimeter of one wall suggests that items have been thrown against it. A painting that has been shredded still hangs on the wall. Stefano takes a moment to examine it, but the subject of the picture cannot be determined.

Several cupboard doors sit ajar, the contents taken. Empty sacks lie on the floor. He shines his light across the kitchen and examines what is left. In a teapot lie the remains of tea and a coating of green-and-white bulbous mold.

A large fabric sofa beneath the only front ground-floor window is threadbare, its pastel floral design vanishing under decades of light. A square table divides the kitchen stove and sink from the living area, but there are three chairs at the table, one of which is broken. On the table are two empty plates with cutlery. Traces of food remain on the plates, now dried and unrecognizable. The house is empty of recent memories.

A faint shuffling from near the back door forces Stefano to turn the torch sharply. He spies nothing at first, but as he moves toward the sound, the boy appears, eyes squinting from the light now in his face. Stefano puts his finger to his lips to signal him to be quiet, though inside he is exasperated that the child did not wait as told. He directs him toward a small alcove under the stairs, and the boy follows this instruction. The child is used to hiding in houses, but he is too afraid to stay near the darkening river alone.

Stefano walks up the narrow stairs to the top level and checks behind him to make sure there is no sign of the boy. On the top floor are several rooms. The door casing of one small room is splintered, the door hanging to the side, as if flung so hard it has been torn from its hinges.

He opens the second door of a room that overlooks the side between the two properties. Lace curtains hang without damage, and a small table is marred only by a layer of dust. A plush rug on polished wood appears to have also survived unscathed, but a mirror on the wall is cracked and unusable. The bed looks inviting, but he has already decided that he can't sleep here. It looks too personal. Though seemingly uninhabited, the room appears to be waiting patiently for its former inhabitant.

With the glow of the sun almost completely gone, Stefano steps cautiously up to the window to view the other house opposite and the river just visible through the small woods to his left. The neighboring property looks well tended: the back lawn has a boxed area for growing vegetables, and the small patch of tiles leading from the back door is swept of leaves. A large barn sits on the far front side of the other house, and beyond that, thick woodlands run parallel with the river. Directly in front of both houses is the shallow wood that separates the houses from the water.

Just inside the entrance to the third room on this floor are drippings of dark stain across the floorboards. He bends down to rub at the stain, and the smell of rust lingers on his fingertips. It is blood, of course. He knows it well. He walks first to the window—partly covered by one curtain, striped in yellow, gray, and white—that overlooks the woods and the river beyond. He should stay here, he thinks, where he can best view anyone who enters the bend in the track that leads to the houses.

There is a metal bed with springs, its mattress leaning against the wall, the insides torn and gushing out of its belly like entrails. He moves his torch across the mattress to see the remains of a red-brown stain in the center where most of the violence against it has taken place. Something crunches underfoot, and his light then reflects pieces of glass, blues and greens, an ornament perhaps, scattered, then kicked untidily to a corner of the room.

Stefano lifts the mattress up onto the springs, damaged side facing down, disturbing its musty fumes of time. The mattress itself, with its evidence of rage, should be something that warns him away, but the thought of something soft beneath him is an unexpected blessing. It is bed he craves now, and he imagines a full night's sleep before commencing the next stage of his quest.

It is mostly silent outside, though every so often there is the groaning of supply trucks, the change of gears, and the squeal of brakes in the distance.

He collects the boy from downstairs and leads him to the mattress. It is barely nightfall, but they are both weary, and Stefano plans to be up before sunrise. The boy doesn't wait for instruction but climbs on top of the bed, its springs squeaking, and rolls on his side to face the wall. Stefano looks at the space that is left for him, at their close proximity. He shared unbearably cramped sleeping spaces with others in times of little choice, but this is different. He needs his space around him. He needs the space to think. He will have to give the bed to the boy.

Stefano visits the second room again at the front end of the hallway to take the rug that is there, and he drags it to the center of the room where they will rest for the night. He lies down, thinks about putting his satchel under his head, but pushes it to the side instead.

"Michal," says a small voice from the gray.

"Is that your name?" he says, startled by the sound of the boy who has spoken for the first time. His voice is tiny like him.

"Ja," he says in German.

"Do you only talk in the evenings?"

"It is safer in the dark," he whispers.

"Is that what your mother told you?"

He is silent.

"And your father? Did you leave him behind?"

He doesn't respond. Perhaps he doesn't know. Stefano is not sure if the boy is German, since he detects something different about the accent. Perhaps he was in a camp; perhaps he only learned some German there. In any case it gives him pause to think about the mother, to wonder if she was foreign to this country, and to speculate about the reasons why they may have been traveling to Berlin.

But Stefano is silent now for other reasons. And it is soothing, the gentle, heavy breathing of a sleeping child that has begun so suddenly. Stefano is glad that someone at least is at peace for now.

Stefano reaches one arm to the floor beside him and fishes inside the lining of his satchel to retrieve a photo. Turning on his back, he places it inside his shirt to rest above his heart. Arms then behind his head, Stefano listens to the rain as it taps the river and pats down the earth around the house, the noise swaddling the house like a warm blanket. It might be pleasant if he were somewhere else, but there is too much to think about, too much inside his head, to enjoy the sound. He shifts several times to find a comfortable sleeping position. He keeps the torch in his hand; it is habit to check the time throughout the night.

Stefano closes his eyes, imagines the cold water of the Mediterranean, and pleads to the air for good dreams to come.

CHAPTER 5

ROSALIND

Tiny droplets of water splatter the window, and Rosalind is transfixed by the glass, lost in the rattling sounds as rain pelts the metal pails outside. The barn doors near the wood bang suddenly in a torrent of wind, the noise pulling her from her reverie.

With electricity to the area yet to be restored, Rosalind ignites one of the lanterns hanging by the front door, and then strikes a match to light the candle on the kitchen table. Candles feature vividly in the earliest memories of her grandmother's place, when she was small, before there were several electric lights installed around the walls. The flames, the smell of wax burning, and the shadows were comforting back then, but now she feels suffocated, the rooms shrinking under the candle's dull-yellow glow.

After the Russian soldiers left, it took several hours for Rosalind's unsteady legs to find solid ground again. She has heard from some that visits by the military can be volatile. Many people were killed or imprisoned in the months after the war. But more recently, there has been less arbitrary policing and more international monitoring. The world is watching as they dissect Germany and share it among the Allies. But it is still too soon to tell whether it will remain this way: silent, motionless. There is still so much hatred for Germany, its sins too vivid and raw to allow the country yet to move on.

Rosalind turns her attention to the photographs on the living room wall: family photos, several portraits, her grandmother, her parents, a large portrait of Monique, and one in particular she wants to hide away. There are three people in the photograph: Georg, Rosalind, and Monique. Georg's wide-smiling mouth and chin are his only features visible beneath a large floral hat—borrowed from Rosalind's grandmother for the purpose of amusement—that shades his face. She wishes it contained only the two of them. She has thought often of cutting Monique out of the photo, but there would of course be consequences.

Georg can do up his shirt buttons, arrange things obsessively; he can remember timetables of trains that no longer exist, and how to set a table. He can't remember that she is his wife, but he will notice that a photo of Monique is missing. It is not worth the risk. His mind is mysterious to her. With a missing photo, he might speculate, he might rage, or, worse, it might help him remember things she wants buried.

One time Rosalind put the portrait of Monique out of sight, but Georg had seen straightaway, as if the portrait were something he depended on seeing each time he woke. He had punched the wall, the spot where the portrait had hung, and damaged his hand. Rosalind hung it back up again, covering the hole.

The barn doors bang again, this time more aggressively. She crosses the room to peer through the front window toward the blackness of the trees and the barn nearby. Its large doors are open and flapping in the river wind. Her conviction that she latched them is quickly followed by doubt. She has been preoccupied lately.

Rosalind opens the front door, and a cool, damp wind pushes past her, pressing the skirt of her dress flat against her legs. On the earth outside, the rain maps out tiny rivers of water that trickle menacingly toward the lower side of her house.

The two properties are secluded here and spaced a short distance apart. Across the track the shallow woodland separates Rosalind from the river. From the doorway of her cottage, during daylight hours, Rosalind can view the water between the trunks and branches. A light mist hovers across the river and lurks in the shadows of the trees that hang above its edges. To the right the wood becomes thicker for several miles along the edge of the river. It was a place she and Monique and Georg would explore as children.

She shivers, not from the cold. She has seen many boats travel the waterways, but she has seen other objects floating in the river also: pieces of houses, broken things, broken bodies. She feels a sense of dread whenever she spies the riverbank at the bend of the river where items are snagged and whenever she sees something in the water that she can't identify. In the months after the war, it was not unusual to see bodies floating down the river, and pieces of their lives—tins, suitcases, sodden paper, the remains of books—following after them. Private, treasured things that belonged to the dead were discarded in the river in the cleanup after the war. Those things, now useless, travel far away with the current.

1934

The barefoot youths walked to the sharp bend, then veered off the track to enter a clearing of yellow grasses stretching all the way to the embankment. On either side of the clearing, two stretches of wood ran several miles parallel with the river. The trio, the owls of Elbe as they called themselves, had come from the direction of the two houses nestled among the trees where the track went no farther. An endless ceiling of blue above the clearing, and the reach of water behind them, would have made the trio appear insignificant—specks of color on the landscape—if it weren't for the bustle and zest they brought with them.

Georg broke from the group, running on long, bony legs and shouting over his shoulder that he would reach the river first. Each summer, he appeared to grow infinitely upward, tall and nimble and seemingly built for soaring through the clouds. He shouted to the others as he ran, marking the start of a race that the girls, who accompanied him, had been unaware of until then. Georg was someone who filled large empty spaces with his confidence. Most who met Georg thought that he was likely to exceed life's high expectations, but he was unaffected by this, and found the lives of others equally important as his own. He was everything that his peers loved and despised at the same time. He could command the room and divert attention from others, yet make those around him feel greater than what their own abilities would ever allow.

He ran the length of the grass in several easy strides, bare feet crushing the grasses that had barely had enough time to replenish after the last time the group had been there. The embankment eased down to the water, and Georg perched on the edge then to slide down the low wall of brown-gray mud. He wore blue shorts that became stained and slimy by the time he entered the water.

Monique ran toward him, wavy brown hair escaping a bright-orange ribbon, tearing at her clothes that were now a hindrance, and discarding them to the breeze. Her figure was shapely, feminine, though her legs were tanned and muscled like Georg's, and her laughter that reverberated between the walls of wood had the rich, throaty timbre of a man's.

Georg was home from a boarding school outside Berlin and he had been craving this time with the girls who spent the summers with their grandmother. The previous year he had forged a close relationship with Monique, based on their shared quest for adventure; their dares were becoming longer, more dangerous, and more exciting. He had dared Monique to climb the tallest tree, jump from the barn roof, dive deeper into the river to catch a sinking pebble, and she would always meet the challenge. It was the thrill of living to every inch of their young lives that drove them closer. At the river there were no homework due dates, no crowded trams to catch to school, no separate sets of rules for boys and girls. There were no barriers to hold them back from living wild and free. Days and nights ran blissfully into one another.

Rosalind watched the others run to the river. She assessed the strength of the current on the water's surface, decided that it was safe enough, and followed, just not as quickly.

The previous year, Monique had nearly drowned because she was not thoughtful like Rosalind. She did not measure things as well or try to understand the importance of inspection. Monique just *did*. Rosalind had saved her from being swept away downstream, Monique screeching and resisting any attempts at help as she was dragged from the river, sodden and miserable. Her dismay was more from the fact she had to spend the rest of the day inside with her grandmother. That she could not return to the water until the following day.

Rosalind grabbed the edges of her skirt and bunched it tightly in front of her as she stepped carefully down the slippery incline to feel the water temperature with her toes. By the time she had taken her foot out again, Monique and Georg had already swum to the middle. She hated that they didn't wait for her.

"Watch the current!" Rosalind called out to them. Though there was little chance Monique would nearly drown again. In the year since her watery near demise, she had grown robust and capable, and as confident in water as a fish. She was everything that Rosalind wasn't.

But they ignored Rosalind's words of warning. They were too busy laughing, too busy with each other. They had stopped swimming now to tread water, and Monique was busy trying to push Georg's head below the surface. Rosalind watched the scene develop into a frenzy of splashing.

She stepped back onto the grass, unzipped her skirt, and folded it neatly in place near the embankment. Underneath her clothes Rosalind wore a new swimming costume that she had received for her birthday.

At fifteen her body was still sticklike, and Rosalind wished for a more womanly shape to emerge. She watched the others ignore her while she unbuttoned her blouse to rest it with the skirt, then stepped carefully down the mud again to enter the cool water five inches at a time.

She swam evenly toward them. Georg grabbed her as she arrived, and he attempted to push her deeper into the water.

"Don't!" said Rosalind, though she loved it all the same. Loved the way that Georg was so strong and so dependable. And Rosalind loved and hated that everyone loved him. She wanted to possess him even back then. She wanted him all to herself.

Monique ducked under the water and came up next to Georg very close, separating him from Rosalind.

"I love you," she whispered. Rosalind thought that she had just heard things, but later when she was thinking about it, helping her grandmother in the kitchen, chopping the vegetables, she knew she was right. And she was trying to picture Georg's face, trying to remember what his reaction was.

"Wondrous" was the word. As if his wishes had just come true.

Present-day 1945

Rosalind stops washing her plate at the sink to listen. She waits for half a minute, hands resting in hot water that has come from the kettle, her eyes fixed to the blackness outside the window. The sounds of the barn doors banging are barely audible against the rain that pounds the pails, loudly now, and smacks the barren earth outside.

She returns to washing, her ears trained on every sound outside. There was a short and eerie period of silence when the bombs and air assaults stopped and the steady flow of tanks and trucks with armed soldiers eased. Noises in those final weeks of war had meant danger, destruction, and death. Now they are intermittent and mostly from vehicles sent to repair cities, the occasional aircraft and military patrol, the calls of wildlife, and the chugging of motorboats. And these sounds mean everything to Rosalind. They give her clues to the changes that are happening in the world outside her tiny sphere, and they remind her that there are still things to fear.

She finishes drying the dishes and sees there is rainwater leaking into the kitchen from the corner of the house. Water seeps between the cracks of the badly patched brickwork that her grandmother reconstructed herself when the house was damaged by air fire.

She checks the time from the cuckoo clock on the wall that stopped chiming sometime during the war years, now with just one tiny clicking sound as the doors swing back to release the bird that hovers expectantly in the air for several seconds, then retreats.

From a cupboard she retrieves bed linen and mats and begins to mop up the water that continues to trickle. If the rain doesn't stop, the kitchen will become a pond, since it sinks lower there on one side of the house. It would not be the first time it has flooded. When she arrived last year, the floor was stained with water, and the stench that met her was putrid. Though the festering damp was not the only cause, as she would later learn.

Rosalind had scrubbed and cleaned and used clay from the riverbank to plug up the holes, but in heavy rain, water always found a way through.

She opens the front door to view the barn doors that swing freely to batter the walls outside, and rain falls sideways at her through the space. Rosalind climbs into a woolen coat and pulls the hood firmly over her head. She steps into rubber boots that are near the door, collects the lantern from the wall, closes the door behind her, and briskly sets out in the direction of the barn. Once she slips on fresh mud but manages to catch herself before rushing inside the shelter of the barn.

Puddles of water lead to the center of the structure. Rosalind holds the lamp above her. The light reveals an eerie emptiness, except for a barrow, a workbench that is absent of tools, and the earthy smell of decomposing hay, once used to feed the geese in winter. Something catches her eye, and she walks closer to examine the floor, avoiding the narrow vertical streams of water that enter through the many bullet holes in the ceiling. Nutshells lie in a small pile near the middle of the space.

In recent weeks, she has become more aware of changes in the environment, of the effects of weather, of the habits of birds: changes that do not inspire suspicion. But the nutshells give her reason to be suspicious this time. Someone has been here. She walks back to the doors and views the dark wooded area beside the river with some dread, fearing what it might hold this night and wondering who has left the shells.

Yellow light that creeps outward from the house's front window exposes a small piece of the track. Rosalind imagines Monique there, appearing out of the darkness, in her pink floral dress, her hair flying wildly around her head, coming home from the town. It was a sight that she had come to depend on once, for company, or news at least.

It is madness, she thinks, or loneliness, these imaginings of Monique. Or perhaps they are wishes. She bolts the doors and makes a swift return to the house, her head bent forward to brace for rain. When she is halfway there, something else catches her eye: a flash of light at a window from the house next to hers. She freezes, rain falling on her face as she waits for something more, something that doesn't come, before continuing back home.

Once inside the house, Rosalind's heart beats fast. She shakes the coat briefly and hangs it back on the hook. Someone is there, someone who perhaps knows about her past. She tries to picture what she saw: the light from a torch. Did she imagine it? She has become more paranoid in recent times. She has heard voices that aren't there, seen things that vanish before her eyes. She has spent too much time alone in her head. Spent too much time alone with Georg.

She must be rational, she tells herself. It is likely to be beggars, nothing more sinister, though they can be dangerous, too. She can't take any chances. She removes the nutshells from the coat pocket and tips them into the sink. Erich has told her to be vigilant, to be mindful of strangers.

Georg thumps the floor from above, demanding her attention, perhaps alerted to the commotion downstairs, perhaps hungry, perhaps needing more drugs. Most likely the latter.

She reaches again for her coat on the wall.

The thumping continues.

She pulls on her coat again and looks up the stairs toward the source of the noise, her hand on the door handle. Georg will have to wait.

CHAPTER 6
STEFANO

A sharp clap startles him from sleep, and Stefano rises on his elbows to see a beam of light charge through the window. A battery of rain sounds across the river, heading toward the house. Stefano crouches, scans the blackened corners, and listens for ghosts, his fingers instinctively reaching for the plaited wire bracelet on his good wrist. When he is certain there are no intruders, he steps toward the window where the air blows wet against his face. The child is still sleeping, too exhausted and travel weary to stir, and yet Stefano is amazed that the sound has not woken him. He leans near to check that the child is still breathing, relieved at the even rise and fall of the boy's small chest.

The roof creaks above him, protesting from the weight of water. And somewhere within the house he senses a change. He is not alone. It wasn't the thunder that woke him, but the door blowing shut—the door he had closed earlier.

It has been rare in recent years that he has not been aware of every movement around him in the night, senses heightened since his first Italian campaign in the deserts of North Africa. But his body desperately craves rest, something lately he finds difficult to fight against, despite the rawness of his nerves that may never disappear. He reaches out toward the dark space that holds his bag, and his hand finds an empty patch of floor. Someone has entered the room and seen them both sleeping. Someone now has his things.

Stefano steps cautiously and swiftly out to the landing to see a faint glow from the floor below, which grows stronger closer to the bottom of the steps and near the open doorway of the kitchen to his right. He stands back a foot from the entrance. The living area to his left is dark and empty, no signs of movement. He moves slowly to peer into the kitchen, but the tip of a rifle, just inches from his face, prevents this, the weapon pushed farther toward him, forcing him to take a step backward. The bearer of the rifle is tall like Stefano, though fair. He appears ominously larger from the doorway, blocking out most of the light now behind him.

Instinctively, Stefano puts his hands in the air. The fair man remains very still, the rifle unmoving, raised toward Stefano.

"What are you doing here?" asks the man in German, louder above the rain.

"Trying to sleep," replies Stefano in the defeated language. There were many things he could have said, but this seemed the most reasonable.

Behind the man with the rifle, in the dim yellow light of a lantern, Stefano can see his bag unopened on the table. He assumes the man has not yet had time to examine its contents.

"Give me a proper answer."

"I am on my way home."

"Where's home?"

"Italy."

"You are a long way from there."

"I came from a hospital in the North," answers Stefano.

"Why did you choose this house?" he asks. "Out of all the houses to sleep in."

"It was pure chance. I did not want to sleep near the main road, and the path led me here. I was going to sleep in the shed behind, but it looked too broken with rain about to fall."

"Roll up your sleeves."

Stefano does so slowly. It always comes down to this. What you are, not who you are, and the numbers on your arm.

"Which prison?" asks the German.

"Sachsenhausen."

"Were you a deserter?"

"No. I was a soldier in the Italian army. I left Italy to join the German army in the North when I realized that the rest of Italy would shortly fall into Allied hands."

"Why were you put in prison?"

"They made a mistake."

"You sound like a deserter to me."

The German continues to stand very still. The rifle does not waver.

"The war is over," says Stefano calmly, holding back breaths. "And you would have seen that I have a child with me."

In the moment of silence, Stefano wonders if this is where it will end for him, and he does not imagine his own death but that of others, of those he has let down. Of the fruitless, senseless way that death might roam.

The fair man lowers the gun, and Stefano breathes out silently, with his brain still wired with fear and memories stretching beyond the ransacked house.

"It doesn't matter now, yes?" says the man lightly. "It doesn't matter what we were before the war ended."

"I want my bag."

"Of course," the man says, and steps aside to allow Stefano room to pass.

He does not move straightaway but watches the eyes and movements of the other man. Stefano is used to tricks. He trusted someone once—someone close to him—and others ended up dead.

The fair man rests the rifle against the wall. "There are no bullets in it anyway. But I cannot be too careful. People still want to harm me."

Stefano walks past him to the table to examine his bag. He unzips it, looks briefly inside, then zips it up again.

"Is the child yours?" the man asks.

"I found the boy on the side of the road, his mother dead."

"And why would you take him if you are going to Italy?"

"I was trying to find him a home."

The fair man is thoughtful, silent for a moment, perhaps attempting to find sense in such a task, which Stefano himself has yet to find. Stefano wonders briefly if he would have been woken, perhaps killed, if not for the child asleep nearby.

"My name is Erich. I was a German soldier," the other man says, "captured by the Russians and then released."

"Released?" says Stefano.

"I agree it sounds unbelievable. I was captured before the end of the war. I helped them with information. For that I was rewarded. It does not mean I was let off lightly. I had to pay for my sins." He does not elaborate, nor does Stefano query. They are strangers yet. "An Italian soldier?"

"Yes."

"Do you have a name?"

"Stefano," he says, viewing Erich carefully as the German moves away to begin clearing pieces of wood that lie strewn across the kitchen floor. He is slightly taller than Stefano, narrower across the chest. Fair hair that is almost white, his skin darkly tanned from months in the sun. It is difficult to see the eyes, in the dim light. He suspects they are much lighter than they appear.

"Do you live here?" Stefano asks.

"Yes. Sometimes."

And then as if Erich has remembered where he is, he explains the house. "It is bad, yes? Beggars, passersby, probably foreign, come here to spend a night. It is disappointing what they do to the place while they are here, while I am elsewhere."

Stefano remembers the violence against the mattress, the picture. It seemed personal to him.

"We should leave," says Stefano suddenly.

"In this weather? I won't try and kill you in your sleep. If I wanted you dead, you would be by now."

Stefano is wondering what he missed when he came in. Was he here all the time? Was he watching?

Erich stamps the floor in places until he hears a hollow sound. With a fork that he has taken from a drawer, he pokes at a board of wood on the floor until it shifts from its position. He lifts away several planks, reaches his arm deeply into the hole to retrieve a metal pail, then tilts it to show Stefano the contents. Inside is a bottle with amber liquid and a small brown paper bag.

Erich smells the small package and passes it to Stefano who does the same.

"It is coffee. Pure," says Erich.

"Did you put it there?"

Erich does not look at Stefano while he opens the bottle.

"No. I just know how people think. And they are not much different from one another. They find the same places to hide things."

Erich puts his nose to the neck of the bottle, and Stefano wonders why squatters would bother to hide these things.

"Whiskey. Good whiskey," he says, this time directly to Stefano, rather than to the spaces around him. From his smile, he is clearly pleased with the find. He sits on the floor and leans back against the table leg.

"What kind of soldier were you?" asks Stefano.

"A soldier on the front line . . . After we destroyed our enemies, we were often sent into homes to check for people hiding. It was either the floor or the ceiling. If we didn't find people, it was usually items. The spaces where they hid things were usually in rooms where they stood, as if by standing on top of their precious items they could protect them. They were wrong."

Stefano wants to ask what happened to the people who were hiding, but he already knows the answer.

"We were the ones to be sacrificed if we were ambushed, blown up," says Erich. "I was part of a group that was expendable. It wasn't my choice."

Erich takes a swig and passes the bottle to Stefano, who sits down also, somewhat reluctantly, with his back against the wall. He is close enough to stretch and reach for the bottle, but he keeps what he thinks is a safe distance between them.

Stefano takes a mouthful. It burns slightly and at the same time instantly dulls some of his worst fears of the man who has handed it to him.

"I wasn't allowed to drink in the war. My parents thought it weak, my superiors, too. There are many good things to the end of the war, yes?"

It is a redundant question, thinks Stefano. It does not require a response.

"Do you have family waiting?" asks Erich.

"Yes. And you? Do you have others here?"

"I am all that's left," Erich says, in a tone that places little significance to such an outcome. "Tell me, Stefano. Did you really fight for Germany?"

"I fought on your side, but then toward the end, your comrades imprisoned me anyway."

Erich smiles. It is disconcerting to Stefano that the German appears so unaffected. Smiles by Germans were often followed by something cruel.

"We are all on the same side now, are we not?" says Erich. "The side of disarray."

Erich takes another mouthful, eyes carefully on Stefano, who does not care to respond.

"I heard what they did to people in prisons. Is that where you hurt your hand? Did they torture you?"

"It was from an explosion."

Erich looks briefly at Stefano's hand and then his face, studying him and interpreting the truth.

"I am going to sleep," says Erich, sighing and standing up, perhaps now bored with the mostly unresponsive intruder. "You are welcome to sleep here. I believe I can trust you. We will save this."

He puts the lid on the bottle.

Stefano remains seated. He is reflecting on the use of the word "we," as if it were the first of more to come.

"You should go back to bed," says Erich. He walks slowly from the kitchen, leaving behind the rifle leaning against the wall. "You can trust me also," he calls out from the other end of the house. "There are no bullets in the rifle. Feel free to check."

Stefano hears the protest of bedsprings, the rustle of cloth on cloth, and then the stillness. He rises and peers around the stairs toward the end of the house where he can just make out the other man's shape through the open doorway of his bedroom, then returns to check the rifle. Erich was telling the truth, but he could have bullets elsewhere. Stefano is still wary.

He treads carefully upstairs, nerves still jumbled at the thought of the German lying below, unsure of tricks and the effects of the alcohol that hums inside his head and swirls warmly through his chest. It has been days since Stefano has had a full night's sleep.

Inside the bedroom upstairs, the boy is still sleeping. Since there is no key in the lock, he shuts the door and slides the rug to lie in front of it, blocking it, alert to the creaks in the house, now that the rain has eased, and one ear trained on the stairs.

But the events of the day prove too much, and several hours before dawn, after his eyes have closed involuntarily, he sinks deeply into sleep.

1936

When Stefano's cousin came back from a victory in Abyssinia, after Italy successfully suppressed those who were opposing Italian rule, Beppe was altered slightly. Not a great deal, just a little less interested in events at home, as if they were no longer significant. Stefano had started showing an interest in a future academic career, with plans to study languages and literature. On weekends he helped his sister Nina make jewelry, bracelets, earrings, and rings with small colored stones threaded with fine silver or copper wire, twisting the metal into loops and plaiting them into shapes. The bright shiny objects would attract the eyes of the tourists.

Thoughts of joining the military voluntarily, which had been in his mind prior to his cousin's leaving, had since dissipated once he found a desire to read books, learn, and breathe foreign words that he would practice on the tourists. But with Beppe's return, and once again craving his company, Stefano found that his enthusiasm to join the military was reinvigorated.

The second day back after a good sleep, Beppe took him out to a bar, even though Stefano, tall for his age, was too young to drink.

Beppe said he was keen to get out of the house; his parents were fighting with him constantly. Enzo wanted to move to the North. He did not like living among "peasants," as he called them. Stefano's father was once one of those peasants, but Stefano did not like to say this to his uncle or cousin. Stefano knew that Enzo's insensitive opinions were not shared by his son. The North was where the money was and where the wealthy continued to prosper. Enzo wanted to sell their house by the sea and head to Florence. There he would buy a business and make real money, he said. When the war was over, Beppe would take over the business, and Serafina expected several grandchildren. The future was clear for them.

Beppe fought with his father about the relevance of war. Over a couple of glasses of wine, Beppe was able to express these thoughts to his intelligent young cousin, whose father had rejected, and mother still rejected, the idea of war and had not openly supported any cause by Mussolini.

"I don't think this war is right, Stefano. I don't see any point to it. For a start half the country we are conquering is desert. And there is little of value there. I can't think why Il Duce is so desperate to retain it that he would risk lives for it. I don't see what Mussolini sees. I can't see where it will end. I can't see us winning. This resurgence by the local people will be the first of many."

"But, Beppe, you were so keen to leave to fight."

"I have seen some things, Stefano, that I never thought I would. I don't know if it is good what we are doing. I don't think it is good at all. If you could avoid it, I would suggest that you never join. I do not want you to see the things I have."

"Like what, Cousin?"

"Things, war, comrades dying. Our leaders do not seem to know what they are doing. I feel that many more of our own men will be slaughtered there, and their deaths will count for nothing."

"I am going to sign up one day."

"You are not!"

"I have no choice."

"You have every choice. You have a family to look after. Without you, what will your mother and sisters do?"

Stefano was confused. "But you wanted me to join."

"Not now that I've seen. Not now that my eyes are open."

Despite what Beppe said, though now with some reservation, Stefano still felt it was his duty to fight. He wanted to do something worthy one day. He felt that he owed his country and those who had already committed to serve.

"What about your studies? You are too smart, Stefano. Not like me whose future was not in books. Do not waste your brain."

"I can put study on hold. I will take books with me to read."

"And what if you lose your head? What will you study with then?"

A wave of sadness struck Beppe as he looked at his fresh-faced young cousin who had idolized him. *What have I done? I am responsible for this. I have encouraged him.* He hoped there would be no war to fight by the time his cousin came of age. Little did he know that there was a greater war to come.

"You need your studies, and people will need you one day."

Stefano thought it particularly odd that Beppe, who had once teased him about his future career and love of languages, was now encouraging it.

"I will ask to be with you. I want to be at your side, Cousin."

Beppe nodded with resignation. His young cousin was smart, but he was also stubborn, a family trait. The more any one of them was told not to do something, the more likely they would. He finished his third glass of wine quickly.

He is drinking too fast, thought Stefano. He was always drinking, but it had once been a joyous thing. It was different then.

Several weeks later, Beppe was called away to another campaign, and a year after Stefano was partway through his studies, he would join his battle-hardened cousin in a new fight in Hitler's war against the Allies.

Stefano loved his studies, but his learning could wait. The future seemed vast.

Present-day 1945

Stefano wakes slowly to noises downstairs: the soft scraping of bristles on oak, pots clanging, and doors clicking shut. The twittering of birds raises the prospect of morning.

He feels groggy, his sleep deeper than most, perhaps due to the whiskey, the travel, the ache in his leg. His back is sticky with sweat, and outside the sun has already spent several hours mopping up from the night before. The boy sits at the edge of the bed, his legs too short to touch the floor.

Stefano's shoulders sag. *What to do with a child?*

"Are you hungry?" he asks the boy.

He nods.

"Is your voice gone again?"

The boy nods again, afraid to make sound in a room filled with light.

Stefano stands, stretches, then moves to the window. A sparkle of silver on the water in the distance and the smells here, tangy and cleaner than the places he has come from. A distant whistle of something mechanical, a factory, a truck, but barely audible, and the sound of a tree being felled somewhere behind him. And closer, the high-pitched, uneven squeals of a water pump lever.

He does not need to call the boy, who is already on his heels before he has reached the top stair. Downstairs the noises have ceased, and there is no sign of the German. His pack and the whiskey bottle sit on the table, where the rifle is now leaning. Stefano peers through the kitchen window with its view of the neighboring house, then opens the rifle to check that it is still unloaded.

The picture that was hanging in strips on the wall is missing. The plates and teapot are clean and put away, and there is a pleasant aroma of coffee, and the scent of something floral through the open window, which takes him briefly to another time, to a small apartment, to the smell of perfume on skin.

He walks to the room at the rear of the house just outside the back door and pisses in the bowl that is stained and browned, though some effort has been made to clean it this morning. He sends the boy in after him, then walks toward the front door to survey the track and the area around it.

Erich's house is square in shape, off-white in color, with a red roof and brown-painted window trims that are peeling in places. Both houses are pretty, but perhaps more from the location. The house on the adjacent property is bigger, long and narrow, with a high-pitched roof. There is a pen for animals off to the far side of it that he did not see before. The noises from the geese make the house seem more amiable.

When he turns to walk back inside, Erich appears suddenly, startling him.

"Good morning!" says Erich. The clothes he was wearing the night before exhibit no crumpled signs of sleep.

Stefano can see the boy behind Erich, unsure what to do, a barrier now between them.

"His name is Michal," says Stefano, and Erich turns to greet the child.

"Nice to meet you, Michal." Erich puts out his hand. The boy's arms remain by his sides.

Erich turns back to Stefano, unfazed by the lack of response. The German is probably used to it.

"I have made some coffee, but first, come! I would like to show you something."

Stefano tells Michal to wait and follows Erich to the rear of the house. Michal obeys this time, his child's sense making him uncertain of Erich.

Stefano is curious but cautious. The pyre of burned items has partly been cleared, and Erich stops behind the shed at the base of the incline.

More woodland behind both houses gently rises upward to a narrow hilltop and down the other side to the main road.

The two men face a large pile of branches and rugs spread across the ground, used as a disguise to hide the small car sitting in the middle of the debris. The lid of its engine is wide open, like a hungry bird, and several tools lie on the ground at the rear of the car.

"This is yours?"

"Yes. I've kept it hidden. Petrol and cars are very much in demand. It is good, yes? I just have to source some petrol, and then it will take me wherever I wish to go. But don't get any ideas about taking it. The Russians will tear it from under you."

Stefano peers inside the passenger-side window as Erich climbs into the driver's seat. The car looks new, the leather seats unmarked.

"Does it work?"

Erich rests his hands on the wheel, sliding them gently over the molded wood. He turns the key, and the car growls to life. While he continues to pump the accelerator, he examines the gauges on the dashboard. Stefano takes a step back. From the satisfaction across his face, it is more than a piece of machinery to Erich. The car represents something he can lovingly control.

Erich turns off the engine.

"Do you drive?" he asks Stefano, stepping from the vehicle.

Stefano is remembering a time with Beppe in North Africa, where he had been taught to drive: a borrowed car, red earth spraying in the rearview mirror.

"Not much."

He helps Erich cover the car with its disguise of rugs and debris, and they return to the house. Once inside, Stefano notices the broken china and pictures that Erich has swept into a corner of the storeroom.

"How long since you were here?"

"A week, just over. I've been traveling to search for work."

"And did you find it?"

"Yes," says Erich.

The house hasn't been lived in for a long time. That much appears clear to Stefano, along with the speculation that the German is most likely lying about everything.

CHAPTER 7
ERICH

Erich has been in control for most of his life, except in two instances, but those events he can bury beneath others. He has watched life as if he has sat above it, carefully and meticulously planning his next move. He looks across at Stefano, a man so different from him. Quiet, thoughtful, Stefano carries many scars, but perhaps no more than Erich. *Surviving is all about the mind,* his mother used to say. *If you have power of that, you will carry on.*

"I drove before and during the war," says Erich. "My father had a nice car."

"What did your father do?" It is the first time the Italian has sounded genuinely interested. It is perhaps the fact that his father had money that piques his attention. Anyone with money in Germany used to suggest importance.

"He was a businessman. He sold machinery, parts. He helped supply factories. He had an excuse not to fight."

It is a small piece of a very large truth.

"He sounds important."

"No," says Erich, his answer assuring there are no more questions. "What part of Italy do you come from?"

Stefano pauses. Erich can see that he is measuring his answer. Dark eyes, dark face and skin, he is as mysterious as Erich chooses to be vague. Though there are other clues to people that Erich can search for in the reticence: the eye movements, the hand gestures, the talking without the use of words.

"The South originally, Campania. But then when the war started, we moved to stay with cousins in the North. My father was dead. My uncle made us go."

Erich sees there are parts missing in the story, parts that don't concern him. The Italian's response sounds truthful. But Erich also knows that it is far easier to tell the truth, but just not give all the truth.

"Then you made the right move," says Erich.

"Did I?" He turns to look directly at Erich now.

"You fought alongside Germany, did you not?"

Stefano is silent from across the kitchen table, the boy now by his side.

"We had a good army," says Erich. "In the end it was simply numbers that killed us." And machinery also, though he doesn't like to think that someone else's machinery caused the end to Germany's power.

"Not good enough," says Stefano.

Erich smiles at first to cover the sting of these words, yet the stranger's sharp edges and wit have aroused more interest.

"In my experience, Italians have had very little allegiance to anyone. They don't know who they support."

Erich is testing Stefano, to see how far he can push him. He can easily bring the conversation back to an even level.

"It is hard when the person in charge has no allegiance to his people."

"Mussolini. A madman, yes? Better without him, yes?" And Erich smiles again, disarming him.

"*Un pazzo* we called him, yes! But not the only madman."

Erich says nothing. His feelings toward his former führer are mixed. One cannot suddenly dismiss a loyalty that has been bred, then fed and nurtured until it has become part of one's blood.

"What does it matter, North, South? No matter," says Erich. "There are no sides anymore."

There is a release of tension between them. Minor, but something. Erich can't explain why, but he feels relief, though he knows, or senses, that at no time did he feel threatened by Stefano. He always had the gift of knowing who might harm him. He was trained to sense it, to assess an enemy, but the gift is not only from training. It is his belief that he was born with an instinct.

"Will it be safe for you there? It is still dangerous from what I've heard. There are still people left to hang, people who did not support the Allies."

"I know that some resistance members are still calling for blood, but the fascists are gaining support again," says Stefano, "and I know a cardinal who will get me safely down south, if I run into any trouble. He has secretly passed Germans through also, some to Africa and across to South America. I will seek his help if I need it."

"Where did you hear about this cardinal?"

"When I was in the hospital, I spoke to some Germans who were there at the end. Some who were caught spoke of those who weren't. They said the Italian partisans, and others who fought the North, will not touch the churches. It is what he believes. It is what I believe, too."

Stefano has answered without blinking, without the look of someone who has forced a response. This information excites Erich, and while his face remains placid, a heady mixture of thoughts and feelings swirls and rises from deep within him. The stranger's arrival is an omen perhaps, though he has never believed in such. Plans are what he needs, and people to advance these. The Italian could be the plan he has been looking for and a gift that has landed here by means he can't explain.

"I would like to help you," continues Erich, "especially as a thank-you for supporting the North."

"I've done nothing you can thank me for," says Stefano, some bitterness in his tone.

"I can drive you to Dresden, to the train, and the boy to the camp. It will save you some time and help your leg." Erich has noticed the limp.

"But the Russians . . . Aren't you afraid they will steal your car?"

"I know the roads they don't travel and the times they do. I can get you there and back without them ever knowing."

Stefano pauses, examines his hands. "Why would you do that for me?"

"Why would I not do that?" Erich shrugs, unperturbed by the question. "It is better to move on. It will accomplish more. Look at it as a fellow soldier helping another."

Stefano is studying him, warily, attempting to search for truth in his words, and the reasons behind them.

"I offer a house, a car, and friendship, with no catch. You have nothing to fear from me. I can also give you food. The boy is very thin. I can get you good food."

Stefano scratches the back of his head with the hand that has the bandage. He looks at the boy, and Erich can tell that the boy is now a problem for him, now a consideration. He does not have the freedom of a single man while he carries the weight of a dead woman's child.

1933

The midday heat weighed heavily on Erich's back, but he liked the feeling of sun through his thick shirt. He lined the rabbit up and pulled the rifle's trigger, but the bullet missed, and the creature disappeared into the thick grasses. He cursed. He could only curse if his mother wasn't within earshot. He was thirteen and heard other boys say such words.

He was hoping to take a rabbit home for dinner. Killing the rabbit would also make his father proud. Erich liked the responsibility of taking care of things around the home, in his father's absence.

Horst Steiner, his father, was working more and more away from home. Sometimes when Erich woke in the mornings, his father would be gone, and he would not see him for days, sometimes weeks. His father was meeting important people in Berlin, his mother had told him. He was working in support of the National Socialists in their military department, as a consultant on the designs being proposed for war machines.

Erich's father, an engineer, had established an equipment-repair business for farms and factories, while designing modifications to existing farming machinery and motor vehicles in his spare time. Horst had seen his parents lose their farming business during the economic decline of the first war and their financial struggles following, and he believed that he would prosper under Hitler, who promised to bring the country back from the gloom.

That day, Erich was disappointed that he didn't come back with any rabbits. His mother was large in the belly. He had another sibling on the way. The new baby would make his third sibling, all younger. He was in charge of the others, said his mother. He did a good job, she said. Though he could not control one of them. His sister, the second, the only daughter, was more troubled. She would wander around the property aimlessly in the rain and return with clothes covered in grass and mud, and injure herself often, and one time she cut her hair off with sewing scissors. Despite all this, Erich liked her best because she was different from him, and because she wasn't afraid of living. She was brave and wanted to be a soldier, though even if she could join, he did not think she would be good at it. She was not a good listener, not like him. She did not like taking orders at all.

His mother wasn't as disappointed about the rabbit because she'd just received a telegram that sat open on the table.

"Is that from Vati?" Erich asked.

"Yes, he has sent some good news. Adolf Hitler has won. His party will now run Germany unchallenged."

"Why is that good, Mutti?"

"Because he will help the people who are struggling to put food on their tables. He will put a stop to foreigners living here and taking our jobs. And he will protect us from those who seek to feud with Germany."

The information his mother provided was interesting, but it was not important to Erich at the time. His mission had been to shoot rabbits.

"When is Vati coming home?"

"Soon. Can you bring in some wood?"

When he woke the next morning, his father was just arriving, horn blazing as he came up the long drive. He had a new car then. Shining, black. He was earning money from the party.

Horst walked in and hugged his wife and patted Erich on the head. Erich loved the way he touched his head. Horst then picked up Erich's brother and sister. He always brought things back from Berlin. He gave Claudine a little painted bear figurine.

That day, Erich stayed in the fields until he killed two rabbits and brought them home. After that he rarely missed with his rifle.

Present-day 1945

Erich has asked Stefano for his map, which he reluctantly withdraws from his bag and spreads out on the table. The German points to the location of the train station marked on the map and advises the time it will take to drive there.

"I can take you," he says. "Save you the walk. The tracks were destroyed, but they have repaired the worst of it to send people out of Germany. It leaves every few days. The next time is Friday."

The Italian looks at the map, expressionless. For some reason, something in the stiff way he bends across the map, not all the way, tells Erich he is not receptive to the information.

Michal, the strange mute child, peers at the map with more interest. When he catches Erich's eye, he looks away quickly. He wears the same silent, disillusioned guise of those Erich had sent away to the camps, those who didn't return, and it bothers Erich that the child is this close; that he is even here. If it were he, the child would have been left to fend for himself, like so many others.

"Is it manned by Russians?" Stefano asks.

"Yes, of course," says Erich. "But they won't bother you with that mark on your arm. They will be quick to see the back of you."

"It is not too far to walk. I passed through there."

"The drive will take the pressure off your leg. I see you have an injury."

The Italian fixes unresponsively upon a point on the map. The air is tense and silent while he thinks.

"And the camp," says Stefano, "there are other orphans there?"

"Yes, they will take the boy. They will try to locate his family."

"That is a generous offer," says Stefano. Though the words don't match the look of disdain, as if he would rather put a knife to Erich's neck than accept a lift from a German.

Stefano explains the offer to the boy: that they could stay a few days, and he will go to a camp where they can return him home.

The boy shakes his head.

"You will be safe there," says Stefano to the boy.

It is an unintentional lie that adults tell children. Erich's mother never used such lines and neither does he. The truth is always there, the harsh realities never disguised with pointless words.

Stefano is slow to respond and does not look at Erich, which suggests he is still mistrustful. It will be up to Erich to earn his trust, to dissolve the tension and soften the belligerence that the foreigner wears as armor around him.

"If we decide to stay," says Stefano, "then I must find some way to repay you."

And Stefano is then staring at him, this time without suspicion or hostility, but with an expression more pliable. Erich pauses, distracted suddenly by the intensity of the gaze and feelings he cannot yet name. Affection is probably too strong, pity too weak: a connection of some kind between potential allies.

The boy begins to whimper, nervously looking around the room. The child can sense a change in circumstance, a shift in the future. He has seen enough of changes that weren't for the better, changes that killed his mother.

But before Stefano has time to reassure the boy further, Michal has fled out the front door to run up the path toward the clearing.

CHAPTER 8
ROSALIND

Monique sways, not walks, into the kitchen. She is like a cat, sultry and predaceous, the way she looks from side to side, searching for distraction.

"Did you like the beets I left for you when you got home yesterday? I thought they would be good for frying with salt and butter, and spinach," says Monique.

"Yes, thank you."

"They were cheap at the market."

Monique pours herself some of the weak tea that Rosalind has made and sits across from her. There is a childlike innocence about Monique, with her high arched brows above deep-blue eyes that always wander curiously, full-dimpled cheeks, and small lips that naturally sit parted, in an expression that to Rosalind always holds a question mark. And it is a face that most have been drawn to. Monique can hold someone's gaze for longer than is necessary, she can bat her thick dark eyelashes without a sense of vanity, and she can steer all the attention toward her.

"Where were you?" asks Rosalind.

"You're not my mother," she says, brushing her dark wavy hair back from her face. "You don't need to ask such questions."

Rosalind looks down at the hands in her lap. Monique has always been willful.

When she looks up Monique is gone. She was never there. It has been like this a lot lately. For so many years she longed for Monique to disappear, but now she strangely misses her. Misses the way she brings life to a room.

They had been close at times, under the umbrella of uncertain futures. But war does that. It brings people closer even when they are nothing alike.

She would not be alive if it weren't for Monique, and she wishes that Monique were here to talk to about Berlin, to off-load the baggage that she carries. To tell Monique what she did in those final moments at the hospital in Berlin, and about the bodies after the bombing, parts of them, nothing that could be identified with a whole person: missing limbs, heads and bodies torn apart, burns that blackened people to something unrecognizable.

Rosalind has seen more debris here, too, more broken people. For a long time she was immune to tragedy, to blood. But she is immune no longer, now unable to deal with the sight of another injured soldier from the battlefield.

Rosalind opens up the front door. She has to push it firmly, the wood swollen within the frame from the rain the night before.

1935

Monique took off on the bicycle, and Rosalind ran after her. They were meant to double, but on the final leg of the journey from town, when Rosalind had briefly stepped away from the bike to collect some elderberries that her grandmother boiled for tea, Monique thought it would be funny to leave her older cousin stranded. She took off at great speed toward home.

"Monique! Wait!"

But she was gone, and Rosalind had to walk the rest of the way to their river house. As she neared the house, she saw that the bicycle had been discarded on its side at the edge of the wood, back wheel still spinning. She could hear voices through the trees and followed the sound. Monique was there, sitting with Georg against a tree. She was laughing at something he had just whispered in her ear. She turned to look at Rosalind, and just for a second Rosalind saw a sliver of defiance, as if she were the older one in control.

"Take these to Oma!" said Rosalind angrily, dumping the basket of berries in Monique's lap.

"I was just having fun with you." Monique looked at her under large guilty lids.

"You should grow up! Stop being so thoughtless!"

"Why are you so mad?" Georg asked Rosalind.

"She left me!" Though she couldn't say if this was really the reason or whether it was the fact that the two people she was closest to looked so good together. She felt suddenly as if she had interrupted something special, as if they would be fine without her.

"It was a joke!" said Georg. "You still have legs."

She felt affronted by this comment. She thought at least he would defend her.

"Sorry, Rosalind," Monique said, standing up with the basket of berries. "That was mean of me about the bicycle!" But Rosalind had already diverted her anger to Georg, who had not sided with her, who sought Monique's immaturity for amusement.

Georg playfully slapped the backs of Monique's legs, and she bounded off through the trees to her *Oma*. Georg stayed sitting on the ground and put his hands behind his head. His hair had grown too long. His shirt was open, and his stick legs stretched out from wide-legged shorts.

"So!" he said smugly. "This is how you spend your last day here. Angry!"

He knows, she thought at the time. He knows how I feel about him. They were sixteen and seventeen. Her feelings toward him had grown stronger with every passing year.

"Do you want to go swimming?" he asked her, while she battled her thoughts on whether to remain angry.

"Yes," said Rosalind, brightening slightly at the thought they would spend some more time alone.

"Go tell Monique then! I'll meet you both on the platform."

Rosalind felt ambushed by these words and walked out of the wood to collect the bike that Monique had so casually discarded. Georg followed her, wondering what he had said to offend her.

"What's with the sad face?"

"I'm not sad," she said, but something had changed since Monique had arrived to interrupt their summers. He was less inclusive toward her, less giving of information.

Georg grabbed her suddenly around the waist, forcing her to drop the bike. He swung her around until she was dizzy, until she was smiling again. He could do that. Change you and turn the mood. Rinse out the bad and make things good again. He kissed her goodbye. Not a long and lingering kiss but a soft and gentle one at the edge of her mouth, his arm still wrapped tightly around her.

He released her moments later and ran home. She stood there smiling a little, watching him, her ponytail frayed from the activity. She picked up the bike again to wheel it toward the house.

Monique was his match, and they shared an enthusiasm that often excluded Rosalind. Her cousin could keep up with Georg, and Georg liked that, but Monique was too immature to be anything but his young accomplice, Rosalind decided. And Monique would never appreciate him like she did.

Present-day 1945

Several yards into the shallow wood, Rosalind turns right toward a thick clump of trees to enter a hidden path that the three of them used years ago. The entrance is dark and narrow and can easily be missed, and a dense canopy of trees conserves the smell of decaying leaves. People could die in here, she thinks, in the thick growth, and no one would know.

Fifteen yards westward along the track, the pathway veers toward a private area of the river, to a small wooden platform extending from the embankment. They would lie here often, in the sun, side by side. Just near the ramp, and nestled into the trees, is a small hut with a gabled roof, not high enough to stand in. It was their secret place once, where they would sit and dream and plan. In a small space, between the hut and the platform, and no larger than a bedroom, is a flat area of mud where several stumps of wood are placed in a circle.

On one of the stumps, Georg sits staring at the barren ground where a fire pit used to be, his elbows resting on his knees. Rosalind sits on the stump closest and watches him. The late-morning sun hits the top of Georg's hair, turning it gold, and his green eyes glisten. He is still beautiful, she thinks. When he finally notices her, there is a lack of recognition not only with her but also with the world at large. Something is wrong today. He appears doleful and teary.

"What is the matter, Georg?"

She reaches to take his hand, but he draws back out of reach to wrap his arms tightly around himself.

"I have to go back," he says, frowning as he attempts to organize his thoughts. He has gone from looking very young to very old in the space of time it takes to frown. "The men . . . They can't do it without me. The Russians are creeping in from all sides. We'll be finished."

"Georg, the war is over. You are safe now. The men are safe now." Though she is doubtful this is true. Most of the men are likely dead.

"She is probably with them," he says.

Rosalind swallows and briefly closes her eyes. She must be strong.

"Do you remember, Georg, when we were small? We would creep out early in the morning to watch the sun rise. Do you remember?"

He doesn't respond, though he is calmer now. She reaches again for his hands and pulls them toward her.

"Georg, do you remember the fire?" she says. "Do you remember singeing your hair with sticks of fire to make us squeal and squirm? . . . You do remember, don't you?"

He clenches his hands slightly, and his eyes rest on her hands; she is hopeful just for a second, before he looks up at the trees. She has lost him again. It is the moments of connection that she waits for.

She bends down to kiss him as she leaves, though he will not feel it, does not even know she exists. She is shaking slightly. It could have been worse. Sometimes it takes much longer to settle him from his memories.

As she returns to the wood, she sees someone running in from the clearing on the far side and heading toward the river's edge. She steps carefully out from the trees onto the embankment to see who it is.

A small boy crouches over the river, searching for something in the water. He has clothes that are stained and torn in places, and a face that hasn't been washed in days, perhaps much longer. His hair is dark and sticks out from his head in badly growing clusters as if at some point previously it was roughly hacked with scissors.

Hooked over one arm is a woven basket, and he searches across the river to the other side before he starts to whimper and places the backs of his fists against his eyes.

She is moved slightly at the sound of his cries, like she would be for a wounded animal. She steps toward him and bends to touch his shoulder.

"Michal!" says a forceful voice behind her, and Rosalind turns her head suddenly to face the gaze of the stranger's frightening black eyes. The boy in the meantime has jumped up and away so that he is out of her reach.

Rosalind looks from the dark man to the boy and back again, momentarily stunned by the intrusion.

"I'm sorry," says the stranger, who has seen the effect on her. "I didn't mean to startle you. He led us on a chase."

"The boy is yours?" she asks.

"Yes."

"It was you in the house last night?"

"Yes," he says. "Did you see us?"

"I saw something."

"I hope we didn't frighten you."

She doesn't respond. Erich said he would get rid of them, and she is confused that they are still here, these beggars.

Erich appears from the woods to stand just behind the stranger, as if they are on the same side. Her eyes pin on Erich, who matches her own rigid expression, before they move back to the stranger.

CHAPTER 9
STEFANO

The woman is staring with eyes that bore deeply into his core before they dart suddenly back to the boy. He feels as if he knows her. She is the face of so many. She has thin limbs and a sprinkling of freckles on her exposed forearms and face. Her hair, hanging in a limp ponytail, is a dull blond, her eyes a pale, crystalline blue. None of her features he considers particularly striking, yet together they blend into something pleasing to the eye. It is perhaps the feline, graceful way she wears these traits that makes this so.

She looks once more at the boy before stepping away with a wary backward glance. Stefano watches her leave in a dress that is oversized, her smallness accentuated by the apron ties around her tiny waist.

In the brief moment that they were connected, Stefano could sense the hostility, and perhaps fear as well, as she gripped hard at the edge of her apron during their encounter. Though it is difficult to know for sure if she was frightened. Women in this country are good at hiding things. Not like his sisters and his mother, who would show anger with their eyes and fists, and joy with their wide smiles and open arms.

She came from the direction of the thick riverbank trees that appear uncharted, and he is curious at what is beyond there.

"She is Rosalind," says Erich once she has quickly disappeared from view, "from the house next door."

"She looked troubled."

"She is not as fragile as she appears. She can take care of herself. Best to avoid them."

Stefano is slightly intrigued by the missing information but turns his attention back to the boy, who is poised to run again.

"Michal, come back to the house!" says Stefano.

Michal looks down at the basket, though he is not really looking; he is avoiding the questioning that he knows is about to ensue. Stefano can see that his legs are trembling.

"Are you looking for something?"

Stefano turns toward the murky brown river so unlike his shining gem in Campania. Willow trees continue to watch them from the other side, pointing their shaggy, twisted fingers at a small boat with a noisy motor that whisks the water into tan-and-white foam. He waits for it to pass before stepping closer to the boy. Insects buzz at the clumps of grasses growing at the base of the embankment, and the smell of rotting leaves dampens the crisp air.

"What is it? Why did you run?"

"Something has frightened him," Erich says.

"Perhaps it was the mention of the camp," says Stefano. "I will try and help you, Michal. Perhaps find other family somewhere." Though he is not sure how, if he can. "It will be all right. We will go back to the house and talk about it."

Stefano reaches his hand forward for the boy's, but Michal is unsure whether to take it, one arm still looping through the handle of the basket and his other small hand hovering uncertainly at his side.

"Come," says Stefano, nodding in the direction of the houses, and the boy reluctantly follows.

As war had raged on, and the future had grown darker, children were not what he envisaged, much less wanted. Michal must be sent elsewhere, and his fate must be in the hands of others who are better equipped to look after him. Stefano's own battles are still not over.

"There is no gas or electricity unfortunately," says Erich, near the front door. "As you are aware from my sudden arrival last night, and from the state of the house, I've been away traveling, seeking work in other towns. But now I am fortunate to have found something temporary not too far from here. Factory work . . . nights, afternoons, could be mornings as well. I have to leave shortly, but I will bring some food back with me late tonight if you can wait till then."

Stefano swallows back words of gratitude. He does not say which way he is thinking, though his decision has already been made.

"The boy can take the other room upstairs," says Erich. "You can boil some water while I am gone. There is a small piece of washing soap in the bathroom. It is good enough until I can bring some more. The boy could do with a wash."

Stefano wonders at the state of the German. He is thin, but he is certainly not lacking any nourishment. He has been cared for; that is obvious by his clothing as well.

"As you can see, my accommodation is not exactly distinguished," Erich says with a half smile. "But you are welcome to it. I felled a tree from the forest earlier. You can chop the rest of the wood for the stove while I am gone this afternoon, if you are up to it."

Stefano nods his thanks, though there is something about all of this that doesn't feel right. He is acting as if he has nothing to lose, thinks Stefano. And sometimes these people are the most dangerous to know because they do not care if they lose you, too. Stefano looks down at the boy.

"But if you want to go in the meantime, I will understand that also," says Erich. "You have choices at least."

Stefano remembers the fields that hold little charity or food, and the roads that hold questions and the likelihood of more dead bodies. Germany holds little appeal now or in the past.

"Do you have enough food to get you through till tomorrow? I may be quite late tonight."

"I have a little."

"Then I hope you are still here when I return." Erich extends his hand, and Stefano recoils internally. He can tolerate him because the war is over and there is no more fighting, but shaking his hand is an acceptance of trust. There is a hanging space of time before he does so.

"See! You have not exploded into a ball of flame," says Erich.

"Thank you," says Stefano, the word finally freed. "We will stay." The boy steps closer to Stefano, perhaps for reassurance. He remembers doing the same as a young child when presented with situations he didn't fully understand, and the protection he felt alongside his father.

Erich smiles, though it is not the smile of a victor, like he has just won a battle, but a slightly and unintentionally smug look of someone who expected the outcome, that things would go his way.

Stefano follows Erich to the front door. "You said 'them' before? About avoiding *them* next door?"

Erich pauses, perhaps reliving what he said.

"Georg, her husband, lives there, too. He has permanent injuries from the war and is very ill. Rosalind is his full-time nurse. He also has a temper, but you are quite safe if you don't engage with him. They keep to themselves. They won't come here."

Stefano watches Erich walk southward from the house, past the clearing, to enter a forest trail that runs parallel with the main road. When he is out of sight, Stefano bends down to face the boy.

"Trust me!" he says to Michal.

Michal grips his hands together and shifts his feet uncertainly while his eyes stay glued to Stefano.

"I don't want to go home," whispers Michal, and his eyes begin to water.

And Stefano is wondering about the dark places that the boy has called home.

"What happened to you there?"

Michal is quiet again. He looks away, tears falling silently, afraid now of his memories that he would rather forget. Stefano feels his heart beat faster, racing to control the rush of emotions he is not supposed to feel: sadness, anger, tenderness.

With his hands, Stefano sweeps the tears from the boy's cheeks.

"I won't let anyone take you where you don't want to go," he says firmly. "Do you understand?"

And the boy nods.

"Friends must stick together, yes?" says Stefano, hand outstretched.

Michal reaches to accept the friendship this time, and Stefano firmly encloses the small hand in his own, feels the innocence and trust this gesture represents, and accepts now that they are bound.

1941

He was in the kitchen with his mother and sisters. His mother put some olives and cheese on his plate, then scooped up some fried tomatoes and peppers, and put them on, too. Stefano had only been awake a short while after a poor sleep.

Teresa was cranky, and he could already tell that she was looking for an argument. Nina chatted about the marketplace and the size of the onions. There was then a debate over the quality that she chose and the man whom Nina bought them from. Her older sister accused the other of buying only from the men that Nina wished to flirt with, concluding that she did not care about the quality.

His mother, however, was silent. She did not look at anyone, eating slowly, with little appetite.

Stefano couldn't stand the bickering between his sisters that interrupted his thoughts.

"Enough!" shouted Stefano, which startled them to cease arguing, but he knew that the moment he left, they would start again.

His mother sat still. She had placed her knife and fork at either side of her plate and stared at the tomatoes.

"See what you do?" said Stefano, pointing at his mother. "All this fighting upsets us all."

"Mamma," said Teresa, back to her grumpy self again. "Why aren't you eating?"

Without warning Julietta threw her face into her hands and sobbed. Stefano looked at his sisters for answers, but both were stunned into silence.

"I can't take this," his mother cried. "I can't take that you have signed up to go to war."

Stefano was not expecting this. She had spoken her fears but had always been logical, less emotional than his sisters. She was a small woman, quiet, unlike her sister, Serafina, who always dominated conversations. Julietta tended to stay in the background. Happy for someone else to take the glory for everything that happened. To see his mother break scared Stefano. Until that time he had not thought about the worry he was about to put her through.

He reached across to take her hand. "Mamma . . ."

But there was nothing to say. He couldn't tell her that he wouldn't be going; it was too late for that. He had already signed himself over to Mussolini's army.

"It is good that your father is not here to see it. That is something to be thankful for. He would not have wanted you to fight for that fascist."

"You had better not let Enzo hear you talk like that," said Stefano, trying to make it lighter but not expecting her reaction.

"That old goat! He would send Serafina if he had the choice."

"Mamma, it will be all right! I will be careful. Beppe and I will be together for this first battle."

"How many of them will there be?"

"I don't know yet." He knew he had to be truthful. He could never disguise things from his mother. She was far too canny not to read between the lines. "The war could go on for years or be over soon. I can't say, Mamma. Whatever it takes to finish it so we can go back to normality."

She wiped her tears as Nina put a protective arm around her.

The despair in his mother's eyes would stay with him for a long time to come. Even when the days were dark and endless, he would always remember them: soft and pleading and hopeless. She must have known something then, something that no one else could see.

What his mother did not know, what he didn't admit to anyone, was that he was afraid. He was not like Beppe who once had yearned for war, for any adventure that took him far from home. And he was not like his uncle, someone who wanted Italy to rule more lands.

Present-day 1945

Michal rests his elbows on the front windowsill to search for small distractions and signs of life, while Stefano rummages through the cabinet drawers, looking for documents belonging to the stranger. He knows it is wrong in any other circumstances, but it is still too early, the wounds still raw, to rest his fate in the hands of a German. Papers and receipts lie loosely in the drawers, some with a name that he doesn't recognize. There is nothing about Erich, no clues, no background, and no piece of information that links Erich to the house at all.

On the walls are rectangular imprints, unmarked by time, where framed photographs and pictures might have sat. Other drawers are filled with things, items from a past: an antique candleholder, an ancient-looking key, a magnifying glass, and a wooden box with nails.

After he chops some wood, he boils some water for washing and from the kitchen window spies Rosalind's house next door. The curtains on a room at the base move slightly, but no one becomes visible. She is odd, he thinks, damaged also, if he believes what Erich says.

He takes the pot of boiled water to the bathroom situated between the main room and the back door.

He searches for a towel and can't find one, but a folded rag from a cupboard will do.

Back in the bathroom he takes off his shirt and turns slightly to examine his body in the narrow mirror leaning against the wall. The scarring from burns stretches down the left-hand side of his body and left arm and flows on to his hand, which he conceals with a bandage. It is not just for vanity that he covers it, but also it is less likely to draw as many questions. The details of it are too painful. With the bandage he can say anything he wants; an infection, say, can end the conversation quickly.

He fills the sink from the pot of water. A razor sits on the edge of the basin along with the soap, washcloth hangs over the tap. Erich is thinking of every comfort. He has tidied the house, and vinegary air hangs in the bathroom. He is meticulously clean, making it all the more curious why Erich was not shocked and upset by the earlier state of the house, by the damage to his things.

Stefano froths the water with the soap, then with soapy hands smears his face and commences to shave. Once finished, he uses the dampened cloth to wipe the grime from the rest of his body. When he looks up, the boy is in the mirror also, standing behind him. Stefano turns to face him, and the boy can see the scars, a look of curiosity only, not horror or pity as is the case with adults.

"I had a nasty accident," says Stefano, continuing his washing. "I lost some people in the process."

The boy looks at him, then looks at his own weary shoes.

"It is your turn next," says Stefano, handing him the cloth.

The boy shakes his head.

"Suit yourself!" says Stefano with a shrug, and he dries himself quickly with the rag, then puts on a clean shirt. His clothes replaced, he returns to the kitchen table. Using a penknife he keeps in his trouser pocket, he opens the tinned meat and beans. In a cupboard he finds crockery and spoons. He divides the glutinous brown contents between two plates and pushes one across to Michal on the other side, who wastes no time to begin eating.

"What did you used to eat?"

"Nettles," he mumbles with his mouth full, and his head in his food. And Stefano is surprised he has answered; he had got used to no response.

"Do you remember the town where you are from? Do you remember the name?"

"There was a big clock outside," the boy whispers, raising his arms.

"In the center of the town? Like the one we saw yesterday?"

The boy nods. So many towns with clocks, thinks Stefano. It is no place to start.

"And the people, in your house. Did you have an uncle, aunt?"

Michal is thinking, but he can't come up with anything. He frowns and pauses his eating briefly as if he can't think and eat at the same time.

"It's all right. You're not in trouble for not knowing."

"My brother would cry a lot," he says, as if he needs to say something.

"And what did he cry about?"

The boy bites his top lip.

"He did not like the dark."

"I see," says Stefano.

"But I do," says Michal, the pleasure of food lowering his shield of whispers. "I can hide in the dark."

"I like the dark, too."

"There is a secret hiding place here that we can hide in," the child says.

"There is?" says Stefano.

"It is a dark place in the wall."

Michal points, and Stefano follows the tip of his finger across the room to the dark void under the stairs. There is nothing immediate that he can see, but Stefano is curious. He retrieves his torch and moves closer to examine the wall, and he recognizes immediately a hidden door. He recognizes it because he hid behind one himself once.

The edge of the door is ajar ever so slightly, and he pries it open with his fingernails to see the secret enclosure within. Under the light from the torch, there are empty jars and tins nestled in cobwebs and brown dust, and just in front of them is a shoebox that is not layered with years of dust.

He lifts the lid of the box to find bundles of letters that are tied up with ribbon. He slides his fingers beneath the ribbon to pull out several of the envelopes, and sees the same handwriting on the front of each envelope, the same name, *Gustav Moulet*, but no address. None of the envelopes are postmarked. He reads the backs of the envelopes one by one. Just one name is written: *Monique*.

He is interrupted by sounds next door, the thumping of floorboards on the top floor and a muffled cry, and he stops to listen for more.

When there are no further sounds, he continues his inspection. A folded sheet of paper falls out from somewhere within the bundle of envelopes; the contents of this brief letter in large and patient, florid handwriting contrasts with the spirited, hurried, and coiling cursive on the envelopes. The letter is from Georg to Monique to say that he can't wait for the following summer. It is dated January 1938. Georg thanks her also for the condolence letter she sent after the sudden death of his father; though he buried a man he barely knew, who was rarely home, and whose coldness made it difficult to form a relationship, the letter says.

But apart from the regret that Stefano can sense from those lines, the letter is mostly optimistic. Georg explains that he is thinking of joining the army and traveling like they (Monique and Georg) talked about, of places far away where the air is always warm. *Where?* Stefano wonders. He would like to know that. Georg mentions Rosalind fleetingly at the end, an afterthought it seems. Stefano is curious. If they are the same Georg and Rosalind from the neighboring property, why are the letters kept here? But he is more intrigued that Rosalind's husband wrote to someone else. He has a sudden desire to know these people better.

A shriek from the house next door forces him to cease further investigation, and he quickly returns all the letters to the box and replaces it within the cavity. From where they are stored, someone doesn't want these found.

"Michal, you must stay here!"

The boy looks fearfully toward the sounds.

"You must agree, yes?"

The boy nods.

Stefano walks outside the front door and searches for movement in the windows of the adjacent property. There is no sign of life within. The house is silent, cold. Its message says, *Stay away*. Beside the front door leans a bicycle, and he knocks lightly on the window beside the door and checks the woods behind him. When there is no response from inside, he peers through the glass. The house is neatly furnished, crocheted covers over polished furniture, and a starched tablecloth edged with lace.

On the far wall is a photograph of a woman with dark hair, wide-set eyes. The portrait, illuminated by the window nearby, seems to leap out from the dullness of the room. The subject appears to look quizzically at the lens, as if she were curious as to why she has been chosen, with lips that are pressed humorously together as if she has just been told the reason also.

Rosalind appears agitated as she steps hurriedly down from the stairs in the center of the room. She stops to think of something, hooking the fingers of her hands together. Stefano raps on the glass, and she turns sharply to spy him through the window before looking back up the stairs behind her. She walks toward the front door and pulls it open with a sense of urgency or frustration.

"What do you want?" she says, her tone something other than receptive.

"I heard a scream. Are you all right?"

She stares at him before dropping her eyes to his feet. The sweet, doughy scent of baking escapes the open doorway.

"Yes, everything is fine here."

He turns to leave.

"Where are you from?"

"Northern Italy."

She looks away. She is too anxious to look him in the eye.

"I don't give to beggars. There isn't enough."

"My name is Stefano, and I am not a beggar. I fought on your side for much of the war, but I'll be on my way," he says, turning to step away. He does not like what she has called him. He has never asked for charity.

She looks at his face. She is observant at least to see the change in his expression from one of concern to one of disappointment.

"I meant no insult," she says.

Stefano turns back, then moves to leave a second time.

"How long are you staying next door?" she asks.

"A few nights."

"Why here?"

He shrugs. "I thought the track would lead to the river, to wash. And then I saw the house. It looked abandoned."

She looks at him briefly to check his sincerity.

"Is Erich there still?" she asks quickly.

"He has to work. He says he will be back later. He is taking me to the train on Friday."

She bites her top lip.

"You should leave before he gets back. There is nothing for you here."

She closes the door.

CHAPTER 10
ERICH

Erich has thought much about the Italian by the time he reaches town, and he wonders about providence, something he never truly believed in till now, and the timing of Stefano's arrival. The Italian could be the catalyst that will move time forward for Erich. With the help of Stefano's cardinal, escaping Europe seems a very real possibility, and the idea excites him.

But there is the question of mistrust and resentment that Erich recognizes, that Stefano can't fully disguise. Erich does not take this point lightly and knows he must change this if he is to gain help. Erich has changed others before, steered their fates and expectations, but this may not be as easy. He does not have the power of Germany's backing. Stefano's trust must be earned with small things, gifts and hospitality.

Today there is a small market operating in the center of the square. The locals are returning to normal business. Most of the stalls look bare and dismal, and remind him of the ghettos he visited, with Germany now turned on its head. There are tables with books, photo frames, cutlery, and farm tools that widows will have no use for. Not just that their men are not there to work, but the fields are destroyed or reclaimed or without crops to harvest. Most of the market offerings are simply for trade—food, salt, spices, paper, soap, as well as basic items, are better than currency. There are handmade linens and prints and other non-essential goods that are unlikely to sell as before when tourists from other parts of affluent Germany used to visit these towns and find such items quaint. The lack of quality in the stalls is not the only difference between before and now. Several army trucks pass through the town regularly, as the Russian unit assigned to the area has based itself in a church on the outskirts of Dresden. One truck is parked in the street.

The sight of the truck makes Erich cautious rather than nervous. He has seen people taken from the street. He has heard accounts of bullying. He has seen it up close. But it is part of war, he justifies. The Germans were no better.

He disappears into the post office to pretend to examine the photos of missing persons on the wall. Some in groups with faces of the missing circled in red; some that a professional photographer has taken; and others grainy or battered from rough confinement in a wallet. Several faces he recognizes.

He hears the roar of an engine and then the sound of it fading. He looks from the window, then steps back out to the street to proceed briskly toward his next destination. Just ahead are an old man with a walking stick and a teenage girl who wears a headscarf. By the state of their worn and soiled clothing, they are beggars, carrying their possessions—possibly their only ones—wrapped up in a sheet. A young local girl walking behind them pulls the beggar's scarf from her head to reveal her shorn hair, and scabs where she has badly scratched her head. The assailant throws the scarf on the ground, spits on it, before hurrying past them. She does not want foreigners here, the ones she was taught to hate, the ones who were placed out of sight in the camps.

The girl is indifferent to the treatment and picks up her scarf. She is used to it. They are Jews, from the reaction by the locals, who have continued to reject them here, still immersed in the fear of association. But Jews aren't Erich's concern. Not anymore.

At a grocery store the owner knows him, and they have a conversation about the Russians as usual. He loathes the conversation, but it is something he has to put up with to fit in, to continue here. They have run out of fresh loaves, but they have several small rolls from yesterday. He agrees to these, plus a portion of pork, cheese, and some vegetables that are close to turning. The price of meat is usually much higher than the quality, and he wonders how much of the good stock she keeps for herself.

"Anything else?" says Erich.

The owner retrieves a package of Russian cigarettes from the front pocket of her apron and places them on the counter. "I have these if you are interested."

Erich wonders what she has traded to acquire these.

"I am."

"You have coupons for all this?" she asks, knowing from his previous purchases that he doesn't.

"I have something better as you know." He opens his hands to show some gold and silver rings.

She inspects all the items, then takes two of the gold rings.

"Only one," he says.

"For all this?" she says with an incredulous edge.

She is aware that he is hiding from the Russians, but while he has something to trade, she is unlikely to give him up, and she still has Hitler's Germany running through her veins.

She pulls out a bottle of vodka from beneath the counter.

"Two and I will throw in this," says the woman.

She is a businesswoman, and a good one it seems, but she is also a survivor like him.

Back in the street the trams rattle through the town. He was here a long time ago, but it is a vague memory now. It isn't home. To Erich, home is Berlin. It is time with his father, brothers, and mother. Home is also duty.

He stops at the pharmacy. The man behind the counter is serving someone else, but when he sees Erich, he is in a hurry to finish the purchase and the conversation. When the customer is gone, he pulls out a package tied with string from beneath the counter.

"Thank you, Elias," says Erich.

"You are welcome. There will always be those who support you. I was very fond of your father."

A woman enters and walks to the counter.

Erich nods to the pharmacist and the other customer. As loyal as the pharmacist is, Erich is uncomfortable that people know him here. He wishes that he didn't have to rely so much on others. He is grateful for the help, but eventually he will have to get rid of any trace of himself.

1937

Erich's father came home one weekend from secret business in Berlin. Erich watched him drive the long laneway to the house. He had been away for weeks. His mother had worked hard to take care of everything needed around the house while looking after their small children. She never complained. She never sought any kind of reward. Erich was shortly to begin his studies in mechanical engineering in Dresden, to follow in his father's footsteps.

His father looked very smart as he stepped out of the car in a black suit and cap that had a silver skull. Erich's mother looked very proud, though she joked about the skull. She had been very happy with her husband, and there was little wrong he could do. He was being paid to develop something for Hitler. Erich wasn't allowed to know at that time. It was a secret, and even his mother confided later that Horst had told her very little.

Erich's father announced that they were moving to Berlin. He had taken lease of a town house so he could see his family more with the promise that Erich could begin his studies there instead. His father said that they would not sell the house and land, that they would come back sometimes for holidays so that the children could run around the wide spaces, and swim and fish in the lake nearby.

Erich's sister, Claudine, several years in age below him, wasn't happy. She wanted to stay at the house. She stamped her feet. Her wild spirit took her to neighboring fields, and Erich had to search far for her.

He found his sister beneath a tree on a hill. With a stone she was carving angrily into the bark. She wasn't just carving her name; she was carving all their names.

"Make sure you spell mine right this time."

She glared at him, but the signal lacked the dislike that she would show for her younger brothers and mother. She had always tried to keep up with Erich but failed simply because she could not sit as still as he did, would not focus her energy on one thing.

Erika, she wrote on the tree spitefully.

"Ouch," he said playfully.

She had carried anger after the first day her papa left. She loved him, perhaps more than she loved her mother. Nene showed very few expectations of her willful daughter, other than the hopes she would marry well and produce children, something Claudine would growl about whenever their father would make a joke of it. Though unlike Nene, Horst didn't mean this. He did not mind what his daughter did, that she liked to paint and draw and dream. He did not seem bothered that she would disagree with him on most issues. For some odd reason that Erich could not fathom, her willfulness and independent views seemed to impress him, and he would quietly listen to her angry outbursts about the way her mother undercooked the beef, the bed linen that smelled strongly of bleach, the poor condition of the roads for bike riding, about the way her little brother pronounced words poorly; in fact Claudine had an opinion on everything. Sometimes Erich would laugh about it; sometimes he would sit and listen with fascination, though not at her comments, but at the way his father would patiently listen and nod and wish her well in any endeavors.

Under the tree Erich talked to his sister about coming back, about holidaying again at the villa, about the benefits of Berlin. He had been there a couple of times on short journeys with his father, and he told her that she would love the color and movement and music. That she could study at one of the art schools there one day. She would find so much more to do. At this she calmed, almost hopeful, returning with Erich and questioning her father on everything he saw there, the restaurants, the art exhibitions, what the women wore. Were there handsome soldiers in uniform?

Later that evening, his parents had disappeared into the sitting room off the kitchen, and he could hear their murmurings. The children had been put in their rooms, the baby with their mother.

Horst's jacket had been removed and hung over the back of the chair. Erich examined the lining, the stitching, the emblems, and the smooth feel of the fabric. While he was distracted by the jacket, Claudine had put an ear to the sitting room door and was shortly reprimanded by Erich and sent away. Though Erich was not without such wiles or curiosity.

The next day when his papa was sleeping late and his mother was busy in the laundry at the rear of the house, he pulled out some papers from Horst's bag. There were architectural drawings of tanks and typewritten reports on their effectiveness, charts of their movement, their ammunition, their speed, their turning circles. He always knew that his father was clever, but on that day Erich realized that Horst was part of something significant and progressive. Erich envisaged his country as the one to lead the world, and a future that was better for everyone. It was on that day also that he was first sold on Hitler's Germany.

Present-day 1945

He arrives at a small brick-terraced home between others like it. He turns the key and lets himself in. She sits there motionless at the window with her back to him. In the early days one would rarely see her still.

"Mother," he says quietly as he walks around to stand in front of her. She has a puckered scar that dips in and out of the lines on her forehead. Dribble sits on her chin. Blue eyes, staring into the street, hold no recognition. She has no sense of time or place, and she carries no memories. She is hollow.

At the sight of her, hands reach inside of him and tug at his resolve, but before they can take hold, he pushes them way. She taught him how to remain impenetrable, to rise above any emotion and only act from conscious, rational thought.

"I've brought you food," he says, but she doesn't look at the packages in his hands. She continues to watch from the window, fixed on nothing. Movement in the street doesn't divert or fill her empty thoughts. She chews the inside of her cheek, then stops, her eyes drooping slightly. She will soon be asleep.

His mother is unable to feed herself and suffers epileptic seizures that have been occurring more frequently. She cannot do any basic functions, but sometimes her eyes roam side to side, as if she were trying to hear. She is fifty and a young woman yet, with scarcely any gray in the hair that frames her face.

Erich tries not to remember her as before. It is about now and forward, not the past. In the kitchen he leaves some medicine from the package for Marceline.

"Vati!" calls a small child hurtling toward him on unsteady legs. He picks up the girl and holds her to him.

"Let me see you today," he says, pulling her away from him to examine her better. One light curl falls across her eyes, and he pushes it back behind her ear.

Marceline walks in. She is efficient, picking up items the little girl has dropped on the way. She had come highly recommended from his German contacts in the town. She was used to servicing German officials, dressing their children.

Now for Erich, she looks after two, his mother less capable than the second. He is not what one might describe as grateful for the help, since Marceline is doing a service and being paid well, but he respects the position she has. He has always understood the effectiveness of delegated and rigid roles. Understanding them made him indispensable to the Reich.

He looks back at the little girl, Genevieve. She wears her mother's smile, her pale skin. She still asks for her, but the crying is lessening.

"You look very nice today," he says, and remembers his sister, Claudine, remembers her dresses always covered in mud. The tug again, harder this time, and the push, the rejection of the memory, more violent.

"Vati," she says, and shows him a picture book that Marceline has bought from the marketplace stalls. Genevieve coughs several times, her small chest rising sharply, though she is unaware of her illness, her interest in the book distracting her.

He was good at taking care of his younger sister and brothers, but a child of his own has been harder, less mechanical. He knew straightaway that he couldn't take care of her like her mother, that he could not bear the emotional load.

Genevieve is pointing to one of the animals in the book quizzically, and he answers her thoughtfully. His father taught him that, to answer seriously and factually. *Children are simply incomplete adults,* he would say. *It is important to help complete them, not treat them like imbeciles.*

He looks at the time. He is already thinking about the Italian, about returning to the river house. It is his gift to watch people, understand and learn their motivations and desires. And he is especially interested in those who might benefit him.

He spends the remainder of the day between the two women, the old and the new, both with different needs. He talks to his mother about the economy, about the town. Though he makes things up. He talks as if Hitler won the war. She doesn't know any different.

"I am leaving after supper, but I won't be back until tomorrow," he says to Marceline. "Please cut me some of the pork and a large piece of the potato pie from yesterday, and more of anything else that you can spare today. I will purchase more items tomorrow. Hopefully there will be more grain.

"Genevieve, you need to be good for Marceline and take care of Oma while I am away. Can you do that?"

She nods. She is accepting of instruction, though she does not understand the world yet, does not even know what she is agreeing to. She will be like him, he thinks, accepting orders from her superiors, without question.

CHAPTER 11
ROSALIND

Georg sits very still on the edge of the bed while she sponges him with warm soapy water. Rosalind is gentle, and she can tell from the way he closes his eyes that it soothes him. Sometimes she passes him the cloth to wash himself, but most times she prefers the task, to feel close. A dusting of fine ginger stubble along his jawline tells her it is time to shave, though she is hesitant. Last time he attempted to fight her for the razor, thinking that she was trying to harm him. Since then she has kept the object out of sight in case he has any more strange ideas.

The geese are creating a ruckus outside, and she leaves Georg to investigate, taking with her a small cup of feed. The birds appear agitated, squawking and rushing at her as she enters the pen. Her attempt to distract and pacify them by scattering the feed on the ground is unsuccessful. She turns to the wood to see if perhaps there are dogs or foxes waiting nearby and is unsettled by the emergence of two people from the trees instead, who stop to view her from the edge of the pen: an older man with trousers held up by rope and a younger girl wearing a dress, soldier's boots that are oversized, and a man's jacket, too hot for the weather.

"What do you want?" says Rosalind.

She has seen beggars before and turned them away.

The man is staring at one of the geese, and the girl stares at Rosalind.

"I have nothing I can spare," says Rosalind.

She imagines the girl is around fourteen or fifteen, with hair that is very short like a boy's. Without the dress it would be difficult to tell her gender, and her expression is haunted, fearful. The older man has a hardened face, so darkly stained and lined it is a challenge to tell his age, his hair white and gray, his shoulders sagging. The size of him says he is harmless, but the face is what she fears. The narrow eyes look sharper than others she has seen.

"You must go."

"Goose!" he says.

"No!" she says.

But the man turns to look at the house as if he might head there, and the girl watches them both. Rosalind can sense that he is wondering whether she is alone, and she feels exposed and suddenly vulnerable to this stranger who might do her harm.

The girl says something in her foreign language, then unlatches the gate and pushes it back to let the man step through and past Rosalind, who is too afraid to move. The girl glances at Rosalind in some way apologetically.

Sensing danger, one of the geese waddles toward her enclosure at the rear as the man moves after her. He fails at first in his attempt to grab at her, then chases her awkwardly on infirm legs. He finally throws himself on top of the bird, which squawks loudly.

"Stop!" says Stefano, who has just arrived.

In the meantime, the thief has thrown a cloth over the head of the goose.

"Give it to me!" says Stefano in German. The small boy stands a safe distance behind him.

The older man doesn't respond at first but then sees the height of Stefano and throws the goose toward the gate of the pen. The bird falls sideways, protesting loudly at her badly damaged leg, allowing Stefano to usher her, risking her snapping beak, back into the pen. Rosalind hastily closes the gate, and the goose limps away toward her tin enclosure, her grumblings more muted now.

"Where are you from?" asks Stefano.

The man steps closer to the girl. He looks worried now, perhaps more so for the girl.

"France," says the man.

Stefano says something in French, and then a conversation between them ensues. Rosalind doesn't know enough French to understand.

Stefano turns to Rosalind. "They are French Jews. The girl is his granddaughter. They were in a concentration camp and then after the war in a hospital in Poland for several months before the man could walk again. The man's wife, daughter, and his two other grandchildren were killed in the concentration camp . . . They are traveling back to France and have not eaten a proper meal in days."

The pair stares bleakly at Rosalind.

"Do they have any other family they can go to?" says Rosalind.

Stefano asks them, then reports their response.

"He says his son who was taken to a different camp might have survived, but he is no longer hopeful, not after the things he witnessed."

Rosalind wills herself to feel something, but she can't. She has had little to do with Jews, has distanced herself from news of their fates.

"I can't help them," says Rosalind.

"They are starving," he says.

"They hurt the goose. They were about to steal it. Why should I offer them any charity? They look at me as if they want to kill me."

"They are starving. People do crazy things. They look at you, at your health, at what you have. They can only envy."

"They would not envy me if they knew the truth."

Rosalind looks at the girl, who doesn't look so alien now, and the grandfather, who appears not as hostile. She is remembering a time on her way from Berlin when she had nothing, when she ate the potato peels she found on the ground.

"They can't have a goose."

Stefano reaches into his satchel and pulls out a chocolate bar, which he breaks, and hands a piece to each of them.

"Can you spare anything else?" Stefano says to Rosalind.

Rosalind walks angrily inside the house to the pantry and cuts a portion of rye bread, only enough for one. She is not yet over the damage to the goose.

When she comes out she hands the bread to the girl, not the man, who is likely to snatch, she thinks. She does not want to touch him. The girl takes it cautiously from her.

Stefano shrugs at something the Jew says in French before he nods in reluctant gratitude to Stefano only, and turns to leave.

"What did he say?"

"He guesses now we will eat the goose that they should have."

"He sounds ungrateful," says Rosalind.

Once the man and his granddaughter are out of sight, Rosalind turns back to check on the goose. It squawks and pecks at her as she tries to examine the leg. She is not sure if it is broken. She still feels only anger, not pity for the vagrants.

"That was generous of you," says Stefano as she walks past him. His words affect her, and she is suddenly ashamed that she hasn't been generous at all. She could have given them more. She has some vegetables in the garden and a bag of rye to grind for bread.

"Have there been many?" he asks.

"A few." Though she does not tell of the ones she turned away.

1938

Monique stopped suddenly and crouched behind a tree, putting her fingers to her lips for Rosalind to be quiet.

She was about to tell Monique to stop being childish, thinking that Monique was playing a silly game, when she saw the reason for her cousin's odd behavior. Georg was in the shallows of the river, shirt off. His hair was cut short on the sides and longer on the top, his normally soft waves flattened from the water. But Georg wasn't alone. Beside him was another boy, this one in a singlet and shorts. They were soaking, the newcomer drenched by Georg, who was splashing him to death.

Monique put her hand across her mouth to stop herself from laughing. She wore shorts and a light-green button-up blouse, and her breasts strained against the buttons.

"That must be Erich," whispered Monique.

"Who? How do you know?"

"Georg wrote and told me he was bringing a new friend home for the summer."

Before Rosalind could process the fact that Georg wrote to Monique and not her, Monique had already rushed forward and announced herself.

"Hello, fellow owl!" she shouted.

Georg rushed out of the water and wrapped his wet body around Monique, who protested with squeals to escape; however, her laughter suggested she was enjoying every moment. Georg then stepped forward and gave Rosalind a brief hug, not wanting to dampen her clothes. She didn't want him to treat her differently, but he did. At the time she had hoped it was because he had more respect for her.

Erich disappeared into the background, but he had watched the whole thing, studied everyone, and seen for himself in the first few minutes the dynamics of the group.

"What took you so long to get here?" Georg asked playfully while he picked up a towel off the ground and furiously dried his hair. Erich also toweled his hair, though his movements were more intentional.

"Erich and I met at a Hitler Youth camp, and he used to live not far from here," said Georg directly to Rosalind. She presumed this was because Monique had known already, and during the hours together on their long train journey, Monique had not bothered to tell Rosalind anything, preferring to write her private letters. "He is almost as clever as me! He is nearly as fast as me at running, too. He is nearly as good looking."

Erich stepped forward, pushing his friend out of the way in jest, his hand out formally to Rosalind. Erich's hand was cold and bumpy from the water. She did not like the feel of it. Monique stretched her hand out to him more eagerly, and their hands touched for longer.

"Nice to meet you," he said, his eyes lingering on Monique. He was good at speaking, his voice rich and deep, thought Rosalind. She could imagine him on the radio.

"Erich is off to study engineering next year."

"That sounds very interesting!" said Monique.

"I want to build machinery with my father."

"That sounds fascinating! What does your father do?"

Rosalind knew that Monique would not find any subject to do with machinery fascinating, but she was good at pretense. Good at making people believe her.

"He designs vehicles."

Erich was not shy, but he was not like Georg, either, who could butt into a conversation without offending. The newcomer stepped back from the group, hardly noticeable to all but Rosalind, to get a clearer view of the overall scene, a habit that she would come to recognize. Rosalind could feel that he was appraising each of them, weighing their value. Once his hair was dry, it was revealed that, like that of most Hitler boys, it was straight and fair, hanging fashionably over to one side of his forehead, and shaved on the sides.

"Tell Rosa what you are planning to do, Georg!" said Monique.

And once again Rosalind tasted the bitterness of exclusion.

"I am joining the military. I will be a member of Hitler's army."

"Do you think you will see actual fighting?" asked Monique suddenly, the alarm in her voice at least genuine this time.

"I hope so. I don't want to do all this for no cause."

The foursome sat on a patch of embankment beside the river and listened briefly to Georg tell tales from the youth camp. Georg had poked fun the previous year at the systems and the Nazi salute they had to perform at the camp, though this year there was a change. There seemed to be more pride, perhaps for Erich's benefit. They talked of the food, which was adequate, and the way they had to present themselves perfectly pressed, up early, beds made. Of teachers who fashioned their mustaches like Hitler, of another boy who had broken his leg sneaking out of a window at night, of boys who were sent away for unruly behavior and others turned away because of their race.

"Their race?" said Monique. "What's that supposed to mean?"

"Where have you been hiding? Siberia?" joked Georg.

"They found Jews in the middle of the camp pretending they were German," explained Erich. "It was humiliating for the officials who had accepted them into the camp."

"If they were born here, then they are likely German anyway, so what does it matter?" said Monique.

"It is about being loyal to one's true race," said Erich decisively, as if he were more in the know about the subject. "And Jews will most likely agree that going back to their own country eventually, which our führer encourages, will be better for them."

"Where is that?" Monique asked.

Erich paused briefly before answering. "Somewhere far away," he said with less conclusiveness, because he hadn't been told exactly.

"Oh, I see," said Monique. But she didn't really want to. They had discussed the laws over the dinner table in Berlin with Rosalind's parents. Rosalind had said it was for the best, and Monique had said it was stupid, but she could not come up with a good-enough reason at the time to say why she thought that way.

"Adolf Hitler has been to inspect our camp," said Erich. "He has torn up the Treaty of Versailles, so Germany can become a free and powerful country again. First we took Austria, and there is talk that Czechoslovakia could be next. The führer said he will fight any country that opposes his decisions."

"I don't like this talk of fighting," said Monique. She had asked her aunt and uncle whether Germany's occupation of Austria meant that her father would be freed. Max had then made further inquiries, but no one could tell him where Gustav had been imprisoned, and whether he was still alive. Though this last inquiry was never mentioned in front of Monique.

"I will give you a tour of our secret hideaway in the woods," Monique said to Erich to change the conversation. "And I will tell you bad things about Georg that you didn't know." She winked playfully.

"Best idea!" Georg said to Erich, encouraging him to go.

Monique linked arms with Erich, and Georg and Rosalind watched the other pair leave. "What made you choose to bring Erich? You have lots of friends by the sound of it."

"He is a present for you and a good match."

"For me?" Rosalind spun her head suddenly around to face him, shocked.

"I thought you needed some male distraction, Rosa. You need a life."

"I have a life!" she said. "I'm starting my nurse's training soon."

"But you need a boyfriend, someone to dream about when you are in that horrible, smelly Berlin. Erich lives there, too, you know!"

"But I have someone. I have you . . ." And it was out before she could control it.

"You never get my jokes," he said. "He's a good friend. I brought him for me, not you!" He looked down, afraid to meet her eyes. She wished she could take back what she had said. Wished that she had said nothing, but it would have been in vain. Her eyes had been saying how she felt for years.

"Let's go find the others!" said Georg. She sensed his longing to dispense with idle conversation.

"No, I think I'll stay awhile here." She felt suddenly awkward and sad. She did not feel like seeing Monique and having her steer their conversations. She did not feel like being insignificant that day.

"No, you won't!" said Georg, and he picked her up and carried her along the leafy pathway toward the sounds of conversation happening deeper in the wood.

She protested weakly, though liking his arms around her, and she turned her face into his chest to avoid the pine needles whipping her face as he ran. Perhaps he was testing her with what he'd just said. Perhaps he really liked her but couldn't say it. She modestly pulled down her skirt, which had risen up when he had lifted her.

Georg stopped suddenly several yards back from the riverbank, and she looked up at his face, at the line of his jaw, at the hollow of his throat. She wondered about his sudden intensity and turned then to follow his gaze.

Monique and Erich were sitting close together, dangling their legs off the platform. They talked in hushed tones as if they had known each other for years. Monique had her hand on his shoulder.

Georg gently placed Rosalind down on the ground and turned his focus back on her, giving her a hug.

"It is good to see my Rosa. It is so good to be here." Though it did not feel genuine to Rosalind, merely a mask to cover whatever it was that disturbed him.

He called out to the couple, who had surely heard them pounding the earth, but they were too interested in their own private conversation.

Monique finally acknowledged them there, and they moved to allow the others room to sit also.

"It feels much colder today," said Monique, who had wrapped her arms around herself and leaned closer to Erich. "I don't think I'll swim today."

"Since when has the cold ever stopped you?" asked Georg.

Monique picked up a fallen leaf and tickled Georg under his nose as he sat beside her.

"Stop it!" he said suddenly. And she appeared shocked at the sullenness in his tone, which he rarely used.

"I don't want you to go to join the military, Georgie!" she said suddenly, perhaps recognizing the change, perhaps even guessing the reason. He was jealous of Erich's attention, something Georg had not prepared for. "Like I told you in the letter I wrote you, I couldn't stand it if something happened to you."

One would expect the thought of something bad happening to dampen the mood, but these words lifted Georg again. Rosalind had been watching him each summer for years now, and never had she seen him affected by something as small as Monique's attention on Erich.

Georg's face brightened. He picked Monique up and jumped with her into the river.

Rosalind sat a foot away from Erich at the edge of the embankment, her legs dangling, her feet not touching the water. Erich was watching them. And no one was watching her. And things seemed different, and Rosalind suspected something awful would come. Not necessarily the war that would alter all of them, but that her relationship with Georg was diminishing to merely childhood fantasies.

Present-day 1945

Even thin-faced and worn, he is handsome, but his dark eyes under a heavy forehead unsettle her, and more so than the fact he is a man, and that the foreign men she has met are volatile, unpredictable, sometimes callous.

Rosalind looks at the boy, at his joyless face covered in dirt. He needs to be washed and fed. And Stefano came to her aid at least. She owes him something.

"Do you have any food?" She knows there is nothing in the house next door.

"We have some rations," he says.

She looks down, pinches her top lip again between her teeth. He is also harmless, she thinks, and vulnerable in a strange country. Erich has seen the surrender in Stefano, has been quickly able to see things that others can't, has been able to smell the air for any traces of betrayal. It is this that probably seals the trust.

"I have some more bread," she says to Stefano. "Perhaps the boy would like some, too."

Stefano looks behind him at the child.

"Thank you," he says. "If you have some to spare. I have money—"

"No," she says, shaking her head. "Please come."

They follow her into the house, and Stefano surveys the room at first before looking upward to the top of the stairs, perhaps to see any sign of Georg.

"My husband is asleep," she says, filling the kettle from a water jug near the sink and lighting the stove.

"Have you always lived here?"

"Yes, and no. I spent many childhood summers here, but mostly we lived in Berlin."

"Were you there at the end?"

"Berlin? Yes."

She walks to the room at the end of the house and quickly returns with a clean bandage.

"You are kind," he says. "Thank you." Though there is an undertone, she speculates, of cynicism in the words. She pushes the thought from her head. It is her nature to overanalyze.

She serves them some tea and a piece of rye bread, and Michal eats quickly, afraid it will be snatched away at any moment. They sit at the table, and the light falls across Stefano, illuminating the small, round sunken marks from his youth, like tiny bullet wounds, around his jawline.

Their talk is awkward, sentences stopped short, in case too much is given away.

The clock makes its sound, and the boy startles.

Rosalind asks the boy where he is from, to smother the jarring silence, but he answers only with stares.

"He does not talk much," says Stefano, who then explains the child's circumstances, before opening the conversation further to talk about himself. He mentions briefly his mother and sisters, and then his capture by the Germans toward the close of the war, when they no longer knew who or what they were fighting for. That by then he fought for nothing but survival. How he was sent to Sachsenhausen, and after the war, he was kept imprisoned by the Russians, just to make certain he wasn't a spy. He says that the walk from Berlin has been difficult with the aching in his lower leg worse than it has felt for months. But it matters not the trail behind him, he tells her, it is the destination now that features in his head.

He is different from most. He carries something that her own soldiers in the hospital in those final days no longer carried. Hope.

"Does your leg hurt now?"

"A little. Sometimes there is pain. Yesterday it reminded me the injury was still there. Otherwise I can walk on it. Just not for very long. Your doctors were good. I was treated at a prison hospital, where German doctors were forced to treat foreign casualties, before I was transferred elsewhere. I fared better than most. It just depended on the soldier who caught you, whether you would be captured and transferred, or shot on the spot."

Stefano looks out of place in the house. Like a piece of furniture too big for the room. He has a warm voice, a smile that never eventuates, that stops itself halfway, and two lines above his eyebrows that don't ever go away. His accent is strange, the words too elongated and musical, or broken, though the fact he speaks German at all is strangely endearing. He has to repeat some to make her understand.

He likes to look at things as he speaks, as if the answers to her questions are in the objects around him. He runs his fingers across the floral embroidery on the tablecloth and examines the cracks in the saucer on the painted tea set. He is looking for clues to the people here, and perhaps appreciating these small things that have been unimportant for so long.

She stops herself from asking about loyalties, anything that might highlight the divide between their races and give him reason to falter.

He looks at her for too long sometimes, and she has to look away. She has treated men like him many times before, men who did not fit in with war, who did not go looking for a fight.

"Where are you?" Georg calls from upstairs. Rosalind looks toward the sound, then back at Stefano.

"I'll be back in a minute." She picks up a bowl that has cold stew ready, some bread, and a cup of water.

Georg sits on the bed expectantly. She does not want him to come down yet. Does not want him to see the visitor. Does not want him to react.

He feeds himself, but oftentimes he finishes only half of it as if he has run out of motivation. He is slowly starving himself to death. He is only hungry for drugs now. The situation is worsening.

"I will come and get the bowl when you're finished," she whispers in his ear. "No need to come down."

"Who's here?" he asks, suddenly lucid.

"A friend," she says.

He looks at his dinner and commences eating, and she suddenly wonders if it was a mistake to leave the visitor alone. Whether he will use the opportunity to steal, though there is so little now of value. She leaves Georg and finds Stefano exactly where she left him, hair too long, curling around the backs of his ears, at the base of his skull.

"I'm sorry about your husband. Erich told me that he was badly injured. Was that from battle?"

He has carved up the air with the question, disturbing the ghost of Georg that haunts her constantly: Georg as he was before the war. She longs to talk about him, to release the past, yet at the same time remain loyal.

"Yes. It was a shock when he returned that way."

"And the rest of his family?"

"Georg has no one else. An only child. His mother died just after he was born, and his father died just before he started military college."

"Is that Georg there?"

Stefano is talking about a photo of the three of them when they were younger.

"Yes."

"You have known him a long time then."

"We met as children."

"He would holiday here with you in the summers?"

"Yes," she says.

"And who is the girl?"

"My cousin, Monique," she says, and she is aware of Monique's portrait behind her, looking down on her.

"Did your cousin come here in the summers also?"

"Yes," she says, and feels her body tense, knowing the question that will likely come.

"Where is she now?"

Michal puts his elbows on the table to rest his head in his hands. He is looking sleepy or bored. She could never understand children.

"We were separated during the war, and she is missing." She turns to busy herself with cleaning the cups they have used for tea.

"Oh, I see. I'm sorry."

And she is grateful that he says nothing more, because to offer any other words is futile.

He stands to look at the photo as if he has seen something, found another clue. Now that he is staring at her cousin, she wonders if it was a bad idea to invite him in. Monique distracts him, distracts everyone.

She explains why she is hesitant to help those passing through, looking for charity. Two months earlier an elderly man and his wife came by. They were German Jews expelled from Poland and looking for a place to live. Their shoes were worn and their hair cut short, and dirt was sealed beneath fresh skin on their hands. She did not feel sorry for them, but she thought that giving them food and sending them on their way would get rid of them quickly. They thanked her for the bread and blessed her even. In the morning when she woke, she found the word "Nazi" written across the door. She had scrubbed it off and later painted over the ghostly writing that she can still see in a certain light.

Stefano says nothing to this. He has now moved to the corner of the house to examine the damage to the bricks, from where water leaked in the previous night. Several different-colored bricks have been roughly patched in the opening.

"I believe the damage was from heavy air fire," says Rosalind. "I was in Berlin at the time. Fortunately, only a patch of wall and a small part of the roof were damaged, though now in heavy rain, water gets through the gaps at the base and under the floor. And the water pipes must have been damaged, too. Only brown water trickles through the taps above the kitchen sink."

"Was anyone here when it happened?" He turns back to the photo briefly before sitting down again.

"My grandmother." Rosalind does not think it necessary to say that when she returned, she had discovered her grandmother dead from sickness in her bed; she had died alone, with no one to look after her in her final days. She has grown tired of talking now that the conversation is about things she doesn't want to remember. The boy is watching her, sizing her up, as if he can see straight into her heart. She doesn't like him here. A child does not belong here, not with her.

Stefano looks at the photo of her grandmother also on the wall, but his eyes fall back on the portrait. She recognizes the look. Everyone looks at Monique that way. With interest and longing. Now Stefano.

"What did you mean when you said I should leave?" he asks.

"What?"

"Earlier. You said I should leave before Erich returns."

She is trying to remember exactly what she said.

"It was nothing, only that the house is not fit for habitation."

Questions. More questions. One after the other.

How long has Erich lived here? Have you known Erich since you were small? Has he always been your neighbor?

"Years . . . Yes . . . Yes." Answers that give away little else but lies.

She must dispense with him quickly now before there are more. Though, some part of her, the part that craves a normal life, likes him just the same.

"He can probably fix your broken building then," says Stefano, changing direction.

She stares at him briefly. It is not a question, but it is begging for comment.

"Erich is very busy these past weeks with work."

"He told me he only just found work."

Something smashes on the floor above them, and this time Stefano does not look past her up the stairs but turns to something on the wall. She is worried Georg will come down, and she heads for the stairs.

"Thank you for food," he says. "I'm sorry to disturb your afternoon." He is perceptive and courteous. She is grateful. Though he can't stay here. Any minute Georg will start shouting.

He smiles quickly and nods as if he knows that, too, pushing the chair in with a screech that sets Rosalind's teeth on edge. Most loud noises do that now. Michal jumps up to stand close to Stefano.

"I won't forget your kindness," says Stefano.

She looks away from his eyes that are too dark and too intense. She is unused to such attention and appreciation, which she can tell is sincere. Appreciation was there, sometimes, from her patients, but it was less personal. In the chaos of hospital casualties, it was blunt or scarce, and death often followed, and there were no thanks for death. And then there was Georg, who perhaps never appreciated her at all.

When Georg left for war the first time, she had been left feeling cold. Then by the time the war was over, the cold had turned to ice. She has grown used to the feeling, but some of that thaws here, as Rosalind warms toward the stranger and his differences. His accent, the occasional omission of verbs and small words that are insignificant anyway in the larger scheme of things, she thinks, are things she looks forward to hearing again.

Stefano leaves, and she returns to Georg to inspect the damage. His plate is in pieces. She is running out of plates and cups. She regrets that she did not sit with him during his meal. It was selfish of her, or was it? Did she invite Stefano in because she wanted to thank him, help him, or just find out something about him? She doesn't know herself anymore, doesn't trust her own perspective.

Georg has several holes on the back of his wrist where he has stabbed himself with the fork. She would like to blame the intruder for beguiling her into opening her door. But it was she. It was the loneliness, the loss.

She hurries downstairs to her bedroom below to retrieve something from a bag. When she comes back up, Georg is gripping the bed, veins extended at his throat, teeth together so tightly they might snap.

"Georg, stop!" she says quietly in his ear. "I'm here." She pushes him back onto the bed and with her arm across his chest weighs him down. This technique seems to freeze him. Rarely does he put up any resistance. With her free hand she injects his arm. In the early days she would give him tablets, but in the state of mania he would sometimes spit them out. The replacement at least is quicker to administer.

His groans turn to moans, and his body relaxes. His head flops sideways on the pillow but with eyes now open, and he looks at her. She feels nothing, she realizes, and can't remember the last time she felt that way. It has been creeping up on her, a slight resentment now, perhaps a restoration of her sanity, of awareness.

She touches his cheek with the back of her hand. His tongue relaxes, and retracts into his mouth, like a snail retreating in its shell. His hair has fallen back from his face. When he is in this state, he almost looks the same as he did. But he is no longer muscular and sunburned. He is gaunt, his skin pasty and flaking. She is remembering how strong he was. How big he was, his long strides across an empty room. Georg. Now small.

CHAPTER 12
STEFANO

Stefano reflects on the conversation with Rosalind, on the evasive way she met questions about Monique, as if the subject were painful, as if there were secrets that she was not willing to share. She is confusing to him, and during the course of their brief conversation, she delivered a contradictory mixture of traits: the edgy countenance of a trapped animal and blunt indifference. Like two different people, he thinks.

She is someone who is lost, who no longer looks to the future, but exists, perhaps because of Georg.

Rosalind was a nurse, though any details were carefully guarded. They talked about the town, about food, about safe topics, touching on families only, both steering much away from themselves where they could. But there is something there, lying deep, perhaps waiting to emerge, about her past that she is not proud of, that should not be spoken out loud.

He leads the boy to the top floor of Erich's house again, the boy's tiny bowing legs dragging tiredly up the stairs, and ushers him into the bedroom at the end of the house with the bed that has linen. But Michal stands tentatively beside the bed, looking at it, perhaps with longing but fearful also of more change, a different bed, a German that comes here, that reminds him of a past, of things to fear.

"You can sleep here," says Stefano. "It is safe."

Michal climbs under the sheet and sinks into the softness of the mattress that engulfs his small frame. Stefano tucks the sheet in as his mother did, then sits beside him.

"I will be here in the morning. I promise."

Michal rolls over to face the wall and closes his eyes. It is a gesture that says he believes him. At least he can sleep with food in his stomach. Stefano meant it when he said to Rosalind he was thankful, but it was more for the boy. He has survived on less. He could do it again if need be.

Inside, the light creeps inward toward the middle of the room, and the walls are fading. There is no lamp that Stefano can see.

He is eager to seek out the letters beneath the stairs. The girl on the wall has written them, and he is compelled to read what she has to say. He is remembering the closeness of the portrait, the largeness of her small features, as if she were in the room, staring back at him, willing him to read her letters, to learn more. She fascinates him even more by her absence.

He opens the secret wall and takes out the box. He slides out the top letter carefully from under the ribbon. Only one in case Erich returns suddenly again. There might be a reason they are hidden, an idea that further fuels his curiosity.

He tucks the letter inside his shirt, returns the shoebox, then examines the empty floor around him. He is trying to picture the damage from before, the destruction, which has now been cleared away. Rosalind said nothing about squatters, only reversed the lie of Erich's employment. One of them is lying, he thinks. Whoever, perhaps, has more to lose.

It is silent next door, though there are lights within. Georg should be in a hospital. But then it is something else that drives Rosalind. Love or duty? And why are the letters kept here at a neighbor's house and not with Rosalind?

He climbs up the stairs wearily, as if he has come home from a long day of work, wincing inwardly each time he raises his bad leg. From the window he looks to the glinting of the river as it falls to a shade of night and the birds whistle their goodbyes to the rays of orange light.

You should be home.

That was the last line of the last letter he received from his sister.

Not yet, he had written back. *Soon.*

Most people displaced have been racing to return home after the war, but there are so many things he has had to sort out in his head, much of which is guilt. Not everyone he loved survived this war.

A creaking sound alerts him in between the chirps and whistles. He returns the letter he had just pulled from inside his shirt.

"So, there you are!"

Stefano turns toward the voice. In the space of a moment, Erich has materialized in the doorway of the bedroom. A band of pinkish-orange light slices across the German's face so that parts are in shade. Stefano can see an eye and part of his mouth, painted in light. He has learned to be a ghost, thinks Stefano. He can enter houses, climb up creaking stairs without being heard. Stefano has fought a different war to know that it is more an art than an accident that he is able to slip in unnoticed.

"I'm glad you decided to stay. I wasn't sure if I'd find you here."

"The choice was easy," says Stefano. "How was your first day of work?"

Erich considers the question carefully.

"The day went as well as any other," he says. "Work is work and best left there. Perhaps you would join me for a drink downstairs before bed, yes?"

Although Stefano was looking forward to rest, to reading, he follows Erich to the kitchen. It is something Stefano must do, in exchange for hospitality.

"I met someone today who will sell me some petrol for the car," says Erich as he opens a linen carry bag and retrieves a small glass flask with milk, and several items carefully wrapped with paper and tied with string: several rolls, a piece of cheese, a quarter of a pie, and slices of pork. The preparation, Stefano notes, looks too meticulous, too caring, to have been done by a grocer.

"Have you eaten anything?" Erich asks.

"A little."

"Would you like something now?"

"No, thank you."

"There should be enough for two days."

Erich puts the food away in a small pantry cupboard behind the kitchen.

Stefano looks down, concerned about the generosity, conflicted also because he is sitting across from a German, who only a few months ago, before the situation changed, might have put a bullet in him.

Erich sits down, pours two small shots of whiskey.

"Why are you doing this?"

"Doing what?" he says.

"This," says Stefano, eyes toward the glasses. "All of it."

"You seem to have a problem with moving on," says Erich, placing his hands in his lap and leaning back in his chair to examine the other man.

It is strange and awkward. Stefano wonders about this relationship, if he can name it anything. Erich seems to have accepted this connection as something not extraordinary, and he seems to be attempting to leave little space for Stefano to hate him. The German is disarming, yet Stefano feels it is too soon to form any sort of alliance, to remind him that he worked for the regime that broke apart Italy and his family and nearly destroyed him. That Stefano must hate him and that he must not forget why.

"No, it is just unusual. Germans aren't known for their sharing capabilities. They wanted Germany and most of Europe all to themselves, I seem to remember."

"The past is done with," Erich says, downs the drink, and holds the empty glass forward to Stefano, as if in some kind of challenge. "Wouldn't you say?"

Stefano swallows some whiskey. The liquid is warm in the back of his throat, and the warmth spreads farther down his limbs.

"Rosalind said you have known each other a long time."

"You saw Rosalind?" Erich says, his eyes locking onto Stefano's.

Stefano explains the attempted stealing of the goose.

"It is not wise to give to beggars, not now."

"They were harmless."

"Then you have not been out on the open roads for very long. Out here, they can be just as bad as desperate people during the war. Charity does not return what it used to. It does not necessarily lead to gratitude anymore. Most who receive it feel they are entitled to more, and people will do anything for food. Besides, Rosalind can take care of herself."

"She is lonely, I think. She is missing her cousin."

Erich's expression is unflinching, yet there is something there—a darkness to the look that wasn't there before.

1941

A new subtitled American film had just arrived at the cinema, and Stefano took Nina to meet Beppe and his girlfriend, Sonia, and their friends Antonio (Toni) and Fedor. Stefano couldn't help but notice the lengthy and appreciative stares by the men as he introduced his younger sister. Nina had grown into an attractive girl of seventeen, more confident and less in her older sister's shadow. She had also grown interesting to talk to: she was socially conscious, curious about the war, and eager to be part of Beppe's somewhat elite group of friends that she had until then been excluded from.

The previous year Stefano's family moved even farther north, to follow Serafina and Enzo again, to support the government, to be closer to opportunity. Enzo had grandiose plans. There was business to be made in war. The North was where they would make their fortune, be close to greatness. In Verona, Stefano had leased a small town house for his mother and sisters, much smaller than their wealthy cousin's.

After the film, they all went to Beppe's apartment, and several other friends joined them. Beppe had moved out of his father's house several months earlier when the tension of their relationship became unbearable. What little time Beppe would have on leave would be spent arguing with his father about everything. After the move, he rarely returned to his father's home, though Serafina often stopped by to bring food and beg him to come home, but without success.

At the apartment, they opened wine and drank and talked. Beppe had served two tours of duty before the start of Germany's war and one since, and he was losing some of his former interest. He tended to talk against the government. They weren't supplying them with enough men, enough ammunition. Their captain made ill-informed decisions. The government was a mess. They were ill prepared to fight the British, and he didn't like fighting the British. He had friends who were English. It didn't seem right they were on opposing sides.

They talked about their dissatisfaction with the current government, and even Nina joined in, suddenly outspoken, and agreeing with the other men, while taking sneaky glances at Toni, who met these with just as much interest.

Toni was still recuperating from a shoulder injury and would not be returning to war straightaway, but he had other ideas, believing that their country's alliance with Germany was wrong. It was dangerous to talk of war with anything but pride and loyalty, but the wine was opening everyone up to find mutual agreement.

One of the men was more serious than the others. Fedor and his older sister had been born in Russia. Their mother, a Russian widow, had met and married a handsome Italian foreign minister during his friendship talks with Russia just prior to the formation of the Soviet Union, and Fedor's new stepfather had brought the family to live in Italy. Fedor's sister had not forgotten her Russian friends and had later returned to the Soviet Union to marry an army captain before the idea of war had even surfaced. Fedor had only recently lost his two young brothers in this war that neither parent had supported. He had heard from his stepfather that many in the government didn't like their leader. He had heard that some were planning to switch sides, to follow those in opposition and avoid further fighting.

Beppe, having drunk too much, was suddenly enraged by other news, of Jews in other countries being sent to foreign camps, of the deaths of other soldiers he had known for years, and he became especially vocal about his hatred for Hitler. Stefano suddenly worried about the darker tone their conversation had taken and pulled Beppe aside.

"Are you certain you can trust these people? Mussolini has spies everywhere."

"Yes, of course! And, young cousin, I will do anything to keep you out of war," said Beppe.

"But it is too late now! Tomorrow we leave. It is my first tour of duty."

"That is why we must trust these people. By the time we come back, I am confident there will be progress made here, and you will not be returning for a second tour."

"Your mother would die if she knew what you were saying."

In fact, thought Stefano, Serafina was so fiercely loyal to Mussolini she might disown Beppe if she knew.

"My mother doesn't need to know anything."

Stefano did not feel so confident. He was not willing to make such a change. He felt betrayed in a way. He was following Beppe into war, and yet he had now learned the full extent of his cousin's true feelings. He hoped that it was merely alcohol. That with his next tour he would feel renewed loyalty. Not that Stefano was overly loyal or supportive, but all this was for Italy. He had to believe it even if his mother, Beppe, and others didn't.

It was time to leave when Beppe and Sonia disappeared into his bedroom, and Stefano had to drag Nina away from a close and private conversation she was having with Toni. On the way home, Nina talked excitedly about the night, while Stefano's alcoholic high turned into a throbbing headache.

"Don't think I didn't notice your attentions, little sister!" he said to Nina.

Stefano had not been expecting the welcoming party on his arrival home. Teresa yelled at both of them as they entered the house, the shrill sound of her voice hurting his head.

"What kind of son are you? You should have been home. Mamma made a special dinner for you. You should have been here. She will not see you for months. And you, Nina! Where have you been? A single girl should not be out so late with those men. You will gain a reputation if you haven't done so already."

Nina was about to protest, but Stefano interjected.

"It was not Nina's fault," said Stefano. "It was all my influence. I kept her there. And *those men* are our friends." He had thought about his mother during the night, but the alcohol and the discussions of subversion had distracted him.

"It is that rogue, *Beppe!*" continued Teresa at Stefano, while Nina snuck away, safely out of Teresa's sight. "Always leading you astray."

Stefano had then gone into his mother's bedroom and turned on her lamp at the side of the bed. She was still awake, lying quietly in the dark and listening to the shouting.

"Mamma, I'm so sorry. Please forgive me."

She looked at Stefano and smiled. She always forgave him. How could she not? Her only son.

He pulled a thin mattress from underneath her single bed and lay on the floor beside her.

"I will stay beside you tonight."

And she smiled again. She loved him. Her Stefano. He always made things better. She would find it hard without him.

And then his older sister crept into the room and lay in bed with her mother, followed by Nina, who crawled in and lay beside Stefano on the floor, snuggling against him like she had done when they were small.

Stefano dozed. At some point someone switched off the light, and he could hear sniffling. Despite Teresa always being angry with him about something, Stefano knew she was sad he was leaving, and that she loved him. Then Nina began crying, too, and then his mother, the crying like a disease that spread quickly through the room. He knew no one would get any sleep that night so they could be together, all of them, for one more night at least. His thoughts turned morbid then at the thought of war, at the thought of leaving them.

Present-day 1945

"Did you know her well?"

"Who?"

"Monique."

"Not very."

"You were neighbors. I imagine you would have spent time together at some point."

Erich pauses, eyes narrowing slightly, and Stefano wonders if he has gone too far.

"You seem very interested."

Stefano shrugs. "A girl missing. Someone you knew—"

"Briefly," Erich says, standing and moving to look from the window over the sink. "I spent much time away. Did Rosalind tell you much else?" He asks this with his back turned.

"Not much. I saw she had damage to the house."

"Did you see Georg?"

"No."

Erich doesn't turn. Stefano can see his profile. His jaw square, his chin slightly forward as if he were gritting his teeth. He turns the tap, which coughs and splutters, and waits for the water to run clear so he can fill his glass.

"I should warn you again," he says finally, his back still turned, "that Georg is very ill, that he doesn't know what is going on around him. You should stay away from him. And Rosalind's nerves are frayed. I wouldn't believe anything she tells you either. She is unpredictable."

"How so?"

Erich turns then. He did not expect a question. He is unused to being questioned.

"She says things . . . She acts strange. She sees things, too. Things that aren't there."

"Ghosts?"

"Sort of," he says. "I brought you these." He puts some cigarettes on the table in front of him along with a packet of matches.

Stefano looks at them offhandedly, but it is an effort not to take one out immediately.

"How did you know I smoke?"

"Some things are more obvious than you think . . . but I must get some sleep, and you look tired. It has been a long day, and there are long days to come. Good night, Stefano."

Stefano suspects it was his questioning about Monique that called an early end to the conversation.

Erich has already reached the bedroom at the far end of the house by the time Stefano commences to climb the stairs wearily. Sitting on the edge of the bed, he rewraps his hand with the clean bandage from Rosalind and replays Erich's earlier words, still curious that Monique's disappearance does not appear to be felt by either of the Germans.

The squeaking of the back door, followed by the faint crunching sounds of footsteps on gravel, interrupts his undressing. He crosses the hallway to the room where Michal is sleeping soundlessly, closest to the noises. Murmurings in the yard below draw him toward the window.

Erich is standing near the back of Rosalind's house, talking with her in terse, hushed tones, the clarity of their words lost through the glass of the closed window. Rosalind faces the house and the window where Stefano is standing. Her face is tilted upward slightly, to speak with Erich, who is a head taller. Stefano does not think he can be seen, but he takes a step back from the window just in case.

Rosalind shakes her head and speaks rapidly before Erich interrupts her. The argument lasts less than a minute before Rosalind rushes away back to her house.

Erich stands tall in the dark. His fair hair catches the silvery light that turns the strands to white. He turns his head sideways to survey the wood up the hill beside him and the rise that peaks thirty yards from the back of the house then falls back down to the main road that can't be seen.

Erich turns his head farther, looking back over his shoulder, not quite in the direction of his house but close, and Stefano has the feeling that he knows he is being watched. Stefano draws carefully back from the window and returns to his room.

He leans back against the cold steel bars of the headboard and lights a cigarette. It rests between his lips while he unfolds Monique's letter from inside his shirt and switches on the torch to read it quickly. When he is finished, he returns the letter to his shirt.

He thinks of Erich then, of the coldness in his eyes, which conflicts with the warmth of his generosity, and of Rosalind and the many hidden truths that lie here, that he wishes to learn.

At some point in the night, when he has tossed and turned himself to sleep, Michal enters and climbs into the bed beside him. It is cramped, and Stefano's sleep is broken oftentimes by the movement of the child, and thoughts of Monique: words on a page, a voice without sound.

17 April 1937

Dear Papa,
I have decided that since I can't see you, I will write to
you and tell you about my life. And if we learn where you
are, I can send all the letters to you, so you can read about
our missing years.
I think about you all the time. I worry that Mama
died without you, that she was alone. I have had night-
mares about it, but Rosalind tells me that I need to calm
down, not think so much.
Last year, when Uncle Max first told me that Mama
died, I cried for weeks. I felt like it was my fault. What
if I had stayed with you, Papa? What if I had told the
police who sent me away that I wanted to stay with you
and Mama? But I did what they wanted, and I won't do
that again. If I find you, I will never let anyone separate
us again.
I miss you more and more, and the more time we
are apart, the more time I have to think of you and wish

you were here, making me laugh at the funny things you say. And I miss Mama so much, too, but I believe she is always watching us, Papa, and that makes me feel that things will be all right.

Uncle Max and Aunt Yvonne are not like you and Mama. They are nice enough, though Yvonne is hard to talk to. She is much colder, and I don't think she likes me here all that much, though she is sour at everyone, even Rosalind. And Max says very little, perhaps because he is afraid to. But he told me that you used to fight with Oma. That Oma did not want you to take Mama away to live a gypsy's life. (She called you a gypsy, which I found rather romantic anyway.) I don't think Oma liked me at first, either, because of you, because she blames you for Mama's death. But I told Oma last summer that you were the best father a girl could have, that you helped everyone, and you showed me how to be brave. And I think she believed me then, because I saw her eyes start to water.

And, of course, there is Rosalind here, always telling me what to do. Always fussing about the way I dress and speak, perhaps because Yvonne doesn't. She can't be bothered with either of us. And Rosalind is odd at times. Sometimes I think I know her, and other times it is as if I don't know her at all.

Max's house in Berlin is nice. It is larger than ours and has a garden, and there is lots of pretty china and silverware, but it doesn't have as many windows, and the rooms are dark, and the furniture, too.

I have made new friends, but Rosalind doesn't approve. She says if Hitler doesn't approve, then I can't have them. But I see them in secret, Papa. Emmanuelle is my friend, but she is scared, and she worries that we may not be able to see each other for much longer. Rosalind has also said that we must distance ourselves because Jews are not like us. It is so difficult to do. I love Emmanuelle. She is sweet and funny, but she says her parents are thinking they will emigrate to America if they can get the money. They worry about their future. These are all because of Hitler's rules.

Rosalind knows I write letters, and she has cannily guessed that I express my true feelings. She is always telling me not to put things in writing. That if someone found the things I write, I would be put in prison. Hitler doesn't like people saying nasty things about him.

We stayed with Oma at her river house again in the summer. It is so beautiful there. Georg, our friend, lives next door, and he is wonderful fun. We have so many adventures with him. He is a fast runner, and, Papa, you would not believe how fast I can run and swim now, too. Next year, when I turn seventeen, I will begin training in typing, and here in Berlin I will get an office job and still see Georg in the summers. And the whole time I will wish for your release and hope that they realize they have made a mistake by putting you in prison.

I will add this letter to the others that I write, and one day you will read them all, Papa.

I love you.

Monique

CHAPTER 13

ERICH

Erich has slept well since he was a child, can cleanly break the connection between night and day. But last night the transition took longer. He was thinking of Stefano in the room above. He was thinking of his eyes, frighteningly dark, that rarely blink, that examine everything around him and follow Erich as he moves.

He tried hard not to think of him there, tried hard not to think where he's been, if he has killed, if he is capable. It is not like Erich to second-guess his own instincts.

But today in the bright light, clearer now, he accepts Stefano is nothing to be feared. Stefano is a soldier with a peasant's heart, he concludes. Harmless, dragged into a war he was reluctant to join. He has lost, though Erich's loss is worse.

He opens the drawer where he laid some clothes the day before, laundered by Marceline. He takes out a crisp white shirt and beige trousers. He does up the laces of his shoes given to him by the Nazi underground, until they are tight and exact. He combs his hair. In the small mirror he takes in his appearance, and just briefly he can see his sister in his face, in the shape of the jaw and the nose that is straight and thin.

He hears no movement upstairs and proceeds from the front door.

Collecting a shovel that rests against a tree at the base of the hill, he walks upward and through the sparse trees above the houses. Over the rise he can see the damaged hamlet that is now empty, the occupants dead, crushed into the earth, then shoveled out again and placed in communal death holes dug in the hills.

The tip of his shovel hits metal, and with his hands Erich dusts off the last remaining earth from a tin box he had buried earlier. He checks through the papers kept inside the container, unfolds another piece of paper to add to these, then commences to rebury the box.

He stops, sensing he is not alone, and looks along the ridge to the thick cluster of trees that bars entry to the deeper wood behind. The wind picks up, and the trees begin swaying, taunting, perhaps whispering their secrets, his secrets. There is nothing there, he tells himself, just the wind and a past he has made disappear.

1939

Erich stood on the sidewalk and watched his father in a small group of other uniforms behind Hitler, who had just arrived to make a speech. The crowd cheered and saluted. His sister, Claudine, was complaining about the heat, her shoes, the crowds, while his younger brothers stood still, disciplined like him. Only the baby, destined for a few more months of life, whined slightly like his sister, reaching for her, waiting for her to take him. With her he always got the attention he was seeking. The grief that would come from his death had lasted much longer for Claudine.

His mother was beaming, he noticed, with adulation in her eyes. His father stood ahead of them, ahead of the crowd, arms at his sides, sweat dripping from under the shelf of hair above his forehead, a small smile, though not a wide one, from the shape of his eyes. Erich detected a frown, too, perhaps from the glare.

Erich felt proud of his father and marveled at the uniforms, at the order, at the control. The people loved him, he thought. The people wanted him.

Then out of the crowd an egg hit one of the soldiers standing off to the side of the selected people on the stage. Erich looked back to see who had thrown it but couldn't, the sun too bright in his eyes. Several Gestapo rushed at the crowd, and someone was dragged to the back through the parting crowd. All the while Hitler kept talking. Erich was disturbed by the incident, insulted for the führer. How could anyone be so brazen, so disloyal? Then he heard a sound beside him. His sister was sniffling, crying. He turned his head not too far, not wanting to disrespect the speech, but his sister needed comfort. He touched her shoulder and then shrank back when he saw. The noises were not from crying but from fits of laughter. She covered her mouth and looked down at her shoes.

"Stop it," hissed Erich.

"I can't," she said back. "It's too funny."

She composed herself eventually, but he was ashamed. He looked around to see if anyone had seen. One of Hitler's security staff, dressed in black, looked directly at him, sneered at him, as if he were the cause.

Erich looked forward, away from him, focusing on the führer's words, the only things that mattered. He talked about loyalty, about greatness, about a future.

Their town house in Berlin was magnificent, with a view of the Tiergarten, and only walking distance from the Reichstag where his father worked. The Steiners' house had gas and electricity and a good heating system, several bedrooms, a foyer, and a sitting room.

"Let's go and spy on Vati at work," said Claudine as she entered Erich's bedroom one night.

"Why would you want to do that?"

"Why not?"

His sister was always doing things that were adventurous or dangerous or stupid, as his mother described.

"I can't. I have to study."

"It looks very dull," she said, her eyes drifting across his mathematics books before she turned suddenly, flicking her wide skirt around her. "Wish me luck then."

"What are you doing?"

"I'm going out."

"Mutti won't let you."

"Mutti won't know. She is too busy with the baby who won't settle. Mutti will not even notice me gone."

"All right then," said Erich, exasperated. "We will go for a walk to Father's work, but I am telling you that it is only for an hour, and then I must come home to finish."

Erich told his mother they were going for a walk. She never questioned him. She trusted him entirely. Claudine, alone, would have been questioned and likely not have been given permission.

They walked past several people who milled on the sidewalk in a heated discussion. The people looked up at Erich and Claudine, then looked away quickly, as if they were guilty of something.

"It is stupid they wear an armband to show their religion."

It was the first time he had heard his sister voice her thoughts on this.

"It is something the government believes is right to do. You shouldn't question that."

Erich had already spoken to his father about it. His father had confided in him that the führer had a magnificent plan to re-create the country, to make it stronger, to make Germany more powerful. But that was all he had told him. There was much that his father was doing that wasn't spoken about.

On the way to the Reichstag, they heard shouting and saw a fire blazing ahead. As they drew closer, they saw that the windows of a bookshop had been smashed, and the books inside had been set ablaze. Erich held his sister's hand and told her to stay close. Several police had arrived on the scene already, standing beside their cars to watch.

"What is happening?" asked his sister. Erich knew the reason for the destruction. He could see more shopwindows broken nearby. It was another of the violent protests against the Jews and their businesses, which happened regularly.

"It is a riot against the government," he told her instead.

"But the bookshop is burning down! It is not against the government. It is against the bookshop owners!"

"Let's go."

"No! I like that bookshop. Papa bought me a book there once. And the police aren't doing anything to put the fire out. We have to go and get Papa! We have to help them!"

"No, Claud! It is too dangerous. We must go home."

He dragged his sister away and home, and she ran excitedly into the house to relate the events to her mother.

"Go get ready for bed," said Nene. "I will talk to your father as soon as he gets home."

Erich stayed in the kitchen with his mother.

"It is getting worse," she said. "It is just a matter of time before they have to do something permanently."

"What is going to happen, Mama?"

"I think the government will have to take even stricter measures. We have to be tougher with their kind. We have to find them a place where they can live safely. And keep our people safe from them as well."

Erich was not sure what to think. He trusted his mother, but he also needed his father's words to verify what she said. Only then could he form an opinion. His father was right about most matters of state.

After all, he had the ear of the parties that made decisions. He had sat in Hitler's office, presented his work, offered advice.

His father came home. He had also passed the bookshop and seen the destruction. But he knew about it before he even left the Reichstag.

"What will happen, Papa?"

"It is not up to me, Erich. It is up to certain members of the government to stop this from happening. They will stop the violence, but they will also find a way to keep these people separate. Any troublemakers will be sent away."

"The Jews you mean?" said his sister, appearing in the doorway.

"Yes, of course."

"From what I could see, they weren't the ones that started it," said Claudine.

"They started it long before now," said their mother, the baby finally rocked to sleep in her arms. "It is just that you aren't old enough to see it."

His sister stood a moment, arms crossed, pouting, then turned away. She was too young to understand at that point. Erich had determined early that his sister would never be a follower, and would be hard to conform, but he could not have foreseen that this minor opposition would be the beginning of her decline. Later, when he looked back, he felt that his parents had failed to see clearly the principles his sister was missing. If they had only seen this back then, had kept a closer eye on her, then perhaps their family would have stayed together, perhaps even his father would still be alive.

Present-day 1945

When Erich returns from the ridge, Stefano has risen, though there is swelling below his eyes from a bad sleep. His hair is combed, but there is still a wrecked look about him that camp survivors do best, a closed expression, a sagging of the shoulders. His skin is damp and glistens with tiny beads of sweat.

"I hope you don't mind. I decided to make some of the coffee you found."

"Of course," Erich says. "Is the boy still sleeping?"

"Yes."

Erich notices that Stefano is favoring his injured leg when he moves to sit down. "How did you hurt your leg?" he asks.

"It was at the end of the war. Your friends marched us from the camp when they feared the enemy was nearing, then shot me when I tried to break away from the group."

Erich wonders at first if it is Stefano's attempt to instill shame, but his expression appears open and honest. There seems no shadow of blame, not toward him anyway.

Through the window, he can see Rosalind walking toward the barn. After his words the night before, he doesn't think she will come here. Georg must stay away, too. He wants to warn Stefano again of Rosalind and Georg, but it will sound too contrived, and he doesn't want any questions about relationships that will test his ability to shade the truth.

He brings out the linen bag that holds the food and retrieves the pie.

"Tell me, Stefano, what did you do before the war?"

"I studied languages, German, French, and English. I planned to travel. And you?"

"Engineering. We were different, yes? Before the war. And more alike then, too, perhaps."

Stefano says nothing. He gives nothing away. Erich imagines he may have been hard to break in an interrogation room, and loyal to his associates.

Erich cuts three small pieces of pie.

"Please eat," Erich says. "One piece for each of us. I will take mine with me. I'm running late."

"Are you working all day?"

"Yes, till quite late," he says, standing to leave. "Good day!"

Erich walks from the door to the track that leads south toward the town. He is relieved to be out of Stefano's sight and to have time now to think. There is something about the foreigner that confuses him, something he cannot yet put words to.

CHAPTER 14
ROSALIND

From her window, Rosalind watches Erich walk toward town, toward a nonexistent job. He has plans, another life, which is why she is curious about his interest in Stefano, why he comes back. Erich hates it here. There is something he hasn't told her. A year ago Erich would have had Stefano imprisoned, or worse. The previous night Erich had reminded her of things, of her obligations, of a past that she wants to erase. He also told her to keep away from Stefano. But she will do what she wants. She will not be eternally bound. He owes her, too.

As she walks toward the gate, only one of the geese waddles to meet her. She checks the other, tries to examine her leg, but the injured goose is offended by Rosalind's needling hand and takes a peck.

"No!" says Rosalind. "I am trying to help you!"

The goose stands, hisses, and fluffs out her feathers, walks a short way and perches on the ground, as if the effort of walking were too much. Rosalind can see that the leg is bent, likely snapped, and unlikely to heal. She scatters the grain in front of her, and the bird forgets her ailment and pecks hungrily.

"You still have your appetite at least."

She then picks up two pails to carry river water for the man-made pond. Monique used to love the job of fetching water for the geese. Any excuse to be gone from the house. Sometimes it would be a long time before she returned, especially if she decided to lie on the platform to catch the morning sun. She shivers. She does not like to imagine Monique lying anywhere.

When she turns to leave the pen, Stefano is there at the fence, watching her. She feels awkward under scrutiny. She is not good with most people, especially those she cannot help. The sick do not focus on her, rather on themselves, their pain. They are easier to deal with. The things they demand are the things she can give.

"Hello again," he says.

"Do you have some advice about an injured goose, too?"

He looks down, and she sees that his lips are now pressed in a line, perhaps amused.

"No. I have had nothing to do with injured geese. Dogs, people, and languages. Not geese."

He is lighter today. He is also careful with the words and works hard to sound them correctly.

"Where is the boy?"

"He is still asleep."

"He is exhausted, yes?"

"Yes. It is probably the first real sleep he has had in a long time."

"You saw his mother. Was she young?"

"Yes, young like you."

And Rosalind is thinking of her own loss, of the grave that sits on the hill. She wishes she could talk to him, tell him everything. Though he is a foreigner, a man, and therefore unlikely to understand a loss like hers, she thinks.

"Where did you learn to speak German?"

"I completed two years of language studies before I signed up for the military. German first because war had begun, and I thought it would be most useful. Then I took my books with me to the battlefield and practiced on the German soldiers. I speak some English, and a little French. Though not as well."

"And what did you want to do with so many languages?"

"A translator or a teacher . . . The world was, how do you say . . ." He looks for the words.

"Full of possibilities."

"Yes," he says.

"Why did you choose to go to war then?"

"Joining someone else's pointless fight was never on my list to do. But not joining would have meant I cared little about the ones who did. I could not sit idle while people, friends, around me were signing up."

It is intriguing to her that he is both studious and brave, and he is caring also. Yesterday she felt he was hiding something. Perhaps it was this. That he is anything but ordinary.

"Do you hate us?" she asks, surprising herself, his answer suddenly important to her.

"Who?"

"Germans."

He shrugs. "I did hate once, but hate now lives in the past. And I prefer to remember the past, not live in it."

This answer brings a sense of relief, though it is still unclear to her why she is so affected, why her heart feels suddenly lighter. Why it is Stefano, a stranger, someone she might have left for dead in another time, who makes her feel this way.

"Are you getting water for the geese?" he says, his eyes briefly leaving hers to look down at the pails, and stopping her from saying something she might regret, a futile apology perhaps for all that has happened.

"Yes."

"Then I will help you," he says, reaching for them.

He walks behind her toward the river.

"You must be looking forward to going home," she says, filling in the silence as they approach the river's edge.

Stefano steps down the embankment and glides a bucket on its side to fill it with water, then passes it to Rosalind at the edge of the slope.

"I'm a little cautious about going home. I'm not sure how I'll be received. Whether I'm a hero or a traitor. I won't really know till I get there."

"What did you do? Was it so bad?"

He passes her the second bucket, then steps closely toward her, their faces only inches apart. Embarrassed by their closeness, she steps away.

"Soldiers who worked for Germany aren't probably looked at with any great gratitude there or here. I have to go back and face enemies in the streets and my family also."

"They will support you."

"I am worried what they will say."

She is intrigued by his candidness. The only time she witnessed such openness was from the soldiers who lay dying, whose affection they bestowed on her, their sins, their truths, in lieu of their wives and mothers who were not there to listen. She heard many stories. Some she remembers vividly. She carried out their wishes. She took their final letters and posted them.

When she looks up at him, he is studying her with unblinking eyes as dark as ink, and she turns away self-consciously.

They return to the house. He walks in front this time, and she looks at the large hands that wrap around the handles of the pails. The limp is not visible today, perhaps due to a night of rest.

She opens the pen, and he empties the buckets to top up the small pond created for the geese.

"Thank you," she says, unsure whether she should invite him in for tea. Whether it is too much, too soon. Whether Georg will be waiting at the table for her when she enters. His reactions are becoming less predictable.

"I'm here for another two nights at the kindness of your friend and neighbor. I could help you fix the leaking wall. I forgot to tell you that building is another one of my skills."

"You have many then."

He pauses, waiting for her response to his suggestions, which she has avoided offering.

"Erich is in town, working again," he says.

She lowers her eyes briefly so she doesn't give anything away. She does not want to reveal the truth. Though perhaps it is that they both know his employment is a lie.

"I have seen some materials in the broken buildings across the road when I was wandering. I can rebuild the wall. I can fix it so there are no more leaks."

"The bricks in the fields across the road belong to someone else."

"By the looks of it, I don't think they will be coming back."

It is a line that hangs for too long.

"It would not be too difficult. I have such idle time. I am not used to being so idle. You would be doing me a favor."

"I . . ."

"But of course, given that I am a foreigner, I would understand."

She shakes her head. "No. It's not that." But there is truth in it. She would feel uncomfortable, perhaps even disloyal. She thinks of Erich, who trusts him also. "You have an injury. I . . . have nothing to pay you with."

"I ask for nothing in return."

She thinks of Berlin in the final days. She shudders. But that was Berlin. This is different. He is different.

1939–1940

Rosalind began her nursing career, not with the desire to heal—oddly enough that had never been her goal—but with an initial idea that was more conceited: that in such a role she would be more appreciated by her parents, Monique, Georg, and by the party. But by the end of the first year, she'd quickly discovered a sense of purpose and a sense of belonging.

She was committed to the principles that the German Red Cross demanded of her: dedication to hygiene, to treatment, and to the preservation of race, and devotion to the führer. Unlike Monique, who, though given work in an office of the Reich Ministry, showed little commitment to anyone or anything.

Thanks to a referral from Erich, Monique now held a position in the education ministry, typing reports and requisitions, and general correspondence that did not include any sensitive material. Rosalind thought this was for the best, given that Monique had previously held concerns about the government. She was not as vocal as she had been in the past on political matters, on imprisonments because of race and her disapproval of war, but her silent rebuttal of the new system came from her willing association with others who did not fit with the German design, an association that her employer had yet to learn about.

Once Rosalind had completed her initial training, she was transferred to a large hospital southwest of Berlin, where the führer himself was said to have once been treated, and she witnessed her first emergency amputation as casualties—those more likely to survive—came in from the field hospitals in greater numbers. The hospital was palatial, with its arched windows and grand staircases. But as the Second World War funneled more patients through its stately doorway, the aesthetics of the building became inconsequential. Under bright-white lights, the overwhelming smells of ether, iodine, chlorine, sulfur, blood, and bedpans disintegrated the building's charm.

Despite the large convergence of the broken, she was not affected by her emotions. Rosalind could treat a person without thinking that she was saving someone's son or brother or father. And she could see from those nurses she worked alongside, from their lack of mental discipline, from their attachments to patients, that her way was the only way. She did not allow herself to imagine Georg on a battlefield somewhere. She could never allow herself to believe anything other than he was bulletproof.

Monique and Rosalind hadn't gone back to the river house last summer because of their work, but they had caught up with Georg in Berlin, before he was sent away shortly after the war began. Georg wrote to both of them often. He spoke of how he missed *them*. Ironically, the collectiveness of this word drew only feelings of exclusion.

When the girls received word that Georg was coming to the city on leave, they made plans to meet at a wine bar. Georg had not yet seen active duty. He had been to Poland to help prepare the area for greater Germany, keeping the civilians in order after the invasion, and witnessing things he did not wish to discuss. Georg was under strict instruction not to talk about the military. They were preparing for something huge was all he said.

Both Georg and Erich wore their uniforms, Georg in field gray and Erich in the attire of Hitler's Schutzstaffel, of which he had just been made a member. Rosalind noticed that many glanced their way, and their eyes did not linger too long on Erich. He was tall, imposing and fearful in black. And his fair hair, combed back severely, called attention to the well-defined and forceful angles of his jawbone and nose.

Erich ordered drinks while Georg lit a cigarette, at home in the smoky, crowded bar. Smoke was part of his life now, especially on the battlefield. He said he had taken up smoking for fun. Though his use of the words "for fun" did not sound as such, the sentence spitting out a more sober but subtle undertone.

Monique arrived late, taller in heels now, and smartly dressed. She wore a navy-blue jacket and skirt and a matching navy hat. Her normally wild hair was tamely twisted and pinned behind her ears. Her cheeks were rouged, and her lips were a brilliant sheen of red, emulating photos of film stars. Beside her, Rosalind felt insignificant and pallid.

Rushing straight from work by train and bus, she wore her plain, striped nurse's uniform, though she had brushed out her shoulder-length fair hair. She was right not to adorn herself. Hitler liked purity, women of natural beauty, and discouraged the use of makeup.

"You finally like skirts now, yes?" said Georg to Monique. "You are all grown up. I did not recognize you at first. What is that paint on your lips?"

Monique threw herself into Georg's arms, laughing. "Stop teasing me!"

"I can't help it. If you are going to paint your face, how will I recognize you?"

"Stop it! I have a very important job, you know."

Monique told silly stories, talked of friends from clubs she attended, her special friends, she called them, and Rosalind noticed that Erich listened intently to this, though he did not question her or make a comment. It made Rosalind feel better, Monique talking about such trifles; it showed that Rosalind and her job were more important.

Rosalind excused herself to go to the powder room, and when she came back, she found only Erich there reading through some notes from a small black pad he carried in his jacket.

"And where are the others?" she asked.

"Talking outside," said Erich carelessly, glancing up at her, then back down at the notes in front of him. He shaded the book with his hand, keeping whatever was written there hidden.

"Why?"

Erich looked up, and this time his eyes rested, studying her. He was reading her, she thought. He took a brief sigh as if his summation were complete.

"I think they are having a cigarette and a private talk. You can go and find them if you wish," said Erich, and Rosalind thought either he had read her panic or he wanted to be alone to write. She concluded it was both.

There was no immediate sign of them at the front of the building, and she searched until she found the pair standing close together in a laneway to the side. Monique seemed very animated. The noisy chatter that spilled out from the windows of the bar masked what they were saying, but there was clearly an argument. "You have to tell her!" was all she thought she heard, though she couldn't be certain.

It was Monique who was facing her, who saw her approach first. She nodded toward her to alert Georg, who turned to look, frowning at the interruption.

"Rosalind," said Monique. "You must keep Georg company! Erich is taking me to a function with some senior officers."

She raised herself on tiptoe to kiss Georg on the cheek before she walked past them. He appeared agitated, brushing the hair back roughly from his forehead, and unable to rest his gaze with his thoughts elsewhere.

"Is everything okay?" asked Rosalind. "What were you talking about?"

He relaxed to some degree, focusing then on her.

"Nothing really. Just about the war . . . I have to leave in a few days . . ."

It told her nothing, but that was Georg. If she pushed him, he would simply change the subject or walk away.

"Why don't we go to dinner?" he asked, brightening slightly and holding both her hands.

"That would be nice," she said.

The following night Rosalind borrowed her father's car and drove Georg to his barracks. He was sweet then, and he held her longer. And this time he kissed her fervently on the lips. Hers was the last face he would see before he left for battle. She knew they were meant for each other. Monique was a pleasant diversion when they were young, but he needed someone stable, someone who could love him back.

The following year Monique was fired from her job. Several weeks after that, she announced her plans to marry Erich.

Present-day 1945

Rosalind is thinking of the water gushing in the other night. She is thinking that she can't afford to get someone to fix it. She would never ask Erich, because he would pay someone to do the work, and then she would feel she owed him something more. He says she owes him too much already.

She agrees to Stefano's offer. It is the look of him that causes her to weaken. A sense that he is too battered for any more fight. She recognized it in others whom she treated: scarred and smaller than they were before the war. She believes she can trust him. He saved a child. It is unlikely he will want to hurt her.

She mutters something about meaning to fix it, but the comment is lame and fades at the end with insincerity. She is not capable. She knows it. Though she is capable of helping load some bricks. She knows the place he is talking about. Houses that were crushed by air fire and bombs.

She directs Stefano to the barn to collect a wheelbarrow. While he is gone she checks on Georg, who is sleeping. From her bag, she takes a syringe and performs the task of injecting medicine to keep him asleep for several hours. She does not want him to wake and come looking for her. Sometimes he does not take to strangers. She does not want to frighten Stefano away, not now that he is doing this task for her. Georg must bear this for both of them.

The squeaking wheel of the barrow alongside the house alerts her to action. She ties up her hair, then an apron, and leaves to accompany the handsome stranger who has somehow landed at her door.

They cross the road to several damaged houses with walls turned to rubble, glass that has disintegrated, and blackened things that lie strewn and barely recognizable: a stove; a birdcage; broken china, the patterns singed; and other objects, covered in black grime and soot. Michal looks at the items, then turns to Stefano.

"Go on," says Stefano. "Find something. There might be treasures there."

And Rosalind shudders, imagining children stepping over the remnants of her house in Berlin, of the faces of her parents in the rubble. She remembers watching men and women, volunteers, pulling out bodies from these ruins. Not long after the war ended, there were many who went from house to house, pulling the injured from wreckages along the road and depositing the bodies in a warehouse in the town.

The boy steps cautiously through the remains, stopping to examine or salvage an object. He is odd. The children she has seen run and squeal. This child is like an adult, careful and quiet, like her, she thinks.

She sorts through the rubble for good bricks with her small white hands, long fingers, with nails bitten to the quick, that look more used to delicate stitching. Rosalind places the last of her bricks in the barrow, and Stefano's arm brushes hers. She draws away too quickly, startled by their connection, and cautiously gauges his expression that betrays no feeling, eyes that are focused elsewhere, unaware perhaps of anything but the task.

When the barrow is full, Stefano raises it to leave and calls out to Michal to follow. Rosalind walks behind for the return journey, examining the broadness of Stefano's shoulders, the muscles that ripple beneath his sleeves, and wondering at the distance that has closed between them in just a day. She wonders also at the warmth of him that she still feels against her arm.

"What have you found, Michal?" asks Stefano as he looks in the basket beside him. "You must be pirate, yes? To find such treasure," he continues in his strange accent, and Rosalind feels the touch of a laugh in the back of her throat, a genuine one, one that comes up from the heart. There is a small spring in the boy's step, his face more animated.

On the way back to the house he keeps checking that the items are still inside the basket. He is excited by his finds: a handle from what once was a walking cane, a brass doorknob, a pipe that is almost intact, and a single red porcelain marble.

They cross a paddock that stretches to the main road. Passing in front of them, a convoy of trucks on its way to Berlin. Several of the American occupants wave to them from inside one of the vehicles. Stefano responds. Rosalind pretends she doesn't see them.

"What happened?" she asks as his limp becomes more obvious across the damp and uneven ground. Though she wishes immediately that she didn't ask. She is afraid of something. The truth, a reminder of what people did, something that might break a fledgling truce. Might remind him again of hate.

"Just before the Russians came, your Germans announced that we were leaving the camp. They knew they had lost the war; I saw it in their faces, but the arrogance was still there. They still hung on to that. They had to have one last victory, and they still had weapons. Even without weapons they could have killed us, most of us too weak to fight. They marched us from the camp. The Germans got more desperate, agitated. Insane is probably the best word. I watched others walking off the road toward some trees. I was skeptical at first, and then I followed. Then they began shooting us in the back, and hundreds fell around me. I took a bullet below the knee, and this, strange as it sounds, saved my life.

"The Germans took off across a paddock to hide from the Russian army about to arrive. When they had gone I dragged myself farther into a wood and lay there, sleeping for some time until I heard trucks. Russian trucks."

He strains from the effort of pushing the barrow, the ground still softened from rain.

"Do you want to stop and rest?"

"No," he said.

"What happened then?"

"When I was in the camp, I would dream about trees that bordered the camp, a symbol of freedom. We thought that if we made it to those trees, we were free. It was a false hope. The Russians found me and put me back in the same prison again. *Ironisch*, I think you say."

"Yes," she says. "It is certainly ironic."

He is strong, hair unruly, and there is stubble on his chin. He has had no woman to care for him, she thinks. Georg is lucky that way. He has someone.

They cross the road, and Stefano begins the task of heaving the barrow up the slope. On the ridge, the ground levels briefly, and he weaves swiftly through the sparse and narrow wood.

At the edge of the descent to the backyard of Rosalind's house, Stefano puts down the barrow and wipes the back of his forehead. She watches him look down at the roofs of their two houses and toward the river beyond the trees before noting piles of rubbish nearby, and something else, too.

"What's that?"

"Rubbish from the cleanup after the bombings."

"There!" He points to the white cross close by, above a mound of earth surrounded by stones. "It looks like a tiny grave."

"I don't know," she says, turning briefly in the direction of the small bundle that Monique once buried. "Since the end of the war, many have walked the road below."

Rosalind is not a suspicious person, but this patch of wood feels colder, even with the too-warm air that blows from the south.

She continues forward to the house, eager to put distance between her and the grave, and Stefano picks up the barrow again to follow.

When they reach the bottom, Stefano empties the barrow at the edge of the house.

"I can check your injury later if you wish," says Rosalind. "To make sure you haven't damaged it doing this heavy work for me."

He nods unconvincingly.

"And the burn on your hand?" She is a nurse now, and it feels good to ask these questions. This was the type of injury she attended to before the bodies flooded in, in pieces.

Stefano looks toward the river, the question arousing a memory. She had seen the mark on his hand when the bandage had come loose, and she could tell immediately that it was a burn. She has also seen him cover it with his other hand sometimes to conceal it. At the table he kept it mostly hidden away on his lap. Whatever is beneath his shirt must be badly battered, she thinks. She can help him, repay him for the wall.

"I took a blast from an explosion in Africa. We were beaten by the Allies. I lost a friend there. I got up and then collapsed. Waking a short time later, I realized I was in the middle of a battlefield."

"You have had much thrown at you."

"Especially explosives," he says in what she perceives as jest, though without the backing of a smile. Instead he stares intently at her. The look of him wild, and too much to take in.

She turns modestly from his gaze to consider his family and the changes they might see. She imagines a man who was once much stronger, before being cut down for reasons that don't make sense anymore. She believed her leaders, the speeches. Believed Germany would win. Georg didn't, and neither did Monique.

"We grew up together here," she says about Georg. She longs to tell someone about the life she had here. For some reason, she longs to tell Stefano. "Georg and I. And Monique. We used to swim in the river and run through the wood like wild children. I used to pray all autumn, winter, and spring for summer to come sooner."

He stands, waiting for more, but she bites her lip. She has said too much. The relationship has changed. Friendship is creeping in.

"We will need some more bricks," he says to cover her awkwardness, and the three return to the ruins with the now-empty barrow.

CHAPTER 15

STEFANO

Michal sits on the ground outside, examining the items in his basket, occasionally looking at Stefano, who is breaking apart Rosalind's wall with a hammer. The existing hastily repaired exterior crumbles and falls to the ground in pieces and dust. A fire burns in an earth pit near the river to cook some of the crushed limestone bricks Stefano collected from the ruins. Stefano also repairs some wooden roof shingles and cleans the bricks that will be used to rebuild the wall. When the limestone is eventually cooked and the mortar is completed with water and sand he has collected near the river, he commences the bricklaying gently and carefully, as if it were fine art, something Stefano had watched his father do.

It is late in the afternoon when he has repaired part of the area that stretches from the floor to the roof. The damage could have been far worse, the kitchen inside ruined, someone killed. Michal has been handing Stefano the bricks and is a patient and willing assistant. They work silently together, and Stefano hides the fact that he is enjoying the partnership, enjoying the little child who, in a brief amount of time, has become attached to him. He appreciates the instincts of the boy, who has most likely had to use them during the war to survive.

"Do you like this work?" he asks, smoothing and scraping away the excess mortar.

"Yes," the boy says.

"Do you want to be a builder?"

"No, a soldier."

Stefano stops a moment.

"Why a soldier?"

The little boy shrugs, and Stefano returns to working.

The sun beats down on Stefano's back, and he wishes he could remove his shirt that hides the scar. Throughout the day Stefano has occasionally glimpsed Rosalind through the cavity into the kitchen, where she is busy cooking and where the smell of browning dough is making him hungry.

With Michal's work complete, the little boy takes the stick that has been used to stir the mortar and draws pictures in the dirt, but the pastime is brief. The distracting smell of food draws him inside the house.

Stefano uses the opportunity to gain some time alone and slips through the woods to the river. Sitting at the edge of the embankment, he lights a cigarette—a habit he took from Fedor—and watches the sun sinking lower behind the trees downriver. When he is finished smoking, he unwinds his loosened bandage and strips off his clothes. He sinks into the water, feels the icy tentacles spread across him to remove the grime and dust, and imagines the girl on the wall, Rosalind, and Georg playing here in the river.

He swims a short way out, floats on his back, then heads again to the side. As he steps up the embankment, Rosalind greets him, holding a tray of small rolls and water.

She looks at his body briefly. She has seen the scarring and looks away modestly to put the tray on the ground. There is no point to covering the hand again with the bandage. He could be accused of vanity, but it is more the explanation that he cannot bear, the lies to cover what really happened. He pulls on his trousers.

"Thank you," he says, sitting once again on the riverbank. She sits down and places the tray between them.

"The boy is sleeping on the couch after I filled his stomach. I thought I would let him rest and bring yours here."

"These are good," he says, his mouth full of bread with jam, though the rolls are flat and hard.

"I don't normally bake, but then I don't normally have visitors who work for me for nothing," she says. "I discovered that Oma had kept one jar of elderberry jam hidden inside an old kerosene tin on the top of the shelf. I'm not even sure whether she remembered it was there. Maybe she did. Maybe she left it for me to find. I will never know now."

She looks away briefly as he eases into his shirt.

"How is your leg?"

"It aches a little, but it is still holding me up."

She turns back as he finishes buttoning his shirt. He is glad she doesn't mention the scars on his body. Instead she talks briefly of the river, of the current, and of someone she knew who nearly drowned there. Of the year her *Opa* died and her *Oma* was left to live alone.

This release of her guard gives him pause to study her longer. She is thin, her clothes oversized, revealing nothing of the body within. She might be unnoticeable in the street, with her dull-blond hair and pale-blue, sometimes-colorless eyes. But she is prettiest in this moment, thinks Stefano, with her expression more open and less suspicious, and her eyes wider with curiosity. He stares back at her, and it is he who drops his eyes this time, her sudden interest in him making him more conspicuous than he wants to be.

When they have eaten all the crumbs from their plates, Stefano stands to stretch out his aching leg.

"I think you should stop work for today," she says. "And I should check your leg before you go."

She looks upon his face longer than she has before, studying him. He is suddenly a patient, someone who needs attention.

"Do you always wear your nurse's cap?"

"Yes, it was hard to leave it behind."

"You should be there still."

"I can't go back," she says, looking in several directions before her eyes return to his leg. "Forget the wall for now. Come back to the house, and I will check your injury . . . see if there is something more I can do to stop the ache."

He nods. There are perhaps two hours left of daylight, time enough to finish, but he is looking forward to rest. He follows her back to the house to find that Michal has just woken, dazed and recovering from his dreams.

"I can see you now," says Stefano, about his washed face.

"It was a challenge to wash his hands and face, but the promise of jam finally made him compliant. But he refused to have a bath. Would not move when I suggested it," she says. "I had to compromise. I am used to washing soldiers who were sometimes difficult. Now I realize they made it easy for me in comparison. The child is quite stubborn!"

She is unused to children, and the lack of affection in her tone reflects this.

"He does not like strangers touching him," says Stefano. "I think he has been let down too many times."

Rosalind is quiet then, watching the boy wistfully, perhaps seeing part of herself in him as well.

"Anyway, I am better with injured soldiers," she says to recover.

Rosalind instructs Stefano to sit down and roll up his left trouser leg. She disappears to the other end of the house, near the room where he believes she sleeps, then returns with a bag that contains medicines and crouches down in front of him. There is no shyness or awkwardness now. She is not afraid of injury. To her, he is just another patient: someone else to heal. A duty. But he doesn't mind the attention.

"Turn a little to your right and stretch out your leg," she commands in a different voice, sterner, than she has used before. He imagines she was direct as a nurse, less frail than she appears.

He does so obediently, and she places her small cold hands around his skin, a slight pressure only, while her thumbs probe the hardened tissue to feel the damage underneath. He winces inwardly, the area still sensitive, and she releases the pressure as if she hears everything that is inside him as well.

The bullet entered through the back of his leg beneath the knee and lodged in the muscle.

"The bullet was removed quickly, yes?" she asks.

"Yes," he says.

"It could have been worse," she says, frowning in concentration. "They could have blown off your kneecap. You have a leg to walk on, not like others."

He nods more somberly. "I suppose I should be grateful then." He means it to some degree, but there have been times when he wasn't grateful, for anything, not even his own life.

She concentrates on massaging and soothing the area. He is no longer a person. She is connected only with the affliction now.

"You have nurse's hands."

She shakes her head, perhaps shaking away the distraction.

"You don't want to continue in that work in a new city perhaps? Away from Berlin?"

"I think perhaps I am destined for something else."

"I think you underestimate yourself. I just don't think people have thanked you enough. It perhaps won't be as bad now, without an enemy to blow up your hospital walls."

She pretends she isn't listening, but the redness on her cheeks tells him otherwise. She takes a bandage out of her bag, applies it with gentle pressure, and pins it together.

"Do you need painkillers?"

"No," he says, glancing at the collection of various medicines she keeps in her bag.

"That should help for today, but I think it would be wise to finish the work tomorrow," she says. "I am certain now that there will be no rain today. The air is too cool, too dry. The geese are quiet."

"They can tell you."

"Not always, but they are mostly right."

"Moni is in the river," says Georg. He has walked into the room and stares at Rosalind. It is difficult to know if he has noticed Stefano at all. But he has noticed Michal, and he stares at the boy, who looks uncomfortable and gets up to stand near Stefano at the table.

Rosalind sighs and snaps the bag shut.

"Georg, go to your seat outside." He stops for a second as if waiting for more, then walks out the front door.

"There is no need to send him away on my account."

"It is not on your account," she says curtly. "It is for him. He likes to stare into the woods at the sun at this time of day. He likes to watch it before it sets."

Any softness that he had seen earlier seems to have vanished.

"Does he not know that Monique never returned?"

"My husband knows very little, but he remembers my cousin fondly. They had a good time together. They were close, like brother and sister. It seems these are the only memories he has now. He talks of the river often. That's where his memories seem to be."

Stefano knows the emptiness of loss. First his father and then, like a torrent, came more.

1942

He had woken from a blast, his head numb, his ears ringing. Through the smoke and dust, people were scrambling to reach a ridge of sand for protection. He climbed over the bodies and found one of the men alive. He bandaged the soldier's open spleen and listened to him cry for his mother, beg for a bullet, change his mind and ask to be saved. Stefano had no more morphine shots. He ran for the medic who was too busy pressing a towel against a neck wound and blocking against a fountain of blood. By the time he returned, after the enemy had paused the shelling, the soldier was dead. He made the sign of the cross, then stepped over other bodies, looked at faces, tried to recognize and remember their names to report back at base. After this, he returned to a savaged and shrunken base camp. The regiment was pulling out. The campaign was over.

It was disgustingly hot, the sun large. Flies buzzed around bloodied bodies carried from the battleground. The stench of scorched metal and flesh pervaded the air and made it difficult to breathe. Tan-colored dust clung to his skin and bedded down in the wrinkled furrows of worn-out men. Stefano had been injured slightly, a gash to his upper body and leg, his shirt torn open, the edges reddened from his blood, which looked worse than the wound the uniform still managed to conceal.

He had written only yesterday to Teresa, telling her that bullets seemed to steer away from him. He should never have put it in words, he thought. He had asked for it. He said not to tell his mother or Nina. They would not cope with this kind of news. It was better they only received letters about the men, and their personal stories and descriptions about the colorful bazaars, with ceramic bowls painted in rich blues and reds and yellows, that he visited on arrival at Tunisia, and the scent of jasmine that carried through the streets. Teresa coped with news. She and her brother weren't close, not in the sense that they shared their emotions, but she understood the nature of things better than most. She could accept his injury and the war as if they were expected and did not think too hard about the future. If her brother lived, she was grateful. If her brother died, it was not unexpected. She loved him, cared for him, from when he was small, but she had a core that was harder than steel. And in some way he loved her for it.

At camp, he expected Beppe to greet him like he always did, but no one had seen him. The cousins had been separated early by a mortar shell that had split the group into two, and on either side of a wall of fire and smoke, men ran for cover in opposite directions. The fierce battle began. Then after hours of warfare, the expressions of the soldiers, vacant and bloodless, told the story.

"Where is he?" he asked his friend.

The man shook his head. Stefano turned to go, back to the scene of battle, but someone grabbed his arm.

"There is nothing there. There is nothing left of him. You won't find any trace."

Stefano didn't know whether he had heard correctly. He studied the dusty field strewn with burned things, a graveyard of tanks and bodies, some that did not resemble soldiers. Where he had just come from, the reality that he had survived, was sinking in. He stood in the middle, mind numb, a lone silhouette. It was not until later that the gravity of the moment had sunk in, of what they had all endured, and he had grieved properly. But all he could feel was rage toward his own country, toward the leaders who led innocent soldiers to their deaths.

While he'd been gone, Stefano had learned in a letter from Teresa that Nina had eloped with Toni. When Stefano read the letter aloud, somewhat offended that his sister had not warned him of her plans, Beppe had laughed. But now Stefano would give anything to hear Beppe's laugh again. His cousin had the ability to put everything into perspective. "It is the best news you will get this year!" Beppe had said. "Worry about the big issues, and let someone else waste their time on the small ones."

The battles in the northern deserts of Africa had been hopeless from the start. Beppe had said that all along.

The remaining men made their way back to Tunisia with heavy losses. He did not speak to anyone on the way to the town where the soldier groups were assembled. After several days in a field hospital and several more months in the northern deserts, he was sent home.

He was not eager to go straight home, his heart still heavy with loss. Instead he disembarked at Florence to walk the cobbled streets where he had spent many nights with his cousin, sneaking out after dark and exploring the city—a journey into manhood, as Beppe had described it, and Julietta had been none the wiser. Stefano stopped at a bar, ordered pasta and several wines, and then wandered near the Ponte Vecchio to watch the river shimmer and to reminisce about the time that Beppe had jumped in on a dare.

His cousin had taken Stefano under his wing. Overly protective, he had even taken a punch for him outside a bar. He had been there always to watch out for him. He had assumed the role of father, carer, though Teresa had told Stefano plenty of times that Beppe was irresponsible. He was, but he also wasn't. He took the role of looking after his young cousin seriously. He was sensitive and emotional, and had cried harder than anyone when his uncle, Stefano's father, had died.

The next day, after sleeping beside the river, Stefano hitched a ride to Verona. Stefano, battle scarred and tired, found nobody at home. His mother and Teresa had gone to pray at church like they had been doing every day since they learned of Beppe's fate.

Even though his mother was overjoyed to find Stefano there when she returned, and over coming days spoiled him, there seemed no relief that he was home. It was tense. The air clouded with unsaid words about the death of his cousin. It was miserable, even more so than in the days after his father died, because of the circumstances, because there was no body to grieve over. Serafina had now convinced herself that her son was still alive, that until they returned the body, she would continue to believe that. His mother had been with Serafina when she learned of her son's death. Julietta told Stefano that Serafina took the loss so badly that she threatened to throw herself off the balcony of their two-story villa.

Teresa had banned Toni from their house because he and Nina had gone against Julietta's wishes and married outside the church, and Nina had not visited recently. This news only added to the oppressive atmosphere that Stefano had come home to. Teresa, feisty and determined to remain single, was unlikely to find a husband. Julietta complained about that in spite of everything.

"What does it matter?" said Stefano.

"It matters. I want grandchildren. I want normality!"

"Mamma, while there is a war, there is no normality."

But it wasn't his impending childless years that caused her sudden outburst.

"I do not want to lose you like Serafina has lost her only child."

The conversation was too deep, too soon. And the reality of his future was all the more depressing because she was closer to the truth of it. He couldn't deal with the tears, though he held his mother. He felt like a statue in Piazza della Signoria, with no more life to give.

He decided to seek out Nina at Toni's apartment, once shared with Beppe. Stefano smiled widely when she opened the door. Nina's belly was round; the pregnancy had only recently begun to show.

She rushed into his arms.

"I guess I don't need to ask what you've been up to," he said fondly.

Nina cried with joy, and Stefano held her for many minutes before they broke apart.

"Why haven't you told Mamma?" asked Stefano. "She is desperate for good news."

"I don't think she will think that way. And you know Teresa . . . She will have another reason to curse at me."

"I think it will heal the broken relationship you have."

She sat him down, and they reminisced about Beppe, and others from the neighborhood who had also lost their lives. Several of their friends had not yet returned from various campaigns, and some were about to embark. Toni was still away in battle, and Nina worried constantly.

"He did not want to go," she had said about her husband, Toni. "He hated working under Mussolini. He was secretly part of an opposition group, but with a baby coming, he has had to conform. Things will change when he returns. They have to."

Stefano liked the sound of Toni. The strength of his anger matched his own. That night he stayed with Nina for dinner, and she had invited Fedor and other like-minded friends, Alberto and Conti. Alberto had been excused from war for failing a medical test. He talked of leaving Italy, bitter about losing a brother in battle. Conti owned several businesses. He was a Jew and said that his relatives had moved from Milan to a small western village after the enactment of the laws that segregated Jews from the rest of society and prevented them from continuing in their professions. Fearful of the anti-Semitism rising, especially after Italy became aligned with Nazi Germany, Conti had removed his name from the Jewish union registry, moved to Verona, and kept his background secret so that he could start his businesses.

The men had drunk until the early hours and spoke of the failed campaign, of desertion, and Stefano told how some Italian soldiers and senior officers had left their postings in Africa to switch sides and join the Allies.

"Then we must do something also to change the course of this war," said Fedor, who had assumed the role of leader without objection. "We can't just sit on our hands."

And at some point in the night, when they were high on thoughts and discussion, they had made a pact to save Italy and stop the war. Though much later Stefano realized that it was youth and inexperience that gave them the false belief they could.

Present-day 1945

The boy sits across from Rosalind in the kitchen. He is absorbed in his collected items on the table in front of him and spends much time picking them up, examining them, and placing them back again in the basket on the ground beside his feet.

Stefano has washed up in the bathroom tub behind the kitchen and looks at the mirror, at the richer color of his skin finally returning. I can survive, he thinks. There were days when he existed on just a few vegetables, but the smells on the stove are making him hungry. Rosalind has fried some potatoes with pieces of *speck*, and the smell of salted pig is making him salivate. She also boils some spinach taken from her garden. She has invited him to stay for supper, payment for all his work.

"I can stay, but if I'm not home by nightfall, my mother will share her best descriptive words."

She smiles. "You have a sense of humor. That is interesting."

"Interesting?"

"Yes."

"You don't think Italians have a sense of humor?"

He can see she finds this amusing also. She tips some water from the saucepan. She has also gone a little pink, though he can't tell if it is from the steam or their banter.

"No. I meant there has been no reason to have a sense of humor. I had forgotten what it sounded like."

He ponders this. She is right. The Allies were dancing in the streets, but he has seen little joy among the defeated.

"Excuse me for being so casual about your generous offer since you have so little. I gratefully accept."

"Good," she says. "I know what it is like to go hungry. When my parents died, I was forced to make do. With few rations after the war, I would spend much time searching for mushrooms, berries, and anything I could make into meals. I became creative. But I'm afraid that meat is still a luxury, and I don't have much of it to offer you."

"I am grateful for anything. Where did you go after . . . ?" he asks.

"After my parents were bombed? I came here."

"You were there at the very end."

"Yes. The hospital was being evacuated, and the city fell in pieces around me. It was carnage, trucks full of casualties who were left to die, some still caked in mud from the battlefields, because even the medics and doctors in field hospitals were being killed. And then the last line of German defense . . . untrained and not the age for such work . . . were brought in also. We worked hard to save many but lost many, too, and then suddenly it went quiet and then noisy again as truckloads of Russians came through. I was luckier than some . . ." She breaks off.

Stefano knows the other dead that she talks about: young boys unprepared for war and the elderly too old to hold a rifle steady were abandoned with firearms and waited, trapped in Berlin for their own disposal.

"Do you have any idea where your cousin might have gone?" He takes another look at the portrait as if Monique might answer the question herself.

"I don't know," she says, looking toward the front door. "She married an officer and moved away. We weren't communicating much, but in one letter several months before the war ended, she said she was trying to get back here. I don't like to speculate. It is difficult with Monique. She may have changed her mind. She was flighty."

Stefano has noted her use of the past tense.

In the photo, Monique sits at an angle, just her head and shoulders visible, and she is turned slightly to look into the lens. The camera loves her. He looks away. He does not want to be distracted from the relationship he is building here.

Rosalind serves up food portions, keeping the chipped plate for herself.

"So, Michal, did you have jam where you were from?" she says curtly, as one would expect from a nurse on duty.

"Yes," he whispers.

"So, you do talk then," she says, turning to Stefano. "I could not get him to speak earlier."

"He prefers to talk in the dark, to whisper. It is his memories he is most afraid of," explains Stefano, "though he is becoming more brave." Rosalind understands. She has been to hell also.

"Do you have a big family?" asks Rosalind.

And the boy is back to silence with his things, though he is thinking, now frowning, remembering.

Stefano asks to borrow the pipe Michal salvaged from the ruins. Michal hands it to him reluctantly, fearing it won't return. Stefano pretends to light invisible tobacco in the pipe bowl and puts his mouth on the bit to make the puffing action, and Michal is absorbed in the display, his expression open. When Stefano gives the pipe back to him, the boy mimics the actions he just witnessed.

During supper Rosalind is courteous; the fact that he is working for her has released some of the tension in their conversations, and her eyes tend to linger on him longer. She doesn't volunteer information, yet she answers everything. She knows a lot. She can describe places in Berlin. She can describe the people, patients she met. But throughout she is looking over his shoulder at the door that Georg has exited. And only a short time later Georg walks inside and sits next to them at the table to stare at the empty table space in front of him.

Rosalind stands up quickly and moves to the bench near the sink. Her own meal not quite finished, she prepares a plate of food for Georg and places it in front of him.

Stefano can see that Rosalind's breathing is more rapid, her movements more erratic. She is nervous about Georg.

"Hello, Georg," says Stefano, but he doesn't respond, his eyes following Rosalind's hands as she fusses with his utensils. Rosalind looks at Stefano and shakes her head. It is best he doesn't speak to him.

Georg is tall with a long neck. His pale red-gold hair is kept short, his features fine: small nose, girlish lips, pointed chin. He might have been handsome once before the scar, before the damage forced his head to droop, his mouth to drool.

Without warning Georg picks up his plate and throws it on the floor. Michal jumps beneath the table in fear, and Stefano stands suddenly, in readiness to protect the others.

"No," says Rosalind to Stefano, stopping him from interfering. "Everything is all right. You must go. I will fix this."

He looks from Georg to Rosalind, attempting to determine whether she is safe. But he must also protect the boy. He talks softly to him under the table in an effort to coax him out. Michal doesn't move, still staring up at Stefano, too afraid. Stefano reaches for his arm and pulls him out gently, then puts one arm around him protectively as he remembers the smashed things next door, an act of rage, and wonders now if Georg was responsible for the damage—not squatters as he was told.

Georg remains seated, his head back to drooping.

"I appreciate what you've done, but after tomorrow, once you are finished, I think you should move on without Erich's help," she says curtly, perhaps for Georg's benefit. "This place is not for you. It was not a good idea to have you here. You should not be staying in the house with Erich."

Her tone and words confound him, giving him the feeling of a cold shower directly after a warm one.

He nods. "Thank you for supper," he says. Though there is still food on his plate.

Georg starts to sob and moan, and Rosalind turns to the sound. It is a long-drawn, desperate cry for help, thinks Stefano.

Michal pushes forward the marble from his basket, which rolls shakily across the table toward Georg and stops in front of him, and everyone watches Georg, curiously, wondering, waiting to hear thunder. And Georg raises his head, crying stopped suddenly, picks up the marble to examine it, then rolls it gently back across the table toward Michal. The boy doesn't catch it; instead he watches it roll slowly off the table and fall to the ground.

Michal moves to pick it up, and Stefano nearly stops him, not wanting any sudden movement, but Georg's expression is now one of curiosity. Michal picks it up and rolls it back toward Georg, but the push is too forceful, and it bounces, landing on Rosalind's plate that still has food.

Georg stares at it a moment before breaking into laughter, and Rosalind looks at Stefano as if she has never seen him before, and then they hear it, too—small gurgles of laughter from Michal. And the laughter continues for several more moments, and Stefano's half smile turns nearly into a full one, and Rosalind, uncertainly at first, can't help but smile, too, to see Georg happy, to hear the joy. And the clock makes its *plocking* sound, and Georg laughs again, when he never once noticed the clock's sound before.

Stefano stands and reaches for the boy and says good night to Georg, who is smiling with the marble that he still has in his hand, which Michal has left for him.

Stefano shuts the door and walks to the dark house next door, listening for sounds of breaking and crashing behind him that do not come. He looks at the boy and wonders at the power of children that he has never known before.

22 April 1940

Dear Papa,
You should see the pile of letters I have for you now. I like to reread them, and occasionally I correct a word here and there. I guess I have Rosalind to thank for that. She was always pedantic about my spelling. I'm sorry it has been many months since I have written.

We did not go to the river house last summer. Georg has left to fight somewhere, though he would not say where. I miss him so terribly. I miss all the wonderful times that we had. Sometimes I think I will go mad if he doesn't send me a letter. He thinks about lots of things. He looks at the bigger picture. He makes fun of the situation. He showed me a paper that is run by an underground organization. It had funny pictures of Hitler in extra-large boots and behind him an army of tin soldiers who had fallen over. He had to throw it away, of course. It is a severely punishable offense to make fun of our leader.

I have a new job as a shorthand typist for one of the Reich officers, which pays quite well. It was Erich, Georg's friend, who recommended me for the job. The education reports I type are rather dull, but I discovered after a couple of weeks that some people in the office have a sense of humor at least, and even joked about the assassination attempt on our führer that happened last year. But when the minister is in attendance, we pretend that life has no joy, and we stare at our typewriters as if our lives depend on it. Perhaps they do. It seems you are punished, shot, sent to prison, for anything these days.

You would not recognize me in my dresses and suits. I sometimes worry that if you are released and we pass each other in the street, you will not recognize me. Uncle Max says I look like Mama, but when I look in the mirror, I see both of you.

I wrote and told you that Rosa is madly in love with Georg, though she always denies it. She is so strange, Papa, like a frightened little mouse too afraid to tell people how she feels.

I do have to tell you that I have lots of friends, and I have grown close to one in particular. He is not what you would expect, Papa. Alain is half African, and he is a performer in an African troupe that sings and dances; there are acrobatics, and their music is truly unique, and the whole show is vibrant and colorful. I have played matchmaker between him and Emmanuelle, my friend. Alain said his father is French, but he does not remember him.

Alain is not allowed in any bars. In fact, he is only to stay with his troupe. Rosalind tells me that I should not be seeing Alain or Emmanuelle. She says that I will get in trouble, and we are not allowed to mingle. But they break the monotony that is this new Berlin, now filled with dreary, awful conversations about war.

Anyway, the war is here to stay for a while yet it seems, though the war for you started long before now. I wish to never hear the transmissions that burst into our living rooms. I heard the propaganda minister, Goebbels, talking about our nation gathering strength, about our future shining victory, and about our desire to trust "our Hitler." With you in prison I see no reason to trust. You saw this coming. I now understand a lot more clearly what you were trying to do. You could see where our country was headed; perhaps you could see that somehow it would become part of Germany. I hope that people out there will remember what you did and what you tried to do. When the war is over, I am sure that people will see sense, and you will be released.

I know that I appear flippant to some, but I care about you and everyone. I really do. I want to make my life count for something, Papa. Berlin is stifling here.

Oh, Papa, why aren't you here?

I wish that you were reading these. I wish that you were writing to me. I wish I knew what was going on. But I am hopeful most of the time. If I'm not, I will go mad, and that would not help anyone.

I miss you.

Till I see you again,
Yours forever,
Love always,
Moni

CHAPTER 16
ERICH

Vivi is pretty with fair hair. Erich kisses the top of her head. She smiles, lips pressed together into a thin line. She has deep dimples of pleasure, so like her mother, and eyes that view with skepticism, those from Claudine. When she looks at Erich, she conflicts him, tests his strength. It is often good to get away from her to keep his head clear of things that link him to a life before.

"Do you have important business?" asks Marceline.

"Yes, I have. I will be back very late."

"I understand."

Marceline always does. She is used to secrets. She was apparently good at keeping them when she worked for other members of the Reich.

"I am boiling some eggs. You can take some with you if you wish."

He thinks about Stefano and the orphaned boy. He nods, and Marceline exits to the kitchen. Erich turns toward his mother at her seat by the window.

He wants to touch her shoulder, to show he is there for her, but it is pointless. The light inside of her is all but extinguished. He thought he would never say it, but he is beginning to despise her being in this room. It feels as if she dwarfs everything in it, drains it of all life just with her presence. He knows there are ill feelings growing toward her, something he has tried to quash.

He has been thinking much about her final decision. Why she did what she did. Why she didn't fight harder. She was so weak in one moment, whereas she had been nothing but strong for all of his life. He moves away toward the door before his thoughts become too vivid. She had always been a constant in his life. When he'd first had doubts toward the end of the war, she had been the one to return him to his path. She had known him better than anyone.

Erich stands beside the door, and Marceline hands him a small cloth bag that holds the eggs while they discuss some household matters. Vivi sits down on the floor. She has grown bored of the adults and has taken a pencil to paper.

"Say goodbye to your papa," says Marceline in an abrupt tone. She does not like that the girl sits on the floor between them. It is not proper.

Vivi jumps up quickly to attention, like she has been taught. She is also being taught not to expect or demand things from people. Erich is teaching her that. Success can only come from patience and study. You cannot expect it from others. Though he learned that from his father, did he not? His father who made a good life, then made a bad choice.

There can be no mistakes if they are to survive this, if he is to successfully disappear, find a new place, begin again. His mind then turns to Stefano. The newcomer has rarely strayed from his thoughts. He worked with Italian soldiers and found them disorganized, purposely sloppy at times. They talked among themselves too much. Many of them resented the Germans, something they couldn't hide. There was one instance where he found some apart from their group, drinking smuggled beer. He had told them all to return to their hut. They had joked in their own language and sauntered away, without respect. Though Stefano is different. He is careful, cautious, and diligent. One can tell this. He let his guard down with his satchel, but now it is never out of his sight. He learns.

Erich stops first at the pharmacy and hands the owner a list. The man puts on his glasses and scans it.

"I will try," Elias says, "but it is getting harder. I cannot guarantee a permanent supply. These have been stolen, and sooner or later supplies will run out."

"You will do everything you can, yes?"

"Yes," says the pharmacist.

"Don't let me down," says Erich, and the tone, though amiable, still carries a certain amount of threat, which Elias detects.

Erich walks briskly along the road near dusk and detours to a narrow path between trees that run alongside the river. The path finishes at a clearing across from which is the gravel road toward the river houses he has grown to despise. But now at least there is something to go there for, and lately a reprieve from the town where he has had to hide or pretend. Rosalind doesn't want him here. He would sooner leave and never see her again. Too much has happened to make some sort of amends. It is easier with strangers now. People like Stefano that he was ordered to destroy. People like Stefano that he has to learn to live with now.

When he arrives, Stefano is washing his hair in the tub at the back of the house. He does not look surprised, as if he has been listening out for Erich this time. He has rolled up his trousers and his sleeves, and his shirt hangs unbuttoned at the front. Erich does not show that he has noticed the scarring up Stefano's forearm and part of his torso with pink puckered skin, though the skin of his neck and other arm is smooth and undamaged.

"Where is Michal?"

"I have put him to bed already."

Stefano's eyes are so black they can't be distinguished from the pupils. He would have been quite handsome once, thinks Erich, if one is not comparing Aryan traits. Even the small indents of his youth do not detract from the fineness of his features and the golden-brown color of his skin.

"You are back early today. How was your work?" Stefano asks. The Italian rubs his hair with a towel, and droplets from the ends of his thick mass of hair darken the patch of ground he stands on.

"It was fine, though I am on double shifts while the factory recovers, and the Russians keep us busy. I have to work late again tonight, but I am back tomorrow. Perhaps we can share a meal together tomorrow evening." Erich is thinking it might then be a good time to discuss his idea of traveling together. "I was paid today, and I have brought some eggs and more bread."

Stefano follows Erich inside.

"I would feel greedy to take your food. I have had something to eat already."

"At Rosalind's house?"

Stefano pauses too long. He has heard the concern in the question. "Yes."

Erich swallows back the lump in his throat and reaches for the whiskey bottle and glasses from the table.

"Then the rest of this instead—"

"I am curious if there is something more in your relationship with Rosalind," Stefano says. The sudden response is a shock and the kind of thing Erich would do during an interrogation: interrupt with an abrupt observation or statement, to catch a prisoner completely off guard.

"Why do you ask that?"

Stefano shrugs, but his look is still intense. "I detect something more."

"Then you are wrong," Erich says bluntly. Erich is concerned about the sudden confidence, the brashness, as if there were something deep within Stefano bursting to show itself. But he cannot afford to show concern. It is better for him if there are fewer questions hanging between them.

"I have no time for Rosalind. The brief visits I have spent with her have only been filled with arguments about her husband. I believe he should be in care, and she says no. Since I spoke my mind, she has been very guarded, very distant in fact. And there is nothing between us."

"She seems very lonely."

"You should stay away," says Erich firmly. "I cannot guarantee your safety. I have to tell you some things . . . Georg is a very violent person to other people. If she tells you otherwise, she is lying. He can take an instant dislike to someone."

"What has he done?"

"He has attacked people, so it surprises me that she allowed you and the child into the house."

"Has he attacked you?"

"Not me personally, but I know of others. It is why Rosalind hides away down here. She cannot leave him alone, yet she cannot take him away either. And she doesn't want my help."

Stefano's dark eyes lock on Erich. There is something in them that looks unhinged, yet at the same time there is emptiness, and longing. He is a contradiction in the way he looks both dangerous and harmless. But it is the grilling, the scrutiny that Erich realizes is happening. Stefano is using the same techniques as he did. The questioning, the waiting, the assessment of lies seem practiced for an Italian soldier who did not want any part in war. It is hard to know whether it is curiosity or probing with some kind of purpose.

And Erich is just as curious. He has not found company so intriguing. There are things he wants to ask him, that Stefano may have seen and witnessed, perhaps different from himself, yet just as brutal. Erich feels himself weakening. Some of the desire to control things, to be in control, is leaving him.

They sit at the table, and Stefano reveals some things with the whiskey. He reveals his feelings toward his enemy, his fear of early mornings because he didn't know what the day would bring.

Finally, he is what Erich expected, someone talkative, and someone with feelings, but strangely enough these characteristics that make one vulnerable are not disappointing to Erich. Not anymore.

"Rosalind appears to have control of him," says Stefano, bringing the conversation back to Georg. "He seems to do whatever she wants."

"Don't rely on that. She gives him something to sleep on the days she goes to the markets. But you must know that he is an addict."

1940–1941

Erich had been withdrawn from university and stood in front of his father, who inspected the party uniform with which his son had just been fitted. It was not an engineering degree that was needed but able, young, and loyal men, his father had been instructed to tell him. Erich was disappointed that he could not follow his father into the private drawing rooms of the führer, and into secret talks about weaponry.

His father had helped design a tank that moved and turned easily. It cannoned high-explosive shells at a range far better than its predecessors, and the engine had been upgraded. But it had a major weakness: it could not yet penetrate the heavy armor of British tanks, and after a battle in France, his father was back, consulting with design engineers.

Erich had hoped that he would eventually be part of this engineering quest, but his first commission was to be part of Hitler's protection squad in Berlin. Erich was given a task that did not put him in great danger. When Erich had asked if he would be sent out in the field, his father had been slow to respond.

"It takes more than rifle skills and a sense of duty to be a good soldier, but, regardless, the führer does not wish it so."

It would be years before Erich would understand the undervaluing his father had just placed on him, so enamored was he by the fact the führer had assigned the task and proud to swear his oath of allegiance. But it was an unusual posting, considering he'd had no training in this area that had nothing at all to do with engineering. He asked his father if he would be under any further supervision.

"I do not think anyone needs training in such areas." He sounded condescending, though Erich had been taught never to question his parents. He was a good and loyal son. He would look after his mother if he had to. "It was my original wish that you work alongside me in the ministry since you have the same mechanical interests and an aptitude for such. I recommended a role for you there, but the idea was rejected. They do not have the time for me to mentor you. And they do not need any more engineers. They have enough contracted for now. I don't make the orders, unfortunately."

Erich was relieved at least that his father had tried. No doubt there would be other positions coming up in the future, and more across Europe once the war was won.

"You will be briefed by someone when you report tomorrow. You are needed to interview and arrest anyone who preaches against the government, including clerics. And you must help organize the transportation of Jews from the city and find those in hiding. You must hunt down all those troublemakers."

Was that sarcasm in his father's voice? His father always spoke gently, but there was something strained, almost stinging, about the tone.

"You will be deciding where to send people who no longer belong here. After an arrest, you will interrogate thoroughly to learn of networks, especially if they are deemed to be political enemies or involved in distributing material that promotes dissent. You will need to gauge who is fit for labor and who isn't. Then later if you prove yourself well in this position, you may see a promotion that involves a foreign posting."

Standing in front of his father, Erich wondered at his father's frown and the sweat that fell down the sides of his face. Horst had a quiet manner and a brilliant mind. Erich wanted so much to be like him. Wanted him to be proud. So why didn't he look proud on this day?

Erich began his first instruction and learned on the job. He also learned that he had a talent for weeding out liars, for spotting the holes in the stories that were spun. And as time went on, his role deepened. Interrogations sometimes led to executions. In one particular instance, he arrested and interrogated a group of university students for subversion. They were later hanged.

And as the role had deepened, his father had noticed the change, had commented on it. Had seen others change in the office where he worked. Had seen superiority and the sense of German entitlement spread like a virus, especially among the young. Horst did not like that his son was in the same group as men that had been recruited from prisons.

Horst suggested to Erich that he should have some free time also. Spend time with friends from university or a girl. But Erich was not interested. Georg was the only one who was interesting, who made stimulating conversation. But with him now in the field, Erich did not feel the need to make other friends. He did not want the distraction of immersing himself in other people's lives. And now that he was finding a liking for the job, he felt a sense of duty to those around him, to lead them, to show them what loyalty looked like. And he was enjoying the praise of his senior officers who suggested, after he'd spent several weeks in the position, that he was destined for something greater. Yet his father's praise, the praise he wanted most, remained the most elusive, and, as time wore on, his father stopped asking about his work altogether.

He took the advice and called on a girl he'd met at university. He took her out to dinner, but the effort was too great. The work involved too much conversation, and the lack of political talk was dull. And the girl looked faded and uninteresting against his real purpose: the tasks he was assigned. He knew there was pressure there, from his mother also, to marry, to procreate, to have a German girl with him once he'd been sent to a foreign place. A woman who would carry the burden of domesticity without complaint, who would make sure his uniforms were clean, his meals cooked. He did not, however, need someone to take care of him. Though he had already accepted it was unlikely he would find someone like his mother, someone strong, loyal, and intellectual.

And then came the suggestion to marry Monique, as a favor to Georg, who wished to protect his childhood friend from herself. She was loose with words and had been corrupted by her Jewish friends and others who were not part of the plan for a master race. Georg had convinced him that she was capable, that she would participate in the role, with no expectations of husbandly comfort or support. The pairing would solve issues for both. Suspicion about her political leanings would fall away from her and her family—good German people—said Georg. The arrangement was temporary, he had suggested. Only until the war was over.

Erich understood. There were lists that he had seen himself. And they were growing longer. Monique's name was on one of them.

"Why don't you marry her yourself then?" asked Erich.

"It's complicated," he said. "She is too close to Rosa. For the sake of our old friendships, I beg this of you."

He understood. He had seen the lovesick look in Rosalind's eyes.

"Besides, with your commission soon in Austria, it would be good for Monique to stay away from Berlin indefinitely."

Erich agreed, though the favor was for Georg alone.

"Do you remember how much fun it was, the four of us at the river?" Georg said over a glass of red wine. His eyes gleamed like gemstones, Erich had thought at the time. "I saw you laugh at Monique's adventures, at her spirit many times."

Erich did remember Monique and those times, but mostly because of Georg, who was both courageous and clever at everything he did. But those times were gone, and Georg was due to leave again for war. Erich had accepted that things were different now. That the path he was on was destined.

Georg's suggestion made sense, and he was one of the few who could influence Erich. But it would mean that Erich would have to take the risk that Monique had indeed conformed. People would be watching. She had promised Georg, who had vouched for it. And that might have been enough. But oddly, it was his father who had been the reason for his final decision. Horst had met Monique previously, and liked her immediately, though he did not give his reasons, and neither did he know anything of the arrangement Erich and Georg had discussed. Only later did Erich realize that his father and Monique had shared many thoughts on the changing Germany, thoughts that were most certainly against National Socialist values.

Present-day 1945

The sky is pink and purple, and Erich wonders if Stefano notices these things. Whether he thinks about the type of person he was before the war. If he has any regrets. Erich has been thinking much of Italy, of traveling with Stefano, of leaving everyone, of finding a new place. He must make decisions quickly now.

"Is it busy in the town?" asks Stefano.

"It is slowly recovering, but as long as there are Russian military hovering, pretending they alone are the sole victors of the war, it will never fully recover."

Erich avoids the Russians. He knows at some point they will come to the house in the city to check on residents as they do, and he hopes to be gone by then. At the moment it is the farmers they are interested in the most, who provide them with what they need.

It is interesting that Stefano has made some sort of connection with Rosalind, he thinks, in such a short time. It is not likely that she has revealed anything, though he cannot underestimate Stefano's intelligence either.

"I think I will check on Michal and retire early also," Stefano says. "You have had a long day. You probably need to sleep also before you return to work tonight."

Erich is disappointed. He expected to spend some of the evening with Stefano before returning later to the town. He wants to question him about the Germans who escaped through Italy, but it is perhaps too soon anyway. He will leave that conversation until tomorrow night. It is best to do these things in the final hours and leave with little notice.

CHAPTER 17
STEFANO

Stefano watches Erich leave for his work, which he believes is a lie. The German shows no wear for the hours he spends in a factory. Stefano is convinced he is sleeping elsewhere but thinks better than to ask the question. He will accept the lie for the house and bed.

Stefano checks on Michal, who is curled up asleep. From the window he sees the lights are on next door, and wonders what else Rosalind does with her time. He returns to the mattress, though he isn't tired and waits impatiently for sleep. Just as he begins to doze, there is a faint commotion of some kind, a protest by the geese, and shortly after he hears a soft knock.

"They are back," says Rosalind in the doorway, holding a lantern.

Stefano doesn't ask. He already knows that she is talking about the Jew and his granddaughter who asked for food earlier.

"One of the geese is missing," she says. "I saw the thieves head west in the direction of the forest along the river. There is a trail there, hidden, that runs parallel with the river. It leads to a hut."

"How long ago?"

"Maybe a minute."

"Go back home. I will meet you there."

"Here, take this," she says, passing him the light.

He enters the wood toward the river. Once he is clear of the trees, there is no sign that anyone has been there. At the edge of the thinning wood are denser trees to his right, and he searches with the lamp until he finds the entrance to the track that Rosalind has described. It could easily be missed with the trees and shrubs forming a guard.

He holds the lamp high to inspect his surrounds. The ground at the entrance of the pathway has been freshly trampled, and he stops a moment to listen for sounds ahead, but the wood gives nothing away. He continues until the track opens up to a small clearing with the hut that Rosalind described. To the left of the hut is a short jetty extending from the embankment above the river. The hut resembles a miniature of many gabled homes. He peers through one of the small grime-stained windows to see that someone is inside.

The door protests with a squeak, and he pulls its rusting metal handle toward him. He has to bend over to enter, the ceiling low. Georg sits in one corner, staring at something through the window that overlooks the dark river, and beside him is a used syringe, which Stefano suspects was stolen from Rosalind's bag.

The scar on the side of Georg's head is inflamed where it has been scratched at viciously. He is curled into a corner, like a guilty child fearfully awaiting his punishment, and clutching something that was white once, a padded piece of fabric. On closer examination Stefano sees it is a patchwork cloth smeared with mud. There are stains on the twelve rectangles of pastel shades and textures, and pictures of owls and other animals stitched within the patches, but halfway down the fabric, the patches are blank and unfinished.

"You must know that I am not here to harm you in any way."

Georg shifts his focus warily onto Stefano.

"Are you all right?" Stefano asks. "Do you want me to take you back to the house?"

"Monique made it," he says, and Stefano is startled by the clarity in his voice, and the lucidity of his gaze.

"Do you want to bring it with you?"

"You must go," says Georg. "Do not come back here."

"Why not?"

He doesn't answer, and Stefano holds the lamp closer to better see his face.

"Are you alone here, Georg?"

Georg shakes his head, and Stefano hears a faint rustling behind the cabin. Georg is aware of things, alert from the drug.

Stefano opens the door again, which does not allow him to leave silently. Hearing whispers, he steps around the corner toward the back. At the sight of Stefano, the man and the girl rush out from their hiding spot and begin to run farther into the wood where the track is thinner, overgrown, and difficult to navigate in the dark.

Stefano follows with the lamp, leafy branches flicking back against him, launched from the pair in front. The man appears impeded, hobbling and barely able to make it into a run. The girl in front of him is calling him to move faster, her voice afraid.

Fearing he is about to be seized, the man turns to face Stefano, holding a knife at arm's length out in front of him. His other hand holds the goose by its broken neck. The girl walks back to be near her grandfather.

"No!" she says to him, her hand on his outstretched arm.

The grandfather, with some reluctance, lowers his knife arm to his side, and the girl is not looking at Stefano but shyly down at her feet.

These are poor, desperate people, like Michal and his mother, who perhaps have no home to go to, and Stefano suddenly understands that it is not just hunger they are afflicted with but that there is no certain end to their isolation and losses. They are outcasts here, everywhere perhaps.

"Don't give up," says Stefano suddenly in French, and the girl looks up while the grandfather watches him with hostile eyes. "There is a displacement camp another thirty miles west from here where you will be fed. You might find a boat abandoned farther along the river, probably your safest way to travel. Take whatever you want from this country. It's yours."

The man's lines seem to deepen suddenly as his face relaxes. He is tired, weary. He is fighting for every inch of his life, daily, protecting his granddaughter, too. It is unlikely they have any other Jewish family left where they are going.

"Go!" Stefano says to them, handing them the lamp as well. "Take this. Don't come back here. Go home to France. Take back what was yours."

The man whose face was hostile crumbles slightly, his lips quivering, his eyes watering, and the years of sadness and hopelessness are exposed. It has been a while since the beggars have seen any kindness.

"Thank you," says the girl, taking her grandfather's hand to pull him away, afraid that Stefano will change his mind. "Come, Grand-père!"

They turn and head farther into the wood. He hopes they make it home safely.

Back in the small hut, it is dark. He can hear Georg's heavy breathing. The German has fallen asleep. He haunts the woods, Stefano thinks, and it is Monique that he comes here for, that he hopes to find.

Stefano walks back along the dark path to Rosalind's house, where the light from a candle flickers softly from within. He knocks on the door, and she answers quickly, as if she has been waiting by it impatiently.

"They've gone downriver. I could not find them in the thick undergrowth. But I don't think they will be back. They know they have taken what they can and will try their luck elsewhere. Georg is in the hut if you are not already aware. He appeared rested."

"Thank you," she says from the half-open space.

"I'm sorry, but the lantern does not fare as well. It is resting in pieces beneath some trees."

She nods, though he cannot tell from the light behind her, and from her silence, whether his buoyancy is appreciated given the circumstances.

"I hope you get some rest now, too," he says as he turns to leave. She reaches her hand to touch his forearm, then withdraws it quickly.

He waits to see if she will say something, but he cannot see her expression or the point of her brief touch.

"Thank you," she says again after several seconds, then gently closes the door.

He waits, wondering, perplexed, if perhaps she wanted him to stay longer, then returns to the darkness that holds no fear. For years it has been his ally.

1943

Toni came back from another commission with a broken arm, while Stefano returned only bruised and scratched but with a hardness and skepticism that weren't there before.

The pair organized a gathering with Fedor—who still refused to sign up to fight—Conti, Alberto, and several other friends. But what started out as an excuse to drink and joke quickly turned into an opportunity to voice concerns about the government and the war. And soon the group was meeting several nights a week.

Teresa had said that Stefano frightened her a little, that he didn't smile much, and that he had developed an attitude. How could he tell her what it was really like? It was hard being compared with how he was before, and though he loved his family dearly and wanted to tell them everything about his time on the battlefields, and what he witnessed, he knew his mother wouldn't cope. Instead he often sought out the group who understood, even Nina. She had grown desensitized to stories of war, exposed to information shared by her husband and his friends. Stefano was aware of how strong she had become, and vocal in support of their ideas, while patiently caring for Nicolo, their busy toddler, who had been named after his grandfather.

The direction of their conversations went deeper at each meeting, and discussions began to fall on ways to avoid a war they felt was unnecessary. It was good to talk about things freely in Nina and Toni's apartment, to not have to worry who was listening in, to share ideas, and to express their hatred of the Axis. Also, to take the opportunity to reminisce about Beppe, whom everyone had known, and whose death had brought this group closer together.

Such discussions could have led to their execution, so to protect themselves the group name of "Il Furioso" was created, as well as false names for whenever they sent messages to one another. Like Stefano, Toni feared that it was only a matter of time before he was called up again. And he was right to worry. Later in the war, injuries were no longer an excuse.

Stefano liked to hold his baby nephew, with more opportunities now that Toni's arm was in a cast, while Nina was busy serving up plates of food.

"Maybe you two should get married in a church," said Stefano, half joking. "That would make Mamma happy."

"My church is in here," said Toni, rolling out his good arm and gesturing around the house. "And particularly in there," he said, pointing to the bedroom.

"Stop it!" said Nina. "Some respect, if you please."

"I agree," said Stefano jovially. "That is my sister, remember!"

"We might still do that for Mamma's sake, Toni," said Nina. "We still believe in God. The priests are anti-Nazi, like we are."

"Most, perhaps," said Toni, who could not deny his respect for many of the priests who had put themselves in danger by speaking out against Hitler. And they were a good source of news. They had switched radio channels to stop listening to the lackluster propaganda from Mussolini and his followers, and they were turning to more facts from the Vatican radio. It was where they had learned that the Allies had landed in Sicily and Rome had been bombed.

The meeting one night turned very serious. Conti's cafés had become important sources of information, where he canvassed unwitting patrons for news, and others who offered it voluntarily. And Fedor had found a way of communicating with his sister in Russia, who passed on messages to her husband in the Russian army.

When they had eaten and talked about the country and food shortages, and the closing of businesses, more important discussions began again.

"I have heard that there is much unrest," said Fedor. "My sources tell me that the Germans are struggling against the weaponry Russia now has access to. The Germans cannot hold their positions for much longer. And now with businesses closing, and being walled in, our country could soon be reduced to rubble. Unless we do something now, we will be destroyed or become prisoners alongside Germany. We must be on the side of who I believe to be the victors—the Allies."

Fedor did not say who his sources were. Stefano believed, that with a brother-in-law in the Russian army, he somehow had access to more information than most on the situation in the East. Germany's turning against its Russian ally had fueled Fedor's hatred for their leader, especially with his sister and his mother's family still living there. He was probably the most passionate and vocal.

"I agree," said Stefano. "People meeting in the piazzas are talking more openly. They are becoming less afraid. Mussolini has lost too much support. We have become too heavily dependent on Germany. It may only be a matter of time before we are only speaking their language." He was the only one of the group who had learned to speak German.

But they soon learned they weren't the only ones to be disillusioned. Conti, who had a contact in the ministry, had heard a rumor that certain members of the government were seeking support from the king to oust Mussolini after the heavy losses incurred in North Africa and Russia and the successful Allied invasion of Sicily. Conti had also listened to many in his café complain about the ruination of their country and the fear of an ultimate takeover by Germany.

And in response to these rumors and grievances, Il Furioso sent anonymously printed messages to villages and towns to fuel the people's fear and to encourage others to take a stance against the current government. Conti was also able to get his hands on a dozen stolen weapons to fight any Mussolini loyalists should civil conflict arise. What they were doing was dangerous, but the air, heavy with dissatisfaction, seemed to lessen any risk.

Whether or not these messages and rumors contributed to Mussolini's ousting, later that month Stefano and the rest of his small group were jubilant when Il Duce was arrested by his own fascist party, without the need for civil war, and a prime minister, Badoglio, was put in place, supported by the king of Italy. Many Italians were relieved and elated by news of a new government, and they celebrated in marketplaces filled with people no longer afraid to speak freely.

But confidence was short-lived after Mussolini was rescued and flown to Germany and the news of Italy's armistice with the Allies reached Hitler. In the days following, confusion about allegiances reigned as Italian battle units on foreign soil disintegrated and many troops were captured by Nazi Germany. Murmurings about an invasion by the German army spread through Il Furioso's underground contacts. Those who had openly been jubilant became subdued when it seemed that Italy's internal war wasn't over. Italy was not yet free. And no one felt this more than Stefano. Serafina and Enzo, and even his sister Teresa, still supported Germany, and Stefano believed they had assisted with Mussolini's rescue.

In the days following, a hostile German army took control of northern Italy, and the king, Badoglio, and his supporters ran for cover to southern Italy, which in days would be completely in Allied hands. SS piled onto the streets, as did members of Mussolini's new Italian Social Republic, based in Salò. These brutal forces began their quest for blood and revenge on those who had betrayed Mussolini and Nazi Germany. Traitors were hunted down, pulled from their beds, lined up in the marketplaces, and shot in front of crowds who pretended they were now on Germany's side once again to shield themselves. Boys as young as fifteen who were deemed traitors, women and men, even the elderly, and some with only minor connections to those who had fled from arrest, were murdered.

But the Nazis didn't stop there. Jews were arrested—from Rome to the cities of the North—and deported to concentration camps in Poland. Villages that had celebrated Mussolini's capture were torched. And the fear of execution and the desperation for survival turned some to betray their neighbors.

Stefano watched on as an old woman was about to be shot for not revealing the whereabouts of her son, the last of the executions in his town that day, and he closed his eyes and turned away before the rifle was fired. The sound of the firing rang repeatedly in his head, and the pain of these senseless deaths crushed his heart as he returned home imagining his own mother lined up in the piazza. The shadow of something dark and terrifying loomed above him and the peace he craved.

His mother saw the anguish in his face as he entered, and she reached for him, like she had many times before. He held her close and assured her there was light ahead, mistrustful of his own words. He feared where it would end and fought hard against the foreboding that the people he loved would, at some point, bear the consequences of his decisions.

Present-day 1945

Stefano is up early and makes some coffee, reads another of Monique's letters, then returns it quickly to the shoebox. Erich could appear at any moment. As he has shown previously, he is stealthy.

The visitor steps outside to inspect the surrounds. There is a strong pine scent from the trees outside, and he listens carefully for human sounds. Rosalind's house is silent; there is no smoke from the chimney. There are several wooden boards nailed across part of Georg's attic windows, like a prison, he thinks. Did he break the glass, or was it to stop him from jumping out?

Michal appears beside him. He looks up at Stefano curiously, his hazel eyes filled with the images of trees, and the boy finds Stefano's hand, holds on to it, fingers curling into his.

"You should be outside, running between the trees. I believe that's what boys like to do. Do you like running?"

Michal shrugs.

"Do you like making things?" asks Stefano, remembering something.

The boy is curious and follows Stefano back inside the house. On the floor, shoved under some old rags and washcloths, is a cluster of yellowing newspapers, with circles of watery damage in places. Stefano drops several of them onto the table and checks the date. On the front page is a photograph of Hitler addressing a crowd in Berlin. Stefano takes one broadsheet and begins to fold.

"This is what I used to do to pass the time when I was waiting for the enemy."

He folds the paper in half and bends it swiftly until it resembles something Michal recognizes. The boy is absorbed, watching Stefano miraculously create an airplane and fly it across the room.

Michal runs to pick it up, but when he tries the same motion, it nose-dives to the floor. Stefano bends down near him and lifts his arm to show him how to make it fly, makes another airplane also, then takes Michal outside to fly them both across the dirt. Michal takes over the play, unaware of anything else around him.

Rosalind appears with some buckets. She does not look across but heads straight for the river.

"Michal, stay here!" he says. But the boy does not hear him; he is chasing one of the planes to the edge of the trees. Stefano decides to follow her through the woods and focuses on the white of her neck beneath hair pulled tightly up into a bun.

At the river he watches her climb down the embankment to fill them with water.

"Can I help you with those?"

She turns around, but she doesn't look surprised. Her face is red and flushed, and there are worry lines around her eyes.

"You must be my guardian angel!" she says.

"Perhaps." And she searches his eyes briefly to see if there is some truth. "Did Georg come back?"

"Yes, early this morning. He came in and went straight to bed. He is still there now."

Stefano nods and watches her. She doesn't drop her eyes this time.

She dips the second bucket in, and he bends forward over the edge, reaching out to take it from her.

She is silent. Lips together.

"Are you all right?"

"Those thieves took the good goose and left the lame one. It is clear she is in pain. That is what you get for charity."

Rosalind leads the way back to the house.

"You seemed upset last night and a little frightened of Georg when he saw us at the table."

"I'm not frightened," she says directly.

"I think you should be. He isn't stable, Rosalind. He needs help. Proper care."

"And where do you propose he get this proper care? If I take him to the hospital, he will be put in a Russian prison hospital I expect, and I will never see him again."

"He talks a lot of Monique."

"Most of the time, Georg doesn't make a lot of sense, as I said."

"And what, if you will forgive the question, was his relationship with Monique?"

She stops and turns to look at him uneasily. "You are suggesting something?"

"No, of course not!" he says. "I was just curious why he talks of her."

She continues walking.

"We were all very close," she says to the air in front, and it is difficult for Stefano to gauge whether she is telling the truth. "He loved her like a sister, like a friend, as I have already told you."

"Does he remember much about his childhood, about the war?"

"Sometimes. He might suddenly ask a question, like where are his shoes. And sometimes he might bring up something from the past. A memory that he describes that goes away just as quickly."

He rushes forward to open the pen gate for her.

"What was she like?" He does not need to say her name.

"I think I am too tired to answer any more questions," she says, reaching for the other bucket he puts forward. "I've hardly had any sleep. Perhaps you are enamored with her yourself. You would not be the first."

"I have offended you. Please forgive me. Do you believe she will come back one day?"

"I think Monique will do whatever it is she wants. Like she has always done."

She brusquely walks past him to cross the pen.

"I will be over shortly to finish the work," says Stefano.

"You don't have to do that," she calls over her shoulder. "It wouldn't have surprised me if you'd left this morning. I thought you would be running halfway to Italy by now after witnessing my husband's strange ways."

She turns, and she is smiling all of a sudden, almost laughing.

"What is so funny?" he asks.

"All of us. Crazy, lost people here beside the river. And now you, like everyone, are curious about Monique. You are just like all men really. I thought you were different. That is what amuses me."

She is smiling and confident, but there is madness there, he thinks, from time alone, from the horrors of war. He is thinking of the girl from the portrait. She is right at least. He is enamored but more curious about her life here, about their lives before the war, about the relationships that were here beforehand.

"Then you don't know me at all," he says.

She lingers slightly, looks at his feet, and then at a point on his shoulder, before finally resting her eyes on his again.

"You should have left, not been seduced by Erich's talk of trains." She turns away, leaving him wondering if there is something more she isn't telling him, that she is too frightened to tell, or whether it is merely her continued bitterness toward her neighbor, or if, perhaps, she herself wants Stefano gone.

As he walks back to Erich's house, he passes the window to see Monique's portrait on the wall. He wants to study it again. He wants to know her. He wants time to finish another letter in his pocket. She is sending messages from far away, and sometimes it feels as if she were talking only to him.

He is alarmed to find Michal inside Erich's house, sobbing into the cushions on the couch.

"Michal, what is the matter?"

He lifts the boy to sit up, but the boy covers his face with his arm.

"Are you injured?"

Stefano gently pulls the arm away to see his swollen eyes.

"Maminka," he says, and he reaches for his basket.

Stefano sits down next to him and pulls him close, so that Michal's head rests against his chest. The child's hair has traces of smoke and earth, and Stefano breathes it in and says a prayer now, a change of heart, for the mother who is perhaps still lying in a field.

They are together in this, both here without their mothers. And Stefano instinctively puts his hand on the boy's head before he has had time to think about the action. He feels the soft fine hair, and strangely, thinks Stefano, he needs the boy as much as Michal needs him. The child is perhaps keeping him level, less bitter, more tolerant.

"You are missing your mamma, yes?"

The child's face is burrowed into the front of his shirt.

"She is probably watching you now. She is probably very proud that you can fly a plane."

The child's sobbing turns into sniffs.

"Michal, I believe we found each other for a reason. Can I trust you with a secret?"

The little boy sits up and looks up at him, wipes his eyes with the backs of his hands to get a clearer view of Stefano. He nods. He is used to keeping secrets.

"I need you to be my soldier. A special soldier with a secret task. Can you do that?"

He nods again. "With a gun?" he asks.

"No gun, but with information that is sometimes far more powerful."

23 March 1942

Dear Papa,
This is a difficult letter for me to write. Forgive me. It has been so long since I found the strength. I feel that I am doing a great wrong by saying anything, by putting pen to paper, yet if I don't, I become like everyone else here. Afraid, paranoid puppets while days turn into nights and nights turn into nightmares.

I promised myself long ago that I would be like you and be strong, but I do not think I carry your fortitude or valor.

As a result of the decision I felt forced to make, I am in Vienna with my husband, Erich.

Things were not right in Berlin when I left there. I was relieved at least when the train left the station and I watched Berlin's buildings disappear from view. Yvonne and Max were there to say goodbye. I would not describe them as loving, but they have been somewhat kind to me, and I feel pity for Yvonne, whose legs ache with disease.

Rosalind was there, too, stoically telling me I had made the right decision, but even as she said these words, I could tell there was a lack of sincerity. But who am I to judge, since I deceive them all about this marriage.

Before I was married, I must admit to you, Papa, that I was not taking war quite as seriously as most. Not that I didn't care about our soldiers being killed; quite the contrary. I cried dreadfully and carried bad news in my heart for days, especially for those I knew, but I suppose in my mind to cope with everything was to fight against Berlin's new laws and voice my support to anyone about those more vulnerable. I was losing friends because of ridiculous laws that told them they were no longer allowed to call themselves German. But I cannot change my feelings.

Emmanuelle, who was forced to wear a yellow-star patch on her arm, and her family were sent away, and our little friendship group fell apart. There were no safe places for them. She and her family were forced to leave most of their belongings in their apartment and took only a few bags, and they were lucky to have those. They were told that new towns had been created for them, but it doesn't make sense that they have to live elsewhere. Emmanuelle asked me to keep an eye on Alain. She had not seen him in the week prior, and she was sad that they could not say goodbye. Since the African show was canceled, many of the acrobats and performers like Alain have struggled to find work. He was, however, lucky to secure factory work for almost a year after that, and after his application to join the Wehrmacht was denied.

Erich said it was likely Alain had been sent to a labor camp. This news made me so angry, and I walked into a *police station and demanded to know where he had been sent to, and they laughed, Papa. They laughed and flirted with me as if I were a dolt. They said he had most likely been sent away with the Jews. They were cruel the way they spoke, Papa. And I told them so. I said that I would write a letter to the British and broadcast it somehow. Sometimes I don't like this Germany anymore. I am worried for its future.*

These inquiries and my affections for so-called "undesirables," and my attendance at "questionable" clubs, as they call them, had caught the notice of more senior people after a report was sent from the Gestapo, and some officers came to talk to me. I was then fired from my government position. Rosalind's warning was right, unfortunately, that I would get everyone into trouble with my inquiries about Alain and my rebellion against ridiculous rules. Yvonne and Max were interrogated about my activities and connections. I think the officers knew that Tante and Onkel were perfectly innocent, but I believe they wanted to scare them into controlling me. And that made my decision about leaving Berlin the right one. I could not do anything to hurt them. I had done enough and felt ashamed that in some way what I did would come back on them. Rosalind, understandably, didn't speak to me for some time.

Erich vouched for me personally, and although I'm indebted to him, I am fairly certain that if not for Georg and his close friendship with Erich, I might now be in prison. It was Georg, my very good friend also, who orchestrated the marriage, and I flatly refused the idea of it at first. But as you can see, Papa, at the time there was no other choice.

While we were still in Berlin, Erich made me agree that I would not attend clubs, and he believes that if I am actively promoting the führer's doctrines, attending parades and speeches, and visibly showing my support, all will be forgiven by the party. But he admitted that it would not be forgotten, since my name is in a file somewhere and will always be. He said that I am lucky I am not in prison.

And so it is that to protect myself, and our family in Berlin, I must continue with this charade, the proposition sweetened, however, with the knowledge of Erich's Austrian posting. He has agreed to help search for you but so far has found no trace, only that you were in prison and then transferred elsewhere. Since I have no control or sway under a Hitler-controlled government, I am not at liberty to search for you myself, I was told.

I'm afraid to write too much about Erich, because I know little about him myself. I can tell you with certainty that he is in charge of a squad who seeks out those against the government and sends them to prison camps in the East. But I can also tell you something else about him, and it is something that was not learned from him, but from wives of other officers. Erich was responsible for finding Jews hidden around the city before and after the mass deportations last autumn, and this I didn't know until after I married him. Knowing of the friends I lost in Berlin, I now find it difficult to look at him, and I feel great shame putting this in writing to you and wonder what you must think of me. When I did raise this briefly with Erich, he brushed me off and reminded me that he was doing me a favor. And we have not discussed it since.

I pray for you, Papa, every day. I feel sometimes you are close by. You are often in my dreams. Mama is there, too. We are in our sun-filled kitchen, and she is laughing at something you say. You would always make light of everything. Oma said that, too. That she did not think you would go far in life because you acted like such a clown, that you liked to drift and dream. But I also know that it is what Mama loved most about you. You were there, always. You found jobs, any jobs. But your focus was on your family. I know that now. I know from relationships that this is what makes them work. To focus on the people, not the things, around you.

Goodbye for now, Papa. I will go back to my table and sew some little flowers on some linen that I bought at the market to make a curtain. Then I will fry some tomatoes and sardines and eat them at the window that looks over the square and the quaint little clock tower that softly chimes throughout the day. I will watch the people, the lovers, the children, and the families that have not been broken apart. And I will sit and dream, Papa.

Yours always,

Monique

CHAPTER 18

ROSALIND

Rosalind sweeps up the mud that has dried to loose dirt on the stone floor that her grandfather laid. She used to sit on the stones in front of the fireplace where they were warm. She would get so warm she would have to put a towel underneath her bottom. Sometimes she would fall asleep on the hearth after drinking a glass of warm milk. Her father would pick her up and carry her to bed. Georg would be there, too. They would play until dinnertime when they were very small. She remembers those times vaguely, pieces anyway. Georg sitting at the table, a small version of his father, listening to conversations, and Rosalind sitting across watching him, marveling at the gold in his hair. They were the very young years before Monique arrived and changed things, and life at the river became more insecure.

Stefano arrives with the strange little boy to finish the wall. She looks at the boy as if he were some kind of gift that she must respect now. He has brought out something in Georg that she has not seen since he returned. He laughed, a sound that was just like the old Georg, and she glimpsed it in his eyes, the return. But this morning he has once again regressed, and he has taken the marble away to the hut in the forest where he hides most things that he treasures.

He is there somewhere beneath the fog. Though deep down she is still unsure. Still unsure whether it would make a difference to their relationship if he did return to normal, whether he might remember things, and whether then she might lose him forever.

Rosalind takes Michal inside while Stefano finishes the wall. She puts some jam on a crust of bread for him. His clothes are dirty, and he has a strong smell of smoke about him, old smoke, oil smoke, not the sweet tobacco smoke she smells on Stefano. While he is eating, she fills the bath with hot water from an iron pan on the stove and tops it up with buckets of cold water from the pump near the tub.

She leads the boy to the bath, and when he sees that she is about to attempt to bathe him, she has to block the doorway to stop him from fleeing. His lower lip drops forward as if he might cry.

"My mother used to bathe me. Did your mother used to bathe you, too?"

He says nothing, but two wells appear in his eyes at the mention of his mother. His legs are scratched and insect bitten, and his limbs are thin. He is not in a good state. If he were her son, he would be well cared for, and something about this thought eats at her, makes her suddenly bitter.

"You are a stubborn little boy!"

And then she thinks of his mother and wonders what she was like. She probably spoke softly, taught him to whisper.

"You can have more jam if you get in the bath. See," she says, her tone softer, bending down to the water. "It is warm and lovely, and I will wash your clothes for you just like your mama."

"Jam?"

"Yes," she says, and feels slightly more confident. "Come on," she says, taking off his shirt with holes and his shorts that are so thin the fabric is see-through in places.

She puts him in the bath, and he sits while she washes him with soap and then with some for the hair. He is delicate, with a sweet monkey face. She marvels at the smallness of his hands and feet.

"Isn't that better?"

Though she isn't expecting a response.

She wraps him in a towel, and he sits near the outside tub in the sun, to eat bread and jam, while she washes his clothes, then lays them on the drying rack.

Afterward she shows him books, and he repeats some words that she says, in whispers, though his voice is slightly louder now, his confidence growing. Michal is amazed by the pictures and colors, and he traces his fingers along the backs of the animals as if imagining the feel of their fur.

When the clothes are nearly dry, she dresses him and then shows him some photos. He studies them hard. She can see that he is looking for his own family among them.

"Do you have a second name?"

"Yes."

"What is it?"

"Nazi bastard!"

Rosalind cringes at the name as if this were personal, as if it has just been said to her.

"Did you know your father?"

He shakes his head and stares at the photos on the wall.

"Who gave you that name?"

He shrugs and looks at her suspiciously. He has sensed a change of tone in the conversation that has turned more serious. He is wary and bright, she thinks. And he has suffered, from the look of him—innocent, an injured bird. She wants him then. Wants him for herself.

"I will make some tea. Michal, can you take the remainder of the grain to the goose? She is in her little house today. You will have to take it all the way to her."

"She will bite me!"

"It is all right, Michal. Watch out for her beak, but I think she will be more interested in the food you carry than trying to chase you away. She is also very tired and may not bother to snap at anyone today." Rosalind does not wish to relate the real reason the goose is staying in her enclosure.

When he has gone Rosalind approaches Stefano to relay her concerns.

"I believe that his mother ran away from wherever she was. I believe that the child's father is German and they were no longer wanted at their home."

She reveals the name that Michal has been given, and Stefano is thoughtful, watching Michal whispering to the goose. Stefano mentions the foreign word he heard Michal use for his mother earlier.

"It might explain it," continues Rosalind. "He is not from here. And the accent suggests that German is not his first language. Wherever he came from, I believe he can't go back."

And Stefano is again deep in thought.

"It is something I can tell them at the camp," he says finally, and this in some small way disappoints her, the thought that they will be gone again, and she will be alone, with Georg, and lonely.

1942

In Berlin, people were feeling the effects of war with the rationing of meat and sugar, eggs, and other essential items, which weren't always available. After Max was laid off when several tramlines were shut, Yvonne had taken to making her own bread using vegetable meal and barley she sourced through a neighbor. Some restaurants were forced to reduce the options on their menus so that portions of beef and lamb were replaced with rice and vegetable stews with fewer pieces of meat, depending on what they could source, and fruit platters were seasoned with saccharin to disguise any bitterness or age. People were going less to the cinema and spending more money on black market coal. Films would begin with Hitler's speeches, more men were asked to sign up for war service, and women had to leave their children during the week to work in uniform and munitions factories.

The rest of the civilians walked around in a state of petrified wonderment under the red, black, and white flags that flapped like dying fish in the breezes that blew from the battlegrounds from the east. These flags supposedly represented greatness, which was at odds with the lessening prosperous circumstances. But even by this stage, Berliners still held the belief that Germany was more powerful than any other country, and they would win the war with fewer casualties than elsewhere.

Rosalind had noticed a change in Monique. She was not as vibrant. There was a darker Monique lately, subdued, with a decline in confidence and an increase in seriousness. It had started the previous year, after Alain's disappearance. Then the loss of her job and the interrogations by the SS after her scene at the police station, which Rosalind still hadn't forgiven her for. And finally there was the news of her engagement to Erich. Rosalind had been shocked at the announcement, since only weeks before that, Monique had vowed to marry no one.

But in the midst of a changing, more somber Berlin, Rosalind's wish was finally granted, which made her forget about everything else. Georg had asked Rosalind, by letter, to marry him. At the time of his written proposal, he was covered in mud and sweat, tired and hungry, with a view of dead bodies and a dinner of tinned beans. He said he had started taking something to make him alert, though the generals didn't approve of it anymore, so he had to keep such a practice discreet. And in that moment that brought euphoria and blissful ignorance of the carnage around him on the Eastern Front, he had written the words proposing marriage, and they could not be taken back.

She had read the letter and told her parents the news. They seemed to take it as a given, neither expressing great surprise with their incurious smiles, shoulder shrugging, and nods, and she could not help noticing that there seemed less fuss than when Monique had announced her engagement and married a week later.

Her cousin would not be in Berlin for Rosalind and Georg's wedding, as Erich had just started his important and secretive posting in Austria. And it was only then that Monique became busy and excited again at the prospect of returning to her place of birth and being closer to finding out about her father. So far, not even Erich had been able to find out any information from telegrams he had sent to various prisons. Monique was certain that once there, they would learn more.

The day after Monique left for Austria to join Erich, who had gone a week earlier to prepare accommodations, Georg arrived back appearing harried and worn. Their meeting was lukewarm, though he seemed talkative about the wedding. He had taken to smoking heavily, something Rosalind didn't like, and he would wave his cigarette hand around while he described things. His face was redder, seared slightly, which brought out the pale green of his eyes, and his slightly more lived-in look made him appear more masculine and impossibly handsome.

She had not been with a man before, so she didn't know what to expect on her wedding night. She'd heard some of the other nurses discuss certain activities, and even Monique had dallied, she suspected. Monique could be as mysterious as she could be open, Rosalind had learned. She could keep secrets well, thought Rosalind.

Though they were different, there was a closeness, a feeling, perhaps more an obligation that they had to keep each other informed about their lives. But after Alain disappeared, Monique told her nothing more about herself, and Rosalind did not wish to detail what happened at the hospital. There were too many casualties, incidents, to talk about. Yet in a strange way, they needed each other. Despite an envy there that Rosalind had carried as a teenager, Monique had brought a vibrancy into their otherwise dreary home, and Rosalind wondered now whether

Georg would have come back each summer in the early days if Monique hadn't been there. She owed her something, she sometimes thought.

It was not until their wedding night that Rosalind wished she had made an effort to be closer to Monique, who was worldly, who would have given advice and told her not to worry so much.

After the wedding, a small affair, Georg had taken her to a hotel for the night, and she had been shy and he perhaps even more so. It felt like they were performing a deed that was required rather than desired. The act of lovemaking was cold and painful, and there was no loving embrace afterward. In fact it had been almost brutish, the way he forced himself harder when she had cried, thinking it was a call for more. If that was a part of marriage, then she would need to be stronger, she felt. After this very brief act, he had sat on the side of the bed with his naked back to her and smoked a cigarette. And when he had walked to the window to view the street below, she modestly eased back into her slip.

Was he all right, she asked, and he had turned and smiled. *Of course,* he said. The response seemed genuine, she thought, she hoped. She loved him so much. She had for so long, and now they were married, and this was marriage, and she had burst into tears. He had stubbed his cigarette out and rushed to her side. "What's wrong? Why the tears?"

"I don't know why," she said, and it was truthful because she didn't understand the feelings of loving and not knowing whether she was being loved back. She could not put that into words to Georg, not at that moment anyway.

"It's a shock the first time," he said, "but it's going to be fine."

She had leaned her head against his bare chest, and he held her and kissed the top of her head. And she had felt his heartbeat and felt comforted, and warm, though the words rang through her ears long after the wedding night. *The first time? Who was Georg's first time?* She had to wonder.

After they had two more nights together in her bedroom at her parents' house, he announced suddenly that he was leaving, his unit about to embark for another battle on foreign lands.

"I heard from Monique by letter," he said as she watched him dress in his dashing gray uniform. He was trying to sound casual, but in the attempt the words had come out forced, unnatural. "She said Erich will be taking some leave at the end of the summer, and they are both keen to catch up with us then at the river houses. Erich said he will use his influence and make sure I have the same week of leave."

"Might you be in the middle of battle?"

"Perhaps."

He had kissed her on the cheek, told her he loved her, and rushed from the room.

Several days later, she found his small brown leather folder, which he carried everywhere, wedged between the bed and the dresser. In his haste he had forgotten it. She looked inside to see if there was anything important and found the papers for his next commission. She also discovered the date of departure for his commission was two days after he had rushed off to leave her. Two days, she thought, he should have spent with her.

Present-day 1945

She stops to view the wall Stefano has created, her skirt nearly touching Stefano's arm. She looks at his hands, wonders at the strength of him, after what he has been through. The corner is a patchwork of bricks in varying shades of brownish reds and whites. But it has been done evenly and with precision.

"If you do not choose to have an academic life with your languages, then I'm sure the damage this war has done could give you countless hours of work." Her words to her ears do not sound sincere, but she was never good at compliments. She means it, though. The work is excellent.

She sees Georg out of the corner of her eye, watching them from the doorway. He looks large, like a predator sizing up its prey. He has the look of defeat most of the time but not today. Minutes later he returns inside.

He is not Georg, not the one she spent time with as a child. And the memories of their marriage are stained with deceit. All this is coming to her. All this in a moment. She wonders whether Stefano has been sent here; if he is the catalyst that will change the course of her future. Wonders if there is a future, if she deserves one, and whether Georg should be part of it. She remembers Erich's advice about sending him to a hospital. She has begun to question her own decisions. Perhaps it is time to take some of his advice.

"I was wondering if you would like to share another meal with me this evening," she says suddenly to Stefano.

He looks at her and doesn't answer straightaway as if he were thinking or calculating. She cannot tell whether he is pleased with the invitation or whether he thinks she is mad the way she lives. Once she may not have cared what anyone thought of her and Georg, but she does now. She is developing feelings for someone other than her husband, a thought that several weeks ago would never have entered her head.

"And Erich?" he says finally, looking up toward the woods on the hill.

She blinks several times at the mention of his name. She saw Erich earlier behind the house, clearing the debris from the damaged shed. They have been bound by the past, but those bindings could unravel at any moment. If Stefano knew her, knew her past, she would lose him, and somehow the thought of losing him frightens her. She does not want him to leave here. She does not want him in Erich's clutches. For some reason that frightens her even more.

"I can't . . . ," she says.

"Why not?"

"It is difficult to explain."

"Is it Georg?"

And she looks at him then, wondering what he sees, what he knows.

"Erich said he was dangerous," Stefano says.

"He is not so dangerous. It is only Erich who thinks that way." She does not trust herself to explain further.

"Then why not? If there is something from the past, maybe the two of you can bring it to an end tonight."

He wears a small thin smile, though it is more a cynical one; smiles he has yet to master. And she thinks that they still need each other, she and Erich. That they made a pact, that they must learn to live with the past, move on, perhaps together in a distant way. But not just that. It is better to watch an enemy, see where he is, than to not see him at all, to speculate.

"Yes. Erich also," she says, her chest tightening with apprehension.

"That is good," he says. "Then this lovers' tiff can be put to rest, finally."

She starts to protest but thinks it will look worse if she objects to the comment. She leaves Stefano to wash her hands in the tub at the back of the house.

"Georg, I have a special request tonight," she says on entering the house to find Georg at the table. She is wondering if the others will set him off. She is becoming more afraid of him, fearful of what he carries in his head. "We are having dinner guests, and I would like you to be on your best behavior. Can you do that?" She is also thinking it would be better he stays sleeping with a sedative, perhaps the dose increased for tonight, though she must be careful. Stock is running low and Erich is giving her less. She can't think what life would be like without the drugs.

Georg turns to look at her. His eyes clear, stubble appearing, a small dribble from the corner of his mouth, and then something hits her. This is not her Georg. Not the one she fell in love with.

He can't see her. He never could. Even before the injury. She thinks of Stefano. Of his dark eyes that see her, really see.

She walks to her room and opens her wardrobe. There are dresses there that belonged to someone else. She takes out one and holds it against her in front of the bedroom mirror: a navy dress with pale-yellow flowers embroidered onto the lapels.

Odd that after all this time she would think about how she will look. It is Stefano of course. Her heart beats strangely at the thought of him, at the warmth of his skin. She wanted him gone two days ago; now she wants him here. She is rash, altered, even a touch mad, she thinks.

She carries a sack and a hammer to the goose hut. There is little food. One day soon, she expects, Erich will be gone, and she will go back to queuing for rations. The thought of it terrifies her, of leaving Georg for hours, without the medicine that will eventually run out, to queue for a few vegetables and sausages that are barely enough for one, and to avoid the Russians again in the streets.

The bird will die eventually. Better it be by her hand than by the hand of a thief.

The goose has hardly moved at all, and she squawks submissively today, a quiet pleading, and graceful, with her long neck and beseeching eyes that turn from side to side to view Rosalind. It is unlikely she will heal. When Rosalind was small she saw a goose with a similar ailment and asked her grandmother if they could take it to the doctor.

No, dearest Rosalind, said Oma. *God has already made his plan for this one.* She had believed her grandmother at the time, though now she can see things for herself: death has nothing to do with God or heaven; death is decided by the living.

She puts her hand out, but the goose does not snap today. She knows it's the end, thinks Rosalind. She is just waiting now.

Without any more thought she throws the bag over the goose's head. The goose flaps around within the bag, and Rosalind feels the shape of her head through the hessian. With a hammer she hits the head, and the goose releases a faint, involuntary squawk but still squirms within. Rosalind hits again twice, harder this time. She has never killed an animal before. She saw her grandmother use an ax on the birds, but she could not bear to kill that way, with such bloody violence. She watched her grandmother kill, then pluck and chop and stuff, and as a child, Rosalind never once considered that she might one day experience it, too.

She sits back on her haunches and hugs her knees to stare at the sack, thinking back to the miracle eggs. The sight of the suddenly lifeless bird within makes her feel ill, but mostly sad.

"I'm sorry," she whispers, and several tears escape.

Rosalind puts one hand on her heart and the other on the sack to feel the contents that are still warm, before realizing what she is doing. She can't afford to attach herself to dead things.

She picks up the bag and heads back to the house to prepare the goose for dinner.

CHAPTER 19
ERICH

For most of the morning, Erich has been clearing the rubbish from the property and depositing it near the broken houses across the road, all the while his mind on Stefano, who is working on Rosalind's property. The clearing is not something he needs to attend to, but he likes to be near, to keep an eye on Stefano where he can. They conversed earlier over coffee. Erich advised he will return at sunrise, and they will leave shortly afterward for the station in Dresden.

At the top of the ridge above the houses, he stopped to briefly watch Stefano working. Stefano did not appear to notice him there, too focused on precision, on the task. He is careful and methodical, smoothing the mortar between each brick with gentle but firm strokes.

Stefano and Michal left earlier with a bucket, heading toward the woodland on the far side of the clearing to collect clay and dry grasses, ingredients to make a crude mortar as a temporary patch to other minor damage in the house's brickwork.

Erich watches Rosalind carefully whenever she leaves the house. She has found reasons to walk past Stefano and to stop and talk. She seems eager to gain his attention. Normally he would think she was suspicious and keeping an eye on him, but just from the encounters he has witnessed, she seems comfortable, even curious like him. The fact she is doing this irritates him. Just the sight of her stirs animosity, the resentment in her face reminding him she knows too much.

Once finished with the clearing, he sets about removing engine parts from the car, and cleaning them. He helped his father do this many times. He could become his father, he thinks. He has much of him: he has his passion for machinery, his fascination for the way things work. He replaces the parts, then covers the car with rugs and once again with branches.

Stefano steps up to the tub near the back door to wash off the dirt.

"Rosalind has asked us both to dinner," says Stefano.

"I can't. I have to work tonight."

He does not want to spend time with her if he can help it. He does not want to be near Georg.

"But you said you are not leaving till late. Perhaps you have time."

"I should get there earlier."

"They are working you hard it seems. You hardly sleep."

"It is a very busy factory."

How one lie can grow to two and two to four, thinks Erich, who must turn the conversation.

"I will be back in the morning, as promised. In the meantime I hope that you will enjoy the evening. Just be careful."

"I sense no danger there," says Stefano. "I believe your dislike is for other reasons. Every time I mention Rosalind's name, it seems to upset you."

Erich remembers the last time he and Rosalind spoke alone. Rosalind turning her back to him to be rid of him quickly. Erich is disappointed in himself that he has exposed certain feelings. He is wondering what else he has shown.

"There are a lot of things in the pasts of people who have known one another in different situations," says Erich. "Sometimes it is better just to move on. To begin anew. We did not have a strong connection in the early years. I see no need to have one now."

Evasiveness was one of his strengths, but he finds himself answering Stefano, not by the means of manipulation, but because he wants to.

"I think that if you can spare time before you start work, then perhaps it is a good thing, for both of you."

And Stefano is looking at him, searchingly. The Italian is commanding and engaging even when he is saying little, even just standing there. He does not have the order, the short hair, the grooming that Erich is used to in those he looked up to, and Erich has been conditioned to distance himself from those who are different in color, in background. Yet at this moment, perhaps for the first time, he questions the motive of such a stance. He questions why Hitler had got it so wrong. The question would shatter his mother if she could read his thoughts.

"All right, I will come," he says. "For a short time. Perhaps we must celebrate the end of the war, at least, even if it was not the outcome some of us would have hoped for."

Erich believes his own words. They are not flippant. He must continue. It is Stefano's company he craves, but there is another reason to be here this evening. He loathes the idea of leaving Rosalind to speak to Stefano alone any longer. She is not as guarded, less cautious. She could ruin his chances to leave with Stefano if he learns the truth. Perhaps it is best that Erich is there to observe, to make sure she says nothing.

Erich suddenly notices that Michal is still missing. He has not seen him since the earlier walk with Stefano.

"Where is the boy?"

Stefano shrugs. "He is just exploring. He will not be far way. I will go to Rosalind and let her know you will be there, too."

1941–1942

In Berlin, shortly after they were married, Monique became a weight in Erich's daily life, and their time together was strained. The foreign posting in the months ahead would likely change things for the better. He would hopefully be traveling often and not have to spend much time with her. He didn't understand people like Monique, nor did he want to. They would make small talk, and he endured it at first. She was charming at functions, and Erich was the envy of many men. There had been whispers at first about her behavior, that she had been naively open to other vices, but they had quickly died down after the wedding, when people saw that she was good enough for a senior officer. She was good at acting, at playing the part of acknowledging her wrongs, should someone accidentally bring up a reference. Though Erich was not completely fooled. There was more to her than she was letting on, and, from past experience, he knew people rarely changed their beliefs.

She was intelligent, he was to discover. He had married her, thinking that she was flighty, emotional, and fanciful, and she would know very little about the world, because of the topics she raised in the early days, the desire to spend idle time at play. But he had discovered that she understood many issues about war. She was curious, too, about people in the party, the measures they were taking in securing all the territories, and the future of Germany. Erich was careful not to provide too much detail, but she would ask intelligent questions, and he told her some things to humor her. Not about his work but about the processes, the German military, the power of the tank that his father had helped design, which he was pleased to speak of because so few people asked. He had misjudged that about her, but it was still not enough to build a relationship, and when conversations ran dry, it might be days before they would find common ground again.

They slept in separate rooms, and most nights he would choose to work late. In the morning when he left for work, his breakfast would be ready, and she would have left for the markets. She was no longer required to work. His position, power, and finances were enough to keep both of them in better circumstances than many.

He rarely took Monique to his mother's. His father was the only parent who liked her, and since he was home very little these days and Erich's mother showed her disapproval of his wife, without even knowing the truth, he was reluctant to bring her. Claudine had grown into an independent, pretty girl, and spent most days away from home with her university friends. They were self-indulgent, his mother had said, and added nothing to this country. Erich agreed. His mother asked if he could find out what she was up to, use his hunting skills. She had asked the same of Horst, who had been quite angry at the suggestion, who had said Claudine was old enough to choose her friends.

Somehow the pair had coexisted, though Erich's job was getting more intense, and his particular work was something he did not discuss with Monique, knowing her previous disposition on those expelled on race, the same type of people that Erich helped remove from Germany. At first, she believed he was simply policing the streets, and part of the security team for rallies and speeches in Berlin, until later learning the truth.

As a member of the Gestapo, Erich was tasked with tracking and interrogating Jews, and hunting down political anti-Nazi activists hiding in the bowels of Berlin. It had taken him all over Berlin, sometimes to the outskirts. His first assignment was to inspect an apartment where Jews were known to live, to take names and verify records. Here he would interrogate them in a style that was neither warm nor cruel. In the early days, before superiority became embedded, it was difficult for those under questioning to dislike him, yet they knew he was there to glean information, to take a mental inventory of their precious items. He would then have to record these people who would, in most cases, be evicted shortly after.

The fate of the Jews was yet to be fully revealed even to him at the time of these inquisitions and removals. He had known that many were transported to camps, but the propaganda within his office did not show the real conditions. It was not until he visited a camp in Austria that he learned the full extent. In those first few months of his employment, he had been unaware of the hard labor ahead for those he had helped remove from Berlin, of the families torn apart, and of the mass executions. In time he found out, but even with full knowledge, he grew to accept these conditions quickly, to become desensitized, even repulsed, by the people he sent away.

Though respectful of orders, some of the SS he was assigned in these early days were crude and untrained in the ways of restraint when it came to controlling a situation. At first he quietly resented them almost as much as the people he interviewed. They didn't like Erich, but they kept a safe distance because he was one they couldn't put into any box. He was too tidy, too careful, too methodical. They used too much brashness and, unlike Erich, were unable to hide the revulsion, which made it difficult to extract information during interviews.

During one of his early interrogations, he was accompanied by an SS officer that Erich considered to have few social capabilities. Erich was able to talk a Jewish man into cooperating, convincing him in a nonthreatening way to assist Erich and advising him that he would have to vacate the apartment for new accommodations on the outskirts of the city. The Jew, the father of the family, with his wife, his mother, and several children sitting nearby, threatened to find a lawyer. Erich patiently told him that there would be no legal representation, that Nazi laws did now allow them such, and that by refusing to talk, they were breaking a law, which meant he would be put in prison and separated from his family for an indefinite period. Perhaps it was the nonhostile tone that Erich used, and the clarity with which he spoke, but the Jewish man calmed down eventually, accepting his fate and agreeing for the sake of his family. But just to prove superiority, the Gestapo member who accompanied him hit the man across the face at the end of the questioning. The Jew then became difficult, and Erich asked that the children be removed from the room. They had begun to whimper, the one thing most likely to distract him.

Erich continued to question the man who held a hand to his bruised face, pretending coldly that there had been no harm done, and the interview concluded quickly. Once outside Erich turned to his associate and said that if he ever did that again, Erich would make sure that he lost his employment.

The Jew, later that night, was taken prisoner and was never to see the rest of his family again. At the time Erich thought he had failed to keep control of his staff and the situation, but sometime later he would come to the conclusion that he was only delaying the inevitable. The man and his family were always going to be separated. And as time went on, and the job became monotonous, the sound of crying offensive, the evasive answers annoying, Erich would find that such brute force would be a necessary part of the job, and that people like his associate served a purpose.

Since the commencement of his commission, Erich had helped remove thousands of Jews and nonconformists from the city, several hundred of whom had been in hiding. He was able to question those who lied about their origins. He was able to spot a fake identity card. He was able to root out hiding spots within walls and glean information from others as to the whereabouts of missing family members.

When it came time to leave Berlin for Vienna in Austria, he had some reservations. He had grown to like the tasks, to like the power and control, and he had earned the respect of fellow officers, above and below his station. His name was known. He was relieved at least that he would not have to attend Georg and Rosalind's wedding to celebrate a marriage that was undoubtedly of little substance, like his own. Monique, on the other hand, was excited about leaving for Vienna. She was "going home," as she called it. But of course, there was no reason for any excitement, as she would soon discover. There were worse things ahead in Vienna.

Present-day 1945

Erich can't help but notice that Rosalind looks different. She has put on a dress that Monique bought in Vienna, and high-heeled black shoes. The dress is too large for her but suits her nonetheless. Her hair is brushed back from her face and held with a pearl pin that he recognizes also. She doesn't wear any face paint, but she doesn't need to. Her complexion is fair, lightly tanned, with freckles across her nose that might appeal to some. She is not stunning, but her eyes are large and luminous, and her mannerisms feminine and delicate. But she is not delicate. She saw much in the hospitals and has experienced much since. He has also seen that she can take care of herself.

She smiles at Stefano. And that is the reason she looks so good, he thinks. It is the smile. Her face is usually stern.

Stefano has noticed the smile, too, as well as the dress and the shoes. He does not hide the admiration with his staring eyes. He has washed out his shirt and damply combed back his hair, so it is no longer loose and curling around his face.

There is no sign of Georg, and neither man raises the question.

The smell of roasting meat entices them to the table where they take their places. Rosalind tells them about the goose she has prepared, the goose with the broken leg, and tells Erich the story of the other goose that was stolen.

"A little charity and they always come back for more," says Erich, and Stefano looks at Rosalind, who glances away, who does not want to be reminded of her generosity.

"I have brought some vodka," says Erich.

"Did you find that also under floorboards somewhere?" says Stefano.

"I have always been resourceful." He rises to get several glasses from the bench. "May I?" he asks Rosalind, who nods.

He pours three glasses back at the table.

"I'd rather not," says Rosalind. "I—"

"Just one," says Stefano, "to celebrate the rebuilding of the wall." She thinks for a moment.

"Thank you," she says. "It was usually Monique who liked to drink."

Erich avoids turning to his right to see Monique on the wall. The mentioning of her is not something he expected. It is not like Rosalind to talk of her cousin, but he can see that it interests Stefano, and she knows this, too, perhaps using it for conversation.

"Is there any word from your cousin?" asks Erich.

"No," says Rosalind, and she moves to check the oven. "Unfortunately nothing . . . With the goose I have baked some potatoes also and spinach, too. I'm sorry that I have not made more. There is so little to take from the garden yet."

Stefano looks keenly between them. He is not interested in hearing about the vegetables. He is examining Monique's portrait; her disappearance still begs for questions. But his attention diverts to Rosalind approaching the table with the food, and the pretty girl on the wall is once more in the past.

Michal sits closest to Stefano. Erich asks the child questions, but he is silent, his eyes darting back to the others, to his hands and to the basket that sits at his feet. He shifts several times, impatiently, the smell of the food distracting. And Erich is remembering his little brothers, who sat quietly upright at the table, who were patient, unlike Michal. He stops himself from thinking and takes a sip of the vodka.

"I owe you a debt," Rosalind says to Stefano as she sits once more at the table. "You have done a marvelous job. I never have to worry about rain again."

As they pass around the serving plates, their talk turns to progress and the reshaping of the country. Erich has brought with him a

German newsletter. The printing firms are starting up again, though the information is carefully worded and distributed so as not to upset the Russians and the Allies. The building work is recovering, and many of the captured Germans are cleaning up the cities, focusing on agriculture. There is much discussed about how they will disperse the labor, where the food will come from in the meantime. The distribution of territories from meetings held in Potsdam confirms that the Russians are expected to stay for some time, and Rosalind's face falls at the mention of this.

The food is nice, Erich tells Rosalind. She thanks him, but from the lack of sincerity in her reply, she could do without his company.

"So, Stefano," she says, "tomorrow you leave!"

"Yes," he says, showing no emotion. Erich can see Rosalind blink back a thought, a small frown between her brows. He can see what is happening here. Lonely little Rosalind has fallen for the Italian.

"Stefano, does your family know you are coming?" asks Erich.

"I have written, but I did not give a date."

"Tell me about your town," says Rosalind as if Erich were not with them. It is definitely Stefano, he thinks, who asked him to dinner, not Rosalind. He orchestrated it, and she reluctantly agreed.

"It is blue and bright most of the time. And yellow and warm."

"I like that you describe in colors," she says candidly, before her eyes meet Erich's and fall away again.

"Rosalind," says Erich, "this is delicious. I don't know why you haven't invited me here before. Why you took so long to kill the goose."

Rosalind's cheeks are flushed as she cuts the meat, her pet goose, into small pieces.

Tonight there is no discussion of war. Stefano is talkative about the village he comes from, about the tourists and the colored glass and silver jewelry that is popular with the tourists, of the buildings that have faced the sea for hundreds of years. He shows the bracelet at his wrist his sister made and sold at markets. He talks and they listen, both of them curious, interested. Rosalind has drunk too much of the vodka, and unsteadily carries out a dessert of baked pears with melted chocolate from the last of Stefano's rations.

Stefano leaves some of the pears to give to Michal, who takes them eagerly, eyes not on any adult but on the food that is scraped into his dish.

"He misses his mother very much," says Stefano.

"And do you think the boy will find his family?" asks Rosalind.

"I'm not sure," he says, and Michal looks away, perhaps content with the possibility that he might not be sent to somewhere he doesn't want to go.

"The boy is attached to you," says Rosalind. "In the days you have been here, I have seen you grow closer." And Erich has seen this also, that Stefano's expression softens when he looks at the boy.

"I saw the way you worked together," says Rosalind. "I saw the loyalty in his eyes."

Stefano searches hers, shiny and animated, the awkwardness of their first meeting behind them.

"They are like that," says Erich, interrupting the moment. "They draw you out, highlight things about yourself you didn't know."

"Are you speaking from experience?" asks Stefano.

And Rosalind watches Erich closely to see how he will answer.

"Yes, I helped raise my younger sister and brothers," he says, answering carefully. And he catches a look from Rosalind, unshrinking, a look that says, *You can't have what I have, not anymore.*

But he doesn't want what she has. He wants something else.

And Rosalind tells them she has an idea and disappears into her room. She returns, wheeling a gramophone on a small trolley. She winds it up, places the needle on the record, and jazz—once banned by the Nazis—pours out of the speaker, scratchy but better than the silence that was about to come. And he thinks of Monique then, not fondly, just that she would have loved the sound, and loved an opportunity to dance.

Erich notices that Stefano has still not drunk his glass and that he is watching everything carefully. Erich is on his second glass, and he is watchful also but caring less, not offended by the music as he should be, and feeling the effects of the vodka. Rosalind smiles at the music, at both of them, and at Michal, who looks curiously at the music box, and Erich likes this new Rosalind, the one who might forget the past.

Erich feels something he hasn't felt for years, the feeling of freedom, of life about to start. He watches Stefano change into someone else entirely: Stefano takes Rosalind's hands and pulls her from the chair to dance, swinging her around forcefully—*furiously*, almost. She is shy and ungainly, and though she tries to be Monique, to be carefree like she once was, she can't be. She is Rosalind and always will be. Then suddenly she interrupts the dance to reach up and touch her throat. And both he and Stefano follow Rosalind's gaze.

Georg is standing at the bottom of the stairs and appears almost normal, his hands casually in his pockets. Rosalind stops the gramophone's playing, and the silence that follows is louder.

Rosalind asks Georg to sit down, but he's not listening, his focus on Erich, who stands up warily as if an unfamiliar dog has wandered near.

"Are you feeling all right, Georg?" Erich asks.

It has been a while since he has faced him. Not since he brought him home from the incident on the battlefield. It has been even longer since Georg has looked him in the eye. The look is primal, and for the first time in a long while, Erich feels fear.

"Get out!" Georg says to Erich before he himself leaves, through the front door, swinging it back on its hinges to slam against the wall, the force of which causes the clock to fall and smash on the stone. The mood in the room is solemn, and that brief time that they had forgotten the past has vanished with Georg.

"It is probably time to end the night," says Rosalind apologetically, not to Erich but to Stefano, in her usual disagreeably abrupt tone, her brightness fading quickly. "I will go and find him. I keep thinking that he will return to . . ." She doesn't have to say the word. It is pretty obvious he will never return to normal.

"No," says Stefano. "Not you. I will go."

And Erich wonders why he should care. Tomorrow he'll be gone, and there will be no one to protect her then.

Stefano leaves the house, and it is just Erich and Rosalind and the child in the room.

Michal has hidden under the table, and Rosalind bends down to speak to him.

"It is safe, Michal. Georg won't hurt you. He is a gentle giant, and he loves children."

Erich watches Rosalind, who has no idea of children and their fears and can't see that the child is not afraid of Georg but frightened of being in the room with them, especially now that Stefano is away.

Rosalind gives up on the boy and stands nervously in the kitchen to wait for Stefano. She avoids looking at Erich.

The last time they were alone, he told her to stay away. He wants to remind her of that, and query her change of heart toward Stefano.

Erich walks to the front window. Near the entrance to the wood, Stefano is whispering to Georg, who is listening, seemingly intently. And then Georg is saying something that Erich can't hear.

He turns to Rosalind. "Do you trust him, the Italian?"

"Why shouldn't I?"

"Have you told him anything?"

"You should not question me," she says coldly.

"Georg should not be left alone with anyone," says Erich. "He says things, meaningless things. But sometimes he tells the truth also."

"I've already told Stefano that Georg makes no sense. There is nothing he can learn. I'm curious, though, why you have taken such an interest."

Erich dismisses the remark and turns back to the window to see that Georg is now gone and Stefano is returning to the house.

"Thank you for your goose," Erich says to Rosalind, who ignores the contaminated gratitude.

"It is a pity the night has ended this way," says Stefano, meeting him just outside the door. "Poor Georg and his demons."

And Stefano watches the other man carefully, waiting for some comment from Erich. There is nothing he cares to add. He will be free of Georg tomorrow also, if he has his way.

"I will see you in the early morning then," says Erich, "and drive you as promised."

"Erich," he says, the accentuation of the name fluid and lyrical. Erich has never heard it spoken that way. Stefano puts out his hand, and Erich takes it, the hold firm, unending. "I look forward to it. To my last night in Germany! Thank you for allowing me to stay, for taking me to the train."

And then he leans forward, holds Erich's shoulders, and kisses him on the cheek. Erich has seen Italians be demonstrative with one another, with old friends, but he is unprepared for such intimacy. He feels unsettled, his heart racing as he feels the lips of the Italian graze the other cheek also: the kiss, the words are strangely full of truths and messages he cannot decipher. *Does he know? Does he suspect what I want from him?* It is Erich who breaks the hold, who turns away to hide any feelings and avoid further intimacy that might weaken him.

It was on this night that Erich was going to tell Stefano the truth about the trains and suggest they travel together. But he can't bring himself to speak. Not now. For some reason Erich senses that he is no longer the one in control.

He walks back toward the town and wonders if his mother noticed the rain clouds from her bay window in the town. He can picture her shutting all the windows years ago in their two-story country villa and ordering Claudine to bring in the washing. The smell of the air, the wind gusts, the brief moments of stillness before the storms that have become more meaningful; small things that remind him of the better times before the war. And perhaps tonight the signs of the approaching storm spell also better things to come.

CHAPTER 20
STEFANO

Stefano is dreaming. It is one continuous war inside his head when he goes to sleep each night. Fire features the most, and he wakes breathless to the reality of his memories: faces in the fire, bullets whizzing past him, running in terror, and living on air, on little else for several nights. The adrenaline was high, and he was luckier than some, completing his missions before madness set in. But his dreams now are perhaps the delayed and resultant madness: nightmares that are disturbed with faces of people he loves, people dead, people still living, and all driving him forward for different reasons.

He had helped Rosalind clean up and carried Michal, who had fallen asleep on the floor beneath the table, back to the bedroom at Erich's. He'd tucked the boy into bed once again. Stefano had bent over him, whispered good night, and touched his soft cheek. He smelled like pine, not the mixture of soil, smoke, and ash where the boy once slept. Then Stefano had waited there, watched him fall back asleep returning once more to the bedroom at the front to get some hours of rest.

Sometime in the night he wakes to a grumbling sky and the boy, beside him again, curled into his back and sleeping deeply. Stefano sits up at the edge of the bed to grip the sides, willing the images from his dreams to disappear. Thunder sounds nearby, distracting him suddenly, and the house shudders in anticipation of another storm. A squall sends the curtain flying wildly up to the ceiling.

He steps near the window, where spots of rain cool his bare chest and bursts of light capture the coiling silver river. As he begins to draw the window closed, movement in the woods to his right gives him pause. He waits several moments to catch the movement again, but when the woods are once more scattered with light, the trees appear alone.

Though Stefano is certain he didn't imagine something there. He is used to watching for people. He checks that the boy is still sleeping soundly, and he waits for the noise of thunder before stepping out onto the creaking stairs, then onto the ground floor. He can see Erich's bed at the back of the room and sees that there is something there: a lump, the shape of a person. He holds his breath and waits for the next flash of lightning to confirm that it is nothing but bundles of linen and cushions.

Stefano walks to the front door, a black space in front of him, his arm outstretched until he touches the door. He runs his hand down the wood and feels cautiously for the handle. *Impatience will get you killed,* Fedor had told him. He turns the handle slowly, one small twist at a time, then steps into the night and shuts the door the same way he opened it. Once it was skill; now it is habit.

Another wind gust and a burst of rain announce that worse is to come. The thunder steps noisily downriver toward him as he reaches the entrance to the wood, and he treads carefully along the slippery path.

He can smell the water, smell the dankness of the soaked roots that fester in the murky shallows as he emerges from the wood to stand at the edge of the embankment. There is movement of something shapeless and white below him as the rain begins its tirade against the world.

A lightning strike across the river exposes someone shirtless, standing in the shallows. Stefano switches on his torch, and Georg turns toward it, eyes wild, staring and unfocused. He releases a bundle of cloth into the water and puts his arms across his face to block the light.

"Moni in the water!" he shouts.

Stefano looks past him to Rosalind, who lies still, floating just beneath the water's surface. Georg turns back once more to Rosalind, and Stefano sees that he is attempting to push her deeper underwater.

"Georg! No!" calls Stefano, who drops the torch to rush down the embankment to the shallows. He pulls at the arms of the other man, but his initial attempts at forcing Georg's hands away from Rosalind are futile, and Stefano then throws several punches. He is unprepared for the strength of Georg, for his inability to feel. Georg finally releases her but turns his attention, reaching for Stefano's throat with both hands and pressing his fingers into his windpipe. Knowing he has only seconds, Stefano's only defense is to lash out wildly at his assailant's face with both fists.

When Georg loosens his grip slightly, Stefano uses the moment to lunge at him, pushing him backward into the water alongside Rosalind. They tussle for several moments in the dark water until, with one arm finally pulled free, Stefano thrusts his elbow upward and into Georg's face, forcing him to release his hold.

Stefano stands up quickly, drenched and out of breath, to wait for the other man to come at him again. They each stand braced in the shallow water, and a blast of light from the sky reveals Georg, a savage beast, teeth gritted and fists clenched. At first it seems he will charge, but part of Rosalind's nightgown rises up from the water, distracting him, and, under the shaft of light from Stefano's fallen torch, Georg looks toward her floating body.

Thunder splits open the night above them, and panic spreads across Georg's face. As if awoken from a dream, he releases a loud whining noise like an animal in pain. The noise continues, louder, piercing through the sounds of rain slapping the water, as he scrambles up the embankment to flee into the wood.

Stefano dives across to where Rosalind has floated to deeper water several yards from the embankment, her face rising just above the surface. He kicks backward, dragging her above him, until he reaches the shallows again and then carries her limp body up the embankment to lay her on flat ground.

Stefano turns her on her side to empty the water from her lungs. Growing up beside the sea, he had witnessed several near drownings and one unsuccessful attempt at resuscitation. Rosalind is still motionless as he turns her on her back to breathe air into her mouth.

She coughs slightly, and as he attempts to sit her up, she retches. Moments later when the spasm has eased, he carries her back to the house and rests her gently on the sofa. He shuts the front door and ignites the oil lamp on the wall above her, the light revealing Rosalind's ashen face and eyes that loom large with shock. Her hair is saturated, stuck flat to her cheeks and neck, and a puddle of water has formed at her feet. She has wrapped her arms around herself and stares back at him, trembling, but she is not yet present, her mind attempting to make sense of the event that just occurred.

Stefano takes the throw that hides the worn fabric on the back of the sofa and wraps it around her shoulders. She doesn't move, tiny and timid beneath the rug, as thunder recedes farther down the river.

In Georg's attic bedroom there is no sign of him, nor in the rest of the house. But Stefano's instinct has already told him that Georg isn't inside. He locks the front and back doors.

He fills the kettle and places it on the stove, notes the puddles he has created on the floor from his clothes, then retrieves a towel from Rosalind's bathroom to pat off the excess water from his body.

When he sits down beside her, Rosalind doesn't acknowledge his presence, but her eyes find something else to focus on in the room, a space of wall that reflects her blank thoughts. He slides the rug away from her and gently rubs her back and shoulders with the towel, then more gently her head. With his fingers he combs the hair away from her face. She doesn't move away or ask him to stop. Her trembles taper, and he wraps the rug firmly around her shoulders.

"How are you feeling?"

"My throat is sore," she says, placing her hand at the tender area.

"What set him off?"

She shakes her head. "Nothing. I just woke, and his hand was over my mouth. He carried me to the river and then . . ."

The kettle whistles, and Stefano returns to the kitchen to pour hot water for tea.

"He has never been like that before," she says, almost in a whisper. "The rage so directed . . . I have always managed to control him."

"He is dangerous, Rosalind."

"If you knew him before the war, you would know that this isn't who he is. This is not the same Georg."

"What is he taking?"

"I don't know what you mean."

She sits up straighter as he approaches the sofa, and she reaches for the cup he brings her.

"You are giving him a drug. What is it that makes him so erratic?"

"It is his brain injury from a bullet, and it is no concern of yours," she says.

"It became my concern when I pulled you from the water."

She puts the cup down on a small serving table beside her, her eyes wide and clear again.

"I appreciate what you've done, but I don't need your advice. You know nothing about me, about Georg."

"He was deranged out there and with a strength that doesn't match his appearance. I believe it is the drug the Germans gave soldiers to make them feel invincible. I fought with some who were taking it, even after they were told not to—"

"You have no idea what it is like to see the person you love shattered, broken from battle, disoriented . . ."

"Was he already addicted before he went to battle?"

"What? . . . I don't know . . ." She shakes her head. "Yes."

"Erich said he was dangerous, and now I have to believe it."

"Be quiet about Erich." She stands up, and the rug falls to the floor. "You know nothing about Erich either! Perhaps it is him you should worry about."

She stumbles when she stands up to walk away. He reaches out to catch her, but she raises her hands to stop him as she rights herself. In the kitchen she puts her palms flat against the table, bows her head, and tries to steady her breathing.

"I'm sorry," says Stefano. "I know it isn't really anything to do with me, but you could have died."

She lifts her head slightly but doesn't turn to face him.

"You cannot imagine what it was like to see him return from war a ruined man—half a man. If you had seen him before, if you had known him, you would know why it is that I want to look after him in this way. He is worse when he is off the drugs. It is impossible to live with him without them."

"And is it Erich who gets you the drugs?"

"Of course! Erich has access to anything," she says, the pain in her throat distracting, throwing away her guard.

"What are you giving him?"

"Opiates to sedate him and help him sleep, and the other you just talked about reverses the first to lift his mood . . . They stop him from hurting himself." She pauses and closes her eyes. "Though lately the second is making him unpredictable."

"How often?"

"As he needs it . . . every few days. I've been stretching it out for longer since it is nearly all gone. It is perhaps the reduction that is the problem also."

"I think you are killing him slowly if he doesn't kill you first."

She puts her hand over her mouth and closes her eyes, the memory of what happened causing more pain.

"Rosalind, I can help you," he says gently.

"No one can help me."

Stefano steps close to comfort her, but she moves away toward the door.

"I can't leave him out there," she says, her voice firm again. "I must find him. He will be feeling wretched. He will remember what he did. Despite his mind, he remembers things between the lapses. He has lucid moments when he knows what he is, what he has done wrong. That is the sadness."

She reaches for the door handle.

"He called you Moni when I first approached him in the water. I presume he means Monique."

She stops and turns.

"As I said, he is confused."

"Is he angry about something?"

She appears annoyed at the questions, shakes her head, and moves again to leave.

"Stay here then. I will find him," he says, his hand against the door to block her exit.

"He won't respond as well to you, not in this state."

"After what I've witnessed, he may not respond to you either."

She lowers her eyes, aware suddenly that he speaks the truth.

"If he comes back in the meantime, don't answer the door. Keep it locked."

Stefano hears her turn the key in the lock as he leaves. He walks first through the wood to retrieve his torch that still sits on the embankment casting an eerie band of light across the river, then along the track toward the secret hut. The rain is lessening as it follows the streaks of light now appearing in the distance.

Stefano finds Georg in the hut, holding the patchwork. He doesn't flinch this time from the bright light that shines directly into his eyes.

"Are you here to kill me?" he says, morbidly calm.

"No," says Stefano gently, pointing the torch away.

"It is probably best," says Georg, turning to him, eyes wide, glassy, but the way he has focused on Stefano, there is awareness as well. "I have nothing now."

"You have much, Georg."

"I want to be alone," he says, and then he closes his eyes and appears to end the conversation.

"I will leave you then," says Stefano.

"She's out there somewhere," Georg says suddenly.

"Who?" asks Stefano.

He doesn't answer.

"Are you talking about Monique?"

Georg is silent.

Stefano crouches in the doorway to be on the same level. He is eager to read more of Monique's letters, to learn more about her. There are things here that haven't been said, that Rosalind has kept to herself, and Erich, too.

"Do you remember her?" says Stefano. "Do you remember seeing her here?"

He waits, but there is no response.

"Do you remember what just happened?"

"You should leave here," Georg responds.

Stefano reluctantly moves to step outside.

"I don't want to be here," Georg says, his voice strangled, desolate. "Earlier tonight, you said that you would help me."

"Yes," says Stefano.

1943

Stefano passed the letter to Toni.

"What is this?"

"I have been called back. I have to report for duty next week."

Toni looked at Stefano curiously. "What do you want me to do about it?"

"That is what I have come to talk to you about. I am not going. I am defecting like you, and I will also have to go underground."

"That is good, my friend," said Toni, patting him on the back.

Though Stefano knew he could no longer fight on behalf of Germany, he still had some reservations about his defection from the army. With the streets full of suspicion and treachery, he was worried about his mother and sisters. He wondered if they would be in danger not only because of what he was planning to do, but also because of the activities that Il Furioso had been involved in so far: the antigovernment messages and the stockpiling of weapons, along with the possibility that someone outside their group would betray them.

Outwardly, Il Furioso was displaying its loyalty to the new Salò government to allay suspicion, the group's members pretending to be excited by news of Germany's successes to others they spoke to in the streets. Privately, they were on edge, and relieved to have not been betrayed during the initial roundup of Mussolini's traitors. But time was another enemy. They would have to make decisions swiftly: either to break away from Verona and make the journey southward to fight alongside the Allies, or to join the resistance in the North.

Alberto was regularly in touch with the north and west alpine partisans who had formed after Mussolini was returned. Alberto would report on the successful activities of some, as well as news of those who had been caught and slaughtered. If the resistance was to win any fight, they would need more men.

"I have been ordered by Salò to go to the Eastern Front, but I cannot fight against my own brothers, the Allies," announced Fedor angrily at the following night's meeting. "We have to do something. We have to commence our own fight against the regime. I believe that we must join our northern brothers in the mountains."

"I agree," said Stefano. "But we also have to think about our families. Remember, they are searching for dissenters everywhere. We were lucky that our names were not revealed during the mass executions. There are some out there who have heard of our true loyalties, and soon it will not be safe for anyone here to leave their doors."

Nina had been sitting quietly, listening, until then. "Mamma and I can take care of ourselves while you fight. Or maybe we can come with you."

"No!" said Stefano. "It is too dangerous, Nina. You must go south. The churches are helping people through. You must convince Teresa also if you can."

"You know that she will not leave here. We do not speak much. But regardless, I am not going without you and Toni!"

"I agree with Stefano," said Toni, catching the indignation in his wife's eyes.

Two days later more Veronese who had links to the resistance were publicly executed. Fury and outrage kept building within their group, and like an active volcano, Il Furioso was ready to burst. This sad news only strengthened the decision to fight alongside the partisans. With their defection to be shortly noticed when they did not report for duty, Stefano and the rest of the group had moved to Conti's to hide temporarily, since Conti had not been conscripted and was unlikely to be tracked. From there they planned their trip to the Alps to join other members of the resistance. Stefano would do this for his cousin, in his honor, and he would make his father proud. He did not want an Italy run by Germany.

And there was no choice now but for their families to leave for the South.

"I'm afraid this has to be," Toni said to Nina. "You cannot stay here, and you cannot join us, not with our baby." And though Nina had objected, her protests were weaker now. She knew she couldn't put the baby in danger, and her going north with the group would be a hindrance to the espionage work they were contemplating.

Radios had been banned completely, and news could only come through Conti's and Fedor's contacts, if they weren't shot first.

Present-day 1945

Stefano knocks softly on the window near the sofa where Rosalind sits weeping. They lock eyes through the glass before she stands to let him in. She has dried herself and replaced her wet clothes with a housecoat.

"Georg is in the hut." Stefano follows her back to the sofa, where he sits close beside her. "He says he wishes to stay there. I think you should lock the door and leave him out there."

"Everything is worsening," she says. "I cannot see that it will ever get better."

"He needs medical help."

"I have been fooling myself about my husband. I don't think our relationship will ever return to normal."

Stefano doesn't wish to talk about their marriage.

"He is afraid of Erich," says Stefano, changing the tone, remembering how agitated Georg was at the sight of him, his hands opening and tightening.

"He is not sure how to be around people. He probably senses that Erich doesn't like him, or perhaps he is jealous of Erich. He might think that he's taking me away. Or worse."

"Why would he think that?"

"Why does Georg think anything strange at all? It is all due to the same reason. All because of a bullet."

"And the drugs," says Stefano.

"He has been growing more unstable," she says. "At first the drugs were making him passive, but the more he took, the more he wanted, and now he reacts badly. He breaks things. He broke things in Erich's house."

"He told me earlier, when I went and spoke to him outside, that Erich doesn't live there. That the house belongs to him, not Erich."

Rosalind's lips press together.

"You cannot take notice of what he says." She turns to face him. "I want to thank you. I know I didn't sound grateful for saving my life, but I am. Some days I think perhaps . . . well sometimes it might be for the best if he would get it over with and put me out of my misery."

"You should not think such things."

She is weeping again, silently, her face turned away so he cannot see the tears. He remembers the sounds of his mother's cries that weren't silent. He remembers the last night he spent with her, and the sadness at being apart from her, Nina, Toni, and the others, the fear of losing everyone who mattered.

Rosalind lies back down on the couch. "Would you stay awhile?" she asks.

Something about her request sounds too restrictive, but he must do what he has to.

"Yes."

7 August 1942

Dear Papa,
I am still in Vienna. Erich made many inquiries about
your whereabouts but to no avail. I've been miserable
thinking about you, wondering if you have been taken
elsewhere. Erich thinks you have been transferred to a
camp far away. I cried for days when he told me. But I
will never give up on you, Papa.

We will soon be leaving for Germany to stay at the
river houses with Rosalind and Georg, and I am praying
for this time to come quickly. It is painfully boring here.
The women I am expected to mix with here talk about
subjects that don't interest me. I can't bear the thought
of going to another function. They are always trying to
impress one another with their wealth and their knowl-
edge of politics, of which there is very little. This tedious
talk is something I bear, and I can't say what I really
think of anything. I want to tell them they are all wrong.
I want to tell them about my friends who were sent away,

about how Alain would climb fences to avoid the Gestapo on the way home from the club. But I bite my tongue until it bleeds, and I think of you and grow another inch taller.

Today I walked to the square in Vienna. It is not quite the same Austria as I remember. There are soldiers in the street, and it is not as colorful. People do not dress up like they used to. Traditional folk dances and festivals are held, but there is a certain formality to them rather than gaiety. And once they are over, we all go home. In the days when I was small, I remember the dances and parades that you took me to. I remember that we would hang around the square, all of us, the whole town, until late in the night. I remember the fireworks. It is a different Austria, one that you will not recognize and one that I daresay you cannot spy through the cell walls that most likely surround you.

Sometimes I see you in the square where the men play cards. I know you liked to tease the older ones who came there, and they would joke that you were the baby of their group. You took me once; do you remember? And you bought me ice cream, and I sat and watched you play cards, and when I got bored, I would run after the pigeons in the square.

The streets here are still beautiful, but I wish you were with me. It is so lonely sometimes.

I pray daily that you are being treated well, wherever you may be.

Love,
Monique

CHAPTER 21
ROSALIND

There is a knot in Rosalind's stomach. She saw the look that Georg gave Erich. *He knows,* she thinks. *He remembers things, perhaps everything.* Part of her wants Stefano gone so that he does not learn the truth, but part of her, the dark part, the part she struggles to recognize, now wants Georg gone also.

He has been getting worse lately. Several weeks earlier he picked up chairs and threw them across the room. Now this, an attempt on her life.

"So, you saw him at least. Georg. How did he look?" she says.

"Placid. The hut must be a special place."

She closes her eyes to block out an image.

"Yes," she says. "We have not always had a great marriage." She is thinking, remembering Berlin. It was the best time they had, but even then it wasn't great. She can't tell Stefano this. How to explain a relationship like that? One built on friendship and then . . . what?

"Monique used to say that love isn't immoral in any form," she says aloud, and then wonders why she said it. Monique used to say such things, and Rosalind would scoff. Though now she is wondering if Monique had it right, whether Rosalind could throw away her prejudice or, better still, drown it in the river. She feels the need to talk to Stefano, to tell him things.

"We met here. We grew up together. After Georg joined the army, we used to meet in Berlin and later married there. I don't believe that he loved me as much as I loved him. I always thought he was too good for me." She stops herself. Stefano is watching, leaving spaces for her to fill in. He makes it easy to talk and does not appear to judge.

"He was a good fighter. He won medals for bravery. He faced battle head-on. The more he left to fight, the braver he got." She pauses. "But it was almost suicidal in a way. He would want to be at the front of every battle. I heard stories that he always put himself in the firing line. That was Georg. He thought he was invincible."

"Of course, you miss him very much, yes? The way he was?"

She contemplates the words, swallows hard. In that moment, she is not sure that she does.

"He was a good man in a bad situation," he continues.

Something about this comment bothers her, some deeper thought that is masked by her aching head and the trauma that has just occurred.

"I should let you rest," he says. "You look tired. You've been through a lot."

He touches her hand, and she instinctively draws it away. She is not used to intimacy, to someone being so close, to someone wanting to know so much about her.

"Please excuse me. I will take something for my headache."

In her bedroom at the far side of the house, she reaches for her medical bag on the table beside the window. Through the sheer curtains she can see the top bedroom window of the house next door, where Monique and Erich once stayed. The sight of it sends a cold shiver up her spine. If only she could forget. If only she could start over again.

She stares inside the bag at the bottle that Erich had brought her *in the event that circumstances are irreversible*. She understood the message and the strength of the chemical. She had outwardly dismissed the notion, but she had kept it just the same.

Deep down she knows why. In extraordinary situations, she is capable of anything. She has been sacrificing for love that is not returned. And perhaps Erich's way is kinder.

August 1942

Rosalind had received a letter from Monique that said she and Erich were spending a week at the river later that month. As promised, Erich had orchestrated that Georg could take the same week, which he'd already been made aware of. Rosalind applied for time off, something she rarely asked for, though she was annoyed that it was Monique who had contacted her and not Georg, annoyed that Georg had not reached out to her first.

Georg advised her later by telegram to say that he would meet Rosalind directly there. They had arranged that Georg and Rosalind would stay in her *Oma*'s house, and Monique and Erich in the other. Meanwhile the cousins' grandmother took the opportunity to visit her son in Berlin, to give the two couples some "marital privacy."

Rosalind was the first to arrive, and she wiped the dust that had gathered on the furniture at Georg's, which had sat empty for some time, and collected fresh wildflowers and placed them in vases in both houses. There were a dozen geese and instructions from her grandmother to take care of them, to feed them the hay from the barn. Rosalind brought apricots and figs that she paid dearly for, as well as a chicken and sugar, and her grandmother had left some bread, jam, and tea for their arrival. The others were expected that evening, and Rosalind prepared a meal in advance.

Erich and Monique arrived next. Monique was dazzling in a pink summer dress, with shoestring straps, and white sandals. Her lips shone with color and her hair was cut just above her shoulders, brushed and much tamer than it used to be.

Rosalind was happy that Monique had moved away and moved on with her life, but there was a selfish motivation to remove the attention that was always on her. She did not miss the troubles that followed Monique, her diversion of Georg's attention, and the sharing of Rosalind's parents. She was relieved that the couple looked happy, and in a rare, unselfish way, she was happy for them, too. Had she been too hard, jealous of how easily Monique approached life, and bitter that she did not carry the same traits that made life more bearable? She felt dowdy next to Monique, her blond wispy hair pulled back sharply so that the color looked more mousy than fair. But that day she didn't seem to care as much. Rosalind was genuinely pleased to see her cousin and had been lonely without her. They seemed to be getting on much better than they had in Berlin.

But if Rosalind had looked deeper, had not been too busy in the kitchen to examine the couple with any great scrutiny, she would have seen that there was something unsettling about their relationship. They seemed content and talkative, Erich keen to go for a swim, like Monique, but they didn't make eye contact when they talked about their life together, and their shared experiences lacked substance. She failed to notice that Monique's sentences stopped shorter than they used to; there were fewer descriptions and exclamations.

"Have you looked for your father?" said Rosalind.

"Yes," said Monique. And that was all she had said, because the result was there in the shortness of the answer, and Erich had moved closer to Rosalind to discuss the weather outside, the sudden burst of heat that arrived with them on the train.

They had already begun to eat when Georg arrived. He did not arrive in uniform, not majestically like Erich in his exquisitely cut, newly issued gray jacket and hat that spelled out clearly his importance and superiority.

Georg had kissed Rosalind and swung her around just the same as when they were younger, and joy coursed through her body. She had loved him always, the feeling stronger than ever.

Georg shook hands with Erich, and Monique now had someone else to talk to, since Erich seemed, even at close quarters, to be in a separate room from everyone else. It was his way, to stay distant, to watch more than participate, and it was something Rosalind found uncomfortable. As if they were always under an examination they were unaware of.

They drank too much wine that night. With wine at least, Erich spoke more than Georg, who smoked one cigarette after another. He looked debonair using his long silver cigarette holder and waving it around casually. Monique relaxed and told about the interesting townspeople in Austria, occasionally glancing at Erich. How they mistrusted her at first but were jealous also of her handsome husband. Erich smiled briefly, but he did not look particularly impressed or buoyed by the description, since validation was something he could manage himself for the most part.

They reminisced, Monique and Georg, including Rosalind in their memories as well. Georg would put his hand on his wife's knee occasionally. Was it possessiveness? Rosalind wondered. She hoped anyway. She wanted to be possessed by someone, to be wanted, desired, pined for.

And then it was time for bed and Monique left first, yawning as she walked away, but planning an early morning swim. Georg seemed disappointed that she was leaving so soon. Erich seemed reluctant to leave at all, much to Rosalind's regret. She and Georg had had so little physical intimacy, and despite the rushed wedding night, she had been thinking a lot about him, about his body lying naked against her, about rubbing her hand across the taut skin on his chest.

Finally Georg said he was sleepy. Erich took the hint and left quickly. When she and Georg were at last alone in the attic bedroom, she changed into the lavender chemise he had presented to her on their wedding night. He told her the food was wonderful. She climbed into bed first, with its soft mattress that sank in the middle, and he took off his shirt and trousers, leaving on just his shorts, and climbing in also. He pulled up the sheet and rolled over to face away from her.

Rosalind lay beside him, facing his back. She traced her finger down his spine. She could see the sun line at the base of his neck, darkened from his days in the field.

In just a few minutes she heard his breathing deepen, the breaths stretching longer, his back rising and falling evenly.

He deserves much rest, she had told herself. He had just come from the front line, something they did not discuss at the dinner table. He'd had the longest journey to get there, an army truck from the field and then two trains. He was thinner, gaunt, she reflected as she lay there.

She switched off the lamp beside the bed and rolled over to spy through the window that looked across to the bedroom where Erich and Monique would be sleeping. Their light was still on. She could see their shadows on the curtains of the room on the second floor at the end of the house. The pair disappeared from view, and then the light was extinguished. She was thinking that tomorrow was a new day and Georg would be recovered from travel and that she had a lot to be grateful for. She dreamed of Monique drowning in the river, screaming for help, not as a young girl, but as she was then, in her pretty summer dress.

She woke to silence.

A shaft of moonlight streaked the bedroom furniture and the empty spaces around her. She was in the middle of the bed alone. She walked to the window to look at the house next door. Monique's room was in darkness. Rosalind stopped to listen for sounds from Georg, but she heard nothing.

She treaded carefully down the stairs, wondering whether he'd moved to the room below, perhaps to sleep alone, and desiring some space. She took pity on him, imagining the cramped spaces where he'd likely been forced to sleep.

He was not on the lower level, and the front door was slightly ajar. She opened it farther, expecting to find Georg smoking on the front bench and staring at the wood, but she was greeted only by the coolness of the night.

She was about to try the other door to scan the backyard, when she heard a voice in the distance, much like Monique's, the sound coming from the woods.

Out amid the trees, she glimpsed the silver beam that stretched across the river; then she veered right to the secret pathway leading to their hideaway.

She was on the narrow strip, where trees leaned inward in an attempt to take back the path, when someone loomed out of the darkness in front of her. Moonlight struck the shock of strawberry-gold hair and the top of his sharply angled cheekbone. He was startled and stopped suddenly so they wouldn't collide, before squeezing past her to rush away. It was only once he'd passed, in the seconds after their meeting had taken place, that she realized Georg was naked.

The past and envy and fear that had dissipated with marriage and time reared repugnantly, replaced only by the dread that there was still more to witness.

She was still standing in a state of shock and fear when Monique stepped into view, startled also by Rosalind's appearance in the wood.

"Rosa!" she cried.

She was wearing a cream satin nightgown, which shimmered and competed with the very star that had illuminated her.

Monique was now speechless in the dark, but she turned her head slightly in the direction of the hut, to the place where the crime had been committed, before turning back to face Rosalind and reaching for Rosalind's hands that were clutching at the air in front of her, searching for something to support her.

"Rosa, we have to talk—"

"How could you," Rosalind whispered harshly, and bile rose in her throat.

"Rosalind—"

"Get away!" said Rosalind, who no longer wanted to see her, who turned then and ran.

"He is wrong for you," Monique called after her.

Upstairs there was no sign of Georg. But she knew he was unlikely to return now that they had been caught. The single thing that had hung over her head for years, the fear, had finally happened. *Why now? Why had he tortured her all these years?*

She packed her bag upstairs, throwing everything into it hastily, except the lavender chemise she had worn for Georg, tossed to a corner of the room. Monique had disappeared to find Georg no doubt. The light in the bedroom next door was then switched on. It was sometime after two in the morning, as she walked past Erich's house, barefoot, uncaring of her appearance at that moment, that she saw a familiar figure on the front bench.

Erich knows, she thought at the time. It was why they weren't talking. And more importantly, he didn't seem to care.

"Goodbye, Rosalind," Erich said.

She ignored him and walked briskly to the station, hatred pumping through her veins, and she waited on the platform till morning to catch the first train back to Berlin.

Only when on the train did she allow herself to cry, telling herself that she would leave Georg, but she knew she never could. He would have to leave her first.

A week later his letter arrived. He told her that he couldn't wait for the war to be over so they could be together. And in the silent messages between the lines, he had somehow made it clear that she was the one he loved. She was comforted momentarily that Monique was just a distraction. Monique had always made herself one, but time would see an end to it.

Rosalind would love Georg still, and she would fight harder. And she forgave him, pushing the truth and the memories deep down, drowning them until they could not be revived. But also deep down was the feeling that sooner or later Monique would pay for the betrayal.

Present-day 1945

Stefano waits for her in the living room. She hadn't noticed before, but his clothes are still wet, his shirt smeared with dirt, and the bottoms of his trousers muddied.

"I have some spare clothes. Let me get them for you."

She retrieves several items from a laundry hamper under the stairs.

"These belong to Georg," she says as she steps near him to unbutton his shirt.

"No, I'm fine," he says, gently pushing back her hands, but she nudges his hands officiously out of the way and continues the unbuttoning. He puts up his arms, suggesting some kind of surrender.

"Tell me, Stefano, did you love someone in the war?"

"There was no time for love."

She peels off his shirt. How many patients did she do this for? So many. Too many. Bloodied torsos. She puts the images away and focuses on the body in front of her.

"It would be best for Georg if I just put him out of his misery. If I just put him to sleep," she says. "It is the kindest way perhaps."

"It is kinder if he gets better care," he says, but she isn't listening. She is thinking about what she wants to do. She wants Stefano to take her far away from the life she has here. Away from Erich and Georg and memories and years of belief and false hope.

Stefano's burn scars, skin pink and puckered, extend up the side of his body to his shoulder and down his arm. She is used to damage. And then her eyes stop on the numbers on his other arm, and she feels she owes him something for his suffering.

"It must have been terrible," she says, laying her hands flat on his bare chest, and thinking of Georg, and remembering that Erich gave her a drug to end her husband's life quickly if it came to it. *Humane also,* Erich had added, and she fights off the image of Georg. She wants to be free of both of them. She wants new experiences, better ones that will block out those that came before. She no longer has control over what she is about to do, and she leans forward, kisses the scarring on Stefano's shoulder, smells the salt on his skin, and wonders if this is what Monique did with men, if she took control.

She looks up at Stefano, who is looking down, his features indistinct in the dim light, then stands on tiptoe and moves her lips close to his. He is very still, waiting for her, she thinks. And his lips, she feels them, close enough to kiss, her hands still against his chest. He moves slightly, a response, willing, she thinks, and her lips are over his now, and beneath her hands his body burns hot.

He turns his head slightly and gently holds her wrist.

"I'm sorry . . . ," he says, and sighs.

"Pretend there is no tomorrow," she whispers hesitantly.

"I can't," he says. "Tomorrow is always the day I'm waiting for, what I dream about."

The words are like a knife in her chest. The rejection, the feeling of being unloved. *Does it ever go away?*

"You aren't ready for this," he says quietly. "You have been through a lot. You must think of your husband. Tomorrow I am gone."

And there is no future, she thinks. There is no tomorrow. There is no Stefano, no Michal. She has chosen her own destiny. And she is crying and weeping and apologizing. He tells her it doesn't matter, that he will stay with her tonight, and she collapses against him, and he lifts her and carries her into the bedroom and places her gently on the mattress. He slides in beside her, arms around her protectively, like a friend, like a parent, she thinks, though she has had no such experience before.

In the night she tells him about the baby they lost, that she had become pregnant on one of Georg's visits. That after a certain particular event by the river, which she can't speak of, the pair became closer. She doesn't give details, and he doesn't interrupt to ask.

And she tells him about Berlin in the final days, of the Russians and the rapes and the rage. She had walked home pregnant, hungry, sleep deprived. People didn't notice, or care. People were escaping Berlin, escaping the Russians who were thundering into Germany in their tanks like a herd of wild beasts, and as she traveled home, the rest of the Allies came in from the west, majestic, as if they had not seen a war. No one stopped to help her. Her own people, desperate now, like animals, she said. Humanity had left, and she feels numb at the memory, but not surprised. There was little goodwill. It was about saving herself and escaping. She was no better than they were, she admits to Stefano, self-ishly uncaring of others at that point.

Her weeping eventually stops, and she is thinking that Stefano is a good man, a man with integrity, and kind. He has sisters, he tells her. He used to comfort them also.

"I'm sorry," she says. "It has been so hard living with Georg. All the secrets."

"What secrets?" he asks, but she is too sleepy to talk now.

Sometime in the night she is aware that he leaves briefly, most likely to check on the boy, and then another time to get up and shine a light on his watch in his bag, before climbing back into bed, but it doesn't matter what he does.

In sleep she can blissfully forget her wrongs. And for the first time in so long, she sleeps deeply.

CHAPTER 22

ERICH

Shadows stretch across the street, and rooftops catch fire in the early morning light that patterns the town in grays and gold. Erich stands at the window to gaze upon the peace. The baker's horse and cart clatter over the cobblestones and head toward the Russian-filled hotel on the outskirts of town to deliver the freshly baked rolls of rye.

Erich is thinking over the events of the previous evening. *To my last night in Germany,* those were the words Stefano said. Prophetic words, almost a challenge. It could be Erich's last night in Germany, too. It is possible.

He steps quietly into the child's bedroom. He thinks of her as "the" child rather than "his" child because he had so little time with her in the first year. At first, in some ways, she was a disappointment, a burden—sickly, awkward, crying for her mother. But by growing rapidly into a quiet acceptance of her new situation, she has also grown on him. She has intelligent, inquisitive eyes. She watches his hands as he speaks, and she looks at body language to form her own opinions. She listens to sounds and repeats them. He must steer her strengths toward superiority, instill in her qualities that would make his mother proud, and keep her loyal to her country.

Hair the color of ripened hay fans across the pillow, and Genevieve's chest rises and falls in loud, shallow breaths. *The medicine has been slow to work,* said Marceline the previous evening. *She needs a doctor,* she also said. That is not possible, unfortunately. She will have to weather the worst of it and prove that she is a survivor like him. His mother lost two babies to fever without shedding a tear. It was nature's way of eliminating the weaker ones, his mother had told him.

In spirit, Genevieve is like him, distant, watchful, but in looks, she is so like Monique that sometimes when she turns to listen, he sees the older version, the raising of one side of her pretty mouth in a sort of contempt.

He touches her forearm and feels its warmth. She moves it away slightly. Even in sleep she is cautious. He doesn't like that she is hidden here, with her future uncertain, transferred from place to place. He must find stability, a home for her like he had when growing up. She has no idea yet what it is like to live freely in the sunshine. She has always lived in the shadows. He wants the golden arms of light from outside to reach across her, too.

Marceline is already up. She has boiled an egg and serves it with some leavened bread cut thinly, toasted and smeared with lard. He eats it at the kitchen table while she pours him a cup of coffee.

"Are you feeling all right?" she asks. "You aren't coming down with something also?"

"I am fine," he answers. "A restless sleep."

She is good to him, but he knows her concern is paid for. Marceline was raised by French parents, but she and her family are more German than French in many ways. They were on the secret German payroll, regularly sending the Nazi headquarters in northern France lists of people who were of special interest, those whose interests weren't aligned with their government.

He leaves and enters the street. Today he will travel with Stefano, but first he must retrieve the tin buried on the hill behind the river house; documents kept there in case his location is ever betrayed. Inside are several sets of false identities, like the French ones he carries for himself and Genevieve, and a list of safe houses for Nazis on the run. But most precious of all, enclosed are copies of his father's designs that have hardly seen the light of day, and that, time permitting, might have changed the state of play in battles to come. They might be something he can bargain with should there be a need.

Erich thinks about the intruder as he enters the track near the river. Stefano appears comfortable with the man he is, neither fearful nor gallant. He is politely inquisitive but not intrusive, as if he has quickly gleaned the information he needs. Most curiously, he bears no grudges. The Italians Erich dealt with were civil but at the same time looked as though they would cut his throat at the first opportunity. Understandably. Stefano has a haunted look like most from the camps, but he carries himself taller than most prisoners Erich has seen since. He likes him, perhaps more than he should.

The photo of Monique drew Stefano more than Rosalind's feeble attempt at attention, though Stefano tried to hide the interest. Erich is not surprised. Monique looks beautiful in the photo. People are drawn to her. They always have been. Except for Erich.

He is comforted in knowing that there are still some Italians loyal to the German alliance. And Stefano, he is convinced, is the pathway to a normal future. He and Genevieve could travel by car to southern Italy, then across the Mediterranean Sea to places where they could roam free. Germans have become prisoners in their own towns. It has entered his mind over several days, but not until this morning has he thought so hard about it, nor has the resolve for his new future been so firm.

Marceline, of course, speaks French fluently, and his French might also pass with the Italians. They must wear German only on their hearts if the three of them are to survive such a journey. And return one day for the new Germany when it emerges, when its power is restored.

Erich opens the front door of Georg's father's house. The kitchen is quiet, the kettle cold. On the top floor, he can see Michal, sunk in dreams, his arms and legs stretched out across the bed, but Stefano is missing. He may have changed his mind, decided that he will walk after all; then Erich thinks about the leg injury and the child. *Why wait for all this time only to walk now?*

He has a sinking feeling, an odd jolt to the heart, at the other thought that enters quickly after: that Stefano spent the night with Rosalind. Rosalind, who told him on the first night that she wanted Stefano gone, to not allow strangers into their world. Rosalind, who claimed that Stefano was still the enemy, would have watched his execution if she'd had the choice. She was fiercely loyal to the party, like Erich, but lacked vision, was easily misguided, and only changed her opinion of Stefano once he'd shown himself better as something interesting, someone who might change the course of her life also. He had perhaps altered both their perceptions of others, of strangers, of people who did not fit with Germany's ideas.

His eyes wander over Georg's bleak and neglected house. He wishes to be free of the misery these walls hold, with the imprint of Monique and Georg, and of times that need to be forgotten.

He walks back outside and squints at the shine off the river that has infiltrated the spaces between the narrow tree trunks. The feelings here are hollow and cold, the sounds of wildlife obtrusive, the houses unfortified. He likes solid buildings, close together, that blend into one another. It is too open here and too primitive.

The house next door is still. He stops to search for the sounds that crack open the stillness, and the smells: the squeak of the water pump, the smoke from the coal burning through the flue in Rosalind's kitchen, doors opening and closing. He is used to patterns; he has studied them.

He has always been good at reading people, at learning their habits in the shortest time possible.

But today the pattern here is broken.

He does not wish to see Rosalind if he can help it, nor see the hostility that hangs in every expression. She has expected everything, food, medicines, even his protection, without showing gratitude. He could be free of her completely today. He walks to the side of her house with a feeling, not so much a sense of danger but an impending change in the wind that might ultimately lead to something he cannot control.

He stands back slightly from Rosalind's ground-floor window and peers through the sheer curtains to view the shapes within. Stefano lies on Rosalind's bed, one arm draped across her.

Erich steps back and out of view. What he has seen alters things. Was his instinct wrong? Is Stefano not the man he thought he was? A traitor, someone dangerous perhaps? But these are the thoughts of people grasping for things to blame. What he feels most is jealousy, something that he did not expect to feel.

November 1942

He was called back to Berlin. His mother was pleased to see him. His father greeted him with a handshake as if they were associates, unrelated. He couldn't help but notice a change, the aging. He knew that his father's work was less about design and more about efficiency with what they had. His father would not enjoy that, patching things, working under the Reich minister of armaments. And at that point, manpower and modifications superseded the need for creativity and foresight.

Horst asked Erich about Monique, who had stayed behind in Austria. He wanted to know more about Erich's wife than his son. Was she fitting in? Did she miss her family? Did she have employment to keep her busy? *She is the type of girl who needs to keep busy; give her a job, maybe children,* he said, more softly, less formally than when he was addressing his son. Horst, always busy, left their meeting quickly.

Erich made his way to an office for briefings by the senior ministry. They needed his help. They knew he had connections as well as a sixth sense. They knew he was an expert at extracting the truth, often without the need for force, because, as they had found, torture did not always work.

There were people underground undermining authority and distorting views. They had tried to find them—a group that had grown in size, but they had been unable to catch any of the ringleaders. He was sent to an address in the city. He was looking forward to this work, to working back in Berlin. He missed it, he realized, places where interrogations were civil, where he did not have to witness the painful extortions at the camp, did not have to face blood.

Erich banged on the door on the top landing. When there was no answer, he ordered the two officers accompanying him to break down the door. And when they did, they found no one there, only traces: a coffee cup that still had the remains of lipstick, an overfilled ashtray, papers and newsletters scattered across the floor. They searched cupboards, pulled out drawers, pulled apart cushions. They did not find address books, but they found piles of leaflets among the papers with anti-Nazi drawings and slogans, and inciting unrest, accusing the government of operating illegally. The leaflets were telling people to reject Nazism. There were also clippings from Western newspapers about the war, articles smuggled in by resistance members, about the campaigns, about Allied successes.

Only a couple of years earlier, Erich had started this work, and he had grown to crave it, like an addiction, the hunt. In Austria there was not enough of this. They captured people, and he questioned, but it was not really a hunt. He was a born leader and interrogator, which had earned him the title of "the pinscher," the rat-catching dog. He was clearheaded, capable, and calm under pressure. He was already someone of importance.

"They've gone," said one of the officers. "There are no clothes in the drawers."

He knew why they had moved location. They were tipped off, and he also knew who was behind the drawings. He had seen similar caricatures before and said that he was ashamed, but she had just laughed and said she could draw what she wanted, then brushed him away like an insect.

Erich would sort out the problem himself. He would see to it.

He did not take the official car. This one was personal. People seemed to sit up straighter and avoid eye contact with Erich when he stepped on a bus to travel home, while many found it hard to look away. He was recognized at public functions, standing near the front of the delegations. He was a celebrity of sorts.

From the bus, he watched the people on the streets, aware that the personal circumstances of some had declined with the rationing of foods, and the threat of Allied air raids hovered. But still the people of Berlin remained stoic and dedicated to the Reich. Small children in nice coats skipped along the pavement and waved at the Gestapo. He was proud of this city and of his country, and of the work he did to protect their futures. He would not let Claudine seek to destroy all that he'd achieved.

He entered his parents' house, greeted by his brothers with enthusiasm, both of them eager to follow their oldest sibling into service. The second brother was then thirteen, the youngest, nearly nine.

"Where's Claud?"

"She is at Ovid's house," his mother answered, in a tone that sounded accusing rather than informative. She had known it, too. That Claudine had become more difficult. She refused to work and disappeared for days at a time. She argued with her mother about small things, about the raising of the children. But mostly she was ungrateful for the new Germany.

His mother ladled some broth into a bowl for him. He reluctantly sat to eat, but his mind was elsewhere.

His father couldn't be there tonight, his mother explained. He was rarely home early, and when he was, he was exhausted. He was a consultant now, an important one, said his mother, though Erich already knew this. Knew that he traveled with the führer and his inner circle. *Like sheep that never quite know the direction,* his father quipped once, and Erich had not at the time recognized the growing resentment.

His brothers were chatty. He was not in the mood to hear about their day. He was only thinking about Claudine and containing his anger.

He didn't finish his dinner but pushed back his chair to leave. His mother nodded. She understood that sometimes things couldn't wait. That he must do what he had to. She respected the duty and pressure that fell on him.

It wasn't a short walk to Ovid's house, but he welcomed the time to think. He knocked on the door, and Ovid's father answered. He held the door only partway open. His expressionless face was less than welcoming. He had never liked Erich.

"Is my sister here?" Erich asked, dismissing any formalities or politeness.

"You will have to wait outside." The older man shut the door, and Erich watched his shadow disappear through the obscuring bubbled-glass panel on the top half of the door.

It was an insult to someone as highly placed as Erich. He could have easily reported the man for disrespect toward an officer, but the older man was not the target of Erich's anger.

Claudine opened the door and stepped outside, wearing a light blouse and skirt. She wrapped her arms around herself protectively, not from the cold but from the confrontation that was about to occur, her expression belligerent. The absence of her coat meant she was not planning to talk for long.

Despite the animosity between them whenever he first saw her, he would always remember the days in the country, her fearlessness, the times she hated their separation, how she had cried when he would leave for youth camps. It was hard to believe they were once close, but he could not afford to dwell on such times. There was the job he must do.

"Why are you here?" she asked.

"I went to the apartment of your university friends. I know what you have been doing."

"What is that?"

"You have been distributing pamphlets siding with anarchy. You have been drawing pictures that belittle our führer. Childish! You and your group . . . It has to stop!"

"Ovid is not involved."

"I know that's a lie. I would have had your friends arrested and spared you and your boyfriend, and not been here tonight, but you have forced this meeting. Even before I was given the commission to seek out the distributors of such lies, I had seen you both go to meetings at places that had been investigated before."

"And what are you going to do about it? Tell on me?" she said with feigned bemusement. He recognized the familiar grin that was once genial, that he had once warmed to, but which now meant opposition.

"Yes. If it comes to that, I will. First, though, I will tell Father. He must be included to make decisions here."

"Go ahead. He knows what I am doing. He doesn't care. Mother is like you! Brainwashed!"

He was angry at the mention of their mother, at the lack of respect. The words about their father fell quickly to the back of his thoughts. He dismissed them. His sister always had a vivid imagination, the gift of storytelling, or lying. It was hard to tell the difference sometimes.

She looked back up the road. It was an area heavily populated with students in accommodations not of wealth. Most houses there were small, with modest furnishings. Claudine liked it better there, she once said. She liked not having furnishings that had been stolen from those put in prisons. She could live with herself better.

She looked down at the cobblestones, which were shiny and black from a light rain.

"You have always wanted to control people and what they think. You can't control everyone, Erich. You can't control me."

"My dear sister, that is where you are wrong. I have the power to control you and stop your friends from illegal practices. If you continue, I will interrogate all the printers, all the teachers and students at your university, until someone reveals the ringleader of this madness and false propaganda."

She shifted then. He had her attention. Her face took on the fierceness of a lioness. It was funny to Erich how he could face men, large and hostile when interrogated, but who never rattled him. It had only ever been Claudine whom he was somewhat afraid of. It was perhaps the thought that he couldn't control her. Despite everything she was given, despite being on the winning side, she was freely making a choice; something that most had accepted was no longer available to them. He had always admired her courage, but he despised her disloyalty.

He decided to take a softer tone.

"Claud, I don't want to report you. You're my sister."

"Then don't. I will not stop doing this. What Hitler is doing is wrong. What this country has become is unrecognizable."

"How would you even know? You were too young to take any political side when Hitler was voted in. Too young to see any change at all."

"I see things more clearly than you. I see the truth, my dear brother. I see the people who are now locked up in prison, intelligent human beings, Erich. Locked up because they either were Jewish or had their own opinion. Harassed, shamed, and persecuted for having one that does not suit the Nazi order. You are too wrapped up in your own seniority to see the damage, Brother, the lies."

"I see disloyalty by my sister. You have brought a very bad mark on this family if this gets out."

"Hitler has made a very bad mark on this country," she says. "First your wife, now me. How will you ever control these women? Her story is still being told in underground circles. It still brings a smile to our faces."

He did not like that she brought this up. It was humiliating that she talked about the incident with others, and he resented being reminded about Monique's past. Things had gone from bad to worse between Erich and his wife.

The two women had seen each other rarely when they had lived in Berlin, but on the occasions that they did, they would gravitate to each other. Claudine had admired Monique when she revealed her experience of storming into the Gestapo's office. Erich had later chastised Monique about mentioning the incident. But his sister had refused to let it go, retelling the story at every opportunity. Even this far away from Berlin, Monique was still a bad influence.

Claudine crossed her arms. He felt himself weakening. For the first time he felt trapped.

"Please, Claud! Stop all this, and I won't say anything."

"You can do as you please, but I will not stop."

"Then I will have you arrested."

"If you can find me."

His heart felt suddenly heavy. The wind was spiked with cold needles, but he was sweating underneath his coat. "Come home where we will talk some more."

"Don't you see, Erich? I'm not coming home. I can't. Not now. Not ever. You should not have followed me here."

"It will kill Mama if you don't come home."

"I know you are lying. She hopes I don't come home. She does whatever it is that this Germany wants from her. We both know that. But you are not a true Nazi, are you, Erich? I wonder what Herr Führer would do if he knew what is hidden there beneath the uniform?"

The last piece was spoken cruelly.

"What are you saying?" he said.

"I know you, Erich. Everyone thinks you were doing Monique a favor, but I know the real reason you married Monique. There had to be something else in it for you."

He was cornered and confused by her words that held more animosity than she had ever used on him before. He went to speak, and then stopped. Ovid had come outside, carrying a suitcase, and Claudine's attention was diverted as he helped her into a coat he brought also.

"If you touch a hair on the heads of Ovid's family once I'm gone, I swear that I will despise you forever."

"Where are you going?"

"Goodbye, Erich! Don't come for me."

"You will be sorry, Claudine! If it isn't me that catches you, someone else will. I won't be able to stop them."

She laughed then, short and brittle.

"By all means come looking, I challenge you, but it is my wish that you never see me again. I loved you once, looked up to you. But I stopped loving you the moment you put on your Nazi suit."

As she walked away into the night, he yelled in her direction, but it sounded foolish even to his ears. He could not afford to lose control. He watched her vanish and felt a moment of bereavement. For the first time he questioned himself. She had made him do that.

The next day he went to see his father at the Berlin office to tell him about Claudine, to seek his advice. If it had been anyone but Claudine, he would have ordered them searched for and arrested without any further consultation.

His father seemed neither alarmed nor surprised.

"So be it. She is gone."

"Your daughter is a traitor, Father!" he hissed. "And something has to be done!"

"And what are you planning then, Erich?" he said, challenging him.

Erich did not know how to answer. He knew what he had to do, but it was difficult to say it aloud, to talk about his sister this way.

"I have lost my only daughter, Erich, and she has lost a family. I think that is enough punishment."

He was protecting the daughter he loved more than anything, and in that moment something else became clear.

"It was you who tipped her off so she could warn her friends!"

"What does it matter now?" he said, defeated. "What good have I done?"

"I must relieve myself of this case," said Erich, shocked by the admission. "I must send someone to find her."

"And what do you think will happen when they do? You have control of this, Erich, and I trust that you will make the right decision."

Erich looked at his father, at the red rims and saggy flesh below his eyes. He was not the same man, he thought. He appeared frail, less important suddenly.

"I lost her years ago," said Horst. "I saw it in her face, and it has always made me ashamed. Ashamed that one so young could see things long before me."

Erich was lost for words, wondering what he had missed about the pair of them. He decided then he could no longer seek advice from his father.

There was only one course. He would need to report her. She must go on the wanted list. And it would undoubtedly bring shame to the family, but it would prove that not even blood would stop him from becoming the best he could be. His loyalty would never be in doubt.

Present-day 1945

Erich returns to Georg's house. He does not want to come back if he can help it. There are traces of him here still that he must get rid of. He opens the door below the stairs to see the box of Monique's letters.

The letters are enclosed, but there is something different about them. The ribbon that holds them is not tied as tightly as he remembers, the letters not evenly together, as they were. Someone has touched them. It is unlikely to be Rosalind, since she would sooner burn the house down than enter it, or Georg, who is aware of so little.

He puts the letters in the fireplace and with matches sets them on fire. He should have destroyed them sooner. Monique had hidden them there, and he had found them. He is not sure why he kept them, perhaps to remind him of her treachery, justification that led to what he did.

Outside the front door, he looks across at Rosalind's house.

There is nothing there for him anymore. He and Stefano had made a connection. An unspoken alliance, or so he thought. But they are not the same after all.

And there is something about the day that feels wrong. Stefano still in Germany, Michal, an orphan randomly plucked off the side of the road and brought here, Rosalind in Stefano's arms, and Erich here, away from the people that matter. Everything is shifted, and no one is where they should be.

He looks up the hill and beyond that to a tall clump of trees that blocks the morning sun, and he heads that way, past the small grave of Rosalind's baby, until he reaches Monique and sees the mound of earth that has been disturbed by the rain, and small piles of earth clumped around the grave. He would not have left it so untidy. He would have cleared every last grain of loose soil. And then he sees it in the trees, a piece of color, of stripes, faded gold and blue, billowing in the breeze, haughtily, taunting him. He walks toward it, to the curtain, and sees the dark stains that litter the cloth as if by the flick of a paintbrush, a work of art on display.

He turns back to the earth and with his hands digs at the soil, compacted now with water, but he doesn't care that his pants are covered in soil, that his arms are stained and streaked with black earth, and he digs down and down, and there is nothing, no body, no Monique.

He senses danger.

Vehicles sound in the distance, the revving of their motors sounding urgent with the speed at which they are coming. From the ridge, he can see them faintly in the distance. He remembers the time that trucks came to his house; there was urgency then also.

He is tempted to dig up the tin, but there is no time; he cannot afford to be caught with the documents if his suspicion is correct. He will have to come back for them later. First, he must return to the town, to Genevieve, to his mother, and then he will return to deal with things here.

CHAPTER 23
STEFANO

Stefano can smell a faint odor of smoke mixed with the citrusy scent of Rosalind's hair. He can feel her slender body beneath the light robe. She had trusted him, and yet it was a trust that he wasn't expecting and did not want. So many people trusted him, and it is a weight of responsibility he now finds hard to bear. During the war, the responsibility of caring for those he loved had proved too great.

He climbs out of bed, careful not to disturb her, checks the watch in his bag before spying Erich through the curtain. He is standing at the front of the other house looking toward the woods before turning briefly to look at Rosalind's, in the direction of her room. Stefano puts up his hand, but Erich does not acknowledge him, instead turning toward the track that will take him back to the town.

Stefano must stop him. He must bring him back. He wonders now if Erich saw him with Rosalind, if he has got the wrong idea.

He throws his satchel over his shoulder and opens the door to hurry toward Erich, but Georg appears, blocking the doorway. He is like a cat, prowling in the night but always returning to be fed. It is perhaps by instinct now, and that likely saved him from doing anything final. But he looks crazed, as if he could still do something dangerous. He is shivering, but not from his damp clothes. He is falling from a great height, coming down from drugs.

Not now, thinks Stefano. He must get Erich.

"Georg," he says, "I told you to stay there until I came."

But Georg bangs his head on the doorframe, and Rosalind now stands behind Stefano, disturbed from her sleep. They watch Georg fall to the ground in front of them.

Stefano looks toward the track through the window by the door, but Erich is no longer in view. He helps Rosalind carry Georg to the couch, and Rosalind disappears into her bedroom, to find the drug that will sedate him, that will send his mind to ignorant bliss.

"I tried to find her, but I couldn't," Georg says.

Stefano doesn't ask. He already knows.

There is a part of Georg that is still there, strong and able, the part of the brain that stubbornly won't let go of life. It is filled with memories, vivid ones that drown out the silent functioning ones, the result of his brain injury combined with the sickness from the drug. It is hard to tell the extent of the damage, what he is really like beneath the chemicals.

"I'm sorry you can't find her," says Stefano, trying to pacify him, but preoccupied with other thoughts. He has lost his only chance with Erich. He has failed.

There is red and purple bruising on the top of Georg's cheekbone from the fight the previous evening, and he turns his bright yellow-green eyes, boyish and innocent, on Stefano.

The gaze falters, and Georg grabs at his head suddenly. He is tortured, Stefano realizes. He cannot unblock whatever it is that stands between his rational mind and the blurred world that has taken over.

January 1944

He had convinced his mother to go south with Nina and the baby, but his older sister refused to leave. Teresa felt it disloyal to be anywhere else but with Serafina and Enzo in northern Italy.

It was the night before his family would leave for their old house in Amalfi, and after they were dispatched, Stefano would go north to help the resistance. His mother knew nothing of his resistance plans. Nina would reveal them only once they were safely stationed in the South. His mother would not leave if she thought he wasn't following quickly. Since the war started, lying had grown easier.

He met Teresa at their mother's house, and when informed of the plan, she had looked at him with disbelief, before trying to talk him out of it. She had argued that his loyalties were wrong, that to unify Italy again they must stay on the winning side. That people were probably watching them. But she did agree, in spite of her dislike for the South—an opinion she had taken from her aunt and uncle—and in view of her sister's and mother's safety, and Nina's closeness to Stefano, that it would be in their interest to leave. Even Teresa did not like that threats to family members of the resistance were a tactic the Nazis were using to lure back any resistance members who had found sanctuary elsewhere. There were instances of family members already killed by the time the underground fighters turned themselves in.

"Then when they come looking for you," said Stefano to Teresa, "you must say I'm a traitor and you have turned your back on me. That you no longer want anything to do with me. That you have no idea where I have gone . . . Do that for me and take care of yourself. It is dangerous here, Teresa. Even for you."

He had always had a fondness for Teresa despite their differences. They had grown up together, and they shared a past. But their futures lay in very different directions. In the past week, Teresa and Nina had grown closer, perhaps with the knowledge that they would soon be apart. Teresa had also grown fond of her baby nephew.

"Little brother, I can take care of myself," she said. "It is you I am worried about. If they capture you, they will kill you. And I hate you for that."

"You can never hate me," he said with a grin.

"No, you're right. I can never hate you, but there are times I come close."

Then she did something he was not expecting. His sister, usually so strong, burst into tears and wept into his chest. "I am so worried about you."

"I will take care of myself."

"I thought Mamma and Nina crazy for this decision, but I agree it is necessary now. While I believe that Mussolini must once again rule Italy, the Germans have methods that put fear into me."

It should have been the last time he was to see Teresa, as she and her mother and sister made their tearful goodbyes to one another.

Back at Conti's place, Toni and the rest of the group were studying maps and discussing something heatedly. Nina stayed behind to help her mother pack, to then bring her back to Conti's, where they would secretly remain until their departure.

"Stefano," said Alberto, who appeared to have no fear of danger, "the resistance needs our help already. We are to make a diversion because they plan to assassinate Pavolini, the leader of the Black Brigades. They have sent us a list of locations that he is visiting, including a dinner being held in his honor tomorrow night. He and his Nazi accomplices have had many of the resistance members shot, their families also. It is a chance to begin."

"Yes," said Conti. "We must do that."

"I don't know," said Toni, who was not normally so cautious. He was trying unsuccessfully to rock his son to sleep. "I want my wife and baby gone before we do this."

"It is an opportunity," said Alberto, disagreeing. "There is nothing linking you at the moment. There is nothing to lead back to us."

Stefano had agreed it was a good opportunity, yet he also felt that it was too early to begin their activities. He also wanted his family gone before they commenced operations.

They argued back and forth for the next hour before finally agreeing on a plan. Conti, Alberto, Toni, and Stefano would all go, along with other contacts they had made more recently. They kept a supply of stolen arms and ammunition in the cellar at Conti's house. One of Conti's friends, a member of the resistance also, owned and operated a small van that they would use for their operations, but the same vehicle and driver were needed to smuggle Julietta, Nina, and Nicolo to a church north of Rome. From there they would be taken farther south. Toni's mother and some members of Alberto's family had already been smuggled in previous days, as there was not enough room for all to leave at the same time.

It was decided that late in the afternoon, the driver would drop Il Furioso off at a forest on the opposite side of the ambush location, along with the materials they needed to complete their mission. The driver would remain hidden in the forest at the drop-off point and wait there until the completion of the mission to drive the group back.

The group's plan was to lay explosives on the roads to blow up part of the road that Pavolini was traveling and thus divert him into an ambush where other members of the resistance would be waiting. They planned it, drew up maps, and it was four o'clock in the morning before they worked it all out. This operation would delay the travel of Stefano's family by several days, since the driver was committed elsewhere in the days following. The timing change had bothered Stefano, but he was too exhausted to think any harder about it. He collapsed on the sofa and woke in the afternoon to Nina telling him that Conti was waiting.

It was a plan that in discussions sounded effective and seemed to consider all possible outcomes. But the mission failed. Not all the explosives worked, blowing up only part of the road. And Pavolini never visited those sites; only several German officials traveled to them, one sustaining a major injury, and the others raising a hunting party immediately to track down the partisans involved.

Il Furioso accepted the failure and safely returned. And by the time the night was ended, the members had covered all loose ends but one.

Present-day 1945

Stefano helps Georg up the stairs to his bed. The man is trembling, erratic, feverish, and feebleminded. Stefano has heard of these cases, but he has never seen the aftereffects of the drug to such a degree.

"His drugs are gone!" Rosalind says, flustered as she looks through the medicine bag she has brought with her to the room.

Stefano remembers the empty syringe beside Georg in the hut as Rosalind rushes downstairs, and he listens to her opening drawers and closing them again loudly. In the distance is the sound of trucks.

Georg is becoming more anxious; he scratches at his arms and shivers despite the warm air.

"Can you give him something else to sleep for now?" Stefano asks as she returns.

"I can try. But there are only tablets left. In this state, he won't swallow these or even drink water. He will fight it. It is a process."

"I will go and fetch Erich in the meantime," he says, "for more of the drug he needs. Do you know where he works?"

"You won't find him at any employment. He lives in the town, not here at the river as he tells you. His address is on the back of Monique's photo on the wall. But you must hurry."

He starts to ask more questions, but the noise of vehicles close by halts any further conversation. Rosalind rushes to the window.

"The Russians are back," she says urgently. "There are more of them this time, and they have guns."

Stefano walks to the window. He does not turn to look at Rosalind. He cannot face either of them right now.

"Stay here!" he commands.

21 June 1943

Dear Papa,
It has been too long. I have so little to tell you, and with-
out any good news, I have not had the heart to write.
I am miserable because of something that happened
recently. I cannot share the details, Papa, because it is too
painful to write them down.

After our last trip to the river houses, things are very
different. Georg is someplace unreachable, in the bowels
of some horrid battle. Rosalind refuses to answer my many
letters. And Erich is very unkind. I have to admit I never
liked him much, and more recently I despise him. And
I have to say that I even fear him a little. I am trying to
sound strong, but I am not, Papa. Sometimes I tremble
when I hear him put the key in the door. He is not the
same boy I met before the war. He is like an animal
trained to perform a task without conscience.

The last time he came home from work, he was
angry, and made me feel as if I were the cause of all his

unhappiness. I feel so useless here, Papa. He takes me less often to his functions and goes alone these days. Not that I want his company, but it is something at least to pass the time.

Papa, this is not the marriage I dreamed about as a little girl. I pray for the day to come when we can go our separate ways. But for now, I must endure.

This city will have only bad memories. Always when I go out, I look for you in the streets, in the square, at the markets, hoping that you have been released, that you have begun some kind of life. I look for you everywhere.

I wish I had someone to talk to me, but it seems everyone I have ever loved has gone from my life.

Love from Monique

CHAPTER 24
ROSALIND

Stefano hurries across to the stairs and disappears down to the next level while the urgent roar of engines sounds on the track toward them. Rosalind steps closer to the attic window. They are not the same as those used for previous Russian visits, but a military truck and a passenger vehicle.

The truck brakes noisily and suddenly in front of the house. Moments later Stefano exits the front door and walks to face the two soldiers who have jumped out from the back of the larger vehicle, with guns drawn. Rosalind watches nervously, her heart thumping hard in her chest. She turns back to look at Georg, who has stopped scratching and is focused on a small photo of Monique he holds in front of him. She only briefly takes this in, because she can't afford to miss what is unfolding outside, and her mind is clouded with indecision, whether to take Georg and run from the back door.

Stefano looks calm as he approaches the soldiers. Another Russian, with a more senior-looking uniform—a fitted jacket with several red-and-gold badges—steps out from the car. The Uniform speaks to

Stefano in Russian. They shake hands, and Stefano hands the officer a piece of paper, which she presumes shows his identity. But she is still trying to process the handshake, still trying to absorb this act of familiarity. Behind her Georg is whimpering like a child. She doesn't turn to look at him. She can already see in her mind that the tears have something to do with the photo. She has urged him many times to articulate his feelings, but for reasons also she is relieved he doesn't. She does not want to be reminded that he and Monique shared something special, something she was excluded from.

Her thoughts are scattered with Georg unsettled, but he isn't what features most this time. The immediate danger lies just outside her house with the Russians. The ones she faced in Berlin were different from these, but the detached glares toward her house are just as frightening. She wonders if they are here on behalf of Erich, if he has somehow double-crossed Georg, and if the untold truth of his drug-fueled rage against the Russians prior to his wounding has surfaced. But the thought comes and goes in less than seconds. It would do no good for Erich to talk. If they take Georg, they will likely take her, too. And Erich needs her silence as much as she needs his. They both have secrets now, and the best they can do is to despise each other silently.

The sudden distraction of another Russian voice confuses her while she processes its familiarity. She tilts her head slightly toward the glass to view the speaker, Stefano, but his back is to the window. He talks in a hushed tone, and the soldiers listen intently. Those from the truck wear helmets as if they are expecting a confrontation. One of them takes out a notepad and writes something down. Stefano is pointing to the track that leads to town.

There is commotion behind her, and the floorboards jiggle. She turns to see Georg's final stride to reach the top of the stairs.

"Georg! No!" she hisses loudly. But he is going down the stairs two at a time.

He is across the floor downstairs, and she turns back to the window to watch him rush out the front door below. One of the soldiers shouts a warning, and Stefano turns and pushes his palm forward to halt him, but Georg disregards the signal and rushes at the Soviet officer.

"Nyet!" Stefano shouts to the two soldiers who have already drawn their guns. One of the soldiers fires his weapon, and the bullet strikes Georg's side, causing him to fall. By the time Rosalind reaches the front door, the Russian weapons are aimed at her. They are halted by another signal from Stefano.

Rosalind ignores them all, uncaring of their guns, and races to kneel by Georg's side. At the sight of him, pale and breathless, she is panicked. With her hands she attempts to stem the bleeding, but it is useless as Georg's blood spills out from between her fingers.

"You have to help me," she shouts, overwrought. "You have to help stop the bleeding!"

Stefano appears beside her with linen from the house, then commands the soldiers to carry Georg to the back of the truck.

"No," says Rosalind, who does not let go of her husband, though it is to no avail as the soldiers are strong and lift him away from her.

She shouts at them that she is a nurse, that she must attend him, but they don't listen. They carry Georg and lay him in the back of the truck. She doesn't know who is holding her arms, but she is restrained tightly enough that she cannot step forward toward Georg.

Stefano says something else to the soldiers in the vehicle, then steps back as this first group of Soviets prepares to drive away.

"No!" shouts Rosalind, her arms released. "They can't take him!" She storms toward the truck.

Stefano wraps his arms around her, and she struggles unsuccessfully to free herself. She continues to shout and call for Georg, and Stefano yells above her that Georg is going to a military hospital and they will do everything to save him.

"It was a mistake, Rosalind," he says. "They thought he was dangerous."

Only when the truck has disappeared does Stefano release her to move away and whisper hurriedly in the ear of the officer who returns then to the second vehicle, which then departs also.

Rosalind is breathing heavily and tears are falling and she is thinking of Georg, bleeding in the hands of the enemy. She will never stop loving him, and she is sorry for nearly giving up. Rosalind doesn't realize she has said her thoughts aloud.

"There is no enemy," says Stefano.

But there is. There is always an enemy. She knows that even more now. There is always someone to hurt her. She is always being punished.

April 1945

Chests rose and fell with the uneven, rasping breaths of soldiers back from the Eastern Front, the German line rapidly disintegrating. The wounded were coming in too many, too fast. Doctors yelled commands above anguished howls. There were so many to suture, so many legs and arms to amputate. Temperatures were checked, wounds packed, and patients cleared hastily from operating tables. Nurses rushed from patient to patient, blood smeared across their aprons, calling the nursing volunteers to bring more supplies and remove surgical dishes stocked with shrapnel and fragments of bones.

At dawn, after a fourteen-hour shift, Rosalind was ordered to check on the new arrivals. She had passed the point of tiredness hours earlier to reach the stage of frayed, ignoring blisters on her feet that burst hours ago. Seconds later a siren sounded to alert hospital staff to commence evacuating patients to the lower ground floor, and the sounds of shelling nearby filled everyone with a grim reality. In those moments that she descended the hospital's marble staircase for the last time, Rosalind recognized that nursing was something expected of her, a choice driven by her sense of duty, by her desire to impress and to stand out finally, rather than something she chose from the heart. And she admitted to herself that she did not do it as well as other nurses. They may not have been as meticulous at organizing the surgical tools, but their ability to care was something that came naturally to them. They knew what to say to those who were dying. They felt more than she did perhaps. She couldn't say for certain, but she was flawed in some way. She recognized it then.

Rosalind entered the basement level and walked toward its only ward, the "arrivals crypt," some called it privately, with a mass of bodies, some with fewer parts than when they left the field. People rushed past her along the hallway. With the evacuation in process, there was much commotion on the floor above her, as trolleys squeaked frantically across the tiles. Those from the basement, those with less chance of survival, would be the last to be moved. The ward's street-level windows were still blacked out with heavy curtains from the night before, and under dim basement lighting that spread sparsely across the room, Rosalind scanned the bodies draped untidily on the dozen beds with soiled linen they had not had time to replace after earlier casualties. Some of the injured had been left on trolleys near the doorway, their flesh torn open, burned and flayed, harvested from battle. The first one she attended was dead. He looked too young for war, plump youthful cheeks and acne strewn along his jawline. A large red-brown stain on the center of his uniform shirt disguised the fatal wound. She moved to the next one. She was picturing Georg at these moments, though she was not afraid to see him. Not anymore. She was told that he was still fighting far away, fighting a losing campaign with no shred of hope.

The injured that had been arriving since the beginning of the year were some of the most gruesome she had seen. And it wasn't just their individual wounds that suggested that battles had grown more savage and desperate, but the sheer number that spilled through the hospital's hallways. Though half in this ward were different from past arrivals, picked up from the streets, boys, barely men some of them. Part of the skull was missing from one patient, and his arm was mangled, as if it had been ground with a pestle. There was so much blood and crushed bone she couldn't tell how many fingers he had left. He was one of the few who didn't cry out, hoping for death, far beyond the reaches of pain. His breathing was steady and his chest undamaged. The next one was missing both his legs, the tops of which had been bound tightly with uniform shirts, most likely by comrades, the medics likely dead. The patient stared at her, pleadingly, through blood-colored eyes.

You make a good cup of tea, but it's not the same as having a healing hand, her mother had said when she was growing bitter with the reduction of food and her husband's lack of employment. And Rosalind wondered then, whether the words were profound, as she approached each patient, whether she had tried to prove something to her mother, to prove her wrong.

Rosalind examined the wounds of the last patient—an old man in civilian clothing—then stood in the center of the room to review the carnage. Everywhere she turned, someone was calling her, and the wailing only exacerbated her unraveling, as well as the shelling that every so often shook the building. She could not do this alone. She went to the medicine cabinet for small tubes of morphine to be administered to several of them, into those most demanding. Each time, the crying and pleading would stop, and the eyes that were roaming in pain were then fixed on the ceiling or off to the side to the spaces beside them. It was simple, so easy to end their suffering.

She felt a kick in her growing belly, disguised by her loosely tied apron. More than ever she knew that she must take care of herself now, and the baby, until she and Georg were reunited. She had not had any contact with her parents since Christmas, a gradual estrangement on both sides as her parents grew more distant, despairing of times ahead and watching their friends and neighbors leave the city. Long before that, to avoid the travel, Rosalind had moved into shared nurses' accommodations nearer the hospital, and she'd not been home since the deluge of battle-wounded soldiers and civilian casualties from Allied bombings began. Her parents were unaware she was carrying Georg's baby, and she felt the sudden need to tell them her secret. She had written Georg the news but was unsure whether her letters had got through to him. She'd not heard back from him in months.

Rosalind took another morphine tube and emptied it into one of the patients, until he was completely at peace, and she suddenly knew why she was in the job now. It had been leading to this day. She was doing what was expected of her: destroying those who were no longer useful to the Reich.

And then she moved on to the next one, a soldier with a bandage to his stomach and his face burned beyond recognition. He begged for help, his eyes unusually bright beneath the black and swollen flesh, and she placed the tip of the needle into a piece of undamaged flesh in his neck, and he looked grateful even before she squeezed the tube. She did this twice more for him until the moaning stopped, and then there were no more calls for help. Her job completed, she was then free to go. Unaware of what had just occurred, a senior nurse walked into the room and directed Rosalind to start wheeling out the men on their trolleys. As though in a trance, she walked past the woman, ignoring her supervisor's continued calls, and Rosalind lifted her apron over her head and discarded it at the front of the hospital. The woman's voice was drowned out by a piercing whistling from behind her, and the crashing of bricks and plaster followed. The ground shook and groaned. Rosalind lost her balance briefly, then walked from the hospital grounds, the sounds of sirens suddenly silent, replaced by shrieks and the distant rattling roar of tanks. She would make it by luck alone, she thought as earsplitting gunfire filled the sky, returned with gold-and-green fire elsewhere.

Rosalind caught a transport vehicle for part of the way and covered the rest on foot. People were fleeing central Berlin, but Rosalind, determined now, strode toward it, toward her home. Mortar bombs dropped close by, and the blasts sent debris in her direction, the earth rumbling and causing her to stumble and reach protectively for the front of her stomach. People screamed nearby and someone white and red was carried in the arms of another. "Are you a nurse?" someone shrieked at her, and then louder as if she were deaf, but she kept walking. Closer to home, she could see familiar streets ahead while the landscape looked strange, missing the height, with buildings shrunken and shattered, and great gaps appearing. She could see into the parklands behind. Small fires were burning, and people pulled at arms poking through from the rubble as she walked to where her house once stood.

"Where are they?" she asked a person standing by, in a deadpan voice.

The voice replied, much like her own, telling her there were no survivors. "All gone," said the woman as Rosalind stumbled across the remains of her house, her parents dead and crushed within the red bricks piled recklessly on top of one another. The only thing that resembled something from her past was a window frame, the one from her bedroom. She was too weary to feel anything and strangely disconnected with the house remains, as if she had left nothing of herself there to damage. And there was no time to grieve for her parents, for the past, for anyone. She and the child, and Georg, who must find her somehow, were all that mattered then.

Someone shouted to her that the Russians had entered the city, and she followed a group of strangers urgently through the streets. Several people disappeared inside buildings until only she and one other remained. Rosalind ran fast despite the pregnancy. It wasn't her life that was at stake here but Georg's child, who she must protect at all costs. A girl, a few years younger, pretty, with hair braided on top of her head, clung suddenly to her arm, seemed to think that Rosalind would lead her from danger. There was no time for introductions as they weaved through devastation. People bloodied and covered with white dust and the crumbled and fiery remains of buildings were a familiar sight at every turn.

The stranger followed Rosalind southwest of the city, where she had entered earlier, and where others were fleeing to, but the shouts in Russian from all directions hindered any escape. The pair ran into an apartment building, first to the basement where it was overcrowded with people avoiding the shelling, and then up several flights of stairs, checking doors until they found one that was unlocked and empty. From the window, they watched the city dissolve under a blanket of dove-gray smoke, and hoped the building would still be standing by morning. There were no more strident voices on the radio to promise a better Germany, just the sounds of artillery fire, which lasted through-out the night.

As light approached morning, shellfire, which by then had been relentless for days, came to a dead end, and the eerie stillness that remained for several hours became even more unnerving. Sporadic sniper shots, short exchanges of gunfire, and terse Russian voices finally broke the silence. Then in the hours after that, amid the dust and smoke and smells of Berlin burning, there were the cries of the wounded, an occasional single gunshot, and more Russian shouts. Trucks and tanks groaned through the streets, avoiding the rubble of bricks that littered the streets but not always avoiding the unclaimed dead Germans who had fallen there.

The girl eventually stopped sobbing of her own accord, Rosalind being too tired to try and console her. She had her own life to think of. She had done her part for Germany, and she had now resigned. The quiet weeping of the girl did not evoke feelings of pity, but rather it grated on her already threadbare nerves. Rosalind had lost one of her shoes in the scramble of the building blasts and the sudden scattering of terrified Germans, and she had kicked off the other one. From sharp broken fragments, her feet were torn and bleeding, her uniform streaked with old blood and ash.

The girl, whose name Rosalind couldn't remember, began sobbing once more while she reported the scenes on the street below: old men and young boys pulled from their homes and shot by Russian soldiers. Rosalind listened, imagined the horror on their faces, and at one point could hear the pleading.

Seized finally by sleep, she dreamed of her parents stepping out of the rubble, then woke abruptly to several rounds of bullets tapping at their building and the crashing of doors below them as they were kicked open.

"We have to get out of here!" said Rosalind, feverishly alert again, the girl woken also and dazed, the night returned. "We must make it to the west of the city." The door of the apartment was smashed in before they had a chance to move. Firing bullets into the air as they entered, two soldiers shone torchlights into their faces. Behind their lights they were faceless, and only their helmets and their voices told her that the Russian reign had begun.

Women screamed from another floor, and a child began shrieking, the noises spiraling upward through the stairwell.

Adjusting to the light, Rosalind could see the men better now, aware of the fury and brutality of their gazes. The older one walked around them, kicking at chairs and smashing in cupboards, and mindlessly knocking over a dresser containing china and glass in what seemed an aimless search.

"Are you Nazis?" the older soldier shouted at Rosalind in German.

She was thinking of her parents. They had likely died quickly at least. And she would die slowly.

"Nazis are gone!" said the young girl desperately, in place of Rosalind, whose voice had frozen.

The soldier repeated this in Russian to his younger comrade. *"Natsistov net."*

The younger one then lifted the young girl up from the floor and pushed her toward the back of the unit.

"No, no!" she shouted. "Please . . ."

The young girl was then dragged forcibly out of sight. Rosalind saw this peripherally, her eyes barely leaving those of the soldier who had addressed her. The young girl's begging turned to screams in a room behind her.

Rosalind could feel the baby kicking again, as if he were part of the fight. As if he were eager to help her.

The soldier looked at the bump in front of her, exposed now without the apron. He had wide and slightly crooked lips, but the yellow eyes, under the meager light in the center of the room, were what she remembered most.

There were only muffled protests then from the room behind them, and a kind of whine that dogs make when they're left alone.

"Ubiraysya!" he said.

At first she wasn't sure if she understood, but he pointed the rifle toward the door.

"Get out!"

She wondered if it was a trick and he would shoot her in the back. There was little choice. She stood up and walked from the room, counting the seconds as she did this.

She walked steadily down the darkened stairs and did not turn her head once to look through open doorways. She stayed close to buildings in the dark, tripping on broken things, and headed to the southern part of the city. She saw that there were others escaping the city, too, while Russians were otherwise occupied with revenge.

Rosalind was going home to the river. There was nowhere else now. Berlin would shortly fall, and the past lives she helped save had counted for nothing.

Present-day 1945

Stefano holds her on the sofa. She is sobbing, and Georg's blood is on her hands. Events from the previous evening are blurred. She remembers Stefano carrying her inside, remembers clearly her own ghoulish appearance in the bathroom mirror, but before that, at the river, there are only patches: images of Georg's hateful expression, the cold water, and painful, crushing hands around her neck.

"You must stay here," Stefano says in his odd accent, the words soft and lazier now, less German.

"I will go tomorrow and see if he is all right," he says. "They will put him in the hospital, but just give it time for things to die down."

"What do you mean?"

"The Russians reacted; they thought they were being attacked. But they have promised me they will look after him."

"You speak Russian," she says, suddenly remembering.

"Enough to make it this far," he says, and she wonders what he means by that. Something about the words he used sounded familiar. When Georg ran out of the door, Stefano shouted something else apart from "Stop." She wants to ask him about it, but her thoughts are still frantic. She is thinking of Georg in the back of the truck, wondering if someone is stopping the bleeding, or if they have killed him, because it is easier. She should be there with him. She knows what to do. She stands to move away, but he pulls her back down to the sofa and puts his arm around her again.

"Georg will say things he shouldn't. He will tell them he killed Russians, and that he wants to kill again. They will put him in prison."

"He will be safe," Stefano says, as if certain. She wants to ask him why he is so sure, and why he is going into the town and not talking about leaving on the train.

She lies sideways on the sofa, and Stefano gets her some water. Monique hangs crooked on the wall. The portrait has been removed in a rush, then replaced. Stefano comes back beside her and is rubbing her back; he is good at taking care of people, but she does not want him touching her. Not anymore. She is being punished, she thinks, for turning her attentions from Georg, for thinking only of herself. And she can see the truth now. That Stefano is not who he says he is.

CHAPTER 25

ERICH

Erich wonders if his instincts are failing him. He misjudged Stefano. The sight of him with Rosalind, someone Erich has grown to detest, makes Erich feel deceived. Perhaps it was merely something a man has to do, something Erich himself has done. But the disturbed grave, he feels, is more than just a coincidence. If Monique was found, then Erich might also be found.

He walks to the pharmacist. It is too early yet to be open. He rings a buzzer at the door. Elias comes to the door in an undershirt and trousers, white chest hair showing, surly, until he sees who it is; then his shoulders seem to widen, and he becomes attentive.

"Come in," says Elias, then locks the door behind Erich. He is more wary and formal with Erich than he is with his other customers.

He reaches behind the counter, takes out a package, and passes it to Erich. The package is smaller than usual. Elias can see that Erich notices this.

"Things are getting harder to come by," he says. "Is your daughter improving?"

"She will survive."

"And the other one, the soldier?" He is referring to Georg.

Erich pauses. "I will need more of the other, too."

"I'm not sure I can supply that for much longer," Elias says, and this time he doesn't look at Erich. Elias's manner is different from usual. He keeps moving his hands around the counter nervously, looking for places to land them on.

"We no longer have access to the original manufacturer, and the stolen supplies are all dried up," he continues. "Our underground chemists have had to improvise as you know, and these drugs are not as reliable as they were . . . Everything is getting harder to source."

Erich says nothing. Yesterday this would have bothered him slightly. Today it is unacceptable. And Elias, who has read the silence, recognizes this also.

"You must give me a week," he says.

Erich nods, takes the medicine for Vivi, and motions to leave.

"I should tell you that my wife said a stranger came in several days ago when I was collecting supplies," says Elias suddenly. "She only just told me because she didn't think it was important. The stranger asked her if there were any new faces in town. She said only his, and he thought that amusing."

"Can I speak to her?"

"She isn't here," he says, looking briefly to the side of him. He is lying.

"Was he Russian?"

"He spoke German well, but she said there was an accent."

"What did he look like?"

"Tall. Dark hair. She had not seen him before. He looked like a farmer, a laborer, and he wore a silver bracelet. She told him that he shouldn't wear it. Criminals will cut off his hand before they ask him to hand it over."

Erich says nothing. He waits for more because he can tell there is still something to come, and Elias is reluctant to speak, perhaps because he is afraid of Erich. Elias has heard things from others about the work he used to do.

"He also asked about a child. He said he had lost a small child with light-colored hair. He also asked if there are places for orphans. When he left, my wife said there was a little boy waiting for him outside."

Erich feels the blood pumping hard through his body and coldness at the back of his neck, the same feeling he had when he returned to his home in the country for the last time. He is convinced more than ever now that the vehicles he saw earlier were coming for him.

"He sounds harmless," says Elias, unconvincingly, his voice brittle and his expression blank and insincere. "I think his questions were harmless. I don't think there was anything in it, but I thought I should mention it to you."

"What else was he doing here?"

"He asked if we had any painkillers. She told him we did not. And then he left."

Erich looks to the doorway behind him. He knows what he must do.

"I need something else from you."

Elias looks over Erich's shoulder to the street, wishes him gone.

He has turned, thinks Erich. He has become weak, afraid to fight, like so many others now.

"What is it?" Elias asks.

"A liquid opiate. Something stronger than before."

1943–1944

Erich had located most of the remaining Jews hiding across Austria in the first few months of his commission. His work since had been to interrogate prisoners at camps, gleaning information about the location of other undesirables, and those who resisted the government. Though the travel was tiring, the position itself had become soft. He still held a small hope that he would be sent to war, to command one of the tanks his father had helped design. But he was convinced that his father had somehow thwarted his plans. That he had kept him away from the front lines.

"You are not a soldier, Erich," said his father more recently, when Erich had put forward the suggestion. "You are merely an enforcer, who must do whatever he is told to do. You no longer have control over your own thoughts. But I can tell you it is not what I wanted for you."

Monique made continual reminders to him to search for her father. Reminders of her continued quest to find him. Erich had not told her the truth. There were some things she didn't need to know.

Upon various inquiries, Erich eventually received a list of detainees from a prison outside Vienna. It was a better prison than most, and he was taken directly to the holding cell. The place smelled of disinfectant, but it didn't mask the smell of defecation. Some of the prisoners had taken to shitting on the floor in protest. They had been punished, their faces pummeled, their noses rubbed in their own excrement. As yet, Erich had not personally enacted such punishments at the larger camps he frequented. And at the end of a day of interrogations, his uniform never looked worn, the labor of the tasks assigned to someone else. But this visit was different. He was not here to interrogate, but merely to observe in a prison not manned by Hitler's men.

The man he had come to see had been ill for some time, Erich was advised, as he was led to a cell that held a single prisoner. The air was warm, which only heightened the stench of bodily fluids along with the staleness of flesh and clothes that had not seen air and sun for many months. Many prisoners had been there for a long time, and Erich had to wonder why they weren't just sent to the labor camps. This was something he would investigate further once more pressing tasks were done.

The man was lying on his side, eyes closed. Shriveled and gray, he looked around eighty, though he was much younger, and had somehow lasted ten years in such circumstances. He should have died by now, thought Erich, but the political prisoners here were treated better than most. He'd had connections. Monique at one time said that one of the fascists who had put him in prison had once been her father's friend.

The prisoner was sallow and shrunken. He no longer resembled a human. Erich scanned the bleak gray walls of the cell, the inhabitant's only vista, and the concrete floor, stained and streaked with matter. When he looked up, the man had one eye open, watching him. Erich paused a moment. He could have said something then. The words were there in his head, the words that might fill the wretch with a moment of peace, if his mind was not yet addled. But Erich walked away instead. If nothing else, he had satisfied his own curiosity.

Monique must never know. Erich needed his wife to do her duties, to not be distracted, and to remain a silent and loyal wife at least, even though it was a marriage of convenience only, as a favor to Georg. He and Monique were nothing alike, and their separations were probably the only thing they agreed upon. The air in their apartment was oppressive. He was glad to leave as often as he did, was pleased when he was called to Berlin for urgent talks.

The next months were spent busily interrogating people who had not been fully supportive of recent measures—of the treatment of Jews, of changed conditions—people who were not happy with the closure of certain venues and the abolishment of certain newspapers, and people who had their own ideas, which were no longer allowed. It was his job to counsel (code for threaten), to ensure compliance from those who were outspoken. And then there were the occasional resistance members who were caught in the mountain ranges between Italy and Austria. Who had taken to theft and minor sabotage but had not been, who Erich thought would never be, clever enough to commit the kind of deed that would overthrow the powers of Germany. As inconsequential as he thought they were, they were still annoying enough to waste his valuable time. They would need to be eliminated.

In the summer he and Monique had taken the train to Dresden and had access to a car to take them to the river house. He had not liked the idea of spending any extra time with her, but he was pleased to be seeing Georg again. Rosalind had been there, mousy as always, looking around her and watching Monique. He had seen the jealousy years earlier, as had Georg. He had been amused by it, Georg less so, more guarded on the subject. But the incident by the river houses had left an effect on Erich that would change the course of his life forever. It was something that would hang low, a gray cloud just above him; even at the crucial moment of interrogation, the memory of that night would attempt to scatter his otherwise arranged thoughts.

As the months passed by, the cloud grew darker. The news of job promotions elsewhere and his desire to work in other areas amplified his growing dissatisfaction with his own role, which had diverged into tedium, and the situation with Monique, even more so, the marriage pointless and regrettable now.

She had acted differently toward him after their return from Germany. The subject of Georg had completely ceased between them from that point forward, and neither did she broach what had occurred, but in small ways the experience seemed to empower her. She showed indifference to the things he spoke about and had become slower to perform the household tasks required of her. But what bothered him most was that the event was another weight on the chain that bound them, in that any knowledge of it outside their tiny river circle would shame him, exposing the lies inside their marriage.

He had just spent the day interrogating several Italian resistance members who had been caught and transferred to a concentration camp. Arriving at the cell, he had found that they had pissed on the floor in front of the door. He had conducted an interrogation in the rooms below to get away from the smell. He was meant only to ask them questions, but they had answered haughtily; they had laughed, and then one of them had spat on him. The prisoner was set upon by several enforcers in the room, but it was not enough. On top of the previous events, Monique, Georg, his sister, and the thankless work, the prisoner's spitting had been the final offense.

Erich had picked up a metal rod and beaten the prisoner so hard repeatedly that the man fell unconscious. Not that these disciplines hadn't been performed before; it was just that Erich had not had to bear the physical side of things. He noticed a trace of blood on his cuff when he took off his coat on arrival at the apartment he and Monique shared.

After a long drive home, he found the apartment in darkness. There were no smells from the kitchen. He had not told her he would be home, but his mother always had meals ready for his father regardless. Monique, in contrast, had grown to be useless as a housewife; there was no point to her being here.

She arrived sometime later, and he was waiting for her.

"Where were you?" he asked.

"Just walking," she said, trying to hide the shock of finding him home. She looked slightly repulsed.

"You have been looking for your father again, haven't you?"

She switched on the light in the kitchen.

"What does it matter?" she said nonchalantly. She did not give him the courtesy of looking at him. She was like Claudine. Showing her contempt, openly then. And the thought of his sister brought even more feelings of rancor to the surface.

She turned to look at his hand that had reached out to grip her arm, before looking up at his eyes with both alarm and disgust.

"What are you doing?" she said. "Let me go."

You must control your wife, Erich, before she controls you, his mother had advised shortly after his wedding. She had seen Monique's flaws, like he had.

He pushed Monique roughly back on the couch. He lifted her skirt, but she slapped him, and his return slap caused her to cease the fight, to look at him differently. It wasn't arrogance now. The look was more fearful.

"Leave me!" she said. "You can't be doing this."

"I know that you are a slut. That you spread yourself halfway across Vienna and Berlin to anyone who looks your way."

"Stop it!" she said, and pushed at his chest. "This isn't part of the arrangement."

"Why now would you fight your husband?" he said breathlessly from the effort of holding her. "It may as well be this way. It may as well be your duty also."

"Erich," she said in a much softer tone. She was becoming subdued, more like she should have been all this time. "This is not what . . ."

But he ignored her and undid his zip, still with his jacket on, still with the uniform that helped suppress those who needed it. Consummation at least would validate their marriage and reduce the power Monique seemed to think she had. She winced as he pushed hard into her, and it was over quickly as she lay there, tears streaming from the sides of closed eyes. He looked down, almost afraid to see what he had done. There was blood on the skirt beneath her, and only then did he return to some semblance of his usual self.

Feelings of revulsion had replaced the anger, and he left for the bathroom to wash her from him. When he came out, she was in the kitchen. She had her back to him. It had to be like this, he thought, but not forever. Time would change things; he knew that and counted on it.

And the only way he could remove the disgust, the self-loathing, was to atone in other ways. He would take vengeance, each act, each interrogation worse than the previous to block out the memory, to create more from which he could draw from to forget Georg, Monique, to forget the past.

He did not return for a month, taking an apartment near the main camp, his job taking him often to northern Italy where partisans had become more active, and they needed someone qualified to take control of the situation. One of the senior officers stationed in Italy had been injured in an attempted ambush. He was in the hospital and would likely recover, but not for some time. Erich was asked to fill the position, which would eventually become permanent.

He was taken by plane and then by car. On the way he was handed the file of information. From a list of names and details, the person he was asked to interview was a supporter of the newly formed Italian guards, or Black Brigades, who patrolled the streets. Erich did not particularly like this group. They were not orderly and organized like the SS had become. The group was made up of members of the police, veterans, and fascist loyalists, and they seldom supplied any important information. Still, they were at least controlling northern Italy to some degree, which then, more than any other time, needed stricter measures, a greater show of force to side with Germany.

The one-legged man, Enzo Silvestri called into the Gestapo headquarters based in Verona, with information that he wished only to give to Erich Steiner, whom he had met once before at a government function, or to someone else as senior. Erich declined to meet him at the Gestapo police station; instead he would pay a visit to Enzo's house to interview him there, as well as the whole family. Erich had found that it was sometimes better to see their surroundings, to gain a better truth, to see through duplicity, tricks, or lies.

The file told him that Enzo had a wife, Serafina, a son, Beppe, who had been killed fighting in Africa, and a niece, Teresa Della Bosca, who was living with him.

An interpreter accompanied Erich to the house, one of the better ones on the street. They had come from money. They owned shops, and they had helped pay for supplies for the Brigades in Verona. Erich established straightaway that they were loyal. But he still had to witness this for himself.

An offer of refreshment by Serafina was declined. Erich never treated such interviews as social, but his manner was courteous and did not fit that of an interrogator. Serafina said she was thrilled by his visit, but a constant flutter of her hands told him that she was nervous also. The sight of SS, especially senior ones, caused anxiety even among those most loyal.

"What is it that you have to tell me?" Erich asked.

"I have the address of someone you might be interested in. A man named Conti Fiore," said Enzo. "I know that he had something to do with the bomb that exploded on the road to Verona."

"And how did you come by this?"

"My niece has been working at his café, and she was asked to place several crates of food in the back of a delivery van. A cover sheet inside the van had slipped away from some boxes, exposing what was underneath. She noticed there was a box marked as explosives, along with several guns, and as she walked away, she heard the word 'ambush' whispered between the owner and the driver. She mentioned it to her aunt that day, but it was not until we heard about the explosion later that we made the connection. I believe that Conti Fiore is involved in the resistance."

"And do you know this man personally?"

"I only know of him. He was a friend of my nephew some time ago. I heard a rumor that he is a Jew, too," said Enzo. "A Jew and a member of the resistance . . . They don't get more dangerous."

Erich was appreciative of the information, but he did not show it, and he didn't care to humor the comment. Though they provided vital information at times, political and social climbers like Enzo, who enjoyed lighting fires as a way to be seen, could be just as detestable as the men and women he sent to the camps.

"And this nephew?"

"My wife's sister's son. He and his sister and mother moved from here to live in the South."

"When did they go?" asked Erich, directing this to Serafina.

"Several weeks ago, we believe," she said. "But I have not seen my sister, Julietta, for months." She pursed her lips, as if she were not only displeased but also guilty to mention her, perhaps even ashamed.

"They supported the Allies?"

Serafina nodded, but she did so to her lap only.

"And where is this niece?"

"She is unwell," said Serafina too quickly.

"I will get her," said Enzo, overriding her, and Serafina tensed. She did not want her niece interrogated.

Teresa walked timidly behind her uncle, supported by crutches, from a room at the rear. Her eyes were red rimmed as if she had been crying.

Erich stood politely to shake her hand, and she sat, rubbing down the front of her skirt, modestly. She avoided eye contact with him until he spoke.

"Conti Fiore . . . You heard him speak about an ambush?"

"Yes," she said. "I mentioned it, but I am not completely sure I heard correctly."

"Had you met him before you worked there?"

"No," she said, but he sensed that she was lying.

"How did you come to work in his café?"

"My brother helped get me the job six weeks ago when the owner of the restaurant I was working for previously was conscripted into the army, along with his sons."

"Do you like working for him?"

"Il signor Fiore is very generous to his staff," she said, her eyes level, the statement unrehearsed and genuine.

"Did he ever talk to any other persons that you thought were suspicious?"

She paused, swallowed hard, then looked at her shoes and shook her head. "No."

She was holding back, a reluctant participant torn between loyalties. But he could live with that. She had given him what he needed, in the silences also.

"I hear that the rest of your family are now in the South."

Her breathing quickened at the mention of them.

"Yes."

"And why didn't you go, too?"

"I am loyal to Mussolini . . ." She regretted this, because she had just admitted the rest of her family wasn't.

"It is all right, Fräulein Della Bosca," said Erich. "I'm not worried about your family. They will have to live with the consequences when the South is once again in safe hands. But in the meantime, this Conti is some kind of ringleader, yes?"

"I'm not sure. I just mentioned what I witnessed to Zia Serafina in passing. That's all." Her aunt did not look at her, ashamed perhaps that she had put her niece in this position. It was obvious to Erich that Teresa had not been aware they would go to the police.

"You did right to do that."

He did not feel it necessary to talk further. The fact that she had some trouble discussing it with him, indicating she was in some way disloyal to her own family by mentioning it, told him that the information was correct. He cared only about the address, about capturing the resistance members.

Present-day 1945

Marceline is surprised to see Erich at the house. She was not expecting him back for hours.

"You need to take Genevieve and go to this address," he says. He hands her a piece of paper.

"But your mother?"

"I will take care of her. Find her another safe place."

Marceline looks briefly at his mother. There is something knowing in the look, something she wants to say, though she would never dare.

"Pack now. Leave immediately."

His tone is terse, but Marceline is used to such orders. She worked for others much harsher. Marceline disappears into the back room.

He bends down to Genevieve.

"You must stay with Marceline. You must be good."

"Mutti!"

"She had to go away for now, but I will see you soon." The little girl's hands are so small against Erich's. He has a desire to pick her up and hold her close, but it would show a certain need that he cannot allow. He stands up before she has the urge to lean into him, to reach her arms around his neck. He takes her hand to follow Marceline to the bedroom.

"Do not take much," he instructs her.

Marceline nods, but she already knows this. She has had to run before, and she is used to packing sparingly.

Erich carries the packed suitcase and places it near the front door.

"Thank you, Marceline, for everything." She nods. She has always been loyal to the party. "I will follow shortly, but there are things I have to do."

Marceline doesn't look to the window where Erich's mother sits, and Genevieve has forgotten she is there. Not that Genevieve has ever had anything to do with her grandmother. His child will never benefit from her encouragement and teachings like Erich did.

Erich opens the door and watches Marceline walk purposefully up the street with Genevieve on her hip.

He stays until they are out of sight, looks once down the street the other way, then closes the door. He moves to the front bay window where his mother sits facing the window. On the pavement outside, some rubbish has been strewn and blows in the wind, without purpose, like the people that pass it. There is nothing for him here.

Erich sits in the chair opposite his mother to look outside, to try to see what she sees. Every day she watches, eyes following passersby. He took this at first to be a sign that her mind was still receptive, but over the weeks he has come to the conclusion that the watching is involuntary. She has become an imbecile, a type of creature she once despised. There is something there, a faint form of recognition, a tiny light every so often, but just a sliver, as if she were teasing him. The same day she committed the murders, she committed herself to a life worse than death, muses Erich.

He traces the hairline above her ear. When he looks down from the window, one man has paused to look back. It unnerves him. He stares back, and the man moves on. He doesn't know many people here, nor does he want to. He trusts no one. His last conversation with Elias has confirmed that he must complete his business here.

"Do you remember when I was small, you told me something?"

Nene doesn't look at him.

"You said that I must always look after the family if anything happens to you. That I must fill the role of my father. What would you like me to do now, Mother? I feel that if you could talk, you would tell me. That you would know immediately what must be done."

She turns, not looking at him, but at something behind him, responding to the tone in his voice. He can see the scarring at the hairline. He touches it briefly, thinks about the moment she took the lives of his siblings and attempted to kill herself. Tears spring to his eyes, and he blinks them away. He can't remember the last time he cried. He takes her hand, bends down to kiss it. And his head stays bowed, not in prayer, but to reflect on all the good that she has done.

"You also said to be merciful to animals, to never let them suffer. You taught me that as well. Do you want me to be merciful, Mother?"

He stands up suddenly and lifts her from the armchair so they are no longer visible from the street. He helps her lie down on a sofa. She looks stiff and uncomfortable, and her mouth moves as if she wants to say something.

He takes a cushion and places it over her face and applies pressure. Perhaps unnecessary force since she is light, but it must be done swiftly and humanely. She makes a sound, beneath the thick fabric and padding, and one hand reaches out to grab weakly at the air, at something she can't see. He presses the cushion down harder and holds it there. There is little resistance until her body becomes limp, and her arm drops suddenly to the floor beside the sofa. He leaves the cushion over her face. He doesn't want to see her again.

He packs a small case, then shuts the door behind him.

There are things he has to know.

CHAPTER 26
STEFANO

Rosalind has stopped crying now, and she is pensive, watching silently from the window, perhaps willing Georg to appear. The soldiers, Stefano has told her, will likely come back to report on Georg's condition.

"Where's Michal?" She turns, her mind suddenly back in the room and her fingers grazing the bruises around her throat.

"He is next door."

"It is probably best," she says, and he wonders why it is best, since there is no Georg here who might harm him.

"I just took him some food," he says. "Fortunately, he did not witness the shooting." Though the boy has likely seen worse.

Rosalind disappears to her bedroom, then returns moments later to retrieve the kettle with boiling water from the stove. She has replaced her bloody housecoat with the dress he first saw her in.

"I'm making some tea," she says, and he finds it odd that she now appears serene. Her face, though, is still damp and reddened from her previous outburst.

Stefano feels the sweat building under his armpits. He wipes his forehead with the back of his sleeve. It is still early in the morning, and already it is too hot. He exits the back door again to survey the area; he wonders about Erich's whereabouts and whether he'll appear.

"I think I will go to town," he says, coming back to the table. "See if I can learn something more." He does not like the waiting. He looks around. He is sure he left his satchel near the sofa. There is no sign of it now.

"Erich should be returning soon. You cannot miss your train . . . I would rather you stay for the moment. Until my nerves settle."

She turns back from the sink and places the tea in front of him, then sits down opposite.

"Thank you," he says, sitting down, though he is still thinking about the location of the bag while he sips at the hot tea. "You are feeling better?"

"Yes," she says too quickly, "but I am wondering what you said in Russian when Georg first came out of the house."

Stefano pauses, trying to remember the words he used.

"You told them the Nazis were gone."

"I shouted something, anything to stop them from shooting."

"It was strange. That's all. The tone. The urgency. As if those soldiers needed to be elsewhere."

"I'm not sure I understand you."

"I heard those words you used many times these last months when I saw soldiers in the street in the town grab someone to interrogate them. It is something we learned to say after the war ended. Though your tone was strange. As if you were frustrated, disappointed. Or a warning to the Soviets perhaps."

He looks at her, absorbs the gentle accusation of collusion, and searches for an answer that will suit her. She is digging. She is deeper than he thought.

"It *is* what I said," he says finally. "I was hoping that my warning would stop him, but Georg did not want to stop. I was just trying to save him, make sure he was not mistaken for a Nazi on the run."

She stares at her cup; there are other things on her mind. He thinks he must explain further and begins to talk; he reminds her how he learned some Russian, and that he loved languages, liked to read, to study words, but she bursts into his explanation to interrupt his attempts.

"It doesn't matter now. Georg is gone. Perhaps Erich is, too."

He takes several mouthfuls of tea, wondering if there is a message beneath the words.

"And soon you will be gone, too, and I will be left here alone."

"I'm sorry," says Stefano, draining the last of the fluid that was thick and black and strong, with too many leaves. Bitter also, like her, he is thinking. Her mood has changed from last night, and he wonders if she is ashamed that she revealed so much and whether she wishes she hadn't. "It should never have happened."

"What was supposed to happen?" she asks.

He looks at her then.

"Just that they should not have shot him. He was unarmed," he says, and looks suddenly wary. "Do you think I had something to do with Georg being shot?"

"I don't know. I lived through a war. I lived through all sorts of disappointment, heard and saw many horrors. I just thought that when the Russians came, you were expecting something to happen, that you ran out to greet them rather than try to send them away."

He opens his mouth to speak in his defense, but there is a sudden pain in his stomach, and he grabs at it. His head feels fuzzy. He tries to stand but finds that the floor beneath him is shifting.

He can just see her through the haze. She sits across from him. She has not touched her tea. Her large pale eyes that emerge from the mist are in sharp contrast with the circles of black that surround them. His hand releases the cup, which smashes to the floor, and Stefano falls to the side of the chair.

January 1944

Stefano watched his mother play with her grandson, and the sight lightened his heart and just briefly blocked out the events they were faced with. Nina wanted Nicolo baptized in a church as soon as they reached the South, and Toni had agreed.

They spoke only briefly of the mission that had gone badly. There was no blame, but Toni vowed there would be no more failures. After the women and Nicolo were safely on their way the next day, they would draft up plans.

In the early hours of the following morning, a truck would take Julietta, Nina, and Nicolo to a church that had been assisting refugees. From there they would be moved southward with the help of the Vatican. They'd had word of others who had been safely transferred to the Allied-occupied territory.

"Finally," said Toni, "the church has come in handy."

"Don't blaspheme," said Nina. "You will come around eventually." Stefano was glad that his mother had left the room and hoped she didn't hear the way Toni talked. Better that she thought well of him now that he was part of their family.

Stefano went to the room where his mother would sleep and spoke to her briefly. She was restless with the excitement of returning home.

"I am sorry for the delay," said Stefano. He did not like that the mission had postponed his family's travels.

"I trust that you are doing everything you think is right," said Julietta to her son. "But you must promise me that you will come to us soon."

"I promise, Mamma, before God, that I will come when I have done what I need to here."

"And what is that exactly?"

He was tired, bits of soil from digging still under his nails from the work two nights earlier. He did not want to explain.

"Mamma, get some sleep, and I will tell you all about it when I see you in Campania!"

His mother at least believed him in part. Nina entered the room, and he hugged them both a little longer than usual, since he had no idea how long they were to be parted, and then Stefano went to speak with the others.

In recent times, Toni and Nina had become more active. Nina would carry messages in the baby's pram and deliver them in cafés. They were fortunately never implicated as members of the southern traitors, but Stefano and others in his group had heard of many executed, and whole villages nearly destroyed in recent weeks. The more death, the more fearless both Toni and Nina had become.

"After the failed operation, the streets will be littered with soldiers, so it is better to have this small delay," Toni said.

Jews were also being successfully smuggled through another local church that had joined their movement. The refugees were set up with false documents, if time permitted, then taken south. With talk now of all Jews being rounded up and taken to camps in unknown destinations, the work of Il Furioso was even more important. Mussolini, once reluctant to dispense with Jews the same way as Germany, had eventually agreed. But with a puppet government and Germany then pulling the strings, he had little to say on any matter of Italian governance.

Il Furioso planned to blow up train routes to Austria and Poland where they had learned most of the prisoners were being transferred. They would do whatever was required.

Stefano had just lain down on the floor to rest a few hours when there was a knock on the door. He crept toward the window while others sat up to reach for their rifles.

"Are you expecting anyone?" Stefano whispered, and Conti replied that he wasn't. Only Fedor wasn't with the group. He had left to say goodbye to his parents who had refused to leave for the South.

Stefano peered out the window. He recognized the visitor as a boy from Teresa's neighborhood and opened the door. The boy told him that Teresa wanted to meet with him urgently. Perhaps she'd had a change of heart and decided she wanted to go also. He hoped so.

"Be careful," said Toni.

Stefano felt that his aunt and uncle would not be aware of the meeting. Despite her beliefs, Stefano knew that Teresa would always be loyal to their mother, even if they fought.

The message said to meet near a bridge, and he headed there straightaway. It was a part of Verona that he rarely visited, and he guessed she had chosen the location because it was far away from both their homes. Whatever it was she was about to tell him was highly secret, and the closer he got, the more he disliked the idea of meeting at all. She was there waiting in the darkness at the edge of the bridge, her face hidden in the night.

Stefano hugged his sister, her body cold and trembling.

"Are you all right?"

"Yes," she said.

"Why are we meeting here?"

"It is not safe for you or me."

He was suddenly alarmed. "What has happened?"

"They came around to ask us questions."

"Brigades?"

"No, an SS officer . . . someone that Enzo knew," she said. "Someone he thought would advance him somehow if he gave him news. Are Mamma and Nina safe?"

There was a break in her then-timid voice when she asked the question. She was breathing heavily as if she were carrying too great a weight. He could sense that she was very nervous, something that his unbreakable sister rarely showed.

"Yes, of course."

She breathed a sigh of relief.

"Tell me, Teresa, what is going on?"

"They know that you and Toni are deserters, and they believe you have already gone south. But they also know that Conti is a focal point for the resistance."

A car turned toward them, its headlights flashing across Teresa's face before it passed them by. In those brief seconds Stefano saw tears streaming down her cheeks.

He gripped her by the arms, the fear of treachery circling.

"What have you done?"

"They are coming for him. I called you away because I knew you would be there. I have seen what they do to deserters."

"What do you mean? Who?"

"We had to give them something. The Nazis are coming for Conti tonight."

"No!" said Stefano, every muscle in his body tensing. "Tell me you didn't!"

"It was either you or him. But you must leave tonight. You must go straight to the church also and follow Mamma and Nina to the South!"

"They are still in Verona!"

"But I said goodbye to them several days ago. You told me they were leaving the following day."

"Teresa!" he yelled. "They are not yet at the church. Mamma and Nina are staying at Conti's."

He had time enough to sense her horror before he turned and ran, sure-footed, his legs taking flight, jumping over rails and fences, across yards and down narrow streets. He had to beat his enemy there. He was thinking of his mother, curled up asleep, dreaming of the Mediterranean, hopeful, and the others, Nina up perhaps to feed the baby, the others dozing, waiting for his safe return.

As he grew closer he could hear screaming, and from his position several houses away from Conti's, he saw Nina being dragged from the house by a member of the Brigades, while another carried her baby.

There was no sign of the others. Stefano slipped unseen down the side of a neighbor's house and crossed the fence to Conti's. He stood behind the corner of the house to peer around toward the street for a closer view. There were two official vehicles parked in front of the house. There were half a dozen Black Brigade members and several SS, all with guns ready. They had been prepared for a battle.

Stefano leaned back against the sidewall. He regretted not taking a gun, having only a short knife, which he kept on him always. Car doors slammed and engines started, and in desperation, and with no time to think, he turned the corner toward the vehicles, with the hope that his appearance would divert attention, halt their departure, and give Nina enough time to run away. But his mother's short and sudden scream and the sounds of unrecognizable voices from inside the house put a stop to this suicidal plan. He was torn in half, helpless, as he watched the first vehicle drive away with Nina and Nicolo, followed by the second.

As he moved cautiously closer to the front door, he was met with the smell of gasoline. Someone shouted something terse, which was followed by a burst of fire from inside the house and the smashing of the front-window glass. Two brigades hurried from the house and headed on foot in the same direction as the vehicles. In their rush to leave, they had not seen Stefano approaching the entrance.

Stefano could see through the window that fire had engulfed the front living room. He wondered then if some of the group had already been taken before Nina, but they could also all still be inside, perhaps wounded and unable to flee. The crackle of the fire turned to roaring as flames caught rapidly, and it became obvious that gasoline had been spread throughout the entire house.

Stefano rushed back to the side of the house where the bedrooms were and called out to his mother. Over the sound of the loud crackling fire and splitting timber, he faintly heard her cries. He smashed at the window glass with his fist and climbed through the jagged opening, pieces of glass piercing him as he entered. The heat and smoke were too much, and he was forced back again to the window, flames threatening to smother him. His eyes and throat were burning, and he could barely see. He climbed back out and fell to the earth coughing, his chest very painful. People from the other houses had arrived with buckets of water. Someone bent down to check on him and yelled that he was badly injured and needed a doctor.

It was only when he looked down that he saw the fire had burned through his shirt to the skin on his chest, and his forearm and the back of his hand were a sticky, blistering mess. He clawed at his chest from the smoke trapped in his airway, and the feeling of suffocation collapsed him to the ground. He began to shake violently.

Fedor appeared and wrapped him in a sheet, and, with the help of a stranger, Stefano was carried elsewhere in the dark. It no longer mattered where. At that point he had lost all thoughts of a future.

He was taken below the grounds of the church that had been assisting Jews escape. A doctor arrived and spread salve across his body and bound the injured areas with gauze. He eventually fell asleep, and sometime in his dreams he heard Nina and his mother screaming but woke to an empty silence and a loss that no words could quantify. His heart ached for his mother, sister, and friends.

By the third day he expected the SS to come, but they didn't. He was safe, said the priest, in a secret passage below the building. He wondered what Nina must have gone through to have not given up the church to the authorities. He closed his eyes in an attempt to block out images of faces in the fire, but for several more nights the pain of what had happened worsened. He tried not to think of Nina and his mamma waking in the night to their deaths. They had paid the ultimate price for his defection, and he was now bearing the blame.

Fedor came to see him often, concerned for his friend and with talk of revenge. He believed that, from Stefano's description of events, their friends were knocked out or shot by the Brigades and SS prior to the fire. It was only Julietta who must have woken to stare into the face of her death, and the image was something he would wake with for most of the coming years.

For three more weeks he stayed like that, was treated for his wounds, and counseled by priests and others loyal to the South. More came, those who supported his cause, and then members of a partisan army offered condolences and something that was much more important: the opportunity to fight alongside them. Fedor and Stefano listened to the stories of the resistance, listened to what they had already done, and how much they had lost also, and the two friends left one night without mercy in their hearts.

Present-day 1945

Stefano wakes to a strange taste in his mouth, a mixture of bile, metal, and tea. He struggles to open his eyes. His head is slightly forward, hair across his face. He goes to reach for his forehead, then realizes he can't. His arms are tied behind him. He is in the barn, tethered to the center pole.

He forces himself to alertness, forces the deadweight of his head upward, and he blinks several times. There are soft warbles from the trees but no human sounds. From the light outside, Stefano gauges it is well past midday. He sifts through the last moments, the tea, Rosalind's vacant expression, and the missing satchel. He is wondering what he didn't see. He twists his wrists within the bindings, but the attempt to wriggle free causes splinters in the skin on the backs of his hands.

Footsteps sound outside. He is expecting Rosalind when the door opens, but it is Erich. Stefano notices immediately, as Erich walks toward him, that there is a slight crack in his demeanor. He is still rigid, straight backed, but the elbows are tight to his sides as if he were tense, his gaze faltering at the sight of Stefano.

"Why am I tied up?" says Stefano, the dullness in his mind slowly clearing. "I need to get to the train."

"You and I both know there is no train. The train line south was destroyed by Allied bombs," says Erich, moving closer. "But I think you knew that. It is why you looked unconvinced when I offered you a lift."

"I believed you about the train," says Stefano cautiously. "And why would you offer to take me there when you knew it was destroyed?"

"You don't need to pretend anymore," he says.

Stefano can see that his captor is trying to sound controlled, but Erich is unnerved, by the way he paces, the way he keeps sighing and combing back his hair. It is a side of Erich that he hasn't seen before.

The door of the barn squeaks open, and Rosalind rushes toward them, looking at Stefano like she did on the first day she saw him, suspicious and bitter. Before Erich has time to reach for her arm, she bends to slap Stefano hard across the face.

Erich grabs both her arms behind her and pulls her away.

"You had my husband killed!"

Stefano feels the sting that is left on his skin. But he has felt worse. Any pain is good pain now, he thinks. It is a reminder that he is alive, while others are dead. He can see that she has been crying again, but there is a determination he failed to see, a determination that most German women carry. The resolve that they will not be made to kneel, that they will still fight. The night before, she appeared vulnerable and frail, but she is anything but.

"I did not have your husband shot."

"Why did you call out that the Nazis were gone?"

"My Russian is poor. As I told you, I was trying to tell them Georg was not a Nazi. That's all. I was afraid that he would be shot. He did that to himself. He came at them. I tried to stop them."

"You knew them!" she accuses.

Stefano sighs. He is wondering whether the war will ever stop for him.

"No," he says, staring directly into her eyes. Though he is aware that Erich is nearby, watching, the scrutiny is worse than Rosalind's fury.

"I don't believe him," she says to Erich. "He shouted at them as if Georg were the wrong one."

"You were confused, upset," defends Stefano. "You are looking for things that aren't there."

She goes to strike him again, but Erich stops her this time and grips her wrist so tightly that the area of skin appears burned after he releases her.

"Did you find the child?" says Erich.

"He is still missing," she says.

"Then you have not looked hard enough."

"He may have left hours ago—"

"Keep looking!" he commands in a tone that sounds much like a threat. "Search by the river!"

"Why do you want the boy?" says Stefano once she has hurried from the room.

"I can see that you have developed some affection for him."

"And you think you can torture him in front of me to extract some information that you falsely perceive to be the truth."

Erich ignores this.

"My first thought was that you might have brought him to cover who you really are, but my instinct says differently. His survival is personal to you. It might save your soul," Erich says with mockery.

"One German orphan is of no consequence to me," says Stefano. He must remain neutral. Feelings must not be revealed if he is to get out of this.

"That is something you can't hide no matter how clever you think you are. You do not wish to lose anyone. It is perhaps that you have lost too many already."

Stefano shrugs indifferently, though there is truth in the words.

"I think that you did not happen upon the houses by chance, that you came here with purpose, perhaps to kill me."

"The war is finished. I see no fight here. I thought we were friends."

"It took me a little longer this time, since I'm out of practice," says Erich. "I am sorry to admit that I believed you about the Nazis being helped out of Italy through the church. It is obvious now what you were trying to do."

"I didn't make that up," says Stefano with a hint of amusement. "Is that what you were thinking? That we could drive to Italy together? That you could escape that way?"

Erich doesn't reply. His stillness shows that he is rattled by the condescending tone.

"If you let me go, both of us can carry on," says Stefano.

"You had this sewn into the lining of your bag."

Erich holds up a gun, and Stefano can no longer feel his penknife against his thigh, which has been taken also.

"So what if I carry one? Wouldn't you if you were me walking through Germany? There are many out there who would still like to see me killed. You included, it would seem."

"I never wanted to kill you. Rosalind did, though. She wanted you gone the first night you were here. That's why she came to collect me. You might as well save me some time and tell me what you were planning with those Russians this morning."

"There was no plan. What are you guilty of that makes you think this?"

Erich doesn't respond.

Stefano swallows. His throat is dry. He is nauseated from the drug. He shakes his head. "I don't know you or care what you might have done. I just want to go home. If there is no train, then release me. Let me go home to my family."

"You were asking questions at the pharmacy, specifically about a child. Why was that?"

"I don't know what you are talking about," says Stefano. "I asked about an orphanage."

"The description matched yours."

"I saw other foreigners in town."

Stefano can tell that Erich is unconvinced.

"Why did the Germans arrest you?"

"It was confusing, chaotic. Since I was Italian, they couldn't tell which side I was on. Prisoners were sent east, some west."

"Either way, Italian deserter or traitor to Germany, they would have shot you on the spot."

"I guess I was one of the lucky ones. Perhaps they were saving bullets."

"Amusing, but it will do you no favors to continue playing this game."

"Look, I don't know why I was sent away on a truck full of Allied prisoners. Why they spared me. Perhaps the soldiers were feeling happy that day, high on the smell of gunfire. As I told you earlier, I was shot by your friendly soldiers as we were marched away from the camp. Then I pretended I was dead. Then I was picked up by the Russians and taken back to the same camp and asked a whole lot of questions again, but they saw the tattoo and eventually let me go. I have been a football to kick around between other nations. The whole of Italy has been."

"Why Sachsenhausen?" he queries again. "Why were you so special? Why not one of the camps in the territories?"

"I don't know. I didn't think to question the German who held a gun to my face," he says, coldly this time, some of his former hostility creeping through.

Erich stares at him. Stefano is aware of interrogation methods. He is aware of the silences performed to threaten, to weaken, to make him speak, to make him accidentally give something away to fill the void. The German asks him more questions: dates, times in Berlin, details of the camp, Italy, the campaigns. He answers everything. He has the responses all stored. He has been prepared for this moment, for the time when he would be questioned. And Rosalind returns, standing back slightly, reporting ashamedly that the boy has gone, and guilty that in some way he was her responsibility.

"You are wrong about me," says Stefano. "I don't know you. I don't even know if Erich is your real name. All I know is you don't live here. That the two of you hate each other. That Rosalind would kill you if she had the chance, but she owes you for the drugs you feed her husband. That you also lie about going to work. That you live in the city."

Erich gives nothing away, but Stefano knows that the last part has cut him, that he expected more loyalty from her.

"You have read me wrong," continues Stefano. "I know some Russian. They wanted to see my papers. I was making polite conversation. I was about to tell them my plans for home when Georg ran from the house."

"No, no, *no!*" says Rosalind, returning to stand close by. "There is something not right about him. I told you first that I was uncomfortable he was staying here, and you wouldn't listen—"

"And then it was you who fed him, who took him to your bed," Erich says louder, steady, and in full control. She shrinks a bit. Perhaps she has seen this other side of him before and knows what might come.

"I trusted him," she says, weaker. "It was not like you think—"

"You can trust me still," Stefano says more forcefully. "All I want is to go home. I wanted to catch that train home. I want to be gone. I can leave now and walk."

"You must make him tell the truth!" she says to Erich.

"This is what I am doing!" barks Erich, his face reddened with anger.

"Please . . . The war is over," says Stefano. "Rosalind says you have a daughter. Please just go to your family and let me go to mine."

Erich turns toward Rosalind's look of bewilderment.

"I never told him that," she says. "I never said anything. He knows you. He must have known that from before. He is lying about everything."

But Erich is calculating; Stefano can tell. He trusts neither of them now.

"You had too much to drink," says Erich. "Perhaps you don't remember. You've had a lapse in memory before."

"No! I remember everything!"

"If I am the person you say I am, what is it that I am supposed to be doing?" asks Stefano. "I had plenty of chances to kill you. And if there are so many secrets, what is it about you that I don't know?"

"Whether you are telling the truth is irrelevant . . . You know things now," says Erich. "You know I am on the run—"

"Which you just told me!"

Erich reaches for something inside the pocket of his trousers and tosses the contents onto Stefano's lap. The paper is crumpled, and the image on one side is not visible, but he doesn't have to see it to know what it is.

"There is more of course," says Erich, "that you need to explain."

10 August 1944

Dear Papa,
It has been more than a year. Where to start? Perhaps at the end. I am in Verona, Italy. What began with an abhorrent event has now become my beautiful accident.

Erich was sent here at the beginning of the year to help the Gestapo. It is his role to help keep the order, to seek out those usurpers, after an opposing government staged its unsuccessful coup last year.

It was not an easy transition for me, unfortunately. Almost the moment we were taken to our new apartment over the piazza, I was left alone again in a strange city. It was even lonelier here than when I was in Vienna. At first, people did not view me as a friend. Few officials here have brought their wives. But because I was carrying Erich's child, he thought it best to be near, perhaps because it would not look so good leaving me in Austria with no one. And I do not think he trusts me in Berlin—I might once again show my disquiet. Perhaps he is right about that.

A child was not something that I had even considered, and the relationship now with Erich is difficult to explain to you. Sometimes it is just too painful to give it any thought, to explain the distance, yet explain in the same sentence how it is that I carried his child. It does not make sense even to me at times. But she is here now, small, not robust, like some, but she is here. She is five months old and lies beside me as I write. She keeps her mind occupied. She is a little thinker, always watching what I am doing and studying me.

I have a book of Italian phrases, which I practice on the shopkeepers. When I first came here, to pass the time I would walk to the piazza in the front of my building and sit on the edge of a fountain there. Sometimes I would take a sketch pad to draw the buildings. But always someone seemed to be looking at me as if I were not welcome, a pariah with a German accent.

One day I ordered some coffee, but a woman refused to serve me. Her husband saw this and yelled at her and sent her away to the back of the kitchen. He gave me my coffee, but there was no kindness in the café owner's service, only a reluctant tolerance. There are some here who are not loyal to Mussolini still and even less loyal to Hitler. He knows I could have reported him. That is why he served me and covered for his wife. Of course, I didn't report him.

The Black Brigades and their wives and others loyal to Mussolini are pleasant enough to me, but I don't want anything to do with them. I know what their husbands are doing to the free people who do not want their country to turn into another Germany. I know that whole families were slaughtered mercilessly when Italy was split. When I do see Erich, he tells me stories, perhaps on purpose, about the punishments for disloyalty, the public hangings to avert reprisals from partisans that hide in cities and the mountains nearby. He has become vile, Papa. I cannot tell you how much. He is so different from the boy I met at the river, but perhaps he was always that way. This has brought out his true nature. And you must also wonder why I carried his child. I have come to the conclusion that the child was meant to be. It is the only way I can justify Vivi's existence.

The first friend I made here was a woman who had lost most of her family. She does my laundry, and we talk often, and she helps me with my Italian. I make her stay and have tea with me, and I pay her extra, which she is embarrassed taking. She is a small woman, a little older than I am. She said she has suffered at the hands of the Germans. But at least I have her to talk to. We struck up a friendship, and she said she would convince her friends to see me, to invite me into their group.

It took several weeks for an invitation to arrive from them, just before Vivi was born. They didn't trust me. I think they had me watched and found out that my husband came rarely. They thought that I was spying for Erich. Of course, I didn't tell them he had asked me to keep an eye on things here, as if I owed him something. But I owe him nothing. He treated me abominably, Papa, and I can't forget that.

Then finally Teresa came and took me to meet her friends. They were very suspicious and talked about my growing belly. The women in the group started to care for me, and I wonder now if it is the child that has made my life better, my acceptance here greater. Perhaps that was part of Vivi's purpose.

There are people here who are not as they first seemed. The women and their husbands appeared to support the war. But it is not true at all. They hate the Black Brigades, who puff out their chests, grinning like morons, and carrying their guns as if they are always about to shoot someone just for fun. Some of the women flirt with them, pretend that they are loyal, but they scowl behind their backs.

I thought I was so alone here, but now I know I am not. I have befriended a group of men and women who are responsible for destroying vehicles and supply routes of the German army. They are no small crimes and carry the penalty of death, but some Italians are also punished for much less, for simply refusing to salute a guard. Murder is a given if you do not respect and comply with the new way of government, the German way.

And I have to tell you something else, Papa. I have been passing on information, learned from conversations with Erich, to the resistance. And on the rare times I am invited to a social function with other members of the Nazi Party, a tiny piece of information slips through. I know where they are looking for partisans and where they are not looking. I have given money for food, medical supplies, weapons, and new identities, contributions that have helped several Jewish families escape to Switzerland and enabled those who wish to remain here to continue the fight. The liberation of Rome by the Allies has given them confidence.

It is dangerous what I do. I have heard what they do to "traitors." The very fact that I am putting this in writing puts me in danger, but I feel it must be recorded, that you need to understand things should anything happen to me, should you somehow, by a miracle, get to read my letters if I am gone. And I pray that it will be me in person who tells you everything, but if it isn't, then these letters will tell you about my life.

But there are always challenges still. I am not always trusted because of my marriage to Erich. Teresa said that while most trust me, there are still some who believe that I am a double spy, and that I am passing on information to my husband. Teresa knows the truth, as do most, so I will ignore their doubt and continue doing this.

Erich rarely comes home now. He is busy. There is so much partisan activity. He goes from west to east to meetings and to camps. It is a relief that I do not see him, and then it is a relief when he does visit briefly and I learn something new to pass on to the resistance.

When Vivi was born, he did not want to touch her. But as she grew, he became more interested. Though I don't like him touching her. I am very possessive of her, and I do not want his ways to rub off on her. I do not know what the future holds, but I do know that when this is over, I will take my daughter away, and Erich will not see her.

Erich asks me about my day. And I tell him what I want him to hear. That people are good. That people are loyal to Hitler and Mussolini and the countries that will one day rule alongside each other.

I have become a very good liar, Papa.

I hope you are proud of me.

I hope that when this madness is over and you have Vivi on your knee, we will share the stories and you will tell me more about Mama, and that Vivi will get to grow up, sharing with her grandfather the same childhood years that I missed with you.

In the meantime I will hide this letter with the others where Erich will never find it.

Loving you, as always—more, if possible,

Monique

CHAPTER 27

ERICH

Erich notices that Stefano's German is not so good now, under pressure, his accent far more distinguishable. It's the nerves; they force one to falter, to revert to who one really is.

The sight of Stefano has again put doubts in his mind. The same doubts and reasons that first drew Erich. He had to be certain of things, of facts. It is his nature. And it was Stefano also, something about him.

Rosalind had met Erich on the pathway back to the river house that morning on her way to see him, to tell him what she had witnessed. She was raving and emotional, something he found hard to deal with. Erich was grateful that at least she did not reach the town and draw unnecessary attention. When he said nothing in response, at first wondering if he should just take the buried documents and leave immediately, she reminded him that he and Georg were close once, that he had a commitment to him, that he must not forget him, and she had opened the lid of something that had been closed for some time. She said that he owed Georg and her, and in some part of his mind, he does. But overriding those feelings of loss and her talk of commitment were also her feelings of revenge. She wanted Stefano punished. Rosalind was of the opinion that the shooting of Georg would prove fatal, or that it was unlikely she would see her husband again.

Erich did not want to kill again. He did not want to murder this man in particular. He likes him, he admits only to himself. But Rosalind is right; there are things about Stefano he feels compelled to know, and if her suspicions are correct, then killing may be necessary. And Erich is curious whether there was any connection between him and Monique, whether he had something to do with the missing body.

After meeting with Rosalind, he had then found Stefano on the floor at her house, on his side, sprawled slightly, his mouth open, frown lines under curls of black. He touched Stefano's neck.

"What did you give him?"

"Sleeping drugs ground and blended into his tea."

"It was more than the usual dose, yes?"

She nods.

"And what do you want me to do?"

"You must find out what he knows. It is your job."

"It *was* my job."

She jumped as the second, louder word leaped at her.

"You have to help me! You have your life still. You have your daughter. Now without Georg, I have nothing. It is the least you can do. Find out what he knows about us. He is hiding something. He was expecting the Russians."

"How do you know?"

"It was the Russian words he used. Everyone used that term when we were lining up. I learned that line. And they seemed . . ." She was looking for the right word. "Comfortable."

"As if they knew him?"

"Yes."

Rosalind had then offered something else that would guarantee Erich's assistance.

"Georg was clutching this in his hand," she said, passing him a small photo. "He didn't get it from my house. This is a recent picture."

Erich looked at the image, disappointed, though he didn't show it.

"I will tie him in the barn, and we will wait for him to wake up," he said decisively. "It may be several hours."

Erich has not yet told Rosalind about the empty grave. Perhaps he never will. She would fall to pieces. She would see things that aren't there.

December 1944

He had been a week at a concentration camp on the outskirts of Trieste, where he had recently been commissioned as a commander. It was a posting he didn't like, that he saw no future in. One of the previous commanders had been killed in a partisan ambush, and the one just before Erich had been called away to another temporary commission elsewhere. He hoped it wouldn't be for too long. The mostly Jewish prisoners were badly malnourished, with enough food only to keep them still working. He did not like to see them from his office, but occasionally he had to officiate over duties, executions.

Though recently, he had become more lenient, not quick to order the deaths of so many, perhaps having foresight that it would mean little in the months to come. He had taken rooms near the camp so he did not have to spend so much time with his wife.

Monique did not cook well. She did not like to look at him, and when she did, she rattled him, just the look of her reminding him that he ended the agreement, that perhaps he was weaker, for a moment. He was also thinking lately that she knew too much about him. She could potentially ruin him. But in the meantime, while he was tied up in Trieste, she did not figure greatly in his thoughts. And she had their daughter to keep her occupied. It was something that he must change once the war was finished, if Monique and Genevieve made it out alive. If they didn't, he would live with that, too. He could put the past behind him when it was time.

There had been very little good news. Just south, the Allies had taken Florence and were still plotting and gaining strength. To the west, Paris had been taken back, and in the East, there was the monumental task of holding the Soviet line. With the help of Allied-supplied munitions, the Soviet forces were making dangerous strides across Poland and into Germany. And Georg was in the thick of it on the Eastern Front. Erich had thought a lot about him. He checked regularly on deaths. He wrote to Georg only recently and heard nothing back. Not that it surprised him. Trains and vehicles were sometimes sabotaged, and mail did not always get through.

From his windows he could see the alpine hills where trees were lined up like marching soldiers, weighed down with the fall of snow, like military backpacks. It had been a place to hide for the Italian resistance. Many were caught there in the summer, and by the autumn hundreds had been executed. There were still many out there, a fact that strangely didn't bother him anymore. There were other things to worry about.

At his desk, he sat down to write a reply to his father. Horst had sent a letter asking for him to return to Berlin. There was urgency in this request, as if he would not get another chance. He put down his pen. The room was uncomfortably warm in contrast to the bitter winds outside, the same winds that whistled through the prisoners' cells and ruffled their garb that was by then little more than threads.

He opened mail and several telegrams that had just been delivered. He read that Himmler had reached the end of the Final Solution and he had passed the final Jews through to Poland to the camps of no return. They were unlikely to survive the camps. Perhaps prolonging their lives, he conceded, was cruel, and fueled the belief that there was light at the end of a very long tunnel. Death was quicker, the future not bleakly filled with lice, disease, and hunger. Sometimes when he looked at the prisoners, he would picture his sister in a camp somewhere, dressed in prison garb, her head shaved. He had learned that she had been sent to Sachsenhausen just north of Berlin.

He read the first transmitted message. It was a formal letter advising that his father had died in an accident, but due to emergencies and lack of men in the field, to please delay a return to Berlin to organize the funeral. His body would be cremated. He didn't recognize the name at the bottom of the letter, though it was on Goebbels's letterhead. He had become more aware of unqualified people being placed in important positions, the führer becoming more erratic with decisions on human resources.

The second letter was from his mother—dated a week after his father's letter—to advise that his father had "died unexpectedly" at his desk at the Reich office. Erich had to read the letter again, to look at the secret message beneath the words, detail that she would never put in writing. She did not give an explanation, but she didn't have to. He had known that his father had not been well. He had learned from his mother of behavior that did not befit such a great mind. That he was less articulate, sometimes rambling. And he often went to visit Claudine in Sachsenhausen, and had been reprimanded for the visits by others from his office. His mother had tried to tell Horst that their daughter was lost to them, and there were greater causes, but he had not listened; she wrote this in a hand that was unsentimental, rational.

His father, his mother informed him, had not left a letter of explanation (a coded message for a much more sinister death), something that disappointed Erich. He would have liked some recognition from him at the very end at least, some encouragement and message of pride in Erich's achievements.

He wrote back to his mother, suggesting she and his siblings return to the country house and when the war was over he would meet them there.

He has perhaps damaged our name, his mother had written also, the words icy, bitter. *But you must fix all that now. You must be what they want you to be. You must not take prisoners. You must fight to restore your father's name.*

Erich folded the letters neatly before putting them into the fire.

There was a knock at the door.

"Enter."

His lieutenant advised that there was a truck filled with Italian resistance members.

Erich briefly looked into the fire and could hear his father telling him that life is a process that we must endure, that it is important to respect and honor our leaders, but within reason. But above that he could also hear his mother telling him to be strong, to ignore the false messages of hope—to forget about hope. Hope is weakness. *It is the doing* that will get him places. Take him where he should go, enable him to be who he should be.

"Shoot them all," he said calmly.

"Yes, Herr Steiner."

There was no more time. They must win the war here at least. They must kill every single person who was betraying them. He would not wait there while the enemy edged closer.

Present-day 1945

Erich turns to Rosalind and asks her to get the medicine bag from the house. She nods as if she has already seen this coming. She is calmer now and exits the barn.

"Where did you get it?"

Erich is talking about the photo of Monique that he has thrown in Stefano's lap.

"I found it in the room upstairs."

"The photo is recent, taken with Genevieve. There was no such photo in the house."

"Perhaps you missed it."

Erich watches him. Stefano's expression doesn't change. There is nothing that gives the lie away. He is used to scrutiny; he is used to lying. And he is lying. Erich would have seen the photo, destroyed it.

"Where did you get it?"

Stefano looks down, very briefly. "I took it from Rosalind's place. I liked it. *Bella ragazza* . . . She is very pretty. What does it matter? When Georg was upset the other morning, I thought it would pacify him to see it. Monique seems to have that effect."

Stefano shifts slightly, swallows hard.

"Did you meet the female prisoners in Sachsenhausen?"

"We were separate from them, but there were times when we spoke."

"Did you meet a girl there called Claudine Steiner?"

Stefano ponders.

"Yes, a German girl. Fair. I met her briefly."

Erich's heart quickens, though he assumes the answer to be a lie. If his suspicions are correct, Stefano would have been told everything about him.

"Did you know her?" asks Stefano.

"Not well," he says. A lie for a lie.

Erich can hear a noise from the house. The slamming of a drawer, something smashing. It is Rosalind. When she is in a mood, she breaks things, like she did in Georg's house. She is unbalanced. He spotted this early, the first time he visited the river, and Georg put up with her because Georg could. He saw the best in everyone, even Erich for a time. But Erich has seen the worst in Rosalind.

"Yes, Claudine and I attended the same school," says Erich. "She was active politically. She was anti-Nazi. She used to scratch nasty things about Hitler into her desk." And Erich would scratch them out, on the desk at home, though he doesn't tell him this. Stefano would not understand about loyalty.

"She must have followed her parents, no?"

"Perhaps." He is thinking that his father had never truly been supportive of the Reich's master-race plan. Horst did not vocalize it, but it was what he didn't say. And Erich has no doubt that his mother knew his feelings, too.

"My father was an engineer," Erich says. "A good one. He designed tanks for the war. He would have had a mechanical company now without the war, and I would have worked with him."

Stefano is staring at him, hanging on every word, and Erich likes this, feels the need to share this. He feels the need to share it with Stefano. He wonders whether they could have been friends before the war. He had picked up signals. Small ones.

Rosalind returns with a medical bag and places it near Stefano.

"What is that?" says Stefano warily.

"It is your end," she says, attempting to sound spiteful, but Erich detects some nerves, too, that lessen the impact of the words.

"Because of a photo? Of a few words of Russian?" says Stefano.

"Because you are not what you say you are," she says. "Because you are pretending to be someone else. And you had my husband shot."

"It isn't true," he says. "I want to go home to my sisters and my mother. There is no reason to kill me."

Erich has been wrong about people before. He was wrong about Monique, about his father, even Stefano briefly. It is unlikely that he is wrong about him now. Stefano had come here to kill him, of that he feels certain.

CHAPTER 28

ROSALIND

Rosalind crouches beside Stefano and from the bag retrieves the vial of liquid that will end his life. It is a lethal drug that Erich had meant for Georg. The fact that she considered giving it to her husband gnaws at her conscience.

"I'm innocent of everything," Stefano pleads with her softly.

She glances at him, and an odd feeling of doubt surfaces that she must quickly abandon. She must never again trust men like Stefano, those who have lied to her. She reaches inside the bag for a syringe. Georg is dead because of him.

"I'm not who you think. I'm not your enemy."

With shaking hands she draws the liquid into the syringe while his words echo in her head. She is remembering his kindness toward her and the boy. And she thinks of Michal then, wherever he is, and wonders about his survival without Stefano, without his mother.

"You should trust me," he whispers.

She is alive because of him.

Rosalind turns to look at him to search for truth. In the moment that she meets his eyes, her vengeance wavering, she feels a sudden jabbing pain in the back of her arm that forces her to drop what she is holding and grip the affected area. She stands, briefly disoriented, and turns to see Erich, just behind her, with eyes that are cold and pale gray, and, more alarmingly, empty. Then as her eyes wander downward to his hand, the situation is made clearer, and the horror of it exposed. Erich holds a syringe, with the remains of dark liquid in its base.

She attempts to run from the barn, but the ground beneath her seems to sway, and she loses her balance and stumbles forward, her hands finding the earth. Then the world is black, then white, lots of flashes in her eyes, and someone moves close, and then she is floating. She is being carried, and then there is nothing. She is once more in darkness.

She can hear voices, and someone laughs as she wakes on the attic bed upstairs. She has to force her eyes to open, and when she does, Georg is there on the side of the bed. He is staring at the empty space beside the bed, as if she doesn't exist. He can't see her, and then he can. He is staring at her, through her. He tells her he doesn't care. That she had this coming; then he is gone and Monique is there in his place. She is asking, "Why?" She says it again, over and over, until Rosalind can't stand it anymore and covers her ears.

She wants to be sick, but she is too tired, and then there is blackness again.

May 1945

She was filthy, no shoes. Ahead of her she could see the other homeless who had fled the city, scrambling from destruction, from the Russian forces, to walk the open stretch of roads, with nothing but their lives. But there was no desire for companionship among them. It was a race to reach the bodies on the side of the road—civilians caught in the crossfire as they fled the city in previous days, and German soldiers still clinging to their guns in a final futile fight—to search their pockets and belongings for food and water. She was like an animal in the wild that must do everything to survive.

Several trucks lumbered and roared toward her. She was frightened at first, but someone yelled they weren't Russian. The trucks were open at the back, filled with Allied soldiers in dull-green uniforms. They called out to her in English, but she kept her head down. She was afraid to look them in the eye. One soldier asked her in German whether she was all right. She didn't look up. The soldiers seemed effusive, celebratory. Several laughed and cheered. They had won, they yelled. The war was over.

The other people on the roads to nowhere in particular were not celebrating. They were like her: desperate, suspicious, and possessive of everything they could find. Compassion had disappeared, replaced by self-preservation. As the night drew near, and the distance between the other travelers grew wider, she stopped to take some shoes off a German soldier who appeared to have shot himself. Sometime after midnight, the moon only half-full, a dog yelped repetitively. She followed the noise and found it tied up outside a house, suggesting that no occupants were inside. She let the dog free to forage like her, then drank from its water bowl as it ran off into the darkness. She scrounged the bin inside the house but found nothing. In the shed there was a sack of dried barley, and she took a handful. It was difficult to swallow, but it was something. Then in a cupboard she found a jar of pickled onions and shoveled them hurriedly into her mouth one after the other. She could not remember the last time she'd had a full meal. In the hospital she had missed many breaks. She was exhausted both mentally and physically.

She slept soundly on the floor of the shed behind the house, then woke with an ache in her stomach and a pain in her chest, and the sound of hanging tins clinking in the breeze. She came out into the midmorning light that was harsh but warm at least. A man carrying pails yelled at her to get off his property. Charity was dead amid a disunited Germany.

She walked quickly throughout the day, and it was dark by the time she reached the familiar track. She passed the clearing near the river where Georg had played with her and Monique, then past Georg's house. She nearly ran the last few yards and then the smell, the dreadful smell. She called out to her grandmother as she entered the door, but there was no response. She has left, she thought at first. Part of the corner of the house was missing and haphazardly patched, leaving small gaps in the brickwork. Flies buzzed around a plate of rotting food. She found a jar of pears, tore frenziedly at the lid, then ate the whole lot and drank the juice. A piece of moldy bread sat in the pantry, and she succumbed to that as well.

But the damage to the house wasn't the worst of it. Upstairs in the attic she found her grandmother. She guessed she had died weeks ago, her face red and green and black, the look of her, a shrunken plum, and worsening in the heat, the sun's rays eating her away.

She had the task of carrying the stiffened carcass down the stairs, the effort so great it made the baby kick and tumble and gave her pains in her back for several hours. She was not strong enough to dig a hole. She had found some kerosene, used it sparingly, then burned the body. Only when the fire had died down did she make a shallow grave and bury the remains.

Trucks flowed steadily on the roads behind her house. Her days were filled with fear, and then Erich arrived with Georg, but it wasn't Georg. There was a patch of hair missing from the topside of his head and an indent in his skull. The bullet, Erich said, had pierced part of the brain. Field doctors had treated the bullet wound, but there was nothing they could do for his mental state. As the Russian army neared, Erich stole a car and brought him here.

They were not wearing uniforms. Erich looked disheveled, casual. She had never seen him like that. He had left Georg with her, almost as if he couldn't wait to get rid of him, and left the drugs as well. She knew the effect of these, knew the danger and told Erich they would not be used. He left some food but not much. He had hidden the car behind the house. People had been walking in front of the car to get him to stop and help them, or try and steal it, and Russian military were stopping everyone. He would come back for it later.

From there, he left on foot through the mountains to his home northeast of Dresden. She would see him again two weeks later with his mother, who also had a head wound. Rosalind did not expect her to live but treated her as best she knew. Erich did not say what had happened to the rest of his family, and Rosalind didn't ask. Their relationship was like that: few questions, fewer niceties.

Over several days she realized that not only had Georg lost part of his mind from a bullet, but he was also addicted to drugs. Drugs that Erich had continued to pacify him with, to keep him quiet and stable, or drugs to fuel him to make him function, to eat. And then after several more days passed and she had found Georg wandering the woodlands, screaming and scratching his skin, she had given him the drugs for the sake of the baby.

She had stood in line for the British food trucks in the town and would return with vegetables, bread, and sometimes tinned meat or milk. It would do, but it was never enough. Hunger was the new state of normal. There was talk in the town that the Russians would be stationed there soon to take over responsibility of the area. At that point no one seemed to be in control.

One day when she was out front putting on shoes to go to the town to wait for more food, she saw a familiar face walking the track toward her, and Rosalind wasn't sure whether to be unhappy or grateful. And the baby kicked her, as if rejoicing, and didn't move again.

Present-day 1945

In the distance she can hear the hum of a truck. It is a sound that she is constantly alerted by, in the silence by the river. She tries to stand up, but her legs give way. She wonders how she walked up the stairs and then remembers, vaguely, that Erich was there. Something he said or did. *What?* She can't remember. She drags herself by her arms along the floor toward the stairs, finding her legs no longer work, and she pulls herself up to lean against the banister. There are smells trapped in her nostrils, of something burning, of chemicals.

Her limbs are weak, and her movement is stiff as she makes her way down the stairs and past the kitchen, stopping when she reaches something sharp and broken, a cup she remembers vaguely that someone dropped earlier, and she finds her legs are now steady enough to carry her to the front door. She is out in the sunshine. She puts up her hand in front of her face because the light hurts her eyes. The gold of her wedding ring is dazzling, blinding almost. Did she sleep a whole day? She doesn't remember. It was this morning that Erich came. It is now the afternoon, she thinks, with the sun low, though she is not certain. She walks to the barn first to find it empty, apart from some ropes left on the ground in the center of the room. Rosalind was here recently—she is certain of it—before the attic. She leaves the barn to walk in the direction of the river, but the hidden track draws her toward it, pulling her with its invisible ties of the past. The truck with Russians is louder, as if it were right behind her now, and she runs, afraid they will crash into the trees and into her, as if there were dozens. She's not sure. Nothing is clear.

And then the noises are gone. They were never here, she thinks, but she doesn't look around. She does not want to know the truth. She doesn't notice the spindly branches that scratch at her legs. She could make this trip blindfolded, she thinks. It was a game they played, she remembers now. They blindfolded one another, she, Georg, and Monique, and they wandered around the wood, calling out and bumping into one another, and falling over laughing. Back in time when they were innocent of disloyalty and deception, and before she realized it was love she felt, which had clouded her judgment.

She reaches the small hut and pulls open the door, which squeals as it swings back on one hinge. There is a faint outline of an owl drawn in chalk on the wall inside, only noticeable to her, because she saw who drew it many years ago, whose small hand took to every task with enthusiasm.

Standing up suddenly, she hits her head on a beam. She hears the sound it makes, but she strangely doesn't feel it. She pinches her arm, which she can't feel either. The skin bounces back in defiance, and she watches it curiously before a wave of nausea washes over her, and she clutches her stomach, where the sickness has pooled. And then come the images, the flashes of Stefano, of Erich, of the medicine bag. It is the drugs, she tells herself. She was given drugs, but she can't seem to hang on to the thought. It is disappearing into the void, deep into her head.

She sits down, her bottom on the cold earth, and she can see the sky and the river from the window. She tries hard to remember what she did here and turns her head to see something familiar. It is part of the quilt patchwork that Monique began for Rosalind's baby, scuffed and streaked with dirt from the ground, the cloth pilled and old looking. It is only half finished. She traces the patterns with her finger. One half is heavy with stitching and the other half blank. Georg would come here and hug the cloth like a child.

Georg. Where is he? He has been taken, perhaps by Stefano. *Stefano.* The Italian should be buried alive, she suggested to Erich, enraged by the killing of Georg. The blankness on one side of the patchwork calls to her. The patchwork asks, no, begs her to complete it. Like the child she almost had. The child that was not completed either.

She fingers the stitching again, the owls made of tiny loops. From someone so eager to leave behind dreariness, who balked at the idea of domestic duties, the stitching is fine and even. War changed Monique. Made her harder and softer at the same time. And Rosalind wants to forget her, has tried. This memory of Monique should have been scrunched up and thrown in the dark corners where she couldn't be found. She is thinking of the photo that the Italian held of Monique and her daughter. Where was that? Vivi looked out from the photo, her eyes daring the camera, just like her mother, the face tiny, but the same.

Erich made promises, and so did she. What were they? She feels suddenly ashamed of things she can't remember. She wishes she could start again, rewind, change whatever it was that happened. And suddenly she is crying. And she is perhaps where she thought she would be, deserves to be. She is so alone.

She hears the rustling of branches that hang across the pathway to alert of any intruders. She can sense that someone is standing outside. The door creaks open slightly, and she closes her eyes. It is the Russians, she thinks. They know her deeds. She will be taken away. She can't look. They will shoot her like they did Georg.

The door makes its final squeak, and Rosalind's name is spoken in a husky voice that she recognizes. A hand, firm and gentle, touches her shoulder. She opens her eyes, and Monique is there, crouching down beside her. She wears a red dress, white satin piping around the collar, and a small black beret, her hair pulled back, as if to display herself better. A shopwindow display, she suddenly thinks, but there are things that mar Monique's beauty. She has a cut above the eye that is swollen, pink, and shiny. The bottom of Monique's dress brushes the dirty floor beside her, and Rosalind worries that it will be stained.

"Rosalind, I will help you."

"Why would you do that?" croaks Rosalind, surprised at the sound of her own voice in the stillness, and she worries it might carry far down the river.

"Because you need me."

Rosalind says nothing. She blinks slowly, but Monique is still there.

"I'm sorry about Georg," she says.

"But you were right," says Rosalind, her voice in a tunnel, far away, as if it weren't hers. "I knew you were right. I knew he didn't love me, but I refused to believe it."

"I was wrong," says Monique. "I was torn every time I saw you together. It pained me to look at your happiness after he proposed, knowing I should have told you about Georg long before then."

"I wouldn't have believed you anyway," Rosalind says, the kindness of Monique's voice forcing her to tears. "It is I who has wronged you!" Though the reasons are still unclear in her mind.

"The war did bad things," says Monique. "Hitler did worse things. He made people suffer unnecessarily. I suffer because I was part of it, not willingly, but that I am called a German now. We all carry that."

"But you always tried to help others," says Rosalind, remembering vaguely. Faces jump in her mind, faces of people she was too ashamed to be around. Though she cannot remember their names. They are somewhere, bobbing in and out of her head, like they are drowning, and she is not quick enough to reach for them.

"Someone had to do something," says Monique. "But I wasn't the only one. There were so many who risked their lives."

Monique looks through the window to the river. Rosalind sees the tiny mole that sits just below her mouth to the side, against skin that is clear. She is an angel, Rosalind thinks, perhaps come to save her, to take her to heaven.

"I hated you and loved you at the same time," says Rosalind, trying to find more words, willing forth those drowning, ghostly images that she can almost see. "I thought you were taking everything from me."

"You had as much as me, except you just didn't notice."

She is right, Rosalind is thinking. She is right, and Rosalind can see that now. There is no one to blame. The past is done.

"Monique, I've felt so alone for years."

Monique puts her arms around her, and Rosalind cries then on her shoulder. She likes the feel of Monique's arms and the floral smell of her, not like herself, harsher, acidic.

"You weren't yourself. I know that," says Monique, her voice soft, syrupy. "I should have tried to understand you better. You were always looking for the faults in people, in things. You were always living in shadows, under clouds. I'm sorry I didn't see that until it was too late."

"I should have been there for you, too," says Rosalind.

"You were. You practically raised me. You lent me your wings."

Rosalind laughs, pulling away from Monique to wipe away her tears. "You grew your own wings. You would have grown them without me."

Rosalind suddenly notices the bandages on the arms that hold her, and then she is thinking, remembering. There was more: Monique in the attic.

Images rise to the surface now: Monique injured, Rosalind watching, angry.

Why?

CHAPTER 29

STEFANO

Stefano is slapped awake, water thrown in his face. He coughs and spits out water, eyes opening, stinging from the light, and a throbbing pain in his head. He comes around slowly to the stillness in the room, to the man who still has him tethered, elsewhere now.

He is told that he will feel better in a few minutes.

"Who are you?"

"My name is Stefano," he says, eyes fighting to stay open.

"The photo of Monique . . . Why do you have that?"

Stefano's head feels clouded as he tries to put his thoughts in order.

He remembers Erich reaching into Rosalind's medical bag, a cloth over his face, something odorous, and fighting the feeling of being smothered under the force of Erich's weight against him. And the memory that came just before that, of Rosalind staggering toward the barn door but never reaching it, falling to the ground, her hands flat on the earth at first, before submitting to it fully, and Erich carrying her outside. Stefano did not see that coming, the tables turned so brutally.

He leans back, nauseated with the sweet, sickly smell of the drug still in his nostrils.

"I told you already." His head rolls slightly on a bar of metal behind him.

"Tell me again."

"I found it in the house."

He is tied to the leg of a large iron bed in another house, his wrists bound again behind him, the ropes anchored to the rim of the bed.

"Where are we?"

"It doesn't matter where."

Stefano looks out the window. They are on the top floor of a house in a valley, the sun low, almost gone but burning brightly. He can see a road twisting upward, and beyond that there is nothing but rolling green hills and the faint sound of a helicopter. He has been here before, just before Dresden. He had chosen it specifically, searched it for clues.

"I underestimated Rosalind," Erich tells him. "She said that she didn't trust you on sight. And I convinced her otherwise. She told me the first night, after she saw you in the wood, that I had to get rid of you. For once she saw things that were there instead of things that weren't."

"And you rewarded her with an injection. I would hate to see how you treat your enemies."

"You should know that Rosalind wanted me to give you an overdose, then bury you dead or alive. I was not ready to give up on you yet. I feel there is unfinished business between us, more words to be said."

"I never found talking worked with Nazis."

Erich looks at him. At first Stefano thinks he will hit him, but he breaks into laughter and wags his finger at him.

"That is why I first trusted you. You wear a cynically honest view of the world. I understand what you are feeling," says Erich, stepping closer. "But now I need the whole truth. I worked for Hitler's protection squad. I interrogated people, I listened to them beg, and most times when I'd had enough, I would order them killed."

He tilts his head and looks at Stefano curiously.

"But you knew all that before you came to the river, didn't you?"

Stefano notices that there is a slight tremble to his voice that he didn't have before. Events haven't worked out quite as they should. Though it could also mean that he is unhinged, that he will not control himself, and may not be prepared to negotiate.

"You don't need to do this. I do not care who you were in the war. I just want to go home."

"To Italy? To your family? To your *mamma* who is waiting for you?"

Stefano's heart pounds against the walls of his chest. He does not like the mention of his mother, and Erich knows this, too. He has probably taunted countless prisoners with the mention of family.

"I will tell you honestly. That I don't know if that is true. I don't know if Stefano is your real name and whether you fought originally on the side of Germany. That much I can't tell since I no longer have access to intelligence. But I can tell you that the other things you said are a lie. You never heard of my sister, Claudine, who was kept locked in a cell of her own, away from other prisoners. When she tried to escape one day, push past the guards to reach her lover in another cell, she was taken away and gassed in a truck." He says this coldly, faster, as if he must speak this way or break.

"I'm sorry about your sister."

"It is what happens to traitors," he says, but he has turned away to say this so that Stefano can't see his face.

Stefano scans the room, the window, assessing the height from the ground. "I have told you everything. There is very little to tell. I was a language student before the war. When I get back to Italy, I hope to pick up where I left off."

"I can't let you go. You have been given orders to find me. Perhaps you gave the orders yourself."

"I promise that you will never see me again. I will go away, and I don't care what you did before. Just let me go . . ."

"Where did you get the photo of Monique?"

"From Rosalind's house. I stole it."

"That photo is not from Rosalind's. She would know. That is a photo you have taken from elsewhere. And why did you give the photo to Georg?"

There is silence between them, gray eyes versus black. Stefano believes they are equally matched in cunning and physical strength. Though only one must win. Stefano can feel the small singular blade inside the bandage on his hand. It has taken him some time, but he has managed to hook the edge of it out with his fingernail, and now he has it between his fingers. It is a sharp-edged blade that he rubs between his fingers to better his grip. He can feel the thick slippery fluid on the tips of his fingers where he has cut himself lifting the razor. It will make it more difficult. He attempts to cut the rope one thread at a time. He must keep Erich talking.

"I gave it to him when he ran to the river hut. I thought it might make him happy. He kept mentioning her."

"And why did you have it? Where did you get it?"

"I met Monique in Italy."

1944–1945

Stefano and Fedor went to the mountains in the North to join forces with the partisans—some who had defected early from the Russian army when they were on the side of the Axis and other Italian members of the resistance. Fedor had plans to eventually seek out his brother-in-law, who was a general in the Russian army.

Stefano had asked among the resistance where Nina and Nicolo were taken, but no one held much hope that they were taken anywhere. They had nowhere to put babies in prison. It was unlikely they had lived. In Trieste, where she was probably taken, many were being killed on arrival.

The resistance was fierce. They freed people from a prison when they made a diversionary bomb. They helped some on the Germans' wanted list escape through Switzerland and others to the Allies in the South, sending them with valuable information about the movements of the armies. They blew up army vehicles, they stole arms, they burned down an automobile factory, and they fired on an SS station in Asolo. They covered the North extensively.

The Germans were raging, and as a show of force, they burned down farms in retaliation and executed people who had nothing to do with the resistance. The SS were ruthless, which drove the partisans to work harder. Stefano had become deft at killing. He had choked and garroted to death soldiers manning checkpoints and others on duty. He had become ruthless without noticing. He was hardened to the sight of death. He did not expect to live out the war that was close to over. He would fill his last days with retribution.

It was during the stealing of firearms that he was shot in the back of the leg and another member was killed. Fedor had killed the SS member who shot Stefano and had carried his friend across his back. Fedor had many contacts, and Stefano was taken first to a house of one of the resistance members in Castelfranco, where he stayed under the floorboards for several hours, then was transported by car elsewhere to a location in Verona until they could find a safer location for his recuperation.

"There is a new member working with our group now," said Fedor as he helped Stefano through the doorway. "I am told she knows you. She says she can help. She has helped other partisan groups also. She knows where you can stay, where no one will look."

Teresa greeted them, making the sign of the cross. "My brother," she said. Stefano heard these words, and they ate at him, stirred up emotions he did not want to feel, and he couldn't bring himself to look at her.

"We have to move him," she said, "to somewhere safer. I know where he can be treated, where no one will look."

Stefano's sister tried to speak with her brother, but Stefano turned his head, closed his eyes, not from the pain, the nausea, or the amount of blood he had lost, but because he was not ready to forgive her. She knew this. She whispered that she was grateful they had found each other. She had believed he was dead. She went to the church sometime after he had left there, and a priest told her the story of Nina and their mother, and of Stefano's survival. She prayed every day that he was safe, that Nina would be found. Because of her mistake, she made a decision then that she would work for the same cause. She wished every day it had been her and not Nina or Julietta.

As Teresa was leaving, he had glanced up and seen the tears in her eyes, the sincerity and pain. She was led away. No one had fully understood their complicated relationship, and no one dared ask. Stefano had a reputation for an explosive temper. Then strangers, mostly women, helped him climb into a trolley to wheel him along dark lanes, and Fedor and one of the women helped him up several flights of stairs. They left him on a couch in a room of a nice apartment with high ceilings and arched windows that went to the floor overlooking a marketplace filled with light. In the distance were olive trees stitched onto hills in seams. Fedor said he had to go get the doctor. That he would be back.

There was a smell of women's floral-scented perfume, and there were photos of strangers, including a man in a Nazi uniform. Stefano tried to stand, but the pain in his leg made it impossible. She entered then, wearing only a nightgown. She had wavy brown hair, and eyes a dark blue, her skin pale, and a very small mole near her lip, on a face that was otherwise unblemished or adorned with makeup. She had been woken in the middle of the night, but she did not seem concerned about the disturbance.

She put her hand on his arm.

"I am Noelle," she said, in a husky voice that he wasn't expecting. Noelle was Monique's code name in the resistance. "They tell me your name is Cosimo."

Stefano had heard her name before; she was the one who passed on information, who had connections and money. He caught sight of another photo, a wedding, of Monique standing next to the man in a Nazi uniform, and her face staring out, not quite smiling but pensive, already planning, he thought at the time.

"That is you?"

"Yes."

There was a soft knock at the door before he had time to question her further.

Fedor and another woman walked in.

"This is Maria," said Monique. "She has not quite finished her medical degree, but she is still a good doctor, I promise you."

Maria gave him a tablet to take with some clear liquor, which numbed some of the pain after several minutes. They helped him up again and carried him to a cot behind a curtained area. They turned him on his side. The doctor unwrapped the blood-soaked strips of sheets around his leg and examined the wound. The bullet had entered the back of his left leg below the knee and lodged in the muscle, narrowly missing the bone. The examination and the removal of the bullet were more painful than the injury itself, but Stefano had endured worse. He would endure this also.

"I'm sorry we have no anesthetic to dull the pain further," said Maria, pausing briefly. "But we must do everything to stop an infection."

Monique reached for his unreceptive hand and squeezed it, while the operation was completed. Once Maria had sealed the wound, she bandaged the leg firmly with fresh wraps from the knee to the shin and instructed him not to walk on it for several days. Fedor said he would be back before the week was over. They were raiding some German storage huts in Milan for medical supplies and clothes. After that, he would come and get him, and they would go north to the Alps and then into Austria to meet up with others, then farther north to join his brother-in-law. He needed him well, said Fedor, to fight the Germans all the way to Berlin. When Fedor and Maria were gone, Stefano lay on his side to face the apartment through the open curtains.

"Are you hungry?" asked Monique.

"A little."

She gave him some cheese and water. She said there was meat also, but he said not yet. He was still feeling ill.

She sat on a chair beside him. He wished she would go away. She spoke about the resistance, about Germany being crushed from all sides. He had heard that some Germans were disloyal, but he had never met one. She told him about her father. She had been through much also.

"You are very quiet, but I hear you speak German very well."

He ignored her, concentrating on the patterns on the tiles.

"I have also heard that your heart is full of hate, and it is why you have not been caught. They say that those who think they have lost everything make the best fighters."

He looked behind her at the photo. She knew where his eyes had strayed.

"Just because you see me in the photo doesn't mean I am one of them."

"You are the one who is helping finance our operations?"

"Yes," she said directly, and her chin rose slightly. He liked that she was truthful, up-front. He liked that about her, but he still had not thawed. She was German, married to a Nazi. Perhaps they had put too much trust in her. And seeing his sister again had reopened old wounds.

"Do you know about a woman with a baby caught in Verona?"

She closed her eyes briefly and nodded.

"I know of the people you speak of. I'm sorry. Is that why you hate?"

"That and for so much more." He guessed that Teresa had told her things.

"It is hard, yes? To go on. My parents were taken in Austria when I was younger for doing what I am doing now. I didn't understand it till now, the magnitude of their sacrifice, the way they stood for justice for the sake of the people. My father is rotting somewhere . . . I do not even know if he is alive. My mother is dead. I could have hated, too. Perhaps I was too young to hate. But whatever happens, you have to find ways to go on."

"Like sleep with a Nazi and lie?"

She pressed her lips together, though she did not lower her gaze. There was some regret with what he said but only a small amount. If she were truly loyal to the resistance, she would have to deal with the distrust as well.

"I don't sleep with him."

There was a cry from another room. A baby. He thought of Nina, and his heart lurched slightly.

"I have to go and leave you to your hate," she said. He liked that she made fun of him, that she didn't offer sympathy.

He could hear her in the back room, nursing and cooing, and he listened. It was peaceful. There were no sounds of bombs here. It was quiet in the streets in the early morning blackness. The crying faded before she returned.

"There is something you should know. That it was likely my husband who interrogated your sister, but I cannot tell you for certain. One thing he doesn't say is names. He just said to tell me that all from the area who had been caught had been tortured and executed, that I should reveal their methods in casual conversation to others here. He thought that by spreading such information, it would deter others in the town. But German methods only fuel them. Perhaps he wants that, too. To draw them out."

"Why do you risk it? Your child," he asked. The question sounded brash.

She crossed her arms protectively, perhaps offended by the question, but she surprised him with her answer. "What would you have me do? Wait idly for the war to end and pray we're not killed, or do something worthy while I wait? There is little choice. I want a future for my daughter where she will never know fear, where she is not told what to think, in a country that is no longer governed by criminals. This risk you mention is for her." She paused and looked at his leg briefly. "You should try to sleep. I will get more painkillers from somewhere."

"I don't need them," he said, but his throat was dry, his voice barely audible. He wanted to feel the pain. It was justified, he thought at the time. He was living, when his mother and possibly his sister and baby nephew weren't.

Monique had pulled the curtain across, and he was alone, except he could hear her busying in the apartment briefly before he heard the flick of a switch and the room went dark. Tears fell then while he lay in the dark. He had not allowed himself any time since the fire to think, but now he was ill and there was time. He didn't like it.

When he woke next, it was the afternoon. The pain was still there, but it was bearable. He sat up, the bandages thick around his leg. He attempted to stand on his bad leg to see if it would take his weight. It did, though he felt a burning sensation as he applied pressure.

A washcloth and a towel had been left nearby, along with a bowl of water, and some soap that smelled like lemon. He put his nose against the soap and thought of the lemon trees in his first home in Amalfi. He washed, sitting on the side of the narrow bed, and with some difficulty put on a clean shirt and trousers that had been left there. He wondered how long he would have to stay. If Fedor had turned up then, he would have hobbled away. He was eager to get back out to their war, to not have time to think.

There was a click of the front door being opened and shut, and then the curtains were pulled back. She had a baby on her hip. She had been out and carried a shopping bag.

In the afternoon light streaming through the front windows near the kitchen, he could see her more clearly. Monique's eyes were much brighter during the day, a myriad of blues, and she was not as tall as he first thought, now that he was upright. Her forearms and calves were muscled. She did not strike Stefano as someone who had ever been idle.

He looked at the door behind her.

"It is all right. My husband is far away at a camp."

"Who is he?"

"He is Erich Steiner. He is the man who interrogates at Trieste."

He felt cold at the mention of the name: the person who had been linked with the deaths of his mother and friends.

"I have heard of him," he said, attempting to stay in control. "He is on our list. The list of people we hope to assassinate."

She stared at him briefly before responding coldly.

"That is good," she said of the man she was married to.

He made a sound as if he didn't believe her.

"You think I am lying," she said directly, with eyes that were hard to look away from. He didn't answer.

"When I met him, I did not think that he was so bad. He was loyal, but I don't think he was aware of his capabilities. He is a monster I believe now. He feels very little."

"How did you become so lucky?"

She smiled then, unforced.

"I chose this path. Who knows, maybe this path was to lead to you. Maybe the path was to have my beautiful little girl."

It was direct what she had said, and he was taken aback by her mention of him as part of her destiny. He was beginning to like her. She was not like anyone he had ever met. She was thick skinned, undeterred, and self-assured.

The baby in pink grabbed at the edge of her mother's navy-blue cardigan to chew on it.

"I must warm her some milk if you will excuse me. And then I will fix you something to eat, and then we will talk."

She returned a little later, the baby put to sleep in another room. She had taken off her cardigan and wore a plain cream blouse and gray skirt, but the cut and fabric looked expensive, he thought. She had put her hair up in the meantime to commence work. She looked the part of a well-connected Nazi wife.

She made him a sandwich with salami and cheese. The bread was dry, but it was the best meal he'd had in days. She also made him coffee with sugar.

He was sitting at the table by this stage, his leg stretched out at the side. She told him he was staying there till the end of the week. No German wives visited her, she said, since very few came with their husbands. And no civilians who did not know of her other activities would dare to call on her unannounced. She told him that the war was looking very grim for Germany. That the Italian Socialists knew it, too, that they had become more desperate, reckless. And those for the South had to be more vigilant. She had heard of unrest. She said that if Germany failed, like she hoped, she might be in danger and have to get out of Italy. The resistance would do what they could, but the pack mentality of people ready to fight anyone with German links might override common sense. He felt for her then. She had suddenly become more believable. She had put herself in much danger. She was perhaps braver than he was, even with his exploits of sabotage: she worked for the resistance, then had to face her Nazi husband. And the fact her husband was an interrogator would mean she was always on her guard.

"I believe it was most probably my husband who interrogated your sister and many of your friends in the resistance. For that I cannot compensate, I'm afraid. But be assured that every wrong he has done I have attempted to match. I have plied him for information, and he has given it freely more recently. I use the money he earns from the Socialist

Party to support his enemy. He thinks that it is me that spies for him, keeping an eye out. He is an intelligent man, but I have learned that he cannot read a woman as well as he thinks. It is probably his downfall. It may even be his undoing," she said, lost somewhere in the future.

"Where will you go after here then? Where is it safe for a German spy?"

"Germany will be the safest place. I am Austrian German. I would not risk staying here. My blood alone is enough to condemn me for some. It will matter not what I have done. There are those that look the other way when I walk down the street, only seeing the façade. Because I have a fake name in the resistance, because I am a secret, many will not know me. They will only see what they want to . . . will only hear my German accent. And my friends may be somewhere else when it comes to it. In any case even if they do plead for me, I think I am safest there back home with my cousin to raise my child."

He was at once concerned for her, at the danger, at the fact she might have to travel to Germany alone.

There was a knock at the door, and she seemed unafraid. She pulled the curtain across, and he heard her call out through the door and a voice respond. She returned a few seconds later.

"It is your sister."

"I do not want to see her."

"You know I went to her this morning. I wanted to learn more about you. She had already told me about the night of the fire, but she told me everything then. How bravely you fought as a soldier, and how you then fought for this cause against the regime. You should know that after the fire she left her aunt and uncle and moved into her own apartment, but she still kept in contact with them because her uncle is a member of the Black Brigades. She joined the resistance herself. She fed information to the resistance also. She has not forgiven herself for the losses of her family. She had no idea that her casual words would lead to such trouble. How her aunt and uncle pressured her for information. And she had no idea that they would then repeat it to the Nazis."

"I can't see her yet." His heart was still aching. He could not look on Teresa's face, which would remind him so much of his mother.

Monique nodded. She understood that he was not ready.

"I will tell her," she said, and closed the curtain.

While Monique was cooking dinner, the cries of the baby interrupted her. By the time she came back from checking on her daughter, the vegetables were burned. She served them anyway with pieces of sausage.

She looked up at him then, an apologetic smile, and he felt a sense of protectiveness, something he thought he would never feel again. And he knew then that it was possible not only to forgive, but to love again as well.

Present-day 1945

"Monique said to find her on the way home," says Stefano, the pain in his head finally easing to some degree. "She knew I was traveling north to join the German army. I did what she asked. She wasn't there at the river. I was going home regardless. End of story."

"No, it is just the beginning. Where did you meet her?"

"We met in a market in Verona. She was buying vegetables. I was walking through the city on the way to the base military camp nearby. She said she was an awful cook. We met at a café a couple of times. She said that her husband was dead. She gave me this address at the river, and I wondered, since I was going home that way, whether there was something more."

"They would have destroyed the photo in the camp. You weren't allowed any possessions."

"The guards weren't so thorough at the end. They threw all our possessions in a room before they had time to sort or destroy them. Some of us were able to retrieve them later."

"Did you sleep with her?"

"No. It wasn't like that."

"You don't have to lie. I know she was spying. I can only guess what else she did to retrieve information. I have read her letters. Was she giving information to you?"

"Why would she do that? What would I have done with it?"

"I don't believe you."

"I was on your side, my Italy. She was not, obviously. She was just as much my enemy as yours. I can see that now."

Erich is saying nothing. Perhaps he cannot trust himself; his tone will betray him. He is humiliated, thinks Stefano. This is likely to bring things to a head. It is what he wants, too, Stefano believes, something that will change the conversation drastically, give him reason to act.

"As I told you, I left when I realized the Axis powers were losing. I did not want to be slaughtered. Resistance members were retaliating against every fascist they could find. I thought it was safer to go north. Germans still believed, some of them anyway, that there was a chance of winning and that they should continue as if they were. But your soldiers fighting in the North had some issues about trust and didn't want to hear about my allegiances. They imprisoned me for my loyalty, shot me on the march, and the Russians put me back in prison. It was a circus."

"And the Russians let you go," Erich says without cynicism.

"The Russians are only interested in Nazis. I told them my family lived in the South, that I was forced to fight or die. They understood that. They had much the same directive from Stalin."

Erich waits for more.

"Then I went to the address. That is the end. You know the rest. I care nothing about her. I thought she would make interesting company, but she was, how do you say, *superficiale* . . . shallow, and there are plenty more out there. From the look of things, it was not meant to be."

Stefano can tell that his facial expressions and body language are being studied. He must appear open, naive even, but still guarded. It is obvious that Erich is used to playing mental games, and Stefano must rise to the challenge, remain strong.

"It is a nice bedtime story, but it is only that. I am used to liars, Stefano. I am used to people who believe they are cleverer than I am. But I believe your intention was to catch me. You were drawing me out, weren't you, into a trap that you never got to set up. Those Russians came too early, didn't they?"

"You may not always be right. Everyone makes bad judgments. You are making one of them now. You obviously made one about your wife—"

Stefano does not see it coming, the punch to the side of his jaw, and the blade slips from his fingers.

20 March 1945

Dearest Papa,

I only have the briefest time to write to you. With most of Italy now liberated by the Allies, it is only a matter of time before they reach here. But it is becoming even more dangerous for me. Although I have been on their side, helping fight against the Italian regime and the Nazis, I am told that it will not necessarily make me safe. I have a German child, and my husband has been responsible for the capture, interrogation, and ultimate execution of many. I will have to leave here soon.

Italian soldiers in the street are still saying that Germany and Italy are winning and that Mussolini will reclaim the South. They continue to lie to the people, but I believe my sources.

My husband sent me a telegram to say he was heading back to Berlin for reasons he didn't say. It is like that with him always. We have separate lives. He stays near the camp; he stays close to his crimes and comes here sometimes to see Genevieve. A handful of times I have had to attend events with him, to show that he is human perhaps, even though I do not think he is. He is smart, calculating. But he feels nothing for me; that much I can tell. I only hope that if it comes to it, he feels something for Vivi.

I have helped many through our operations. I have passed information. One man, Cosimo, has been here hiding. I have to say, Papa, that I have never felt anything like I feel for him. He has been here a week now. We have spent so many hours talking. I admire his bravery, his support for the Allies. It is hard to explain love, but the pain in my chest that we will soon be parted, me to Germany and—

CHAPTER 30

ERICH

Stefano sits on the floor, perspiration on his forehead, his lip bleeding. He was not expecting it. That was always the best part of the job for Erich. The surprise, when they did not see a punishment coming, which rids the prisoner of any self-importance.

There has been only a handful of times where he used such a method on a prisoner. Mostly, he has been a spectator. He left it to others, though later it gave him some satisfaction, some way of releasing a frustration, an anger that grew larger over the war years.

The last months on the run have at least given him cause to think of the future, to know that all is not lost. That others are there hiding still with the words from Goebbels's final dedication to the führer ringing in their ears. "We feel him in us, around us."

"Why have you brought me here to this," says Stefano, "if you are so certain I want to kill you? Why didn't you just kill me when I was tied up in the barn?"

There is something Erich is going to say, then he changes his mind. He cannot say for sure. First it was to be far away from the Russians in case they returned to the river houses. But now that he reflects, it is

Stefano also, he concedes. There is still something about Stefano that attracts him that he cannot admit openly, that he has been fighting to admit, even to himself.

But this should have been over with. He should have killed him on the first night he found him. He should have known better, trusted those first brief seconds when Erich had seen something fierce and hateful in his eyes before Stefano had time to hide it. Stefano was never on the side of Germany. They are still at war. He can see that now.

"I needed to know what you are doing, who you are working for. How much you know of people in hiding. It is my job to study people, to know."

"It *was* your job."

"You are wrong, Stefano. There are still many of us out there loyal to the führer's cause, though circumstances have stalled the inevitable. Germany will be strong again one day, and I plan to help make it that way in time."

"You should forget that fantasy, go back to your family. Or I could still help you leave Germany through my contact in Italy. I know that is what you were hoping for. We can put this event behind us."

"Please spare me your tricks. I know what you are doing, filling me with false hope about your contact that doesn't exist."

Stefano is undeterred.

"There is no enemy to fight, Erich, no greatness in Germany. We are all equal now, and there is no more war on the horizon. Only the people who matter should be on your mind like they are on mine."

And somehow these words reach Erich, and he looks at the marks on the wall near the kitchen. He remembers the day the marks were made. There are names written there, in children's writing, and a measurement beside each one. Stefano follows his gaze. He sees things quickly, watches for them, like Erich.

"Was this your house?" asks Stefano, and Erich is thinking then, remembering.

"Yes," Erich says, unreserved, wishing suddenly to give Stefano something before he is killed. To make him understand, view the world through his eyes.

"This is where I grew up. This is where I watched my mother work hard every day and my father design his machines. This was once a place of wonder, now . . ."

The sounds of the trucks rush through his mind. He had entered the wood, and he knew he could run fast enough to reach the other side before they had left their vehicles. But he stopped because it felt cowardly to leave his mother alone with his younger siblings. I should be there, he thought. He stopped to watch from behind the trees and wait for the trucks to leave. They would find nothing there, no papers linking him or his father. His mother was safe, he thought, and he would return to her.

And then he had heard the sound of a pistol being fired, the noise from somewhere in the house. He waited in the forest. He heard their loud Russian voices, their boots on the stairs that led to the children's bedrooms. And then there was laughter and the Russians calling to one another. They left quickly then and climbed back into their trucks. Erich did not wait for them to reach the road but ran through the back door.

"It was here where I realized that I was on my own to fight. That I would have to survive and start again, but also to keep the hopes of my mother alive—"

"Not your father?"

He turns to Stefano. He is thinking he might hit him again because he has reminded him that his father was not like him. They were two very different people, and his father knew this, perhaps had known it all along.

"My father hated politics and hated being drawn to one side, I realize now. He did not see the world through Germany's eyes. That was his downfall."

Stefano looks away.

"You don't believe me."

"I find your conclusion confusing," says Stefano. "It sounds like he knew what was coming before you did."

Claudine flashes in his memory.

"My father had a brilliant mind, but he was emotionally weak. He hanged himself the day that Claudine, my sister, was executed for distributing anti-Nazi leaflets, for turning against us."

"You must concede that Hitler led your family and the rest of Germany over a cliff."

"Hindsight tells us where we went wrong. It is the case here," Erich says dryly, refusing to concede anything. "We can learn from it."

"And the rest of your family? Did they fail you, too?"

The words burn because Stefano is getting close to the truth. He looks again at the writing on the wall by his brothers and Claudine, then imagines them dead. Nothing but pencil marks to show they existed.

"The Russians were looking for me. I was on the Allied list of those wanted for war crimes. And Russian soldiers came to my house just after my mother had told me to run, to disappear. But I didn't. I stayed nearby. I never planned to leave them. And my mother, thinking that I had gone and not willing to be interrogated or worse by Russian hands, shot my young brothers in the head, then shot herself. The Russians found their bodies first. I heard laughter, and they fired off guns, which sounded celebratory. When I came out from hiding in the wood and returned to the house, I found my mother at the top of the stairs. She was the only one alive."

He feels light-headed and sits down. The room feels unbearably close to the dying sun, and the heat through the glass window burns. He hasn't eaten anything or drunk recently. He is suddenly thirsty.

"I'm sorry," says Stefano softly, and Erich feels again a touch of regret at the thought that he will shortly kill the man who, until today, he'd begun to feel an affection for.

"I have lost family, too," Stefano says. "I'm not a spy, Erich."

He doesn't like the way he says his name, the intimacy with which he uses it, the way it clouds his judgment.

"Why does Rosalind hate you so?" asks Stefano.

He had taken his mother in his arms to Rosalind. He could not take her to the town, not himself. Rosalind had treated her as best she could. He owed her for that.

"She dislikes everyone."

"She hated you because you were in love with her husband," says Stefano, the softness in his voice gone.

Erich stands up to move closer, his fist clenched. "Who said that?"

"She told me."

"Monique?"

"Rosalind."

"I don't believe you."

"Last night she told me."

Erich is remembering Georg. Damaged now. Not the man he was before, tall, beautiful, arresting. A magnet for women, he remembers, when they first met, and jealous of those who looked at him.

His fist lands in Stefano's face, but Stefano's arm is suddenly thrust forward, and in the moment of confusion, Erich does not see the thin strip of steel that suddenly wraps around his neck. He feels a pinch of his skin and then something sharp cutting into his throat, tighter and twisting, forcing him backward and down to the floor. He reaches both hands for the weapon he can't see at his neck, struggling to get his fingers beneath it to free himself. His feet slip from under him, and he is in Stefano's lap, and he reaches up behind himself, one hand to grab Stefano's wrist, the other to claw at his face. The wire is tightened again, and he can no longer breathe.

There are sounds that he realizes are coming from him, strange gargling noises. He kicks out suddenly with his legs and scratches at only air now, grabbing on to life.

And then looking up behind him, he sees Stefano's face, the burning sensation of his gaze. As the room begins to fade around him, Erich sees that the bracelet of finely woven silver is missing from Stefano's wrist.

March 1945

He ordered the execution of the last of the partisans who had been kept in the cells. They had already been tortured over several weeks, and the SS had gleaned nothing. The prisoners had not broken.

He was only ever there for the questioning. When they no longer answered his questions, he sat for light torture methods—breaking of fingers, threats of hanging, and water. The other methods came later, when he was no longer in the room. He left it to others to break the prisoners. It could take hours, days. He did not wish to witness the last moments of their lives.

But there were more important issues to deal with. Personal ones. It was pointless sitting there waiting for an uprising. He could smell it in the air; he could smell the fear from his own men, the nervous excitement of the prisoners in previous days.

Like a tidal wave, the Russians had washed over former German strongholds, had crossed the border of Germany, and were breaking apart the country to get to Berlin. He could see the end, they all could, but any Germans or Italians who admitted this, who took the time to speculate, were shot. He could see the fearful silence in the faces of the civilians also.

He looked across the yard at some labor prisoners pushing a trolley full of coal to warm the officers. The faces of these prisoners looked so shrunken, flesh starved of sustenance, until they were no longer distinguishable from one another. When they had been lined up for inspection, a job that was harder than it looked, they no longer resembled people, he thought.

He stared at the piece of paper in front of him. It was a single piece of information taken by one of his enforcers during an interrogation elsewhere, information that had come to hand from the interrogations of women, relatives of the active resistance. He had been given an address of a safe house, at his own address in Verona.

He was thinking of everything Monique had said to him, all the times she had lied, pretended that she was content, all the while betraying him. She was not bound by blood or love, but she had a duty like all German women, and this betrayal had the potential to humiliate him in the worst possible way. The war might soon be lost, but he wanted to leave at least without dishonor, without being stripped of his rank for failing to see the enemy that had been in front of him all this time.

He knew the German propaganda—that Germany would still win the war—was false. He did not believe in hope. Italy was about to crumble, and he would not wait around to see it.

He called in his lieutenant, who viewed him cautiously.

He knows, thought Erich. The descriptions of Noelle, her cover name, and the child; everything matched. And he felt a fool. He was renowned for getting under the skin of others, for finding out things without torture. He put people at ease, but at the same time they were scared of the control, of his calm, of the paradox of his cold stare and amiable tone. Yet there he sat, a subject of humiliation.

She had wronged him, and there would be consequences.

On his desk was a list of offensives and military placements, which included Georg's unit. Erich would find his old friend one last time near the front lines.

"Send a message immediately to my wife. Tell her that I have moved and that I will send further word later. Then send a car to pick me up to take me north."

"And who is the replacement?"

"It is you for the time being. Do not advise Berlin."

He did not tell his lieutenant that he was not coming back. The mood in the camp had been more somber, the sound of bombing and air raids constantly sounding in the dead of night, and the reported losses of men growing daily. The lieutenant looked uncomfortable with this order and hovered unsurely.

"I will send word. Out now! Follow your orders."

"Yes, Herr Commander."

Erich pulled out papers from the desk, threw them in the fireplace, and watched them light. Evidence now was the newest enemy. Nothing to say what he'd done, what his wife had done. He then walked to his car, choosing not to call for his driver.

Reaching Verona late into the night, he drove along the streets, scouring the addresses of those messengers who had been to see him, who had been paid for work by the Germans as informers. They had not only been reliable but had offered other services, too. He stopped at a house, knocked, and waited outside. Two men appeared, and he told them what he wanted and negotiated a price. He didn't haggle. There was no time. In less than a month, they would be his enemy. The men left on foot, and Erich killed some time by driving around the streets. By then Monique would have received the message. She would feel safe, relieved. He eventually stopped the car.

He walked up the stairs casually and unlocked the door to his apartment. Monique was there, face flushed. She wore a dusky pink satin dress, as if she were about to go to dinner, and forced apart the lines between her eyes to smile. She was not pleased to see him. He knew that immediately.

"Erich!"

"You are surprised."

"Of course! I just received a strange message that you had gone."

"I had to come here first before I left Verona. I had to see Genevieve." But it was not the only reason.

The curtains were closed at the back of the room. He walked through and opened them. The room had not changed, though there were medicines on the sides and washed bandages. There was also a smell of disinfectant and blood, but there was also something else: a faint leathered, earthy odor of men returned from battle. He had lived with that smell for years.

"Have you been hurt? Was Genevieve?"

She had followed him into the room. "Oh no, Frau Russo called by, and as she left she tripped and cut her foot on the edge of the radiator. I treated her, and she rested for a while."

"It is a lot of medicine."

She looked at him, put her hand to her throat, and shrugged. He left the room and surveyed the kitchen and dining area, the plates and cups. There was nothing remarkable to note, except for her dress and the fact she was wearing perfume.

"Is anything the matter?" she asked, the frown reappearing.

He took a deep breath. "Of course not. I just haven't been here in a while." He did not say that he had no plans to see it again. "Where is Genevieve?"

"In her room. I will get her."

"No, I will go to her."

He walked in and saw that she was sitting in the corner of her cot. She crawled across toward him, her tiny face exploding into a grin as she pulled herself up to stand. He felt the back of his throat thicken, and his heart beat unsteadily at the sight of her. He must not weaken, he told himself in order to do what he was about to.

"She has been walking," Monique called out. "I have to watch her all the time now when she is out of her cot. It is a shame you weren't here to see her first steps."

He bent down and kissed her downy hair, while breathing in the sweetness of her. It wasn't just Genevieve he was absorbing but the memories of his siblings. It was one reason to be away from her. He marched from the room.

"Would you like some tea?"

"No, thank you."

She fidgeted with her fingers and watched him uneasily, unable to meet his eye when he turned to stare.

"Is there something wrong?" she asked.

"Monique, it is becoming dangerous. I'm not sure if . . ." He couldn't bring himself to say the words, to say that Germany was losing. "I will send word when I reach Germany, if I think you should leave here. It might be wise to take Genevieve to your grandmother's soon. It might be safer there."

He looked behind him as if there were something he hadn't done, something that was still not right about the place. *Had he missed anything?* His senses said that he had. He looked at her, at her shoulders, at her crimson-colored lips. His beautiful wife, as she was referred to. But he could never see what others could. Her mouth was open slightly. She was breathing rapidly, perhaps a mixture of fear, of the unpredictability, and all he could do was feel relief that he was on the threshold of leaving.

"Goodbye, Monique," he said, but he was thinking of the name Noelle that she had called herself. It suited her. He could have called her by that name to let her know she was exposed, but it would be a clear warning. She was intuitive and quick thinking and likely to find a way to protect herself from what he had planned.

At the bottom of the stairs he stopped to look up and down the empty street. Two men, the ones he had met with on his way here an hour earlier, waited just inside the entrance to the building.

He did not make eye contact with the men. He put on gloves to walk outside in the cold.

"Kill her," he said, "but leave the child." He did not know what would happen to Genevieve. It was a small regret that he wouldn't see her again, that he was leaving her care to chance.

He had hired local men rather than ask members of the SS to arrest and then kill her. It was better not to have an official order or interrogation record that would link him to the embarrassment that was his wife. Better to eradicate the problem swiftly to make it look like a senseless murder of a lonely woman, who perhaps brought men into her apartment. The dress she was wearing would suggest it. Perhaps a jealous lover, some might say.

He did not think about how they would do it. He had hated the sight of blood since he was a child, but he had hidden this fact from the soldiers and SS that he worked alongside. It would be seen as a weakness. Perhaps it was a variation of the same weakness he had inherited from his father. Horst had not thought his son to be a soldier, as someone fit for battle. He hated his father for this, and for leaving him, for failing to fight also. And yet he loved him, too, for being right, for knowing his eldest son better than anyone.

He would eventually go to his mother and siblings. He was looking forward to speaking with his mother, who balanced the world around him. Who kept the floor beneath him solid.

Erich drove all night and most of the following day past broken train tracks, and houses and empty fields braced for devastation, guided by road maps and flashes of light in distant skies. He arrived the next day at a military base in Germany and requested a transfer to one of the units. The captains didn't ask for his reasons, too haggard and uncaring to query his motives and desperate for reinforcement; any recruitment protocol had been forfeited by their heavy losses.

Erich slept briefly the second night on a cot alongside other men who had lost the desire to speak, who no longer noticed his badges of superiority, and he was woken early to climb on the next truck that would ferry him to the front. He was given a military pack recovered from someone dead, since no new ones had been issued recently, then was squashed between used and weary soldiers. As he neared the battalion's base camp, the sky above him grew dark with battle dust, and streaks of fire lit up the horizon.

He was led to an area where officers rested between battles. He was so close he could feel the vibrations of heavy vehicles and ground fire, in smoke that smelled like melting iron and burning fat.

He asked after Georg and found him in a tent alone, frazzled, thin, and sunburned. He did not have the skin for the sun, but under the redness, the cuts, and the dirt, he was still dazzling. He had always been so unlike anyone else, so capable, and someone who looked to no one else for support. It was perhaps these qualities that Erich drew strength from, which he was attracted to. But there was a hardness about him then that Erich had not seen before. He was distant and seemingly indifferent to Erich's sudden appearance.

Beside him on the floor were Georg's medals for bravery, for valor. Erich felt a small resentment then; these were medals he did not have.

"Congratulations on your latest medal! I hear you have done extraordinary things . . . saved many of your men on the field."

Georg said nothing. He was lying back on the bed with a cigarette in his mouth. There was a new confidence about him, or an old confidence like in the early days before that one time, in the river hut, when things changed for them forever. That one time Erich had tried to forget but couldn't.

"I wanted to see you, make sure you are all right."

"As you can see, I am," he said, and drew back on his cigarette and stared at the ceiling, finding an anchor there that might hold him away from Erich's gaze.

"Georg—"

"I have a war to fight. I have a wife to get back to, a baby on the way. And you have a family, too. There is nothing to discuss."

Erich was surprised at the coldness, though it was little wonder. After that last summer together, Erich had left without a word. He wanted to forget. He could not have that hanging over his head, not with the future he had laid out for himself. Georg wore the signs of battle weariness but not only in the eyes. He was wired but wary, perhaps even a little paranoid. It would be pointless talking to him, and then Erich also had to wonder. Would he say something? Was he dangerous? With a few words he could undo everything that Erich had ever accomplished.

Georg was drugged up, fueled for battle, with something that had been used widely, stopped, and was now passed around the soldiers as their last line of defense. Generals turned a blind eye, especially when soldiers showed little fear of dying.

Georg sat upright and jumped up off the camp bed. "I have to go. You should probably go interrogate someone else. Maybe a little Jewish girl, or an old man who is handing out a funny cartoon."

He walked away, carrying his helmet under his arm.

The insult was felt. Georg was the better man, he was saying.

Anger exploded inside of him, and Erich took off the rifle that was flung over his shoulder. He lifted it and aimed it at Georg's head as Georg walked toward the group of soldiers ahead, marching to the front line.

Shots rang out from elsewhere, close, and the soldiers ducked and slammed their helmets on. No one could see Erich in the tent with his gun aimed at Georg. No one would hear the shot; it would be lost among the other sounds. He kept his finger there, on the trigger, his hand trembling. He could end it right now. One bullet and Erich would kill the one piece of the past that he'd found no rational place for in his head. The gun followed Georg's unusually disordered movements as he rushed forward, broke in a different direction, then stopped. Erich had not killed anyone in cold blood before. He had ordered executions but never actually pulled a trigger on a man, woman, or child.

Georg turned to look back at the tent as if he had sensed him watching. Erich wanted to hate him, and yet he couldn't. There was something so defiant about Georg, something unbreakable and decisive, more qualities that he needed, that he might need again, that he hadn't been able to get from any other relationship.

Erich relaxed the trigger. He felt himself weaken. He couldn't kill the only person who had ever truly understood him. And there was no need to kill the past. The past would die naturally in war, would disappear among the consequences, like everything else.

There were more gunshots, louder now. The fight was too close.

Someone yelled that they needed everyone out on the field, and his father's tanks roared over tracked and trampled earth. He put the gun down to watch the machines, to remember the images on paper, the excitement on his father's face when he received his first tank commission. Only yards from Erich, in the space between him and Georg, a grenade exploded, shaking the ground and spitting fire and earth into the air. The German army was being driven back. From his pack he raised the binoculars to see whether Georg was all right. Many were running through the smoke, and it was difficult to see. And then he was there in his vision, and Georg, perhaps aware that Erich was still watching him, turned at that point, again in his direction.

Then another bomb, followed by the sounds of gunfire, and Erich saw blood burst out from the side of Georg's head before he fell.

Present-day 1945

He is slapped hard across the cheek, but he is not roused fully from the fog inside his brain until water is thrown across his face. Erich opens his eyes a fraction and spies the green diamond-patterned linoleum on the floor of his mother's bedroom. His chest jerks suddenly as a kick lands hard between the shoulder blades. He coughs and then gags, and pain extends down his back and through his legs. He is on his side on the ground, and his wrists are bound tightly behind him.

Stefano pulls him roughly upright and slams him back against the wall. He can picture where he is even before he opens his eyes. Erich's head hangs forlornly to one side as he assesses the pain, deals with the discomfort. Out of the corner of his eye, he can see drops of blood on the floor and part of the split rope that once held Stefano.

He raises his head slowly, unwilling to see the person who has finally beaten him. Stefano is sitting in front of him, cross-legged, dangerously tranquil. He has tricked him. It was the first thing the SS thought of, to take off the shirts and trousers of prisoners, and everything else that wasn't anatomically connected, to search the body thoroughly, so they had nowhere to hide weapons or riches. He feels anger mostly against himself, for this failure of procedures, and wonders in the same instant whether, deep down, he was hoping that Stefano was his equal, hoping still for time in Italy, or elsewhere, a reprieve until he returned.

"I suppose you want to know what happened to Monique," he says between small coughs. His voice is hoarse, his neck sore.

But Stefano says nothing. His dark look makes him appear like a madman, and Erich looks away briefly, to gather his thoughts. He can feel the tightness of the ropes on his wrists and feet. Stefano's gun is on the table, far from reach. For the first time in his life, there is no plan. He is the prisoner now.

"I can tell you that she's not coming back," he says more firmly. "Whatever you had hoped to find with her, she's not here." He thinks of the grave interfered with, perhaps by Stefano, and waits a moment for a reaction that doesn't come. "But I am more than certain she wasn't your only reason. You came for both of us."

"Tell me what happened to Nina Della Bosca, the wife of Antonio Venturi," says Stefano, who stands up suddenly. Erich's heart beats rapidly from the sudden movement. He casts a glance to search for the silver wire, fearing that it will be used again. "They were in a house you had burned down in Verona. The woman and her baby were taken by the Germans."

Erich remembers them.

"Is that why you have come to find me? To avenge?"

Stefano doesn't answer. He stands, moves to the window, in profile with his hands together, as if in prayer, staring at the shadows of late evening that Erich's parents once enjoyed.

"You were never on Germany's side," says Erich. "Admit that you fought for the resistance."

"I don't have to admit anything to you," he says, still looking out the window. "But I will tell you this: I was never in any concentration camp. I was never caught. I lied about that and most things, except Monique. I knew her. She told me all about you."

The conversation is too casual. It is unsettling. It is what he was like himself. They are alike, and this thought that once drew him disappoints him now and fills him with apprehension. He knows it will not end well. He underestimated an opponent. He has lost, caused by an emotional reaction at the mention of Georg. He knows everything, he thinks. *Monique. The traitor.*

"If you promise to kill me quickly, I will tell you everything you need to know."

Stefano lowers his eyes but doesn't respond.

"I can tell that you are a man of honor," says Erich, encouraged by the silence. "I also believe that without the baggage of war that we were forced to carry, we would have been friends."

Stefano turns and paces thoughtfully before he sighs and looks at him directly. "I will be merciful, but only if you give me everything I want."

Erich tells him then, about entering the house, about making Antonio and the others stand against the wall, about several women and several men and a baby screaming. Erich told one of the men to get the baby, while the mother begged that her child be kept alive.

Then the SS had found some maps but nothing else. They decided to shoot all but Nina and her baby. They took them in the car. If anyone had all the information, it would be the wife of one of the partisans.

And if anyone was likely to give up information, it would be the mother, for the life of her baby.

But she had surprised them. She knew what was coming: a fate far worse than the bullets she had seen used on her husband and friends. And she knew that any information must die with her. But her mistake was to believe that they would not kill an innocent baby, only her. She grabbed a gun from one of the soldiers and shot herself upward through the chin before the car even got to the prison entrance. She knew it was pointless to shoot the officer driving; she was outnumbered, and her baby would most likely be killed in front of her. Nina was quick thinking and clever. Erich had admired her for that.

Erich had been in the car behind her when it happened. The first vehicle stopped, and Erich went to inspect inside. The baby was crying next to its dead mother in the arms of one of the officers. Erich hated dead ends. Everything must have an ending, good or bad, his father used to say, a completion. And with those words ringing in his ears, he had ordered the immediate death of the baby, then had its body tossed over a fence. They died, all of them, but the task that evening was not completely unsuccessful. They had hoped to find a list of other cells, but they had at least killed one of them.

Erich looks up at Stefano, who has not said a word.

"I have no mother to go home to," says Stefano after a long pause. "I lied about that, too. She was with my sister and nephew the night you took them. My mother was still alive when your men set fire to the house."

Erich is dreading what is coming, but it is inevitable, he sees. They have both lost their sisters and mothers, but such words are weightless now. And it is not yet over. He still has more cards to play, more information to withhold if necessary, and perhaps more that will get under his skin.

"So, you can kill me now. Shoot me in the head. You have what you want."

And if his bluff is called, what does it matter? He is thinking about Genevieve, about Marceline. They are left to fate now. And the information that is buried, a list of safe houses, of places where other Nazis are hiding in Germany, will never be found, nor an address that Genevieve and Marceline will be at now. And his father's designs will never fall into the hands of an enemy. They are buried, perhaps to be dug up at some point in the future when Germany is different, when the German soldiers, his father, others will be celebrated. In a way he has won. They will not get all that they want. They will not find the others who will celebrate his name. He wants it over with now.

"I'm sorry things didn't work out for you and Monique," Erich says in a condescending tone. He feels some of the fight return, his power to demean. "You were in love with an idea. Monique would not have loved you. She was only in love with herself."

Stefano laughs hoarsely, as if the sound has been trapped deeply for too long. Erich is taken aback. He has never seen him smile so widely— a smile with teeth that overlap one another, many of them, vicious.

"You know," Stefano says, coming close, so close that Erich can feel his breath. "I dug up something interesting from the hill, something very dear to you."

It takes Erich only a second to realize what he is saying. He is thinking about the missing body of Monique, but that is not what Stefano is talking about.

"I had watched you walk to the ridge. I had seen you open the ground, check something. I was curious, so when you weren't there, I went to see what it was. I'm pleased to say that the contents are now in Soviet hands."

Erich swallows. He feels the first pang of hopelessness that he has witnessed on the prisoners. He understands something about them, has a sense of what they felt. He fights to repel the feeling, to regain control. And looking at Stefano, Erich has lost, he thinks.

He is thinking of his father, of Claudine. It was why his father hanged himself. He had gone to visit Claudine at Sachsenhausen, to try to help her, to plead her case, only to learn on that final visit she was already dead.

"Was it you who found Monique's body also?" Erich says.

"What body?"

Erich is confused. Rosalind had not witnessed him bury Monique on the hill, and Georg had lost his mind completely that night, disappearing in the woods near the river. Who could have seen, and who would have bothered taking her since? After he walked down from the hill, Rosalind was there in the house with Genevieve. She said she couldn't look after Genevieve, couldn't live with her. Couldn't look at her because she was so like Monique. The child was crying, distraught. Erich did not want to take her, but there was nothing else to do. He would take her, raise her, and teach her to be like him. He hadn't wanted her at first, but he had quickly grown an attachment. She was of his blood, after all.

"Why didn't you kill me before today? There were plenty of chances. You had weapons."

"I had to find out where you had hidden Vivi before I released you to the Russians."

"And what will happen to her?" says Erich. He is not so in control now, and he knows his voice reveals this. He doesn't like that Stefano uses the same abbreviated name Monique used for the child. It is too familiar.

"Does it really matter?"

He is cold, thinks Erich. Much colder than he could have imagined.

"So now you can shoot me!" shouts Erich.

Stefano smiles.

"Your arrogance amuses me. You will have to live with your past a little longer. The Soviets, I believe, have a few things to discuss with you."

Erich feels nauseated at the thought of the Russians and what they might do to him.

"I shot and killed hundreds of Nazis. You, on the other hand, shot no soldiers, only ordered the execution of many. You took the coward's way, Hitler's way. You made others do it, then looked the other way and wiped your hands of any knowledge. The Soviets don't look kindly on cowards."

Erich remembers the blood. He hated the blood. Stefano is right. He never fired a weapon at anyone.

"Do what you want," says Erich. "But make sure that Genevieve is looked after, is sent to a good German home."

"No one can replace her mother, the person who loved Vivi most. A woman of courage who did not deserve a coward like you."

Erich's head is buzzing with memories. *Confused, the war nearly over, still so much to do.* He remembers the name Stefano, not uncommon, in a file somewhere, another interrogation. Stefano, Teresa Della Bosca's brother, and a name that was unimportant at the time. He feels a weight pressing against his chest, the air around him thinning. He is remembering the last letter written by Monique, where she talks of *him*, a man she was falling in love with. Cold tentacles of terror spread across the back of his neck. He should have seen this. Cosimo. Stefano. The same!

"You are Cosimo!"

"And *you* are finished."

Stefano picks up the gun and slams it into Erich's temple.

CHAPTER 31

ROSALIND

"I thought you had left me," says Rosalind.

Monique ponders the statement.

"What do you mean?"

"I thought you had died."

Monique looks away.

"Part of me did."

Rosalind follows Monique's gaze across the darkening river toward a violet horizon.

"You didn't tell me that Erich came back," says Monique. "Why didn't you warn me he was close?"

The question is like fire, sizzling and blistering; it causes her consciousness to fade and recede slightly, into the background, as if repelling the words.

"I don't know," Rosalind hears herself saying, as if her conscious self has broken free to take control. "Partly because I felt I owed him something. He brought Georg back to me. We had both been loyal to the führer. In some way I thought that bound us. And that it was something that kept us separate from you."

Monique stares at her thoughtfully.

"He did bad things," Monique says.

"So have I," Rosalind says. She is remembering the last days in the hospital in Berlin, the death of German soldiers. Merciful, she thought at the time, but she knows it was also murder in another form. It makes them equal in a way, her and Erich.

Rosalind studies Monique's injuries.

"What happened?"

Monique looks at her, her dark brows almost together, her eyes becoming duller at some inner thought, at memories of her perhaps.

"It doesn't matter now," says Monique. "The past is the past. We must start once more at the beginning. We must start from now."

Thoughts filter through: pleading, crying, blood. She remembers Monique with blood dripping down her arms, begging Rosalind to stop. She closes her eyes. "I hurt you," she whispers. Images disperse, and others enter: Georg on the bed, his back to her, distant, always somewhere else in his mind.

"When did you know about Georg?"

"Before he knew himself, I think," Monique says.

"I hated how you hung around those clubs. But you saw things that I couldn't."

"It doesn't matter."

"The irony," says Rosalind. "Georg . . . Erich—"

"I have to go," Monique says, her head cocked, ear trained on something Rosalind can't discern. Her hand touches Rosalind's and she leaves it there a second, her eyes searching Rosalind's. When Monique pulls her hand away, Rosalind can still feel her hand there, the warmth. She was always warm. And she, Rosalind, always cold. "But I will be back."

"Why did you never tell me . . . about Georg?" asks Rosalind.

"He made me promise. He knew that you weren't ready for the truth . . . wanted one day to get the chance to explain. He loved you once, Rosalind. You have to know that."

But not now.

Monique opens the door, and she is gone, the door bouncing shut, a dull thud as old wood meets old wood.

"I have to tell you things," says Rosalind quietly when she is gone, but she can't remember what they are. She shuts her eyes, sinking slightly, imagines the murky depths of the river, but other images consume her thoughts. She flows from dreams to wakening, to delirium, though the episodes are coming less now, and memories appear and are not so quick to disappear.

And surfacing in her mind, those final days after the birth, patches that she can't quite piece together, followed by another memory that emerges clearly and boastfully above everything else, an introduction to the trauma that she caused. *She tries hard, but there is something not right with her,* she heard, listening through the wall to her parents' room. *She thinks too much; she thinks too darkly. I don't think she should be a nurse. She does not have the empathy, the strength of character. Monique would make a better one.*

"But I do try, I do," she pleads to ghosts.

July 1945

Rosalind was in Georg's house. There were photos on the wall, pennants and silver trophies from athletic competitions, and there was a vase in the shape of a fish, the tail stained in blues and greens, and eyes with each side painted gold. This last one was a present from Monique, something she had bought from a bric-a-brac stall with the money she earned sweeping a café on the corner of their street in Berlin. Georg kept it on his side of the bed.

Rosalind's first screams during the contractions had sent Georg shrieking and stomping the floor in their attic bedroom. Monique said it was best for Rosalind to stay in the other house, just until after the birth. Monique said that Georg was confused, erratic, and unreachable; it was better to be away. The baby was born in Georg's childhood bedroom instead, which was sweet, said Monique to make her cousin feel better, a short time before the truth emerged about the fate of the child.

Monique was efficient, quick, comforting, though Rosalind didn't want her there. She wanted Georg. She wanted her mother then. She had never thought of her mother before, had never leaned on her emotionally. Yvonne was incapable of being leaned on, but it didn't matter. She had still needed her there.

And then Monique took the child away, and Rosalind wondered if it was because of her cousin that the baby had died. Monique was not looking Rosalind in the eye. She told Rosalind she was sorry it happened. She had tears in her eyes, but Rosalind didn't believe the sympathy was genuine. Monique also told her she loved her, but that was also a lie, thought Rosalind. She was not there for her. It was always about herself.

Her baby was dead, and she had not yet come to terms with the strange situation she had found herself in. She should be nursing a healthy baby, but instead it was Monique again who was there, always blocking the sunlight.

Monique told Rosalind that she must allow herself to grieve, that coming to terms with losing the baby would allow her to face the future, a future where she could try again, return to some kind of normal. *There was no kind of normal!* screamed Rosalind inwardly. Not now with her baby dead and Monique back from the dead, where she had imagined her, who had arrived in the weeks before her contractions with a healthy little girl in her own image.

Rosalind looked at Monique who was tired from helping with the birthing, and quite ordinary without the dresses and the makeup and the hats. She looked like a farmer's wife, a scarf around her head, apron on with stains of Rosalind's blood. The roles were reversed. It was

Rosalind who was claiming the attention finally, but it was attention that she didn't want.

And she wondered whether she should tell Monique the truth about the near drowning years earlier. How when Monique was first struggling to reach the surface, Rosalind had paused to watch her from the edge before diving into the river to save her. That she had thought, just for a moment, it was the answer to all her problems. If Monique drowned, Rosalind would no longer have to share Georg. But she had dived in and she had saved her, and she wondered then as blood fell between her legs, the skin of her belly still swollen, whether things would have been different, whether Georg would have loved her more.

The morning following the birth, Monique had brought her tea in bed. Rosalind hadn't slept. The combination of lack of sleep over several nights and the loss of the child had put more fissures in her fragile state of mind. The sadness that had nearly choked her had passed, and she was left with a feeling of numbness. She pinched herself as Monique sat on the bed and spoke of things she did not want to hear. She thought of her mother and father. They were good people, but she had never felt wanted by either of them. They never told her she was loved. And there was the strange irony of Monique, whose parents doted on her, but she had lost them. And she had moved on, stronger than anyone. How different Rosalind's parents had been compared to how they were after Monique arrived. They were lighter, laughed more, when Monique was around.

But that morning there was no organization to her thoughts. There was no logic; there were no feelings of goodwill—there was no time to think on Monique's qualities. Beside her, distractingly, was the glass vase that she wanted to smash. There was just one random image after the other. The memory of telling Georg that he was soon to be a father and the smile on his face that did not mean anything. That did not register. A child, a living, breathing person created from his own flesh and blood, would have healed him, she thought.

And Georg had arrived to see the dead child and his eyes had come alive and he had reached for the boy at first and then recoiled and that had hurt Rosalind; it had burned into her memory. Even a live one perhaps would not have been enough.

Monique carried the baby carefully as if it were alive. Monique, with her healthy child sitting nearby: the sweet little girl, with downy hair, watching, unaffected by what was in front of her, eating her toasted bread and watching her mother with wonder, soaking up everything about her so that she could be just like her. Rosalind shuddered. The erratic thoughts continued. She still couldn't sleep. She paced the floor again that day, looked again and again at the dead baby, which was changing color, becoming not so soft or flexible. Perhaps it wasn't hers. Perhaps hers had been taken.

Then she did sleep briefly that night, and in the morning the baby was gone and so were the bloody towels now bleached and hanging on a line between the two houses. There was no trace left of him, her child.

When Monique returned to Georg's house, Rosalind was waiting furiously in the kitchen and had screamed at her as she entered, demanding to know where she had buried the child. Then Georg walked in and looked at Rosalind as if he had never seen her before. It only fueled her anger, and she pulled pictures off the wall, one by one, smashing them.

"Be quiet," he had said, and she had run upstairs, back to the bedroom she had shared briefly with her baby.

Monique had followed, and so did Georg.

"You stole him from me," she had screamed at Monique. "Your child is probably his, isn't it? Georg was mine, and you stole him. You chased him until he gave himself to you."

Rosalind had seen for the first time the redness in Monique's eyes, the dark circles. She had not slept either, because of her guilt, thought Rosalind.

"Rosalind," she said quietly, "you are not thinking straight. You are in shock. You need to sleep. You need to rest. I will give you something to sleep."

"Leave me," Rosalind screamed. "You are not to touch me!" And she was standing on the bed, and Georg covered his ears and ran from the room. And now it was worse, thought Rosalind. He hated her.

"You had an affair with Georg and you ruined my life and I will never forgive you," said Rosalind.

"You still don't understand . . . I'm sorry . . . I should have told you," said Monique, quietly, eyes closed to a memory. "But the truth was hard, and Georg made me promise—"

"Leave Georg out of it," she yelled. "You use his name because he can no longer defend himself."

"You have to stop giving him the drugs," Monique said, then continued more harshly. "You are making it worse for him. He will never repair."

"Leave me! You will never find your own man. You are a whore! Not satisfied with Erich, you had to take Georg."

Monique was silent and still, and she straightened her back and brushed down her skirt, which never needed brushing.

"You think you know everyone," shouted Rosalind. "You think you know me. You don't even know your own husband."

"Rosa, stop now! Please! Enough! We are on the same side. I—"

"You didn't know that it was Erich who had Alain arrested. That he was the one to round up your friends, and then he pretended he knew nothing. Not even Georg knew about it. But I did. He trusted me. He could see that I didn't approve of your friends. That I thought like him."

"You have to stop this!" said Monique firmly, and Vivi climbed up the stairs behind her. Monique left to take her daughter next door, and

Rosalind could hear Monique telling Vivi that Mama would come to get her soon.

When Monique returned, she broke down and cried, and Rosalind felt nothing, perhaps more hatred because her cousin was becoming the victim, as if she had been wronged somehow.

"This war," Monique began, "has changed everyone for the worse, but the truth was always there. It has been there in front of you all this time with or without a war."

"Get out!" Rosalind shouted.

Georg came back then. "You know nothing!" he shouted before going down the stairs again. As if the light had turned on briefly, after all the darkness. He was there somewhere, and Rosalind realized that she must focus on him now, help him get better, but she could not do that with Monique, not after what she did. And Georg needed his drugs, the drugs that Monique was against.

Georg left then. She heard the door bang. She knew what that meant. That he would be gone for hours. He would sit in the river hut until night. He needed his medicine, and she would take it to him.

But Monique was on the stairs, stopping her from going past; they tussled on the top stair, but Monique pushed her back into the room.

And then came the lies, the poisonous lies.

Rosalind didn't want to hear them. She had already heard from Erich about what Monique had done. How Monique had betrayed Germany and supported traitors with the money he gave her. And she was suddenly proud that she knew something that Monique didn't know: that Erich was close by, in the very town where they collected their rations. She called in on him weekly to collect the drugs for Georg, but she hadn't told him of Monique's arrival. Rosalind had felt some duty to keep her cousin safe, but that was no longer an option.

Monique had killed her baby, and now she was saying vile things about her husband. She was admitting to the adultery.

"Yes, I loved Georg," she continued while Rosalind was perched at the edge of the bed, looking beyond the trees to the river. Monique was thinking that Rosalind had calmed, but she was unaware of the thunder that reverberated within her.

And Monique continued talking, cruel and calculated. She was crying the words that were coming out of her mouth.

"That night you saw me and Georg on the path, it was not what you thought . . . Erich had left our bedroom, and I followed him. I already knew about Georg . . ."

Rosalind was covering her ears. She could feel the truth deep, deep down inside of her. She was remembering something, just vaguely, Georg touching the hand of another man at a restaurant they were meeting at, and Georg's face falling at the sight of Rosalind's early arrival. At the other man, uniformed, scurrying away like a mouse, disappearing from her sight and then from her mind, willfully. Georg had asked Monique about the secret clubs that didn't discriminate; he had asked her to take him with her next time he was in town, but he never got the chance. The clubs were closed, Monique then married.

"I never suspected them. I never loved Erich, and it wasn't the marriage you think . . . It was a ruse, to protect me, and one of the conditions from Erich was that I tell no one of our arrangement, our pretend marriage, which might affect his position in the party . . . and Georg begged me not to say anything about him . . . all these secrets a burden . . . and I was worried about you, and I was angry at Georg when I saw them . . . It was unfair, you unknowing."

The lies were becoming more vicious. Monique said that she caught them, Georg and Erich, together in the river hut that night. That she had known about Georg but not about Erich and it shocked her, but it also made sense then. It didn't hurt because she didn't love Erich, but she loved Georg like a brother and he loved her, and she had known his secret since they were teenagers. And he had told her that she was the only one he could ever admit it to; otherwise he was doomed.

Rosalind didn't want to hear any more. She hated the truth, but Monique wouldn't stop. She told her that after learning of Georg's marriage proposal, she had arranged to meet with him in secret, the night before she left for Austria. Georg had just returned from battle and was due to see Rosalind the next day to begin plans for the wedding. Monique had tried to talk him out of it, because it would cause Rosalind suffering in the end. He said Rosalind didn't need to know, that he would cover it well. Monique was unable to convince him, but she would be there for both of them when the time came. And that time was now, she said.

Then Erich did something so terrible as to take away her rights, but for the grace of God, Monique was rewarded with Vivi. And Rosalind was reminded that she, herself, had been punished without a child.

Monique said that they could start again, the three of them, like they were children, living here, with Vivi, her daughter. *Her living daughter,* thought Rosalind. And they would both try to help Georg recover, and wean him off the drugs.

Just for a moment Rosalind thought about it, and then the glass vase glinted, the golden eye of the fish staring at her. *It sees the lies,* she thought, and Monique took a step closer near the bed, and the idea, the plan, had barely settled, and the vase was in her hand, and she crashed it to the side of Monique's head, but it didn't break, and while Monique was doubled over, her vision blurred, she hit her again on the back of the head. This time the vase smashed to pieces, and Monique stumbled forward, slamming into the post near the stairs. She stood up unsteadily, hand across her forehead, eyes half-closed from the pain. And Rosalind still had the base of the vase, glass daggers jutting from its solid-glass base. She lashed out at Monique, who put her arms across her face then and edged closer to the stairs before tripping backward and landing halfway down.

Rosalind's thoughts were clearer then. She ran to the window to see whether Georg was anywhere nearby. And she dragged Monique to the bottom of the stairs and wrapped her in a curtain from Georg's bedroom before dragging her toward the barn. And she could see the back of Vivi's head near the window as she did this, and it hadn't occurred to her what to do with the child. She dragged Monique into the barn, then bolted the door. There was still no sign of Georg. He was unlikely to check there.

She took the bike, in her nightgown, and in daylight rode into town to fetch Erich, and she failed to notice that she was bleeding through her nightgown, and Erich didn't care, didn't bother asking what happened, whether her baby lived or died.

Erich didn't go straight to the barn. He went first to see Genevieve. And she was there, crying for her mother, arms outstretched from the side of her cot in the living room, and Rosalind had felt the hardness inside her give a little. She breathed in deeply and suddenly, as if brought back to life, and she saw with clarity and revulsion what she had done.

She told Erich that Monique was still alive, that they had to do something to help her. And she followed him as he crossed to the barn, watched him lean down to check on her and report that she was dead. Rosalind had asked if he was certain, and she had wailed and said she wanted to see her, to check her, to make sure she would live, and Erich had shouted at her to get the shovel, and she did because she had no better plan, no way of stopping what she had started.

She then followed Erich a short way as he began his ascent of the hill behind the house, and he had stopped and turned to look at her, warned her to stay away with just a glare, and she remembered what he was capable of, what he used to do. Rosalind could hear the child crying, and she reluctantly returned to the house. She tried to comfort Vivi, but the child was calling for her mother, and she wouldn't listen.

Erich came back to the house to clean the dirt from his hands and did not look at either of them but made to leave without his daughter. Rosalind couldn't let him do that. She could not look at Genevieve every day, after what had happened, and she told him to take her away. And he picked up the child and took her, though he didn't want to. He said it was important for Rosalind's own sake to never talk of what happened, to tell no one. It was a threat, veiled. And he had left with Vivi.

The next day she had walked along the ridge that eventually ran into deep woods, until she found Monique's grave, and then she had returned and sat near the other grave, above the houses, that had a cross and a name, "Georg," which she had given the boy, the name that Monique had carved. She had cried then, grieved for losses. Grieved for her meaningless life.

Present-day 1945

She stares, trying to remember the past days, Erich's betrayal. It wasn't the first time. First there was the taking of Georg, who was not his to take, and now injecting her. Why not just kill her? There is nothing to tie her to him anymore. He has broken the bindings.

Where did he go? She no longer cares. He can't hurt her anymore. She won't let that happen.

The door of the hut opens again, and she blinks back the fog that is in her eyes. It is the tiny boy, Michal, with his basket over his arm.

"I've come back to get my basket," he whispers in his peculiar accent.

And she is wondering where he has been, if he has been in the house, what happened to him.

"Are you leaving here?" she asks.

"Yes. They're taking me to a new town."

"Who?"

He looks to the side and fiddles with his fingers before his eyes settle on hers again. He is still wary of questions, of adults who ask them.

"I hope it's nice there, wherever it is."

"I have to go now," he says.

"Goodbye then."

He puts down the basket, steps into the hut, and wraps his skinny arms around her neck. He squeezes her so tightly that her face is pressed hard against his, and she breathes in the scent of youthful innocence. She closes her eyes to burn the touch and smell into her memory. *A child. How beautiful to have a child.* When she opens them again, Michal is gone.

He was never there, she thinks, and she weeps because nothing is real anymore and everything is gone. It is the needle. It is the medicine. She has imagined sweet Michal, and Monique's forgiveness. She cries because she so wants to tell Monique she is sorry. Monique, who was loyal to everyone she loved, who cried for Rosalind's dead baby, genuine tears and genuine pain. She can see the sadness now. See Monique crying, wishing that her baby had lived, while she bathed Rosalind through her fever, her madness, her paranoia, her misunderstanding of everything.

She remembers now the violence in the attic. It was Rosalind, the cause of Monique's pain. She wishes she'd had the chance to tell Monique she loves her. That jealousy does strange things to people. That she is flawed, badly. She wishes she had been the daughter her mother had loved, and wonders briefly about Vivi, where she is, whether she will have her mother's nature, her smile.

Her feet meet the river. She used to be afraid of the cold, but now she welcomes it. The sensation says that this is real, not imagined.

She treads briefly, then sinks below the surface. Through the water she can see the pink sky that swaddles the remains of the sun, before turning to float with the current, like Monique used to do.

She imagines that her name is being called, muffled by the water above and the sound of her bubbles. It is better here, she thinks, in the cold, in the shadows where she is hidden from ghosts. And the current pulls her downward and toward the bend where she can disappear forever.

CHAPTER 32
MONIQUE

July–August 1945

Monique woke up in the dark, wrapped in fabric, her head in much pain. She fought the curtain that covered her face and sat up to feel the sticky wound on her head. She pulled a piece of glass out from the side of her hair. Blood had streamed down both arms, and she remembered Rosalind's face, a stranger, controlled by madness and fury.

She could hear voices, crying, shouts by Rosalind.

"Where is she?" said Erich.

She lay back down, pulling the curtain over her face again. The latch was lifted from the barn door. She didn't hear him walk near, but she sensed him there.

The curtain above her was bloodied. He did not pull back the cover, not straightaway. He never liked the sight of blood, the sight of wounds. For someone who appeared so in control, he was too cowardly to kill innocent people himself, ordering others to execute instead.

He slid the bloodied curtain back to see her face, and she feigned unconsciousness, with a piece of glass gripped tightly and concealed in her fist. He put his hand inside the curtain and fumbled for her wrist and with cool hands held tightly.

"Is she alive?" said Rosalind hysterically. "Please God—"

"Silence!" said Erich loudly, and Monique's heart missed a beat. And Rosalind whimpered.

"She's dead," said Erich in the cold tone he had used on her in recent times.

"I don't think she is. I think she has just lost consciousness. I saw her chest moving before. Let me see. Let me check her! She needs the wounds bound." And her pitch was high, and she was still close to the madness that Monique had witnessed in the bedroom. But it wasn't Rosalind she was fearful of anymore. Erich knew she was alive, and he was planning to dispose of a live body.

She felt his arms burrow underneath her, lifting her from the ground to walk from the barn.

"Get me the shovel!" And then he shouted it again, because Rosalind had perhaps not moved the first time.

And he had it in his hand, the metal blade digging into her shoulders, crushing her as he walked.

"Where are you going?" said Rosalind.

Erich didn't respond, not at first, not until she said it again, her pitch higher still.

He kept walking, and Monique forced her body to loosen, her head to fall to the side, but inside, her heart pounded, her mind raced. She heard Rosalind behind them, protesting weakly, sobbing, asking if she could see her, asking if she could examine the wounds back at the house, and then Erich stopped suddenly, a moment of silence; then the walking recommenced, and Rosalind's pleading faded into the background along with the notion of wriggling free of the curtain and hopes for escape.

Her face was covered, but she still kept her eyes shut, arms pinned to her sides between Erich's arms, her body jolting with each of his steps.

At first she thought he was taking her to the river, but he turned and stumbled, his knees bumping into her as he inclined. And then his movements became more steady, long strides deeper into the darkness while branches raked her legs, until finally he laid her down on the hard earth. She imagined the trees somewhere on the ridge above the road. And the sounds of digging were harsh as metal hit the soft earth, and she knew then of his intended crime. She could smell, beneath the metallic smell of her own blood, the dankness of a freshly dug grave.

Her head pounded from where Rosalind hit her, and from when she fell, and the cuts on her arms were stinging. She was depleted of strength, and her shoes were missing from her feet.

She pulled the curtain partway down from her face, and in the dark she could see him near, several yards away. She watched his profile, his face fixed on the task. The sight of him suddenly brought out the reality of the situation, and she was trembling now, her arms and hands. Shock was taking over.

Scrambling free of the curtain, she crawled, then ran, the sliver of glass in her hand forgotten and falling somewhere in the confusion, and she stumbled across the hilltop toward the faint and distant house lights between the trees. The sound she made was feeble and strained, an attempt to scream, to alert Rosalind and Georg that she was alive. Alive! She must stay alive for Vivi.

She felt him grip the back of her leg, drag her backward, and she called out, *"No!"* and wondered if it was loud enough before Erich's hand covered her mouth, suppressing the sounds that were little more than groans. He lifted her partially off the ground, one arm pinning her arms to her body and the other over her face, and she was too weak to do anything but squirm beneath the grip.

"I can't let you live. You were always so blind to control, to order. You lost the war for us, people like you: my wife, who betrayed me, who betrayed Germany, who turned Georg against me. You told him what happened, what I did to you."

And the hand was so tight over her mouth that she could not shake her head, could not deny or defend. Could not tell him that she never told Georg what he did to her, that he had worked it out for himself that Erich was a monster, a man hired for the lowest of work, hired to entrap and order the executions of innocent people. And she could not remind him that she was never his in the first place, his grip so fierce that she could barely breathe, could not say any of it, and all fight left her, and for the second time she lost consciousness.

She woke to weight above her and felt vibrations through the ground, a thud each time the soil fell on top of her.

She screamed and pushed upward, but she was wrapped tightly in a curtain under the dirt, and her screams were trapped in the back of her throat, and she would die here. The wriggling had forced the curtain down slightly, and cold earth was on her face and near her mouth, and she clamped her mouth shut. She felt the last breath within her fighting to leave her body, and the digging slowed, and there was no air, and she still held the breath, held the last precious breath, not giving up, though she knew she would have to. She remembered the time that she nearly drowned years earlier, when she had held her breath until Rosalind came, and she hoped she would come again. Monique would forgive her for what she had done, and she could fix this.

The thudding stopped, replaced by a silence and the realization that she would never be found here, that even her grave would never be seen. She felt dizzy from holding her breath, and she thought of Vivi and hoped that she would be loved.

Then the earth moved, footsteps above her, and then scraping sounds like an animal burrowing. Vibrations frenzied then. But she was fading, the fight leaving her body, her mind turning to elsewhere, to the river shimmering under a bright sun. She had run out of time, and she closed her eyes, released the final breath. And suddenly the curtain was pulled away from her, and she was gulping back air greedily. She was lifted and placed at the edge of her grave, and she vomited back in the hole, spat out earth. Georg sat on his haunches, watching her come back to life, and she opened her mouth and sucked in more air when she tried to speak. Georg had picked her up and carried her through thick trees and bushes until he was near the river. He carried her into the little hut, gently leaned her against the wall, and sat watching her, shocked at his discovery.

She had shaken the dirt from her hair and wiped the dirt from her mouth. She could not see him in the dark, but she sensed he was upset, and she reached up and put her hands on the sides of his face, and he reached out to touch her, too. And Monique knew then that the connection between them was still there, a bond that was unbreakable, a loyalty that takes years to build. She would have sobbed into his chest if she could, but he was ill and sedated, and she knew there was little time, and fear of Erich still gripped her.

"Georg," she said, "I need you to do something, but the others in the house can't know what you are doing. You mustn't let them see you. Can you do that?" He stared at her in the dark, and she had no idea if this would work. "I need you to spy through the windows, like when we were young, to see what they are doing, and if the little girl, Vivi, is still there with the others." And he sat there for a moment as if he hadn't heard. She said it again, and suddenly he left. She waited, not knowing if he understood under the haze of his illness, and when the door had opened a short time later, her heart had leaped, expecting Erich. But it was Georg.

"The little girl has left with the man," he said clearly. And she didn't know whether to hug him or cry that Vivi was perhaps still alive, but gone also, and to where she did not know. "The other one is still there."

She had instructed him to do one last thing, to fill in the hole that he had found her in, and she wasn't sure if he had understood, but she had left him then, kissed him on the cheek, but she felt he wasn't looking at her anymore, that he was lost somewhere else in his head.

And she promised then that she would never give up on him, that they would be together again.

She had swum partway up the river. Then it was some British soldiers in a truck that she flagged down on the road to Dresden. She was badly injured and shaking uncontrollably, and they were shocked at her state. They were also surprised when she begged them to take her to a Russian military base just north of the city. A German woman was not safe alone, they said, and there was no mockery in their tone. They gave her a blanket and some water and took her to the destination, hesitant. They did not leave there until they knew she was safe, until she had safely delivered the lines she was told to say in Russian. She was taken to a hospital nearby, where she was later reunited with Stefano in another base with Fedor, north of Berlin, and away from the eyes of the Nazi underground suspected of operating near Dresden. She was to wait there until Stefano completed his mission to find Erich and her daughter. But after a failed attempt to capture Erich, with Georg shot by accident, Monique had rushed down from Berlin with Fedor.

Arriving in the afternoon, they had learned from the postmaster that the boy he brought with him, Michal, had delivered a second message from Stefano, and something else. From Georg's bedroom window, Michal had seen Stefano dragged to the barn unconscious, and, not knowing if he was alive or dead, Michal had run to a place inside the wall under the stairs to hide. He had heard footsteps in and out of the house several times, and then, after he heard a car leave, he ran up the track toward the town.

He was orphaned, the postmaster told Monique, and had come through the town with Stefano several days earlier.

And Monique had been moved at the sight of him, had taken his hand and told him that there would be no more secret messages, and no more reasons to run.

OCTOBER 1945

CHAPTER 33
MONIQUE

At the hospital, Monique kisses Georg softly on the cheek. He has tears, and she is so glad that he remembers something. He will love Italy. She knows they both will.

"When you are a little better, I will have you moved so you can come and live with me. The doctor needs to monitor you for longer."

Georg remembers her name. He remembers many things. He remembers her in the river. The process of remembering is slow, many memories lost.

She holds his hand. "I promise I will come back for you. You will come and live with us. Do you understand?"

She pulls out a postcard of houses on the Mediterranean and an address. "This is where I will be taking you."

He stares at the writing and recognizes some of the words. He is getting better at reading.

"And what of the owls of Elbe?" he asks.

"Yes, one day there, too, when Germany is better."

He starts to cry again, and she cradles him.

Seeing him upset is making her cry also. She doesn't want to show this in front of him. She knows that her tears will distress him further. Monique is hoping the recovery is not too long. They delayed their journey to be with Georg while he recovered from the gunshot wound, and his withdrawal from the drug, the result of which is still making him moody and anxious at times. Even though he will be there for several months yet, he is over the worst of it, the doctor thinks, and is healing slowly but steadily.

It is an hour before she drags herself away. She hates seeing him alone in the bed, but she will make good on her promise. He is her family; he is part of her.

CHAPTER 34
STEFANO

Stefano is wearing a white shirt and black pants, his dark hair slicked back, the sides cut short, his stubble gone. He no longer resembles the man who lived in the forests and mountains, who nearly starved to death, who fought not just with guns, knives, and fists, but sometimes a silver wire, too, against the enemy. In front of him is his friend Fedor. If not for the war, they agree they would not have made so many friends, and it is something to say, to stop the talk of losses, to see a greater good.

As Fedor walks away, vowing to see him again, Stefano lights a cigarette and leans against the driver's side door.

His sister Teresa has written from Amalfi, and he holds the letter with one hand, cigarette in the other. She is preparing rooms for him at the house where they had lived with their father. When she had first returned, she had discovered other people living there, but they have since relocated. It is a little run-down, but she has been painting walls and planting vegetables. She says that the lemon tree is still there. The meat vendor at the markets is back to selling lamb, though lean, and she is planning a feast for his return. She is looking forward to seeing him, to seeing everyone. He reads the letter again. He can tell that she was crying when she wrote it, as she did when she found him again. Mistakes were made. Appalling crimes committed. And the consequences for these were high. But these events, his history, he must place now in the past, not to forget but to enshrine, so he can focus on the living.

He had almost given up hope of hearing from Monique, thinking she had changed her mind, and had been planning his return to Italy, when Fedor told him what had happened, delivering the message personally about Monique's injuries at the hands of her husband and cousin. The Russians had brought her to a hospital in Berlin, and Stefano rushed to her side, alarmed that she was torn and bruised. But she was not distraught about her injuries, just that Erich had taken her daughter. They both had reasons to find him.

She told everything she knew about Erich to Fedor, who passed it on to his brother-in-law in the Soviet army, also keen to capture Erich Steiner and other SS who had so far evaded them and believing that most had left Germany by then. But they now had some idea where Erich was, and their plan would have to be clever in order to capture him. Stefano would find him and her daughter, he told her. Monique said that Rosalind was the key to unlocking the mystery of his whereabouts. Fedor had tattooed Stefano's arm, along with several others, during their time in the resistance campaign to prevent the Allies or other partisans from mistaking them for the enemy in the final months of chaos and misjudged loyalties. And Stefano fit the picture of a broken, weakened man returned from a German concentration camp, eager to be home. He had begun his quest, his head full of revenge, for his mother, sister, and friends and for the treatment of Monique. He was not sure, if it came to it, whether he could bring Erich in alive.

On the morning that Rosalind gave Stefano the drug in his tea, Erich was meant to be there, to be captured, after Stefano had sent Michal to the town the previous day to deliver a written message, with just a date and a time and coordinates, to the postmaster, who was a spy for the Russians. And although Stefano wished Erich dead, had dreamed of it, the Allies wanted him alive, wanted information, and wanted him put on trial. A fate that would likely see him hanged.

He thinks of Michal. Did he use him? Perhaps it was in his mind: something to help his purpose, the boy a guise. But he did not expect to care the way he did. This is something not even war can remove from his heart.

On the night Stefano spent in Rosalind's room, he had crept out to dig up the tin that he had seen Erich bury on the hilltop. He had taken it to Michal, woken him up, told him that he must stay at the house for his own safety and watch over the tin until Stefano came to collect him in the morning. To not come out of the house if he heard any gunshots, and in an emergency to deliver the tin and another message.

Stefano is not excited about the future. It is not the word to use, but there is something now that he can build from: a family pieced together from different puzzles that will form a new one, a new future, a patchwork of their own design.

March 1945

Stefano was in the secret cavity at the base of the wall that had been cut out and then replaced with a door. One might have seen the line around the section, the point of difference from the rest of the wall, except that the bed in front concealed it.

Stefano opened the door slightly to listen better once Erich had retreated from the partitioned area and entered his daughter's bedroom.

He climbed out of the enclosure and out from under the bed. He stood at the curtains, his gun ready. This was his opportunity to kill the man who he believed had taken the lives of his mother and friends and most likely Nina, too.

Monique stood there, staring at the room that Erich had entered, her hands twisting together. She turned then, looked directly at the parted curtains, directly into his eyes. She shook her head.

So much of him wanted to burst through and put a bullet in Erich's head, a knife to his throat, but he honored her wishes and vowed that there would come a time. He retreated back under the bed and into the wall. He did it without sound. He had been sitting at the table opposite her. She had been reading aloud the letter she was writing.

When she got to the part about her feelings, he had reached across the table and held the hand without the pen, but they were suddenly interrupted by sounds from the stairwell, evenly spaced, fine leather shoes making a soft shuffling sound at each upward step. He'd had just enough time to hide.

When he heard Erich leave, Stefano had emerged immediately. Monique raced straightaway to check on Vivi.

"I should have killed him," he said.

"No. Not here, not with Vivi. He may have told someone he was coming here."

"And we could have disappeared before they got here."

"Who knows who else he had waiting outside to collect him. Erich always has insurance."

She was right. There was too much risk. But there was something else about Erich's goodbye, as if he were certain he wouldn't see her again.

"I'm not feeling good about this," Stefano said, looking around the apartment and wondering what Erich had seen, sensed. "He sent you a message and then turned up anyway. It is strange. You said he always has insurance. Perhaps this time it was the message to let people think he wouldn't come here."

Stefano could see from Monique's trembling hands that she was uneasy about his visit also. It was quiet outside. Too quiet. The sight of a Nazi vehicle in a quaint cobbled street sent people indoors.

Monique went to speak, but Stefano put his finger to his lips. He thought he heard something and stopped to listen. A rustle outside, clothing perhaps, trousers brushing together, faintly audible, followed by a creak of the floor and silence. He sensed there were people there, waiting.

Stefano pointed to Vivi's room to send Monique there, but as she walked past the front door, it burst open and two men appeared, the one in front leading with his gun only inches from her. Stefano fired into the first man, hitting the intruder in the shoulder, just before the intruder fired his gun. The injury skewed his aim upward, causing his bullet's release into the ceiling, and plaster rained on them from above. Monique rushed forward toward the bedroom with Vivi, while the injured man turned his attention fully onto Stefano. The second intruder, also armed, retreated back outside the door while Stefano emptied several bullets into the first.

Ignoring the pain in his leg, and the first man down, Stefano charged outside and crashed into the second assailant, standing on the landing of the stairs, before he had time to raise his weapon. Stefano threw himself down upon him, attempting to wrestle the gun free. The man head-butted him, the sudden pain not enough to halt Stefano, but the wound in Stefano's leg was now weeping fresh blood.

As both fought for the gun, Stefano pushed the barrel of the assassin's weapon into the man's neck, crushing his windpipe. The assassin grabbed Stefano's wrists to pull him away. He was strong, and Stefano could not maintain the hold. The assassin twisted both Stefano's arms and was able to turn him on his back to lie above him. The barrel of the gun was forced into Stefano's throat, and he could feel himself weakening.

A burst of gunfire and the man suddenly slumped forward on top of him, blood spurting onto Stefano from the assassin's head wound. Monique stood behind, holding the weapon belonging to the first man.

They had come badly prepared, like so many working for the Nazis' underground. He was relieved that it wasn't the SS.

Taking the assassins' guns, they hastily packed a bag, which included the letters she had written to her father. The sound of gunshots had drawn others, and the Gestapo was certain to arrive soon.

Monique picked up Vivi, who was now wide awake and clinging to her mother, and they ran to another house to call Fedor. With the car's lights off, Fedor drove Monique and Stefano to an abandoned villa in Garda, at the base of the mountains that led into Austria.

They were guided to a small sitting room at the front of the house. A tiled floor led to large glass doors and a balcony with views of the dark lake and mountains, and the only lights shone from houses across the water. There were two mattresses on the floor, on either side of the room, where others had spent nights on the run, and several woolen blankets, a lamp, and a small gas cooker, along with some provisions. Stefano was able to swap his bloodied shirt and clean the assassin's blood from his skin.

It was decided that they would stay there only until early morning, when someone else would guide Monique and her daughter northward, and she and Stefano would part ways.

"Thank you," said Stefano to Fedor.

"Have faith, my brother," said Fedor. "I had word from my brother-in-law that it is now just a matter of weeks before this is over." They discussed the plan to take Monique and her daughter into Austria. From there she would have to make her way back in the direction of Germany. It was a loose plan, the fact that Monique would have to go it alone for much of the way. They had already decided that the assassins' attempt was not Nazi ordered, and it was unlikely they were looking for her, which meant it would be safe to catch the train from Austria to Dresden. However, Allied aerial bombings would be her biggest problem, forcing a slower journey home, when she eventually made it across the Austrian border. Fedor taught her several lines in Russian in case she was faced with Russian soldiers. She was also to mention the name of his brother-in-law, who would help her and guide her to Fedor and Stefano. If she didn't remember the lines, he could not guarantee her safety. Russian soldiers could be brutal, he told her, and not in the mind-set for tolerance. She repeated the lines until they were perfect.

Stefano left Monique to prepare Vivi to sleep on one of the mattresses, while he walked with Fedor to his car. Fedor would return at first light with supplies for their journey and for Monique's.

"I trust this place is adequate," said Fedor, raising his eyebrows in the direction of the villa, a small smile on his face. And Stefano pushed his friend in jest, and thought of Monique, wondering if love was possible and if the night held something that he had had barely time to dream about in recent years.

"Tomorrow, Brother, I will return with more ammunition and provisions for our journey, and we will continue the fight, to the end," Fedor said to Stefano.

"To the end," said Stefano, and the two men hugged. "We still have much work to do."

Stefano watched him climb into the car and disappear up the track. It was a friendship that had been forged in blood and grief and wine, but it would undoubtedly stand the test of time if time permitted.

Stefano returned inside to boil some water on the cooker to make some coffee, while Monique fed her daughter some of the cheese and milk she had brought with her. While she rocked Vivi to sleep, Stefano opened a tin of food with his knife to share between them.

Vivi had curled up asleep with several blankets, and Monique had draped her coat over her for extra warmth. The baby had cried at first as they had left the Verona apartment; the gunshots had terrified her, but the exhaustion of the event had finally caught up with her.

"Where will you go next?" asked Monique, sitting with Stefano on the other mattress. She shivered from the cold, and Stefano took off his coat to drape around her shoulders.

"Fedor and I will go north to fight with the Russian army and enter Berlin. I will find Erich Steiner, too. I will kill him."

"You do not need to kill him. It is too easy. Death is too easy. Break him. Take away his control, the superiority he believes he has. But it is dangerous what you do. He is calculating and likely to be prepared for anything. I don't want it to be *you* that dies in the attempt."

"I don't want to die either," he said, spooning some of the beans and meat into his mouth, before passing the spoon to Monique to do the same.

"The Germans are desperate," she said. "They will stop at nothing."

He smiled. "You don't have to worry about me." And it was then she saw the blood on his trousers.

"Oh, your wound! Let me help you."

He lifted up his trouser leg, and she bound his leg again with torn strips of clothing. He watched her do this, her hands working carefully and gently, her face furrowed in concentration. The coat around her shoulders did not completely cover the satin dress beneath. She had admitted feelings for him, he remembered, in her letter. The last letter she would write to her father.

Vivi began to cry again, and she went to her on the other side of the room. Half an hour later the child was quiet and sleeping.

"I think it was a nightmare," said Monique.

They shared more of the hot coffee from the same cup and discussed Fedor's plan for the following day.

"I hope to never see Erich again!" she said.

"If I have my way, you won't."

Stefano was still angry at the mention of him, at the fact that Stefano had come so close to killing him. His heart was racing with anger, fear, and something else. He had developed strong feelings for Monique in the week they had spent together. He had never met anyone like her; he was unnerved by her suffering and dazzled by her resilience.

She had saved lives with the information and finances she had provided to the resistance.

Something else he remembered feeling at the sound of Erich's voice, amid the hatred and thoughts of killing, was the feeling of envy that someone had staked a claim on her, someone who had never deserved her.

She had seen him thinking deeply and reached out to hold his hand.

"You are cold without your coat," she said.

Her eyes were dark in the dim light, her hair pulled back with a piece of string, her face glowing yellow. She held his gaze, daring him almost and knowing what was in his thoughts. They sat on the mattress opposite each other. He put down the cup and moved nearer to her so that their faces were close. He felt frightened and excited, but the feeling that overrode all others was the desire to hold her, to never let her go, to protect her and her daughter.

He leaned forward and kissed her softly, and she returned the kiss, cautiously. He placed his hands on her shoulders and slid back the coat from her shoulders to feel her skin, to rub his hands on her back. She drew closer, putting her arms around his neck shyly, and he reached over to turn off the lamp. Behind her he unzipped the satin dress and pulled her downward so they would lie together.

Slowly and shyly shedding their clothes beneath the blankets, they still had hours before they would separate, before someone would come to take them elsewhere. He would not rush this moment, which might be the last time he was with her. He tasted the buttery sweetness of her, explored the secret creases of her body with his hands, and kissed the silken expanses of her skin, and they held each other and loved more than he had thought possible.

Naked, they wrapped themselves in blankets and sat on the balcony, warmed by each other and forgetting for a moment they were still at war. They stayed there talking about themselves, about their pasts;

shared their real names; and speculated about a life they might continue together one day. Until it grew too cold and he carried her inside to lay her back on the mattress and enfold her cooling body with the warmth of his own once again.

At some point she left to check on Vivi, and he could marvel at the shape of her against the light from the night sky through the window, the curves, as she stood to go. And she returned to become entwined, each afraid of release, until the early morning light spread across the inner walls of the room.

They dressed and waited for the car to come. The driver would take her as far as he could, and she would have to walk with Vivi into Austria. Stefano feared for her safety and could not bear the thought that he might lose her, too. Though they professed a desire to be together, the pair did not make any promises, unsure whether they would survive the war and whether their destinies would intertwine.

It would be three months after the war was finished when Fedor would come to him in the Russian barracks outside of Berlin, where Stefano had chosen to remain and work, unknowing of Monique's whereabouts, but still with a glimmer of hope that a message would come. And when it did, it would be the beginning of his final quest to end his own war once and for all.

CHAPTER 35
GEORG

The hospital bed is hot and uncomfortable. Georg touches the scar on his head and does not remember much from before. His memories that span the length of his life are still few, though the earlier ones feature most. He can remember his name being called over and over, playfully by the river. He reaches for these memories that he knows were special.

Stefano has been to visit him with his friend who spoke Russian on his behalf to the doctors who are looking after him. He did not learn till later that Stefano had known Monique, and when he spoke of her, of the girl that he remembered, more memories had come through. Monique, who shared his thoughts, was like a sister, maybe closer. Their relationship was always difficult to explain: something more than friendship, better than blood.

There is a German-speaking doctor who comes and checks on him, who says there are treatments. Georg is still ill from his injuries and the drug toxins in his body, he is told. But the brain injury, from the gunshot, may never be fully cured. He can't remember his father or an image of his mother. Many memories are possibly lost forever. He will need to make new ones. Only some of them filter through now.

There are soldiers in the beds next to him, mostly Russian, recuperating before being sent home. They talk among themselves, and he is glad they don't talk to him.

Beside him two soldiers play a game on a small board near their beds. One is missing his left arm, the other most of an ear, the remaining piece of flesh resembling a dried fig.

He stares at the postcard of the sea.

Sitting at the edge of his bed is the girl who is in most of his dreams. The girl from the river.

"Where did you go?" he asks, remembering that last time in the hut, her hair was covered in soil and she was injured, and then she was swimming in the dark in the river, disappearing, taking the good feelings that she had brought away with her.

And she tells him about how she swam as far as she could until she felt it safe, and she met soldiers who drove her the rest of the way. She describes things, small things in greater detail, and there are things about her that he could watch all day—the lifting of her hands to her eyebrows when she thinks, the color of her, the pinkness of her cheeks when she is animated.

He remembers all those things, those small things that seem so familiar. He remembers her bursting through the surface of the water to greet him, rubbing the water from her eyes with her fingertips, and smiling, her face close to his as though they were twins, joined.

"And the boy? There was a boy. With a stone I think, brightly colored."

"Yes, the boy is Michal," she says. "You remembered! He was quite the soldier, took a message to the postmaster for Stefano, clever, brave. He understood the importance of the mission for someone so young. He told the postmaster, 'The parcel has gone awry,' and the postmaster then brought Michal and the message to Fedor and me, after we had just arrived at the Dresden barracks from Berlin. We had gone straight to see you at the hospital, but you were sleeping, and then to the river houses, which were empty." She stops then to look at him. There is something she doesn't want to say, and he suspects what it is.

"The girl, Rosa . . . ," he says, though he is afraid, afraid that she is near.

"She is gone, Georg."

And he feels loss and relief, though he cannot yet find the thoughts or memories to justify these, and somehow the way Monique says these words, at the finality, does not beg further questioning.

She bends to wrap her arms around him, and he likes her there, and she tells him that she will be back, she promises, and he knows she will keep her promises because she is Moni from the river. His little owl. And she stands and turns quickly. He watches her go, and then he turns to see the soldiers still playing their game.

The one without the arm looks at Georg and points to the game.

Georg shakes his head and looks away. He closes his eyes, and he is thinking about Monique and what she just told him. A memory surfaces, pushes through the fog that still fills in much of his mind. He remembers her and another man coming to the hospital after he was shot. He wishes she were still there so he could tell her this, tell her he wasn't sleeping, that he saw her there, in a red dress and a beret. But she is gone, and he is hoping that he keeps the memory for later so he can tell her then when he is at the place on the postcard.

He lies down and falls asleep and dreams of a time in the army, of soldiers on fire and people flying in all directions to escape the bullets. He wakes up in a sweat. He prefers to be awake to stare at the postcard, to dream of times ahead.

July 1945

Georg was at the river hut. He was crying. He couldn't remember why he was upset. He felt sick. He grabbed his stomach. Many times he had felt this way until Rosa, the girl, injected him with medicine. His head was throbbing, so much that it jumbled his thoughts.

There were voices. He could hear Rosa. He knew her name now, but back then she was just the girl from the house, the one who gave him medicine that made him feel better.

He crept along the path. He knew the paths well, all the hidden ones that no one else walked through, in the thick trees by the river.

"She is still alive!" said Rosa.

And then they talked.

Rosa stood there. She was wearing almost nothing, blood down her legs. She was crying, and then she turned and ran.

And there was the man, Erich, whom he hated, who carried a bundle to the hill. He watched this through the trees. He thought about running at him, yelling, to frighten him away. Sometimes bright-white lights that confused him filled his head, made him forget what he was about to do. He had walked back to the hut when he heard the voice of the other girl, Moni.

And he climbed up the hill through the brush where there was no pathway, and he saw the girl, Moni, sleeping, and Erich rolled her in a curtain like she was an object and placed her in the hole. He threw earth over the top of her, and Georg knew this was wrong, that people did not sleep in the earth.

When Erich left, he scrambled toward the earth and dug and dug until he found her, plucked her from the ground, like a flower. And she was gasping and shaking.

"Georg!" she said.

And he suddenly remembered things about her, things he'd forgotten, of times years before.

And he knew what he had to do. He carried her to the hut where it was safe for them.

And he sat and watched her. Her face was only partially in light from the stars through the window. He hit his head to try to remember other things, to make the jumbling in his head stop.

She reached for his face. Her hands were gentle. Then she described what she wanted him to do.

"Can you do that?"

Yes, he could, but he couldn't make the words with his mouth.

And he did what she said. He went back toward the house to see the man leaving with the child. Then he looked through the window to see Rosa, who was crying and grabbing at her arms. He returned to tell Moni what he saw.

She hugged him, and it was strange and wonderful, and he didn't want her to let him go. He felt so good then for a short time.

And then Moni left to sink in the water, and she was gone. And he filled in the hole like she told him and then stayed in the river hut through the night until the other girl came to collect him in the morning.

CHAPTER 36
MONIQUE

Monique leaves the room and stands outside, tears falling. She hates seeing him like this. Georg, so capable, so beautiful, so strong yet so tortured these past years. She wipes her face. She is not known to crumble. She does not want to show this side. When the last of the tears are dried, she walks outside.

She can see Stefano across the road, leaning, arms crossed, against the car, a piece of paper gripped in one hand and flapping in the breeze. He still doesn't smile, not widely like her, but she can tell that he is happy, the expression lighter at the sight of her. She loves him, though she hasn't yet told him, not since the letter. She doesn't need to. There has been no announcement, no discussion about their love, only where they will live and where they will raise her Vivi. It is simply that they will be together.

He walks around to the passenger door and opens it for her. It is a car, he told her, that he "borrowed" from Erich. She kisses him on the cheek as she climbs inside, and he touches her back.

They drive past a town that is just charred remains and fields of earth interrupted, waiting for a fresh chance of life that will come.

"What's that?" says Michal from the back seat. He has been talking more, and he is pointing at some children playing in the rubble. Monique has sent a photo of him to the Red Cross in the hope that they can find something, along with an address where they can reach her if they do. Though she is not hopeful. From the small amount they have taken from Michal, and the stories she has heard of others cast out of villages and towns, it is unlikely he has any family alive, and unlikely that they will claim him. Those children with German fathers are not welcome in their mothers' countries, and she hates the thought of what it would be like to grow up being hated. She and Stefano decided that they will take him, where he will not feel different, where he will feel only acceptance and love.

"Just some children," says Monique, "having fun."

"Broken," says Vivi, repeating a word she has heard, sitting next to Michal, who clutches his basket on his lap.

"Yes," Monique says. "The houses are broken."

It is a simple observation but one that is too layered yet for Vivi to understand.

Vivi's hair appears almost golden at the tips with the sun through the window behind her, and she looks curiously at the world outside, to a place of wonder, and a future that is vast.

Monique smiles at her, at the innocence, and then turns farther to smile at the person who is holding her daughter's hand.

Gustav Moulet sits there, the third person in the back. She looks at him. He is a stranger for now. Not so talkative. There is too much that he holds on to that he may never say, but he is looking at Vivi, and the crinkling of his eyes and the gentle hand that holds his granddaughter say enough for now.

EPILOGUE

Owen sits beside the old woman, another one who was recently carried out from the back of an army vehicle, rounded up like a vagrant. She watches him carefully, her mind still sharp, her thoughts hidden behind raw, sagging lids full of rheum, and skin flaking with age and the subhuman conditions she has been forced to endure.

It is difficult to know what to do with these who have no family left. By the time they set up nursing care facilities to cope with the volume, the infection that riddles her body will likely have claimed her.

Outside the window, a patch of dirt that was more recently a playground is patterned with dark heads, colored skirts, and thin, browned limbs. The doctor watches the children making the most of a new day and a clear sky and chasing one another noisily. Children had been found in the woods, some from camps across Europe, and some simply living on the streets, while the Red Cross sought permanent accommodations for them. Some would undoubtedly be sent to Jewish and other orphanages; others, if they were lucky, to homes, and luckier still if living relatives were found.

"What is a young man like you doing in this place?" the old woman says in jest. "You must have drawn the lucky prize."

"I am lucky," says Owen in her language. "I came in when the war was nearly over. I volunteered. My brother, however, was not so lucky. A Lancaster pilot killed in 'forty-three."

The old woman considers him for several seconds before nodding, quietly acknowledging their differences and their sameness.

"I'm happy now to go to God," she says. "I'm tired."

"You mustn't talk like this. We will take good care of you and then place you in a proper facility. You might finally see people you know."

She looks around her at the beds filled with the old and terminally ill.

"You are young," she says. "Optimism works best on the young."

She sounds cold, but Owen knows that patients and others like her here shroud their hearts in rigid practicality: the words a defense against emotions they are too exhausted now to feel. He saw the destruction, a country in pieces, when he first arrived, and was shocked by it, but nothing could compare with the full knowledge of what many of his patients had been through.

He had worked first in a makeshift tent hospital, treating mostly Jewish prisoners, the handful that survived. In his first letter home, he could not put into words the sheer scale of hopelessness that he was met with: people who had lost everything except their human shells. Then after that he was sent to an English POW hospital treating German patients that were nothing like the indestructible force he had heard about abroad. Then finally he was sent to a displacement camp near Hamburg; his time here coming close to an end, his parents wanting him home in England by Christmas.

One of the nurses approaches the bedside. She says there is someone he should meet out front, someone who wishes to volunteer for work here.

Owen smiles warmly at his patient and squeezes her hand in both his own before standing to leave. Her grip tightens briefly before her release, as if she were attempting to catch as much of him as she can.

"I'll come back and check on you later," says Owen. And he means it. Each of the people he cares for means something to him.

He leaves the ward and walks the long hallway toward the front of the house. This house that had once been occupied by soldiers is now part of a camp for the lost. Outside there are fields of tents surrounded by more temporary barbed wire: fences erected no longer to keep people in, but rather to keep people out. The medical hut is a target for looters.

A young woman stands facing the front window in the foyer. From the back of her, there is nothing that gives much away. She wears a long skirt, with a wide-sleeve blouse tucked into her tiny waist, and a scarf around her head covering her hair.

She turns as he approaches, and there is blond hair at the edges of the scarf above her forehead. She is young, pretty, with eyes the color of pale topaz.

He puts out his hand, and she looks at it briefly first before she carefully takes the greeting.

"I would like to volunteer here," she says, hands formally back at her side.

"It is hard work. Doesn't your family need you at home?"

"There is no family," she says directly. "I am all that's left."

There is an instant understanding of why she is here. He has seen it in others. Others who want to make amends for things they weren't directly involved with.

"I'm sorry," he says sincerely.

"I have my life. I'm grateful for that."

"Can I see your papers?"

"I have none. My name is Rosa, and I was a casualty nurse in Berlin. I have had several years of experience. Everything, my records, too, was destroyed in Berlin. My home is gone."

These are words he is used to hearing, but there is no self-pity in her voice, something that, to Owen, makes her strangely endearing and fearless. From the moment he stepped on German ground, he told himself that he was not here to judge the common people, but to heal the injured. He has met with many like Rosa, but none that have brought about the intrigue he is suddenly feeling now.

"As you are already aware, there is no money in it for you, I'm afraid, but I can give you a bed and food, and see what your skills are like at least. Until I agree to any permanency."

She nods.

"Are you any good at making beds?"

She bites the top of her lip and looks down.

"Yes," she says seriously.

When she looks up again, she sees that he is smiling. Her cheeks redden, and Owen feels a quickening in his chest. Though he can't help noticing there is history and sadness there, too, behind the modesty.

"Don't worry. You'll get used to my poor attempts at humor. Your other skills will be used as well, I daresay. We need all the help we can get.

"When can you start?"

"Whenever you wish," she says. "From now."

"Good," he says, reaching to shake her hand again, and eager to feel it once more in his own. "From now, it is."

ACKNOWLEDGMENTS

Special thanks to go to Jodi Warshaw at Lake Union Publishing for her intuition, advice, and expertise. To have such a professional and supportive team makes the book journey far more enjoyable, so a huge thank-you for the production work by Nicole Pomeroy, the art direction by Rosanna Brockley, and the marketing by Kelsey Snyder, and PEPE *nymi* and Riccardo Gola's fabulous cover design work. Thank you also to Tegan Tigani and the editing team for their extraordinary work on this multilayered, complex text, polished to completion.

These are fictionalized events and characters for the most part, and certain geographical license has been applied to suit a particular point in the story. However, the backdrop is based on historical accuracies and set during the turbulent times of Europe directly after the war. Much of the World War II nonfiction I've read over several decades has highlighted the many tragedies and challenges for people who endured during this period and those that didn't. Several books rich in detail have helped create the setting and atmosphere for this particular fiction. The *Berlin Diaries 1940–1945* by Marie Vassiltchikov allowed me to see the scale of fear by Berliners and their declining circumstances under Nazi rule. Keith Lowe's *Savage Continent* gave me insight to the postwar chaos in Europe that followed World War II. For some, the war didn't end after the surrender by the Axis, but a new era of hunger, retribution, and reclamation added to the horrors of this period. To understand the chaos of displacement and untested loyalties, and in some instances the hands of fate for the Italian resistance, Sergio Luzzatto gives a chilling account of their activities in Italy to fight Nazi occupation in *Primo Levi's Resistance*.

I extend my thanks and appreciation to the administrators of the German Federal Archives, and the State Library of Queensland for the ease of access to research material; the United States Holocaust Memorial Museum for their extensive archive of information to educate writers like me; to the Holocaust Research Project also for its contribution and the records it makes available to read; to the aerial reconnaissance collected by the RAF during World War II and now held by the Imperial War Museum; and to the staff and guides at the Auschwitz-Birkenau Memorial and Museum in Poland for their dedication to education, and their preservation of history.

My thanks and love to those who have supported me throughout: to Oscar Liviero and Stella Lindsay (a former newspaper reporter, WREN, and evacuee during the Blitz), who have dedicated countless hours to critique, advise, and encourage; to Brian Curran, an RAAF pilot in World War II; and to others whose sufferings and sacrifices make me forever grateful.

ABOUT THE AUTHOR

Gemma Liviero is the author of the historical novels *Broken Angels* and *Pastel Orphans*, which was a finalist in the 2015 Next Generation Indie Book Awards. In addition to novel writing, her professional career includes copywriting, corporate writing, writing feature articles and editorials, and editing. She holds an advanced diploma of arts (writing) and has continued her studies in history and other humanities. Gemma lives with her family in Queensland, Australia. Visit www.gemmaliviero.com.